will sweep you ... dventures await you. Fro ... and the thrill of discove ... nknown and encounters with creatures that could prove to be the staunchest of allies or deadliest of foes, here are sixteen brand-new tales of those intrepid sailors on the seas of space:

"The End Is the Beginning"—Were the Smoothskins mere legend meant to frighten the kits, or was there some truth behind the Great Lie—a truth that an adventurous kit might discover for himself?

"Pyrats"—They had evolved, taken over the spaceways, and now they were preparing to give humans a one-way ticket off of Earth. . . .

"A Matter of Faith"—Was it mutiny or common sense to question your commanding officer's orders on a mission into the unknown?

More Imagination-Expanding Anthologies Brought to You by DAW:

OCEANS OF MAGIC *Edited by Brian M. Thomsen and Martin H. Greenberg.* In thirteen original tales some of today's finest navigators of the magical realms—including Tanya Huff, Kristine Kathryn Rusch, Mel Odom, Fiona Patton, Rosemary Edghill, Mickey Zucker Reichert, and Mike Resnick—set sail through uncharted waters to distant lands where marvelous adventures await. So grab your treasure map and plot your course to mist-shrouded isles of enchantment in tales that will take you from a dock waif rescued by John Cabot for a voyage into dangers that might only be escaped by magic's grace . . . to a sorcerer awaiting the last days of Atlantis . . . to a spell-spawned encounter with a true Colossus . . .

MY FAVORITE SCIENCE FICTION STORY *Edited by Martin H. Greenberg.* Award-winning, career-changing, classic stories by such masters as: Theodore Sturgeon, C. M. Kornbluth, Gordon R. Dickson, Robert Sheckley, Lester Del Rey, James Blish, and Roger Zelazny; personally selected by such modern-day greats as: Arthur C. Clarke, Anne McCaffrey, Frederick Pohl, Connie Willis, Lois McMaster Bujold, and Greg Bear. Each story is prefaced by the selector's explanation of his or her choice.

SILICON DREAMS *Edited by Martin H. Greenberg and Larry Segriff.* Such trailblazers in the field as Julie Czerneda, Jane Lindskold, Kristine Kathryn Rusch, Gary Braunbeck, Jody Lynn Nye, and James P. Hogan introduce us to some of the next possible leaps in the development of intelligent life, some of them in startlingly unexpected forms. Here are triumphs and tragedies, cautionary tales as well as visionary ones: Could the last android in existence be preserved from terrorists able to strike at any time and place without warning? . . . An intelligence that began life in an old man's left foot soon learned the most important truth of a created being's existence—enchancement was everything . . . An alien-built being, how could it resolve the conflict between the knowledge of its original purpose and its loyalty to a human friend?

OCEANS OF SPACE

Edited by
Brian M. Thomsen
and
Martin H. Greenberg

DAW BOOKS, INC.
DONALD A. WOLLHEIM, FOUNDER
375 Hudson Street, New York, NY 10014
ELIZABETH R. WOLLHEIM
SHEILA E. GILBERT
PUBLISHERS
www.dawbooks.com

Cover art by Masterfile Corp.

DAW Book Collectors No. 1218.

DAW Books are distributed by Penguin Putnam Inc.

First Printing, March 2002
1 2 3 4 5 6 7 8 9

ACKNOWLEDGMENTS

For C. S. Forester, Nordoff and Hall, Robert Louis Stevenson, Herman Melville, Dudley Pope, Patrick O'Brien, and their SF brethren, H. G. Wells and Jules Verne, and many others who have so eloquently sailed seas before.

CONTENTS

LEGENDS OF THE HIGH SEAS AND SPACEWAYS

PROTO-PIRATES OF THE GALAXY AND BEYOND

Sails ho, matey!

Welcome aboard!

What lies before us is the vast ocean of the cosmos where the annals of voyages of outer space freely mix with legends and adventures of the high seas both metaphoric and actual.

Some of the sailors are honor-bound officers of navies, others pirates, both practitioners being human or alien (well, at least alien to the likes of me).

Keep a watchful eye open, for no one can anticipate what we might come across when we be sailing through *Oceans of Space.*

LEGENDS OF THE HIGH SEAS AND SPACEWAYS

Legends and the sea go together like moonlight and romance. Mermaids, buried treasures, mysterious islands, and far-off destinations need not be earthbound any more than the metaphoric "fish story" of two guys in a bar trading whoppers needs to be a human tale.

An engineered mermaid, castaways in search of a home, or the sea monster of the cosmos—all can exist as legends of the spaceways.

ZEMBLA

BY DENNIS O'NEIL

NO breeze stirred the Caribbean, and the water was so still that it reflected the stars. He stood on the flight deck of the aircraft carrier anchored off St. Thomas and thought that Janice would love to swim here because Janice loved both swimming and the sea, and then he remembered the letter that burned like a cinder in his pocket. It would have been a "Dear John" letter if his name had been John instead of Bernie: at that particular moment, *Seaman* Bernie Hobbs, United States Navy.

Janice, his steady date for four years, the girl who became all soft and touchy-feely when he called her his "little mermaid," dumping him for a college kid!

"Sucks, man," he told the night and considered, briefly, running to the stern and jumping into the sea. Then he decided, *no*. He would not kill himself. Instead, he would become . . . he didn't know what, exactly, not at that moment. But something! Something great!

He lifted his gaze to the stars and thought: A *poet. I'll become a poet.* Why not? He'd always gotten good grades in English and sometimes, parked in front of Janice's mother's house after a movie, with frost on the windows, listening to the tick of the cooling heater, when he would whisper the few lines of Elizabeth Barrett Browning verse he'd memorized for extra credit, Janice would sigh and tell him that maybe she could stay out another five minutes. . . .

A poet. *Outstanding!*

But then he remembered what he knew about poets. They seemed to be mushbrains, weepy females like Browning or losers like Edgar Allan Poe—didn't he die a drunk in a gutter?

Okay, scratch the poet idea. What, then? A businessman? In a brown suit lugging a worn leather briefcase, shoulders slumped, glasses sliding down a nose full of enlarged pores, worried about the trade-in value of last year's Buick? How great could a businessman *be*? Not very. Scratch the businessman. So what else was there?

Not knowing, but vowing to himself to give the question further thought, he turned, proceeded smartly to the ship's island, went through a hatch, and down a ladder. Crossing the hangar deck, still moving smartly, going toward the forecastle, he met Larry Stephens, the bright little guy from St. Louis who was always reading and listening to newscasts.

"Hey, man, ja hear?" Larry Stephens asked, obviously excited and needing to share news with *someone*. "Those weird lights in the sky over Madagascar, remember I was telling you about them? Well, they're *alien ships*. From another planet. NASA is pretty sure."

"Yeah, cool," mumbled Bernie, not pausing, not even looking at Larry Stephens, being rude and not giving a shit.

In about twenty years, after he'd attended hundreds of lectures and read a lot of books—probably way more than Larry Stephens ever read—and even written a few, he would wonder whether meeting Larry Stephens that night might not have been what Dr. Carl Gustav Jung called *synchronicity,* which, if true, might explain both his later achievements and his eventual fate. Or—and this was both wilder and more appealing to his hard-science training—some undetected quantum event had generated a portal to a parallel universe, providing entry to a spaceship which landed next to him on the flight deck long enough for a strange creature from another planet (with powers and abilities far beyond those of mortal men, maybe?) to tell him, "You can fight it if you want, but you'll lose. You're a poet. Start looking for your gutter!" If this latter explanation were true, the visitor would next have had to have tampered with Bernie's memory and done some major meddling with probabilities, but such pranks might be lagniappe to an alien of even modest powers and abilities.

No ship landed and no alien announced his destiny, not in *this* universe, which was the only one he had any access to, after all. Instead, he descended into the crew's quarters belowdecks, mostly ruing the day he ever met Janice but also mulling over what Larry Stephens had told him. Spaceships. Aliens. NASA. $E=mc^2$. Well, Larry Stephens hadn't mentioned that last—Bernie remembered it from General Science Class in his sophomore year—but it seemed to fit with what Larry Stephens *had* said. But why? Because it was *scientific*. The rest of it—spaceships and aliens and NASA—that was all science stuff, too, wasn't it?

He stopped outside the hatch leading to his sleeping compartment and listened to the rumbles and growls and whines of various machines that operated the huge ship even when, as now, she was at anchor and had his big idea, his life-changer. A scientist. He would become a scientist.

Outstanding! A scientist.

Okay, scientists seldom were famous—there was Einstein and Carl Sagan and he couldn't think of any more—

(Not then, not standing outside a sweaty-smelling sleeping compartment, he couldn't, but after two years at the university he could compile a pretty good list: Newton, Bohr, Oppenheimer, Hubble, Tesla, Heisenberg, Archimedes, Franklin, Salk, Curie, Broca, Mendel. Copernicus, Lovelock, Crick, Watson, Darnell—)

And scientists didn't get girls like athletes did—

(But by the time he completed graduate school, he'd had a round dozen affairs with women ranging from the flaxen-haired assistant television producer to the mousy little education major who, in certain circumstances, was not so mousy.)

And scientists didn't make much money—

(Depends on how one defines "much": the week he got his Ph.D. he received offers of two hundred thousand a year plus starting salary from two privately-owned biotech outfits in Northern California, which was not exactly movie star money, but wasn't exactly burger-flipping money either).

By the time he remet Janice, he was doing very well indeed, even by movie star standards. There was the salary, of course, which was by now comfortably over twelve mil a year, not counting stock options, and the book royalties, and the lecture fees, and the consultantships and that column on the net, actually written by a grad school assistant who was paid nothing more than the great man's occasional presence, and some little thises and some little thats and a few et ceteras. . . . He was doing just fine. The *world,* of course, was rapidly going to hell—considering the effects of global warming, the metaphor wasn't all that metaphorical—and he wondered sometimes how closely his own prosperity was linked to the world's decline; scientists were pretty shabby saviors, but they were all the saviors people had and people were desperate to be saved, or at least given a reprieve and a bit of hope.

So he had plenty of money, and women weren't exactly a rarity around the old lab either. But none ever satisfied him, except in a way that, while certainly pleasant, was usually pretty damn gross. Often, as he was engaged in one of those grossly pleasant encounters, he would wonder what an encounter with Janice that didn't occur in the vicinity of a gearshift lever would be like.

Then, one night, in the midst of a very heated moment, the obvious occurred to him.

"I could find her—my mermaid," he blurted as he was

rolling off a bed. His companion wriggled farther under the sheet and said nothing.

The next morning, he asked a private detective to locate Janice and, it being the age of computerized instant information, the detective called five minutes later with Janice's married name, cell phone number, address, e-mail address, bank account and credit card numbers and amounts, driving record, favorite restaurant, divorce lawyer, medical history, shoe size . . .

Wait a minute. . . . *Divorce lawyer?*

He sent her an utterly charming e-mail—the grad student certainly *did* have talent—and, after a day's electronic negotiation, a plane ticket to St. Thomas in the Virgin Islands. He remembered that the white sand beach was spectacular. And Janice had always loved beaches.

She'd changed in twenty years, which was only to be expected, but he had no trouble recognizing her; a certain physical characteristic was unmistakable. It was her right front tooth—a good ten percent larger than her *left* front tooth, and two shades yellower. He knew that—he'd *always* known that; he knew it from the moment he'd first seen her in the school cafeteria, using the tooth to gnaw on a hangnail. He also knew about the eyes that went one way and the knees that went the other, hands like catcher's mitts, thick ankles, hair the color of the stuff that was left in drainpipes after a bad storm. . . . Nobody had ever accused Janice of being pretty, but, when his friends wanted to compliment his girlfriend, they called her "cute." At seventeen, which was her age when she'd sent the letter to the aircraft carrier, the tooth, eyes, knees, hands, ankles, and hair may have, in fact, combined—alchemically?—to produce *cute.*

At forty, however—

"I'd know you anywhere," he told her, perversely pleased not to be lying.

"You, too!" she answered enthusiastically, in a voice that was as cute as everything else about her.

He pulled his sunglasses down from the top of his head to their proper position on the bridge of his nose and looked around: Janice, sand, sea, sky, sun, hotel, old people, young people, guard towers, more sand, and Janice again, unchanged.

"Shall we go for a swim?" he suggested.

"Oh, I don't go inna water anymore," she replied. " 'Sbad for my skin, the salt and all. You go ahead, you wanna."

"Perhaps a bit of lunch, then?"

"Maybe a little," she said, and giggled, and somehow he knew what she would say next and he hoped, desperately, that he was wrong, and wasn't. "A girl's gotta watch her figure."

Over appetizers, she told him about "husband numero uno," the college kid, who never graduated, who held a series of dead-end jobs and was drowned when he fell into a septic tank. Over salad, she told him about "husband numero *dos*—that means two in Spanish." A drunk, but she loved him anyways, only she couldn't stay with a drunk, could she? (It was to end her union with old *numero dos* that Janice had hired the divorce lawyer.) Over salmon steaks, she told him about noisy neighbors, television shows, potholes, her skeevy sister-in-law, the refrigerator repairman who overcharged her, vaginal deodorant—the words pounding, as relentless as the surf. Finally, over New York-style cheesecake, she asked what *he'd* been up to these past twenty years.

"I heard you went to college after the Navy and you was some kind of scientist," she said. "What does a scientist do, anyway?"

Well, she asked and, dammit, he was going to tell her. He was a biologist—actually, two *kinds* of biologist, if one counted the number of doctorates he held—who worked in the private sector and had been one of the people credited with the first successful clone of a human being. Next, he helped devise the growth acceleration process that developed a human from germ cell to fully mature adult in the nine months nature needed to create a squalling, smelly, utterly helpless infant. That, a few years ago, got him his Nobel. Now, he was working on human adaptation—that is, altering the human genone to make people smarter, stronger, healthier, and able to cope with diverse environments. This last was potentially very valuable as the Earth's ecosystem changed, making the planet increasingly unhealthy for mammals, forcing humankind to consider other worlds or adapting to changes on the home world.

"At the moment, we're looking at the possibility of extensive undersea farming—"

"It pays real good, huh?" Janice said around a mouthful of cheesecake. "On a scale of one to ten, how rich would you say you were?"

He watched her chew. Had she understand a word he'd said? Had she ever *heard* what he'd said? If he had to bet, he'd bet no. The old Janice, the teenage Janice, had always been a really great listener. What had happened to change that? Who *was* this woman? She *looked* like an older Janice should look, but— It was as though some armature at her core had shifted and twisted, altering her polarity. Or as though some alien entity had entered her—

Could that be it? Those spacecraft that Larry Stephens mentioned on the night Bernie had decided to become something instead of jumping off the stern of the aircraft carrier had never been seen again, despite the most earnest efforts of both the scientific and military communities to locate them. So had they just given our solar system a peck on the cosmic cheek and then flitted away—pursuing an intergalactic equivalent of a college kid—or had they left behind a spy or two?

"So what we gonna do next?" Janice asked through the napkin she was using to remove cheesecake from the vicinity of her mouth. "What'sa plan, Mr. Scientist Man?"

Please don't giggle, Bernie thought. Janice giggled.

"Could I have that napkin, as a memento of this wonderful occasion?" he asked.

"I guess so," Janice replied, reaching across the table to hand him the cheesecake/saliva/lipstick-smeared linen.

"Wait right here," Bernie said, rising. "Don't budge an inch." He hurried from the restaurant, stopped at a boutique long enough to buy jeans and a sweatshirt to wear over his bathing suit and took a cab to the airport. Five hours later he was back in his lab, programming his various computers to answer any call from Janice with the words *"Die alien scum"* before breaking the connection.

Then he began working furiously. He worked without stopping for seventy-two hours, ate, slept four hours in the front seat of his car and returned to the lab for another seventy-two. It was not possible to do the kind of precise, demanding intellectual toil he was engaged in while exhausted and semistarved—he knew that—but he did it anyway. He had no idea why. But at the end of the week, Project Zembla was, except for necessary tweaks, begun. Now, he had to wait.

"Why 'Zembla'?" Jerry Hines asked a month later, as they were leaving the lab. "I would have thought you'd want to call her 'Ariel.' Not that it's any of my business."

And it wasn't; Jerry was the businessman half of their partnership. But Bernie answered him anyway, with a series of his own questions.

"You really want to name her after a character out of Hans Christian Andersen by way of Disney? Would you want her to be *cute*? and *sing*?"

"Nothing wrong with cute." Jerry shrugged. "So what's a Zembla?"

"Henry Hudson spotted a mermaid off the coast of Nova Zembla sometime in the sixteenth century."

"Where the hell is this Nova Zembla?"

"Damned if I know. I like the sound of the word."

"Liked the *sound* of the *word*? That's the lamest thing

I've ever heard you say. Are you a scientist or some kind of dumb *poet*?"

"Poets are losers who end up in gutters."

"And that's not you," Jerry said, grinning, lightly punching Bernie on the bicep. "Gotta run." Jerry nodded a farewell and loped toward the parking lot. After four seconds he stopped and turned. "Hey, Bern," he called. "I almost forgot. Where'd you get darling Zembla's DNA? Who's she a clone of? I mean, I was kind of hoping you used *my* sample, but probably not. You used your own, am I right?"

Who's she a clone of? Bernie felt momentary panic—

"That'll be my little secret," he shouted to Jerry, winking.

—panic because he couldn't *remember* where he'd gotten the seed DNA. He'd performed that part of the procedure, according to his records, at about three a.m. the third night of his marathon work session while he was thoroughly zonked by a potent cocktail of fatigue, neurotransmitters, adrenaline, and genius. There were a dozen possibilities, a dozen samples of DNA arranged by a code name and number only he could decipher, in a refrigerated vault in the lab. Which had been chosen by the work-crazed maniac he had been that night?

Five minutes later, he answered himself aloud, "None." The samples were all neatly arrayed in the vault, their seals unbroken. Then he saw it, neatly folded and lying at the end of the sample rack: a dirty napkin. He lifted and unfolded it, and saw a square cut from the center, where the smears were heaviest. Cheesecake would have been in that square, and lipstick, and, of course, saliva.

Maybe Janice was possessed by an alien, maybe not. Or maybe one of those undetected quantum events had catapulted him into a parallel universe years ago, at the senior prom maybe, in which Janice had always been the person he'd met at St. Thomas instead of the person with whom he'd shared those achingly sweet moments listening to the heater cool. No matter. In a few weeks, the incubation period would be over and he would have *his* Janice, created by his genius from the raw matter supplied, albeit unwittingly, by the cheesecake eater—accelerated from microscopic wriggler to fully-formed woman in less than a year, thus fulfilling the specifications demanded by his client, the United States government, but tweaked and shaped to his own needs and dreams. Oh, he had no doubt that he had also*lutely* tweaked and shaped to the sizzling shores of hell and back during his creative frenzy.

All he had to do now was wait.

One question nagged at him: Why had he taken the napkin from Janice? He was certain that he had not consciously intended to appropriate Janice's DNA for the Zembla project. But he not only took the napkin, during what must have been a fugue lasting at least two days, he carefully transported it to the lab and preserved it in the vault. For what conceivable reason? Surely, his subconscious must have had *some* motive. Maybe Zembla herself would provide the answer when she finally made her debut.

She emerged from the incubation tank sticky and stupid—no surprise there—and fully-formed and breathtakingly lovely. Not perfect: the right front tooth was noticeably bigger and yellower than its mate, and the hands were disproportionately large. And not exactly human: slits ran down either side of her neck—gills. But these minor imperfections—if having gills could be considered an imperfection—only emphasized her overall magnificence.

Bernie felt pride throb in his chest.

After every expert from every country currently friendly with the United States had given her every kind of test anyone had ever heard of and she'd been paraded in front of a herd of generals, admirals, congresspersons and, finally, selected educators, pundits, and reporters, Bernie was at last given quality time alone with Zembla.

By then, before Zembla could talk, before she could even stand without wobbling, Bernie was in love with her.

She was a quick study. Speech she mastered in a month, grammar in three, the high school curriculum in six. She learned everything as quickly and easily as extraterrestrials and aliens in movies learned English: life imitating art, without benefit of a script doctor.

Personally, she was a delight: sweet, friendly, calm, her voice softly musical, her smile quick and infectious. She seemed to have only one serious deficiency.

She wouldn't swim.

She would get into the pool at the lab, sink down to almost the bottom and stay there, expressionless, her gills pulsing slightly. On one occasion she walked, not swam, to the shallow end of the pool, stuck her head up into the air and asked if she could have something waterproof to read.

"You won't even try a little dog paddle?" Bernie asked her.

"I don't want to displease you, but I don't *feel* like swimming here," Zembla answered.

"You didn't feel like learning calculus either."

"That was tedious, but at least it was easy."

"Do you know what the problem is? With swimming?"

Zembla frowned. "I am afraid of failure. I was created to be an amphibian. I'm afraid that if I swim badly, I will disappoint you and everyone else."

"You've succeeded at everything you've tried. How can you be afraid of failure? You've never experienced it."

"But I have learned about it. It is a frequent theme of the comic strips entitled 'Cathy' and 'Doonesbury' in the newspapers."

"You said you don't feel like swimming *here,*" Bernie said suddenly. "How about somewhere else? An outdoor pool. The ocean."

"You've shown me pictures of the ocean—"

"But you've never seen the outside of this building."

"Our schedule calls for you to remain under constant observation for at least three years. On the other hand, if we were following our schedule, your whole vocabulary at this point would consist of 'goo goo.' "

"Why would that be?" Zembla had difficulty understanding the concept of irony.

"Never mind," Bernie replied. "Not important. I've got a few chores to do, paperwork stuff. It'll take the rest of the morning. I'll see you later."

Bernie's chores did take the rest of the morning and all the following day and the morning after that. Nobel Prize winners, he discovered, are not immune to bureaucratic paranoia. But finally, after a call to the White House, he had the permissions he needed.

The morning was bright and brisk, a late September day too late in the season for most swimmers. Smuggling Zembla out of the lab was easy; Bernie simply put her in the back of his station wagon under a blanket and drove, waving, past the reporters who continued to keep vigil outside the fence. Not much of a challenge at all: it had been 214 days since Zembla's existence had been announced and the journalists weren't really expecting a story anymore.

At the first stoplight, the station wagon was joined by three humvees festooned with aerials and satellite dishes and containing a total of twelve Navy SEALs wearing clothes purchased an hour earlier at a place called The Casual Shoppe. They were armed with collapsible, laser-aimed assault rifles and semiautomatic pistols loaded with the latest, top-secret "smart shells." The admiral who had assigned the SEALs, an officer renowned for his skill at clandestine operations, apparently assumed that nobody would think there was anything peculiar about a convoy consisting of a station wagon and three brand-new, absolutely identical military vehicles with government plates manned by grim men in sunglasses, all wearing identical T-shirts with the words "I'm With Stupid" splashed across their broad chests.

As it happened, nobody did. The convoy arrived at a small marina a few miles from the lab and stopped at the end of a long pier with only two boats tied to it. Bernie got out of his wagon—the SEALs had already formed a defensive perimeter around it—opened the tail-gate, and helped Zembla out. She stretched.

Bernie stopped breathing and gaped; in the lab, she was attractive; here in the sunlight, she was magnificent, even clad in the shapeless, hideously pink housedress he'd borrowed from an assistant.

She looked upward. "Sky?"

"Yes, Zembla, sky."

"Yes," she said, nodding as if in confirmation

She lowered her eyes, squinted at the horizon and moved slowly toward the pier, the SEALs moving in lockstep with her, still maintaining their perimeter. Bernie joined her and waited while she stared at the water.

"The sea?" she asked.

"Actually, the bay. The sea's a couple of miles out."

Again, she nodded, as though her most profound suspicion had been confirmed.

"We can go have a look at it,' Bernie said.

"Yes," Zembla replied.

Bernie, Zembla, and two of the SEALs got into the nearest boat. One of the SEALs started the outboard engine and, with the other boat bouncing in its wake, the small craft chugged away from the pier.

"They wanted to do this with coast-guard cutters and helicopters and submarines," Bernie told Zembla. "But I told them that would defeat the purpose. You'd be even *more* self-conscious with all that around. They *did* insist on the guards. Sorry."

Zembla did not seem to hear him. She was squatting in the boat's bow, staring out at the bay.

When they were a mile from shore, the SEAL helmsman idled the engine and the boat stopped and swayed in the waves.

"This far enough?" he asked.

"Okay," Bernie said.

A SEAL produced a life jacket from under his seat, moved forward, and slipped it over Zembla's head and shoulders; he thumbed a toggle and it inflated.

"I didn't authorize that," Bernie protested.

"Orders," the SEAL said.

"Have you stopped for one second," Bernie asked, "to consider how ludicrous it is to give an inflatable life jacket to a creature who has *gills*?"

"Protect the government's investment," the SEAL muttered, taking off his Casual Shoppe clothes, revealing a gleaming wet suit. Bernie glanced at the other boat and saw that its SEALs were already wet-suited.

Zembla reached into the water and stirred it gently. Then she lifted her wet hand and rubbed her cheek.

"What do you think?" Bernie asked.

Zembla smiled. Then, quickly, she swung her legs over the gunwale and slipped into the bay.

The SEALs were out of the boats in less than a second and, treading water, formed a circle around her.

Zembla raised her arms and, suddenly, vanished beneath the waves; the life jacket, now empty, surged upward. A moment later, the pink housedress floated up beside it.

"What the?" a SEAL shouted.

"Search and recon," a second SEAL ordered.

"The SEALs' hands were full of sleek, waterproof weapons as they widened their circle.

But they did not have to look far. Zembla's head, chin tilted toward the sky, came out of the water a few feet outside the SEAL perimeter.

"It is wonderful," she said, staring directly at Bernice.

"Hold it right there," a SEAL said, thrashing toward her.

Zembla vanished again, and surfaced a dozen yards to the north and, as they changed direction, vanished, and surfaced, and vanished—

The SEAL formation was broken, military discipline forgotten, as the men swam erratically, at first trying to grab Zembla, and then, when that was clearly hopeless, trying to anticipate where she might next appear.

The game continued for ten minutes. Bernie sat in the stern of the boat, watching, enjoying himself immensely.

Finally, the SEAL helmsman popped up next to the boat and, sounding like a sissy asking for help with a schoolyard bully, said, "Make her stop."

Zembla surfaced beside him. He reached for her; she glided away. "Is this . . . *fun*?" she asked, laughing.

"Not for them," Bernie replied, gesturing toward the SEALs who were swimming toward her, their faces glistening and grim. "But for you? Yes, sure, of course. This sort of thing is what fun *is*."

"I'm glad to know that."

Hands reached for her. She twisted, dove, surfaced on the other side of the boat.

"Thank you for creating me," she said to Bernie and went underwater.

Bernie and the SEALs waited, but Zembla did not reappear.

For the rest of the day, as the sky darkened and a cold wind swept in from the sea, the SEALs swam and searched while Bernie shivered, hugging himself, gazing at nothing in particular.

Finally, when the only light left was a thin line of bluish glow on the horizon and the waves had risen high enough to splash over the gunwales, the SEALs clambered into the boats. Two of them flanked Bernie and pointed their waterproof weapons at him.

"Is this necessary?" he asked them, and got no reply.

As he was climbing onto the dock he'd last seen ten

hours earlier, he was stopped by the SEAL helmsman, who grabbed his shoulder roughly and actually snarled, "Your ass is grass."

"I thought people only did that in bad novels," Bernie said as he was shoved into a humvee. "Snarl, I mean."

Guarded by SEALs with guns drawn and aimed who obviously didn't care anymore about being clandestine, Bernie was taken to a military base, incarcerated and questioned: by majors, colonels, generals, admirals, men in dark suits, men in light suits, men with their white shirtsleeves rolled up above their elbows and, after a week, by the Secretary of the Navy and the Attorney General of the United States. Between questionings, he was locked in a small room with an adjoining bath—not a prison, exactly, because it was nicely furnished and he could get any creature comfort he wanted by simply asking for it, but not *not* a prison either; the door was always locked, and there were no windows. He thought a lot about Zembla and the year of captivity he had helped foist upon her.

When he saw her again—and he was absolutely certain that he would—he'd ask for her forgiveness.

The night before his court-martial, while on leave to attend an uncle's funeral, one of the SEALs got knee-walking drunk in a Norfolk bar, lamenting his fate and the suckiness of the Navy, and sharing the reason why he was to be tried in the morning, which was that the mermaid babe had escaped. This he told to to eleven of his newest best friends, one of whom had a cousin who was a stringer for the *New York Post.*

The story was on all the morning newscasts and material for variety show comedians by nightfall. By then, dozens of Zembla sightings had been reported: she'd been seen in all seas and oceans, in all the Great Lakes, in twelve rivers, and in a tank at the Coney Island Aquarium.

Bernie was released the following day and taken to

his lab, still under guard but without guns pointing at him. The Secretary of the Navy was waiting.

"Get busy," the Secretary said.

Bernie got busy, doing science the way it was *supposed* to be done, slowly, meticulously, with excruciating precision and tremendous fussiness. He was bored silly, but he got the job done—he *was* still a genius—and, fifteen months later, a begilled embryo was growing in an incubation chamber.

"What you gonna call her?" Jerry Hines asked him. "Zembla junior?"

"I was thinking 'Ariel,'" Bernie said.

"Changed your mind, huh? Where'd . . . *Ariel's* DNA come from? Or is that a top secret again?"

"It is, but I'll tell you anyway. You. Your DNA. You're gonna be a father, Jer."

It was a modest enough gift to give Jerry who was, after all, a good guy.

In late March, a year and a half after Zembla's departure, with Ariel decanted and prospering, Bernie noticed that the lab was less populated—fewer miscellaneous people lounging around. Then, startled at his own obtuseness, Bernie realized that the miscellaneous people had been government agents and their absence meant that they weren't watchdogging him anymore.

The day he'd been awaiting had come, as he knew it must.

Getting the boat was no problem, requiring only a few calls on a phone he'd made tap-proof and a large sum of money, Nor did he have any difficulty eluding any snoops that still might have been watching him. He simply established a routine: every weekday, he bought a pizza and went eat it while sitting on a bench near the marina. So, if a government spy happened to observe him on this Thursday, he or she would think the geeky scientist was just doing his usual thing and, Bernie hoped, go violate someone else's civil rights.

Bernie ate his pizza, stretched and yawned elaborately, and sauntered onto the dock. *Just your basic old geek stumbling around, his head filled with equations and stuff. . . .*

He leaped into the boat, started the engine, and chugged out into the bay. He looked back at the land: no other boats, no helicopters, no guy in a trenchcoat jumping up and down and yelling into a cell phone . . .

After three hours, the engine coughed, sputtered, and quit, its fuel tank empty. Bernie stood, and, struggling for balance, scanned the horizon.

Sky and sea and nothing else.

He cupped his hands around his mouth and shouted, *"Zembla!"*

The water absorbed his voice, instantly deadening it.

"Well, okay," Bernie said. "I know you're here. I know you're waiting for me. I *feel* it."

He kicked off his shoes, lowered himself into the water and began swimming. What he was doing was not rational, nor were the feelings which prompted it—the yearning, the willingness to sacrifice everything simply to be with his beloved. Not at all what would be expected of a Nobel prizewinning biologist. More, perhaps, what some mushbrained poet might do.

It wouldn't take long to find her, or for her to find him, and then they'd be together.

YOUNG AS THE MOUNTAINS

BY C. J. HENDERSON

"The tragedy of age is not that one is old, but that one is young."

—Oscar Wilde

BOLLATU stood at the water's edge, staring out toward the horizon. The sun had just begun to shatter its edge, spilling across the vast Northern Ocean of Byanntia. Dawn—not the best time to push out in search of the great fish. But then, that had only been an excuse anyway.

They voted nay, thought the old chief. *All of them.*

Bending his back, the Kuzzi warrior threw his still-powerful limbs into the job of sliding his hunter's skiff across the hard-packed blue sand and into the water beyond. He reached the lapping waves by instinct, his eyes not seeing the ocean before him, his conscious mind not actually concerned with the hunt. Throwing himself into the moving boat with accustomed ease, Bollatu landed lightly in the center, managing the maneuver without wetting any of his fur.

What did you expect, he asked himself with a bitter tone. *That they would accept the judgments of a failure forever?*

The chief was the oldest of the Kuzzi, a proud warrior who in his elder years still stood an even eight feet high. A short coat of horizontally-striped fur covered his body, as it did all of his people. The blue, black, and gray markings were a natural camouflage which allowed the Kuzzi to blend well with the planet's landscape.

Bollatu did not differ from the rest of the Kuzzi in

any remarkable way. His head was surrounded by the same thick mane, the usual single black stripe parted his forehead and muzzle. His chin and jaw were covered with the typical longer fur of the Kuzzi mane, setting off his muzzle and hard, blue lips, his shoulders broad and chest rippling with thick layers of muscles.

But Bollatu felt different that morning. As his skiff followed the morning tide out to sea, for once he felt much older than the rest of his tribe. He felt tired. Weary. Betrayed.

It's you that's betrayed them, his mind whispered in the dark recrimination. *Led them astray, forced them to eat the lies of the past. Murdered them—*

"Enough!"

The chief sat back in his boat, closing his eyes, letting his mane cushion his head against the rear panel seat. Still close to shore, the current rippled gently against the sides of the skiff. The sound was smooth and pleasant—relaxing.

They voted nay, the voice from the back of his mind repeated. *What do you have to relax about?*

Bollatu sighed. His was a nomadic warrior race that had lived on their planet since the beginning of time. Their cherished story cycle gave them a history extending back through a hundred and twelve thousand cycles. Over all that time the Kuzzi had formularized their way of life. Their population had always remained small due to the ravages of the Gr'Nar, frightful beasts that returned from a generational hibernation to destroy everything in sight. Over the centuries the Kuzzi had learned to calculate the coming of the creatures. They knew when to move to avoid their coming and to where. When the Gr'Nar arrived, they would slaughter the plainsherd, but never the Kuzzi. The nomads were too clever.

Then others had come, outsiders from the stars—the Earth'ings. They had come to Byanntia and built permanent homes. They went where they wanted, did what they wanted, acting like children lost in the dark. Some of the younger Kuzzi had been concerned. The Earth'ings would swallow their world, they said. But Bollatu had said, no, leave them be. Soon will come the Gr'Nar and the Earth'ing bones will litter the sand.

All had agreed. Of course, Bollatu was correct. None could resist the Gr'Nar. The greatest Kuzzi warriors—even in groups of a thousand—had been devastated by the fearsome god beasts.

Let the Earth'ings plow and build and roam. In twenty-two cycles they will all be dead. It had been a time of great laughter.

But the years had passed and the Gr'Nar had come, and had not destroyed the aliens. The god beasts' arrival had not even driven them away. A few pawfuls only did the Gr'Nar kill. Pawfuls! The usual cycle of blood had been reduced to a few days. A single Earth'ing had stopped it—cold and final. And then, the alien had not even shown the Gr'Nar the dignity of slaying them. He had turned his back on the god beasts, allowing them to slink off to their lair.

"You knew the creatures would come back to plague your land and sons, Jacob Matson," snarled the warrior in confused contempt, "and yet you let the Gr'Nar live. Knew the deaths would have washed you in glory. And you let the beasts live."

Bollatu sat upright in his skiff. Rage boiled his blood, steamed the water within his brain. He had been so certain, positive the Gr'Nar would sweep the plains free of the Earth'ings. But he had been wrong. And now for the first time in all of Kuzzi history, a chief had been removed from his station.

Bollatu stared out across the endless water. Only a pawful of times had there ever been a vote. Seven times throughout all their generations. Seven times the entire nation had been brought together to cast their stones—blue to retain their chief, black to send him out. Not one blue stone had been cast for Bollatu. Not by his smoke mates, his sister, his children—not even his wife had thrown for him.

Why should they?

Bollatu frowned. Why was it his fault the Earth'ings had triumphed? Millennia of tradition said they would fail. None could stop the Gr'Nar—ten thousand grandfathers wagging their collective fingers down through the centuries had said so—

And you listened to them. . . .

Disgusted, the former chief threw aside his thoughts. It was over. Fine, let the next chief do better. Tired of self-pity, annoyed with simply drifting, Bollatu picked up the double-bladed oar next to him and thrust it into the water. A smooth stroke pushed him forward, followed by another the next second. The oar shifted from side to side, silently slicing the water, the skiff effortlessly gliding faster and faster toward the horizon.

"Good day for fish," whispered the elder Kuzzi, as if fishing was what he sought from the Northern Ocean that day. In a tone still thick with anger, he looked over the side of his skiff and muttered, "Are you hungry down there?"

Setting aside his oar, Bollatu pulled up his line and cast. Securing the cast's handle in its notch in the cross brace before him, the Kuzzi held up the hooked end of his line for examination. Having not really come to fish he had, of course, brought no bait. A thin laugh grumbling through him, the elder worked his mouth, pulling together a thick wad of mucus and phlegm. Spitting it onto his hook, he cast the wicked curve of barbed metal into the ocean, shouting—

"Well, eat this!"

And then Bollatu laughed. No sooner had his hook sunk but a few feet beneath the surface when his line jerked. Something had taken him at his word, impaling itself on his invitation.

Everything dies that listens to you . . .

Laughing again at his own cynicism, the elder warrior watched as coil after coil of line dashed out over the stern. Something big and fast had decided to challenge him. Reaching for his hauling gloves, he told his hidden foe—

"I accept."

His heavy, resin-woven gloves in place, Bollatu hauled on the line. Of course, he was not trying to drag whatever had taken his hook to the surface. This was only the opening lunge in a duel he expected would take the next half hour or more. The rate at which the coils of line had snaked overboard told him he had something big, a fellir, a houlta—twenty pounds' worth, at least. Whatever it was, it had to be made aware that it was in a struggle. The Kuzzi's opening tug would let it know there was a new force in its life, and then the battle would truly begin.

As the elder warrior worked his line, easily letting a few yards play out, hauling them back in, letting them out again, he began to relax. The sun was warm on his fur, the occasional splashes churned up by his struggle refreshing. The fish began circling the skiff, going deeper and deeper, trying to find a direction from which it could not be pulled back. Bollatu easily kept the line from tangling against any of his vessel's edges, his still strong muscles easing the line around and around.

Slowly the elder's cares were being left behind—forgotten. The contest had shifted his focus away from the internal. As his fingers stiffened, he would hold the line secure with one paw while flexing the fingers of the other. Then he would let his line play again, pulling the fish short with his refreshed paw while loosening the digits of the others.

Then, finally, the line went slack. Bollatu's hidden adversary was heading for the surface. The warrior's forehead ridged, his lips smiled. He had tired his foe to the point where it could think of nothing else to do but to run straight toward its captor.

"Come to me, swimmer. We'll prove I'm not dead yet."

The water broke, shoved to both sides by a leaping form. Water caught the light, surrounding the fish in reflected dazzle. Bollatu marveled at his prize.

"A geldiffa—this close to land."

The elder laughed, pleased with himself. Seeing his enemy, he could tell the great fish weighed forty, forty-five pounds easily. Then, in the background, Bollatu noticed the distant shore, discovering he had traveled much farther than he had realized. The warrior did not care, however. What could that matter? Forward, toward the end of his line, that was where his attention was demanded. The geldiffa, all blue and yellow stripes, hit the water again cleanly, gliding below its surface, racing for the bottom.

He's trying to throw the hook—he's done this before.

A real adversary, decided Bollatu with a grunt of admiration. A worthy foe. This would be a battle worth fighting.

The Kuzzi found himself repeating the steps he had already made. First playing out and hauling in the line, working it around his skiff as the fish went deeper and deeper, constantly switching directions as it again tried to find some space of ocean that did not connect it to Bollatu's line. The warrior smiled with a child's sincerity. He had not been so happy in many a year.

Then, once more his line went slack. Again, the geldiffa was racing to the surface. For a moment Bollatu's breast swelled with pride. In his moment of despair, the gods had sent him a challenge, a sign, an opportunity for redemption within his own eyes. It was a small thing, but life was assembled from small moments, and he was in no position to argue. Then, his split second of joy was dashed.

Instinct sent his free paw to the bottom of his skiff, feeling for vibrations. His eyes scanned the water around him. Something was wrong. To his left, the ocean was beginning to swell. It was a signal—the geldiffa was returning to the surface. No longer trying to escape Bollatu, instead it was running from something else.

"What in all the gods . . . ?"

Bollatu's mouth froze open in amazement as the geldiffa broke the water once more, not merely leaping this time, but shooting straight upward into the atmosphere. Before his prize catch had begun to sink back below the waves, the water beneath the fish boiled and then split apart, shattered by the arrival of a massive black form.

"Chuln'fa'ulu!"

Bollatu sat in his tiny skiff, his boat and himself dwarfed by the incredible monster swallowing the ocean before him. So gigantic were the chuln'fa'ulu that their skins were used by the Kuzzi to make their central meeting tents. The nomads did not hunt the great fish, of course. They only salvaged their carcasses on those fortunate occasions when one of their dead drifted into shore. Even the Gr'Nar-killing Earth'ings had been impressed by the size of the largest creature Byanntia had to offer. Unable to pronounce the beast's Kuzzi name, they had labeled them "Melvilles," claiming the word to be a compliment.

There was no way to stop chuln'fa'ulu. The records spoke of insanely daring bands of Kuzzi, twenty, thirty boats' worth, going out with spears and throwers, looking for the glory of being the first mortals to slay a godfish. None had ever succeeded. Few had ever returned.

All these things flashed through Bollatu's mind as he watched the chuln'fa'ulu break the surface. He smelled the terror of the geldiffa—*his* geldiffa—as it struggled upward, flopping desperately, only to fall pitifully back toward the ocean and the waiting jaws below.

"Nooooooo!"

The godfish's jaws came closed, Bollatu's prize disappearing from sight. With a casual shrug, the massive beast turned and headed back beneath the waves. The elder warrior stared, his mind numb, emotions racing. He had been so at peace, actually happy, and then . . . there was no sense he could make of the moment playing out before him.

Had he been given his purging moment only so that he might be punished further? Was he naught but a toy of the gods? Was he to be scorned by not just his tribe, but by all life as well? To have snagged the geldiffa as he had, surely it had been a chance at redemption. Now, was it so easily taken away?

Is what you allowed so easy to walk back from? The elder winced, his stomach churning with fury. *Was your mistake that minor?*

At his feet, his line was disappearing once more. Second after second more coils disappeared over the side, leaping into the air two, three at a time. Without thinking, Bollatu's paws reached out.

"No," growled the Kuzzi, his anger smashing reason. "Not this day. Not to me."

His left paw grabbed at the disappearing line, carefully catching a straightened segment, not one of the snapping loops which could slice his paw in half with a motion. The elder gave the line careful jerks, testing the great fish, gauging how far down it intended to sink. The line stopped.

"Not far," muttered Bollatu. As the line limped, he asked himself, "Coming back so soon? Why?"

The warrior reeled his line back in as quickly as he could. Four hundred yards he returned to the floor, refusing the notion of cutting it, of backing away from the challenge he had made.

Retreat, the back of his mind questioned with a sneer. *To where? Why?*

He sensed tension in the line. Knowing the geldiffa had already been chewed to bits, he realized his hook had reestablished itself somewhere within the chuln'-fa'ulu. Perhaps it was lodged in some swollen abscess, wedged between two teeth where it was striking some nerve, serving the great fish a pain it had never known.

"Not used to being hunted, eh?" taunted Bollatu.

The warrior's mind reasoned quickly that it was impossible for the chuln'fa'ulu to understand what was happening. Unlike the geldiffa which had been harvested from the ocean for aeons, the godfish had no instinct for such impunity. Still retrieving his line, Bollatu watched the water, waiting for the chuln'fa'ulu to return.

Again the ocean boiled as the great mass broke the surface, hurling water in all directions. The elder left off gathering his line, his paws closing on his spear. Made as a boy, carried throughout his life, it had served as his staff of office for more than thirty cycles. Carved from the straight trunk of a young stinger tree, it possessed weight and cutting power. Filled with authority and memory, it spread confidence throughout its owner.

The godfish made a wide circle, then began moving toward the skiff. Was it somehow following Bollatu's line back to the boat? Did it know they were enemies? Did it matter? Pulling back and planting himself as best he could on the pitching floor of his vessel, the warrior shut one eye, watched his foe's progress, gauged his moment, and then threw.

The spear dashed forward, slamming through the thick black skin of a monstrous eye, sinking nearly two feet into the vision of the onrushing horror. Terrible as the attack was, however, if the chuln'fa'ulu noticed any pain, it was but a moment's distraction at best. Onward came the godfish, jaws wide as a cavern, water rushing over the terrible rows of broken teeth.

"And so it ends," whispered Bollatu. Still standing, balled fists at his sides, he waited for the monster. His skiff rocked wildly as it tipped upward over his foe's lower jaw, Kuzzi and vessel flipping inside the massive mouth. The skiff swirled, twisted by the miniature whirlpool created within the godfish's maw. Then, motivated more by anger than either desperation or self-preservation, Bollatu suddenly jumped to the back of his craft with force, pushing its prow upward into the roof of the great mouth.

The sharp edge dug deep into the soft lining, the skiff's transom wedging against the bottom of the gullet.

The elder was thrown sideways as the godfish thrashed against the sudden pain. Bollatu instinctively sank his claws into the side of the chuln'fa'ulu's mouth, hanging on against the churning current. His oar fell from the skiff, bouncing off his shoulder. Grabbing out, the warrior snatched it from the air. Digging its pointed blade into the chuln'fa'ulu's throat, Bollatu pushed himself toward the great mouth before him.

The warrior laughed as he staggered forward. His skiff had jammed the godfish's mouth open, and now it could not dive for fear of drowning. A fish, he thought, afraid of drowning. The idea made him giddy even as he fell repeatedly, thrown about effortlessly by the chuln'fa'ulu's panicked thrashing. Water crashed against Bollatu as he struggled toward the flapping lips before him. Despite the wedge blocking its throat, the chuln'fa'ulu still strained to close its great mouth. Reaching the doubled rows of the godfish's horrible teeth, the elder found his line once more. He could not see its end, buried somewhere beneath the constant rush of ocean falling in and out of the open mouth—could not determine why the creature had noticed his hook.

Nor did he care. At that moment, all that mattered to the warrior was escaping the beast's gullet before he followed his geldiffa to its bottom. Poised to dive out into the ocean, however, the godfish thrashed once more, sending Bollatu falling against its lower jaw. Eleven spikes tore into the elder's side, the great teeth ripping skin, piercing muscle. Blood sluiced out of him, the taste of it sending the chuln'fa'ulu into wilder spasms.

Bollatu dug his oar into the godfish's mouth, pushing himself off the tearing rows. None of his wounds were terribly threatening, but several were deep and all were painful. Pushing himself erect, however, the warrior sneered—

"Best you can do?"

—and then dove outward into the welcoming ocean beyond. Bollatu landed feetfirst, dragging his oar behind him far under the waves. The chuln'fa'ulu passed overhead, plunging the ocean into darkness for the long moment it took to glide by. Not having taken in a deep enough breath before jumping, the Kuzzi struggled his way back to the surface. When his head broke the water, three things caught his attention instantly. The first was that he was now much closer to shore. The second was that the end of his line was floating several yards in front of him. The third was that the chuln'fa'ulu was nowhere to be seen.

What happened?

Had the skiff been dislodged? Had the tremendous pressure of the godfish's straining jaws finally snapped the vessel? Had his hook come loose as well? The warrior reached out for the floating line before him.

"Where are you, thing?"

As if in response, the godfish's great body shattered the ocean's surface some distance to his right. Such a quick return told Bollatu that his wedge was still in place. He reasoned that the chuln'fa'ulu must have dived in an attempt to clear its throat with a rush of water. Unable to remove the blockage, it had hurried back to the sky for another breath.

Bollatu bobbed in the water, taking in his own deep breaths, watching his adversary. The chuln'fa'ulu floated with the current. Although its remaining good eye was trained directly at him, it made no move to continue their struggle. It did not try to submerge again, nor did it attempt to make for the open sea. As the warrior's strength began to return to him, he looked upon the godfish for the first time without anger.

The monstrous beast glistened in the sunlight. As it gasped one short breath quickly after another, the elder realized what must have happened. He could see that the chuln'fa'ulu's mouth had reached the point where it could almost close. Bollatu knew his skiff had shifted, perhaps even shattered. Now it was wedged within the godfish's throat. The elder realized it was only a matter of time before his adversary would swallow one wave too many and choke to death.

Suddenly, his anger drained, numbness gone, Bollatu felt a great surge of pity of the dying beast before him. Graping his line tightly, he began pulling himself toward his victim. Sad, sorrowful notes trembled from deep within the beast, drifting across the ocean. Returning to the chuln'fa'ulu's side, the elder pulled himself upward—paw over paw—until he reached the bristling rows of teeth once more. Straining with all his remaining power, trying not to excite the still flowing wounds along his side and abdomen, the warrior pulled himself up onto the hardened ridge which served as the godfish's lower lip.

"And what would you all say," wondered Bollatu of his former tribe members, "if you could see this?"

Half jumping, half falling, the warrior cleared the jagged teeth by inches. Standing, he made his way backward through the dark gullet until he found the blockage. Indeed, his skiff had been dislodged by the chuln'fa'ulu's dive, but that had only made things worse for the godfish. The vessel had followed the downward water flow and wedged itself farther back in the creature's throat, leaving only the slightest of air passages.

Bollatu shook his head sadly. Not caring what might come next, laughing at his former inability to understand Jacob Matson, he whispered to himself—

"No wonder they all threw black." Looping his line around the still solid center spar, the elder added, "If I could have seen this moment, I would have thrown black, too."

Pulling against the horrible weight, the elder strained to free his shattered vessel. The movement tore at the lining of the godfish's throat. Blood oozed as the creature exhaled harshly. Bile rushed up from its stomach in cascades. Bollatu ignored the smell, ignored the pain in his own body, ignored the derisive laughter within his head.

Instead he merely struggled—step by step—toward the thin line of light so far away. A great cough shuddered the beast. The warrior fell to his knees, almost losing hold of his line. Fighting to maintain the tension he had created, the elder felt his left glove finally eat through. Blood leaked from his paw, but he ignored the accompanying sensation. On his knees, he crawled onward, dragging at the skiff.

"Move, damn you. Move. Move."

Digging his heels into the floor of the chuln'fa'ulu's mouth, Bollatu drew his remaining line into a loop and tossed the loop end forward. Snagging it around one of the godfish's teeth, he threw his weight into pulling on the line, using the great fang to increase his strength. For a long moment the warrior strained, his eyes fast shut, heart racing, breath held deep. And then, the godfish coughed once more.

Instantly Bollatu was thrown from the chuln'fa'ulu's mouth. The elder hit the water at a bad angle. His left side going numb, he sputtered violently, gasping for air. The Kuzzi floundered, his good arm tangled in his line. Something was attached to it, weighing him down, dragging him under. Then, a shadow appeared over Bollatu's head, and the remains of his skiff were returned to him along with a shattering flood.

* * *

Max L. Kornev, captain of the *U.R.S. Canton,* was an insatiably curious man. When he noted that passage had been booked on his vessel for an alien being, he saw an opportunity to not only brighten some of the dull travel hours ahead, but to accomplish what he had come to space to do in the first place—to meet another life-form for himself.

"That's a hell of a story." His tone not revealing whether or not he believed what he had been told, he added, "back on Earth we'd called it a 'whopper.' "

In the grand tradition of the oceangoing vessels of his past, Kornev had requested Bollatu's company at his table that evening for dinner. The chief had accepted, knowing that if he were to travel among humans, he would have to learn to deal with them. Attempting to do so, he inquired, "Is that a good thing, or a bad one?"

"Depends, I guess," answered Kornev honestly. "Probably good this time."

Bollatu nodded. When he had awakened on the beach, he had laughed for a long time. How he had managed to drift all the way back to shore without drowning, he did not know. Nor could he say why his bleeding wounds had not attracted any predators. Perhaps, he had thought, he had endured enough bad blessings for one day.

"Can I ask you a question?" Bollatu nodded in response toward the captain. "I noticed your ticket was purchased by a Jacob Matson. Isn't that the guy you said killed your Gr'Nar?"

"Yes," answered the old warrior. When Kornev gave him a look even the Kuzzi could interpret, the elder answered, "For some reason I cannot explain, once I realized I had survived, I felt it necessary to tell the tale to the man who had destroyed my ability to lead my tribe. He asked me what I was going to do now that I was no longer chief."

"What'd you tell him?"

Bollatu made a "tsking" sound, moving his tongue against his teeth. Giving the captain a look the man understood, the old warrior answered his question.

"I told him that on the morning I had gone to the sea, I felt old. I had left my people—gone to the ocean to die. The ocean spit me back. Thus I was free to do as I might."

Bollatu answered Kornev's next question before he could ask it. "The big tooth, the one that snarled my line, it washed up on the shore with me. I traded it to Matson for passage on your vessel."

Kornev raised an eyebrow. "He bought you a Rim Circle Trip. That's a lot of ticket for a tooth."

"He came, took my world. I told him that I would leave to take his heavens."

The captain smiled. Did the alien know how much this Matson had done for him?

Then again, thought Kornev, considering what Bollatu did for Matson by sitting back and letting humans get established on his planet, maybe the price wasn't all that steep.

The captain paused for a moment, staring out the observation port built into the close wall of the dining room. In many ways it was a senseless luxury, but it was one he delighted in. Staring out at the endless sea of stars, he thought that, maybe, he knew what the alien before him was feeling.

"There was a poet on my world," said Kornev, pouring himself and his guest another drink. "Emerson, they called him. He once said that 'few envy the consideration enjoyed by the eldest inhabitant.' Good thing you're just a kid, huh?"

Bollatu smiled.

"I do feel young," he answered, surprise in his voice. "As young as the mountains."

Man and Kuzzi laughed, banged their glasses together, drained them, then laughed once more.

THE END IS THE BEGINNING

BY ANDRE NORTON

THE two kits settled in front of the Teacher watched the unrolling of a tape so old that it was, in portions, dim, while the front of the machine's screen was scratched beyond any possible polishing. Most kits believed that the instructional device was one tool used by the now-vanished Smoothskins to spread what the Commander often called the Great Lie. However, the tapes could still provide some degree of entertainment, and one could think up many questions based upon the actions witnessed therein with which to baffle both Big Ones and other less-observant Littles.

"Why the Great Lie, anyway?" Marguay muttered, watching a scene wherein some type of creature supposedly—impossibly!—raised itself high into the air.

"Because of the Far Flight," Porky replied in a bored tone, as he lifted his right hand and licked the fur on its back. Then he began to recite, and Marguay joined in the ritual they had learned by rote from the time their eyes had fully opened and they had started exploring beyond the nest.

"The Smoothskins went out to the stars,
And the People went with them.
Long and long did they travel.
Among them were those who were close to the People,
And wished to draw nearer,

Desiring to share speech and duties.
Thus they used magic taught by the great Machines
And strove to make the People as they visioned.
So did the People learn to walk as the Smoothskins,
Use forepaws as hands, and—"

"What are you doing here?" demanded a voice from the doorway. "You two are on duty—why this hiding away and looking at parts of the Great Lie?"

Mam Sukie stood in the entry port to the compartment. Marguay hastened to shut off the machine, thinking ruefully that there was probably no trip to the Lookout for them now.

"Scat!" The ruler of the kits smacked each of the truants hard as they slunk past her. "You for litter-box duty—right now!"

Marguay waited until he was (he hoped) beyond hearing distance before he hissed; then he glanced quickly back over his shoulder. A Little must not forget that the Big Ones were able to walk very softly, and never more so than when about to bring a kit "to order," as they called the meting out of such discipline.

"There are no Smoothskins anymore," Porky huffed, panting a little as he strove to match his brother's pace. "I wonder where all of them went?"

"Don't be a weanling!" rebuked his companion. "You've heard Harvey often enough—they all up and died, and then they were shoveled into the converter."

"But—Father Golden says that when we die, we go out to the stars. Where did the Smoothskins go—to the stars, like us?"

Marguay hissed again. "Those clunkpaws? Hardly! Maybe that's just another part of the Great Lie. You want to meet one of them?"

Porky rumbled out a growl. "NO! My mam, she says they sometimes kept kits in *cages,* and other times—"the tubby Little's voice dropped to a near whisper, "—they did bad things to us. It was only because more and more of them died, and they did not have many small ones of their own to learn their tricks, that we People at last were given all *this,*" he threw wide his furred, clawed hands to encompass what lay about them, "for our own selves."

"Hey, you!" Ahead stood Wilber, and he was mad. He was almost Big in size, too, so the Littles felt it wiser not to tangle with him, even though they were two to his one.

They hurried on to the smelly place. Tippi, a small gray she, was already tilting a pan into one of the waiting cans. Her whiskers twitched as the he-kits joined her, and Maggie, her companion, snarled:

"What were you doing that Mam sent you along?"

"Looking at tapes," Porky answered before Marguay could stop him.

"Waste of time," Wilber commented, "all the Great Lie—never could be stupid stuff like that anywhere. Get to work, you two."

As he cleaned under Wilber's sharp eyes, Marguay thought about what he had found the last time he'd gone roving. There were many compartments where the People did not go very often, and a few of them held fascinating things. Some of the unknown objects were amusing to roll around and jump at when one was very small, but when a kit grew older, he could make even more interesting finds.

Not all the People were able to do as much as the Smoothskins, though more and more kits now being born were able to use machines easily and think harder ideas. Marguay's own mam, Knottail, had been able to open the box-things that had many pieces of paper fitted inside them. Lines of black dots marched in rows across those sheets, and a kit could learn to tell what they meant. A lot of the marks—most, in fact—dealt with the Great Lie, and some told their tale so convincingly as to make one believe the past had happened in just that way. And there were instructing devices, too, almost like the

Teacher except that they unrolled different stories. Marguay had every intention of going back to the last compartment he had found only yesterday and tinkering with the machine in that chamber—one of those pages with the Smoothskin-scratches told how to make it work, and the determined Little had almost been able to get it going.

Tippi was using a brush and catch-tray to sweep up crumbs of spilled litter; not much of the pan-sand remained anymore, and what might be saved must. Careful as the cleaner was, though, the job could not be spun out to excessive length, or Wilber would march the duty-doer off for another job. Marguay *had* to get away before then!

He and Tippi were out of the older kit's sight now, and the she-Little stood up, brush and scoop in hand, and looked at her partner.

"You going to the play-place?" she asked.

The Big Ones might call the room set aside for amusement "the play-place," but they themselves were always there, and thinking up tasks for Littles to perform—mostly the jobs no small kit wanted to do. Before he thought, her striped companion shook his head.

"Then will you go sneaking again?" she persisted.

Marguay's ears flattened in annoyance. What did Tippi know about him—and why? He had never noticed *her* very much; shes had their own affairs.

"I don't sneak!" he retorted.

"No?" she shot back. "Then what were you doing up on the top level yesterday?"

How had she found out where he was?

"Get to work, you two!" Wilber roared.

Both the Littles started guiltily and speeded up their labors. Marguay glanced at his fellow helper as often as he dared, wondering. How much had she learned? If he slipped away when they were through here, he must be careful she did not follow. He knew he wouldn't have to worry about pursuit by Porky—that well-rounded yellow fellow would be on his way to the mess hall by then, ready (as always) for a snack.

When the pair had finished their nose-wrinkling job and Wilber had reluctantly told them they might leave, the would-be explorer did not shoot away in the direction he wanted to go. Instead he followed Porky for a little way; then he slipped into one of the side passages, listening intently and looking back now and then. Luckily, none of the other People, Big or Little, appeared to be coming to retrieve him; so after making two more way-turns, Marguay went for his goal.

Less light shone up in this high passage. The inquisitive Little had overheard several full-growth kits talking about whether the illumination in some parts of their home was eventually going to fail. He was also aware that Commander Quickpaw had Big Ones working with him all the time, hastening to learn more about the objects the Smoothskins had used long ago.

Marguay shoved aside the compartment door and jumped up to the seat before the long shelf on which stood a machine with a dark screen. The box-thing—*book,* he corrected himself—that he had found yesterday was still open, and it was held outspread to the page he wanted by a Lie-thing. This was a figure, very heavy for its size, of one not unlike himself. But when had any of the People ever sat so, a ring in one ear, and—the he-kit pushed the offending object away from him a hiss—wearing a *collar*! Except for those adornings, though, the statue was not altogether of the Lie—the Little knew three of the Big Ones who were colored like this. But he could not let that problem trouble him now. Giving the false-kit-figure a final shove off the book, Marguay settled down to find out what he could manage to do with the silent machine.

What, he mused as he pored over the scratch-filled page, if he were able to make a *real* discovery—and the Commander were to learn that it was he, Marguay the

Little, who had performed the valuable deed? Suppose—

"What are you doing?"

His reverie shattered, the striped kit reared back and nearly slipped off the chair onto the floor. No longer did he hiss, as he had done to the statue—this kind of scare deserved a real spitting.

Tippi paid him no attention. Crouching slightly, she launched herself and leaped to the shelf that held the perplexing device. She then nosed against its blank front as if, by so doing, she could smell out its purpose.

The fur rose along Marguay's back, and his tail expanded and lashed. "Get out!"

His work-mate continued to ignore him. Seating herself in a calm curl, she patted the face of the machine; if she had any fear of it, she showed none.

"New Teacher?" she asked, as conversationally as though they were both in learning-litter. "You had better tell One-Eye. Remember what happened to him when he was a small kit and started up that chittering box? He was never able to shut it off either—and his eye got hurt." Still paying scant attention to her companion, Tippi bent her head intently and began to study the row of buttons below the blank square.

The hero-in-his-dreams could stand this insolence no longer. Wanting to do battle, or at least chase the intruder off, he slapped at her, claws out. She dodged the blow with ease, but Marguay's hand struck against three of the buttons.

Sound answered the blow. Tippi jumped back as they both heard a hum—the noise the Teacher made when coming to life. Two of the buttons the he-kit had bumped now showed green, not in a steady glow but a pulse that flickered very fast. The last one in line was red, and it did not move.

Down the machine's face-front now scrolled lines of the Smoothskin words, but these were gone too fast for Marguay to puzzle them out. And then, almost as strident as the battle-cry of a Big One, a voice shouted:

"Mission accomplished! Destination located! Assuming orbit!"

The two kits crouched together, for not only did the device repeat its message over and over, but a change was occurring in the compartment itself: the very walls were echoing the hum made by the machine when it had awakened. Then another call commenced, reaching even above the double din of voice and hum:

"Orbit alert—landing in twenty-five hours! Orbit alert, orbit alert! All systems go, faults negative—"

The noise in the walls continued. Marguay hurled himself down from the seat, Tippi following behind him so closely that she nearly bowled him over when she landed. Both intrepid explorers streaked for the door of the chamber.

They got no farther than the next deck down. On that level, the two found themselves in a most un-People-like crowd and confusion. Big Ones were racing for the section in which, it was said, the Smoothskins had sat in council when they were here. Other full-growth kits were also gathering; and mams were trying to catch Littles and having a hard time doing so.

Marguay and Tippi had been separated in the ever-growing press of People, and the he-kit shivered as that loud voice began to boom its announcement again.

"Orbit alert! Orders obeyed! Landing in twenty-five hours—"

Unable to pull free, the young adventurer was borne onward into the assembling-place of the Smoothskins. Bright-hued lights now flashed from many of its surfaces on which few now hurrying in had ever seen any life before.

Marguay squeezed himself as small as he could, trying to escape being stumbled over by Big Ones. Certain of those full-growth kits were standing by the machines and, as the Little was pushed forward into the room, he heard Commander Quickpaw roar a series of orders that sent them all into seats before the newly lit screens.

What were they trying to do? Marguay saw clumsy-appearing hands press down on buttons. Below some screens, lights burned red, and the commander leaped from one to the other of those machines, shouting at the Big Ones stationed there.

More hand motions, and the red lights disappeared. Commander Quickpaw watched closely for a short time; then he turned his head to hiss at those crowded in behind.

"Out. The ship is landing."

Ship? That was part of the Great Lie!

"Come," Father Golden waved his arms, urging the mass of People toward the door. "Our Learned Ones must be left alone now. There will be Cries to the Stars in the Great Assembly Place. Come!"

Slowly they obeyed. Mams carried very Littles in their arms, herding larger kits before them. The Big Ones came after. A husky full-growth routed Marguay out of his crouch, pulled him to his feet, and kept a hand on his shoulder until the group was out of the hall of many machines.

They regathered in the large compartment where the Big Ones always met to decide what was best for their kind. Now, however, the room rang to the voices of kits from the new-weaned to the white-whiskered.

"The Lie!" Marguay heard over and over again. "The Great Lie!"

Father Golden held up his hands and fairly war-screeched for their attention.

"Brothers—Sisters—we who are the People! The She-One of the Stars has remembered us, for we have come to the end of our far-faring such as the old tales foretold would be. Strengthen, then, your hearts; arouse in your inmost beings the courage of our kind—"

"This is the Great Lie—the lie of the Smoothskins!" A cry that ended in hissing interrupted him.

"Those who littered us," the father continued, unperturbed, "and those who brought them forth, birthing upon birthing beyond memory-reach—yes, they named as falsehoods the sayings of the Smoothskins. Yet if they—and we—lulled our fears asleep, as a mam quiets her kits, with the belief that that story was a falsehood, then the fault is ours. Yet I say to you that the mighty Star-She whom even the Smoothskins once served is with us still, and that there will be a new life for us all. It may be very strange, but we are the People, and we will survive!"

Overcome with shame, Marguay hunkered low, hoping to avoid Father Golden's sweeping gaze. The young kit wanted fiercely to close not only his ears but his mind in some way so that he could neither hear what was happening here nor remember what he and Tippi had done.

The crowd began to disperse. Certain kits drifted away with frown-creased brows, as though they strove now to make themselves believe a history long firmly denied. Others drew near to Father Golden and began the Cry to the Stars, the Plea to the She Who ruled them.

Under cover of the movement, Marguay slunk as far away from the rest of his kind as he could. A Lie that was truth—and he and his playfellow had *made* it so!

The erstwhile adventurer concealed himself in a storage place that looked empty, but something stirred in the shadows there, and Tippi mewed softly. Then she was beside him, her tongue touching the spot between his flattened ears, smoothing his fur. The two kits curled together, taking comfort from the warmth of each other's bodies; yet in spite of this reassurance, whenever that booming voice proclaimed another measure of time as the hours passed, they shivered.

At last, though, Marguay decided that it was better to look forward and not back, and he spent the rest of that longest of nights trying to recall the many wonders that had appeared on the old worn tapes. "There will be many things we have never known," he mused to his curl-mate, "and some we could not even dream."

"Those creatures in the air," Tippi agreed, catching his enthusiasm. "And all that green stuff outside—someone must have planted a very big water-garden!"

Both kits summoned from memory all they could, not only of what they had learned from the Teacher but also from the stories that had been told them about the old days of the Smoothskins. Some of the tales were less than pleasant.

"If the Furless Folk are waiting," the he-kit said, "we must hide. The People are free now, not slave-ones to be caged as the Smoothskins used our litter-sires."

He felt Tippi's shudder of sympathy. "Yes—hide," she agreed.

All too short a time later came the call for the People to assemble. When the two youngsters joined the rest, they were led to another compartment where a weblike substance was being woven across the floor. The netting, they were told, was to keep them safe while the ship landed. Marguay reflected that parts of the Great Lie must not have been taught to all kits, for he had never heard of this hold-fast, though the Big Ones in charge seemed very sure that such must be used.

The he-kit could never afterward remember that landing. He roused, sensing Tippi not far away. Cries, mews, and hisses filled the air as those about the two also wakened; then came Big Ones to free them all.

Hand in hand, Marguay and Tippi joined the crowd growing around the port that had never been opened. All watched apprehensively as the Learned Ones struggled with centuries-glued seals. To one side of the door stood Commander Quickpaw and a group of warrior-People who carried curious metal rods. The young he recognized those—one had been pictured in the book-box he had pored over. Such weapons could make a being fall down and be still—sometimes forever.

When the port was opened at last, the commander and his soldier-ones were the first to exit. Alien air flowed in after them, and Marguay lifted his head high to sniff a heady mixture of odors—unfamiliar, but enticing—mingled together.

Time passed, but the remainder of the People were forced to wait and wait. At last came the word that they might go, but they were warned to stay together, with the rod-bearers keeping guard abut them.

This place had no—no *roof,* was Marguay's first discovery as the kits stepped down a tilted walkway to the green flooring ahead. And that material was not flooring, either, but a substance that was soft underfoot. Then something moved, and a nearby he-Little grabbed at it. A moment later he raised a hand that clutched a small creature, near as green as their footing, which kicked until the kit crunched it.

Tall green-and-brown plant-things stirred when the breeze blew against them. The stalish atmosphere of the ship was gone now, and the People, ever sensitive of nose, reveled in the myriad fresh scents.

Five suns later, the ship's passengers and crew had established an outdoor living area. Scouts had discovered water that ran freely in streams. It had also been learned that the small beings in the grass (that, Marguay learned, was the name of the floor-growth) could be safely eaten. Two of those who explored—though all the People were under strict orders not to venture far from the camp, no matter what intriguing phenomenon beckoned for their attention—sighted much larger animals. And there were, indeed, living things—*birds*—that traveled through the sky itself!

Commander Quickpaw might have designated his Big

Ones to reconnoiter this new world, but once again it was Marguay and Tippi who made the great discovery.

The youngsters had undertaken to follow for a little way the stream, in which yet another kind of living being moved swiftly about. A day earlier, the he-kit had managed to get one out with his hand and had taken it back to his mam, who pronounced it excellent eating—better, even, than those tiny furred beasts that ran squeaking through the grass. Two of the other mams had then asked him to catch more of the water-wrigglers if he could.

Marguay had already flipped one of the creatures out of the stream. Now his companion, belly-down, was attempting to equal his skill, when a high-grown bush on the opposite side of the water began to shake. The kits glanced at each other, startled. Could this be one of the bigger animals the scouts had reported?

A moment later a—beast?—fell, rather than worked itself, out of the shrub. It scrambled on two hind legs down to the stream, then thrust its head in, gulping and choking. Though it bore patches of unkempt reddish hair on its body in places, far larger areas of bare skin were visible; and its head was not shaped as were the heads of the People.

Marguay and Tippi edged back from the water. Though they were not yet frightened enough to run, they had no idea how fast this creature could follow. The young he-kit longed for one of the weapon-rods.

Suddenly his companion caught at his arm with one hand, and with the other pointed excitedly at the drinker. Marguay saw what had caught her eye. Around the thing's thick throat ran a bright red band, and from this collar stretched a heavy leash that trailed back into the bush from which it had emerged.

The young explorer had no more than sighted that controlling device before the shrub once more rustled, then swayed. The leading-line snapped up and tightened, jerking the creature back out of the water. The patch-haired brute was held captive so, pulling at the prisoning collar and clasping both hands around the leash, but it was not left long to its struggles.

For around the shrub stalked a Big One—a very Big One, taller by far than the largest full-growth the kits knew. His fur was a tawny color with black spots in bold contrast. He, too, wore something about his throat, but his neckpiece was no slave-collar. It was a broad band of metal nearly the hue of the pelt on which it rested, and it sparkled in many places with bits of bright color. Encircling his forearms were a pair of similar glowing-and-glinting bands; and in one of his ears gleamed—a gold ring!

Marguay's mouth, already opened in astonishment, drew in a pleasing spicy odor from the stranger, borne across the water upon the wind. But the newcomer had halted abruptly to stare back, and he was now looking at them so intently that the small he-kit felt as though he had been lifted up by one of those clawed hands and was being turned round and round for inspection.

The two-leg beast that the stranger held in check raised its head. Matted and tangled hair covered most of its shoulders and blunt face, but there was still something about it—

"Smoothskin!" Tippi shouted.

The brute was not really one of the ancient aiders-of-the People; yet it was similar enough that Marguay could see how his companion might make such a mistake.

In response to the she-kit's outcry, the one who held that half-beast in check called back to them. Nothing about his voice or stance seemed threatening as he did so, and slowly the two Little explorers advanced once more to the water's edge. They had not understood what he had said, and he was *very* tall indeed, yet all their senses told them he was kin.

Pulling his unwilling captive with him, the alien Big One entered the stream to splash across. Both kits waited courageously. Their noses wrinkled at the smell of the brute-thing he led; still, his own scent, beneath its exotic spicy tang, was as familiar as their own.

Again he spoke. Marguay shook his head but answered in his own language: "Come—see our commander, the Big Ones—come."

The stranger obeyed, giving frequent jerks to his charge's leading-line as he moved; and in this manner the pair of junior adventurers brought him to the encampment. Several of the guards fell in around their prize and his "pet," but those soldier-kin offered no raising of rods.

Thus Antimah of the Tribe of Rammesese, in the service of the Great Goddess Bast Herself, came to sit at a council meeting with the People from afar. Some of the attendants drew sketches with sticks in the dirt; others returned to the ship and brought out maps of the starways, pictures of their vessel's interior, drawings of the Smoothskins.

Marguay, however, slipped away from the crowd that stood watching the momentous meeting in wonder. Once more in the ship, he ran unhesitatingly to the compartment he had discovered, and there he caught up that statue-representative of his kind who wore golden adornment much like that of this splendid newcomer. When he had hurried back, he held high the figure and dared to interrupt the commander himself.

"Look!"

All heads swung toward him, and look they did. For answer, the stranger moved first. Coming to Marguay, he lifted his hand, palm out; and, fixing his eyes on the statue, he bowed his head.

Then he turned. Tossing to one of the guard-kin the leash of the Smoothskin-That-Was-Not, the living model of the figurine opened his arms wide in a gesture that could only mean full welcome.

Above them shone Sol, and underfoot was the soil of Terra. The far-farers as yet had that to learn; but for them, the end of their flight was also the beginning in a world that the Smoothskins, in their time of power, had near destroyed. For the People, sent forth without their consent, had touched the outermost reaches of the heavens, and now their years'-lost home had received them once again.

NICOBAR LANE

The Soul Eater's Story

BY MIKE RESNICK

It seemed that I had been alone for millennia.

I can remember the creation of the galaxy, the white-hot gasses coalescing into suns and worlds, the ever-increasing black hole at the very epicenter.

I can remember the first tentative attempts of starfaring races to populate the worlds of the Milky Way. I remember the laughably small ships racing from planet to planet, and ultimately from system to system.

I remember the explosive wars, the death-dealing weapons, the campaigns, the englobements, the explosions and implosions, the lifeless bodies spinning off into space to take up their eternal orbits.

But what I mostly remember is the aching loneliness, the terrible, frightening knowledge that I was finally the last member of my race in a cold and impersonal galaxy. There was no one with whom I could share my hopes and my fears, my dreams and my longings and my terror.

I'm sure that I had a beginning, a birth, but it was so many billions of years ago that I can no longer remember it. Once, so long ago that I can hardly recall it, there were others of my kind. We floated through the void, fed upon the vast dust clouds, touched in a way that I cannot begin to explain.

Then, one by one, they vanished. Killed, I presume, since otherwise we are eternal. It seemed that one moment the galaxy was filled with us, and the next instant there was only me.

And so it remained—for days, for years, for centuries, for millennia, for time past measuring. The loneliness closed in around me, became almost tangible, beat me down and dulled my perceptions. Oh, there were still ships traversing the void, but they held no interest for me. They were not my kind, and I was not theirs, and communication seemed futile. I fell into regular but mindless patterns, moving from one feeding ground to another, trying desperately to forget the past until at last I succeeded, and then trying just as desperately to remember it.

And then one day I sensed something different, yet similar. It was a small metal ship, barely a thousandth of my own length. It was not unlike a hundred others I had seen and attempted to avoid—but this time I was struck by a loneliness as deep and bitter as my own. I knew it could not belong to the ship, which is an inanimate thing, but rather to the being that commanded it. I reached out a mental tendril, and was appalled.

The pilot, indeed the only being aboard the ship, thought of itself as a "man." Its name was Nicobar Lane, and it was a professional hunter—which is to say, it killed things for its livelihood. I had hoped two starfarers might have something in common, but I could not force myself to make contact with the killer of so many things, let alone consider forming any kind of personal bond with it.

The ship had seen me, or possibly Nicobar Lane had sensed my presence, I did not know which at the time, but there seemed only one thing t do, and so I did it—I fled at many times light speed. He followed for a few moments, but I darted into the parsecs-long dust cloud, and he pursued me no further.

I was safe, and he was gone—and yet . . . and yet, there was *something* about him, something more than the loneliness. Self-appraisal, perhaps. Not exactly regret, for he had no regrets about his occupation—he felt that he was the best of his race at it, and probably he was—but regret that the needs and economics of the galaxy should *require* a being who was so skilled at hunting and killing. Of all the beings of all the galaxy's many races with which I had formed a fleeting bond, only he was totally, painfully, tragically honest with himself.

There were complexities there, complexities of such a nature that I suspected no one else had ever noted or analyzed them, that Nicobar Lane himself had no idea they were there or that he was anything other than a skilled killer of animals with a vague sense of dissatisfaction concerning his life.

He intrigued me—a totally honest being. And a lonely one. By rights I should have fled halfway across the galaxy, lost myself in the Greater Magellanic Cloud where he could never find me . . . but I was as curious about him as he was about me.

So I remained in the area, feeding locally, making only a perfunctory effort to hide—and before long I found him again, or perhaps he found me, I am still not clear which. This time he was not alone. He had another of his race with him, an old man whose every thought and every emotion welcomed Death. A beam of some sort leaped from his ship. I analyzed it, saw that it could do me no harm, and made no attempt to avoid it. Instead, I let it drive through my molecules, concentrated on the men's minds, and let them feel what I had felt.

It killed the old man, but I felt no regret, for he wanted nothing more than to die. But its effect on Nicrobar Lane was electrifying. I could not separate all his reactions, but primary were pain, and pleasure, and surprise.

And then fury.

I had not meant to hurt him, only to share at the most basic level what he was doing to me. For the moment that we were in contact, I found to my surprise that it was not the pain that had elicited his fury, but rather the pleasure. Even he did not understand what he had felt or was feeling now, but he knew that it made him uncomfortable, and that I was the source of it, so he turned his rage upon me. I fled but remained nearby, in case his fury should dissipate—and after a time, it did.

We met again, and again, and again. Each time we shared the bond, as he came closer and closer to leaving his past life and joining me in the present. And each time we met, I perceived yet a new emotion: shame.

And, along with the shame, one more reaction: guilt.

Still, neither the shame nor the guilt stopped him from flying into the vast interstellar void to approach me. He had to break away a number of times to refuel his vessel, but each time he came back we intertwined our emotional tendrils—and yet never once did I perceive him to be free of the shame or the guilt.

And then came the day that he approached me out by a red binary, and I discovered that he had an alien being with him, a being that was neither lonely nor honest, but simply filled with a sense of purpose—and that purpose was to kill me. I was sure Nicobar Lane would not allow this to happen, so I made no move to flee.

Then a beam shot out, and I felt pain such as I had never known before. The agony came close to burning all my neural circuits, but finally it subsided enough for me to try to bond telepathically with Nicobar Lane and find out why he had done this, or if it had been done without his permission.

What I received shocked me almost as much as the burst of energy. In the past, he had thought of me as the Dreamwish Beast and the Starduster and a host of other appellations—but now, with a cold fury fueled by his shame, he knew me only as the Soul Eater, and there was no shred of mercy in his thoughts, only an overwhelming desire to end my existence, as if that would bring peace to his own.

I knew that I must flee if I were to remain alive, and in my panic I did not bother to analyze whether remaining alive was a worthy goal for one such as I. I began racing toward the rim of the galaxy with Nicobar Lane's ship in hot pursuit. When I reached it, I realized that I would not have the energy to cross the enormous void between galaxies, and there was no food for me between the Milky Way and Andromeda, so I turned back and headed toward the Galactic Core. The ship matched my every move, and as I neared the black hole that filled the Core, I changed my angle of approach and let it slingshot me into another universe.

The ship followed me, but I noticed a difference when it emerged. The alien was dead, and it was just him and me, alone in an unknown universe. He took up the pursuit again, I fled again, and finally, when I was almost out of range, another beam of deadly energy shot out and struck me.

I could bear no more pain. I had tried to form a link with this most unusual of creatures. I wanted only to bond with him, to share his loneliness and his sorrow, and this was the result: he had all but killed me. I was in a new universe, but it varied only in detail from the one I had so recently departed. There were none of my kind here. In fact, Nicobar Lane and I might well be the only two living things in the whole of this new creation—and his sole desire was to destroy me.

I had the energy to race away again, but to what end? An eternity of loneliness? Or, as my energies lessened, a painful death that had been anticipated for days or months or years? Better to have it over with right here, right now.

I came to a stop and turned to him.

You have won, I tried to say. *I do not know why you have grown to hate and fear me, because I have never tried to harm you. I was lonely. You were lonely. We are two thinking beings. I thought that was enough. Evidently I was wrong, though I still do not know why. Go ahead and end it now. I will not run again.*

Then the strangest thing happened. It was almost as if he could not only read my thoughts but see into my very soul, and I could respond in kind. He stared at me in his viewscreen, a score of conflicting emotions crossing his face.

Finally he reached for a control, and I prepared for my death.

"Ah, hell," he said, and fired a pulse that seemed to engulf me in warmth and—dare I say it?—love. I felt it, analyzed it, returned it mentally . . . and finally, for the first time in aeons, I was no longer alone.

We approached the black hole again, and soon emerged into this, our universe.

We remain at the edge of civilization, just close enough for him to get fuel for his ship when he needs it. Then we race off to the Magellanic Clouds, content with each other's thoughts and company.

I know that Man is a short-lived race, and soon he will be gone, and I will be alone again.

But having experienced the bond we shared, I may be lonely again, but I will never be without hope again—for now I know that the Maker of All Things has not forgotten me. I have found this warmth and intimacy once, and I will find it again and again until the stars come racing back and the universe implodes into a single atom.

And even then, at the very last nanosecond of existence, what is left of me will still remember what is left of him.

EDITOR'S NOTE

In 1981 an NAL editor by the name of Sheila Gilbert published a novel by Mike Resnick entitled The Soul Eater.

In 1992 a Warner editor by the name of Brian Thomsen reissued The Soul Eater *under Warner's* Questar *imprint.*

Now Resnick, Gilbert (now at DAW), and Thomsen return to the scene of the crime to publish the other side of the story.

PROTO-PIRATES OF THE GALAXY AND BEYOND

If there is a sea to sail on, there will always be pirates there bent on plundering, whether it is the sea of Columbus and Blackbeard or a sea of time and space.

The asteroid belt, the spaceways, and far-off makeshift settlements are all akin to island hideaways and the merchant lanes of the Spanish galleons.

Sometimes the pirates bear cutlasses, other times proton torpedoes, and yet other times lawyers and lawsuits.

In all cases they strike fear into unwary sailors and plunderees.

Yo ho! Yo ho!

MESSAGE IN A QUANTUM BOTTLE

BY TOM DUPREE

PEARED undisturbed, but newly fashioned, buffed to a great silver splendor. MacLendon found it first, resting behind our last rum cask, and had the first mate's lips not been so parched as the sun slipped over the yardarm, there it might be still.

Thank God that Houghton had the devil in him, man, so we all said. Our first mate ordered the final hogshead broached, to the lusty cheers of every last man aboard, and when MacLendon pulled the precious cooperage from its resting place belowdecks, out rolled the bowl, or goblet, or flagon, or whatever in perdition it was. So surprising was its appearance that MacLendon froze in his task, and nearly all thought of the drop was gone for the nonce.

Which chest of plunder had it fallen from while we had been busy lapping up gold and jewels like so many starving dogs? How many months had it lain in that dark corner, with only the rats for company, while we plied the Indies and plucked the treasures from a dozen islands and a hundred merchantmen sails? We could not tell, for it glinted like new, even in the fading light.

Here were men who had rounded the world, enjoyed fifty lifetimes' worth of adventures, watched human beings walk on hot coals, sleep on beds of nails, and disappear on a rope into the air, endured the most devilish typhoons blown their way, stolen fortunes from pirates and princes alike, fought alongside each other at the doorway of death, and been the secret envy of all the poor sods who were lashed to dull drudgery for the rest of their pale, quiet lives. Here were men who had done and seen everything that could possibly be done and seen from the base of a mast. Yet not one among us had ever beheld the like of this simple silver bottle.

Such workmanship—true it was, sure and bright. The smithy who forged it can ship out with me any day—nay, he could grace any of the finest establishments in London. It was not steel, that much we knew, for it lifted so lightly that I imagined it might float away. And no one, not even the thirstiest among us, had ever beheld a container like this: curved at the neck and then widening toward its base like the hips on a luscious barmaid, the bowl large enough to hold grog sufficient to make a man forget the events of an evening upon arising the next day. Darby said it was the kind of bottle a man rubbed to get a genie. I said something better popped up whenever I started rubbing, and the lads roared with me.

We could not see inside, but there seemed to be something there. It rustled as we shook the bottle. But opening it was another matter, one that eluded all challengers as surely as that ancient sword buried in the stone. The gentle neck led up to nothing: no screw or stopper could we find. We yanked and twisted and pulled at the neck, but the thing held as fast as a harpoon thrown true. Finally the Moor, a man so powerful he can go up the rigging using his hands alone, brought his heavy cutlass to the task as requested, set the mystery on deck, and lifted his weapon skyward as if to chop off a head. He grunted with the effort and we felt the force of his blow through the deck. His aim was true, yet the Moor, who had sent dozens of men to their reward each with one mighty swing, was unable to make so much as a dent against the damned thing. It made to roll leeward with the waves, but Magee picked it up and held it to the burning sunset.

"Lads, this chippy's sturdy enough to protect the Crown Jewels!"

"Aye, or the family jewels!" said the Scot.

Magee reared back his head with that big laugh that had called us into many a battle, lifted his hand in mirth, and slapped the neck of his silver toy. Suddenly the air began to shimmer and crackle. The hair rose on the back of my neck and one of the boys howled at Magee over

Look into its manufacture, possibly a presumptive metal based in one or more of the indeterminant standard-state elements; an unprecedented bezium-heisium post-inert alloy is the closest hypothesis this council is willing to support. This would in theory allow a dual-state existence, one that could attach and propel itself across great vistas of time and space. The theoretical purpose of such a device is unclear. The technology is, frankly, far beyond our own. But let us engage for a moment in a thought experiment. If controlled randomness could somehow be applied toward a codified purpose, possibly by employing a third *quantum element which we do not yet understand, and if this experiment could be repeated using precise admixtures of indeterminants, the here-not-here unit might be utilized as a metaphysical probe, to witness and even record firsthand knowledge, heedless of Newtonian-age boundaries. It would be an information vessel free to wander anywhere and anywhen, perhaps governed by connective defaults, perhaps the slave of coincidence. Data could be gathered and stored in countless formats—written, audiovisual or further sensual, digital, even pure thought—and retrieved in the manner most appropriate for, or attuned to, the needs of the sender. It would be the ultimate search and sift machine. Of course, there would still remain the problem of retrieval back to the point of origin in space-time, but whatever technology created this device would surely have addressed this issue.*

* * *

ride in the uncommonly bright starlight, period, paragraph.

I never fail to marvel at the splendor of the heavens in this thin atmosphere, period. We stand on the shoulders of those who have gone before us, comma, and this rich display issues from the very highest vantage point, comma, built from the labor of countless brave and resourceful pioneers, period. I am closer to the stars today because I stand on the shoulders of these unnamed and unknowable men and women, period. My only constriction is the breathing unit over my nose and mouth, comma, but it does not hinder the eyes or detract from the ravishing view, period. For those who have become jaded by the grime and congestion of terrestrial destinations, comma, the answer is celestial, semicolon, the star sea, comma, as close to a paradise of rest and contemplation as one is likely to find, period, paragraph.

I glide along on a sandship, comma, a self-propelled model of the latest design, comma, softly pushing its way across the vast, comma, gently undulating granular plain. An unexpected pleasure is the midrange hiss of the sand as it is displaced by the ship, comma, the only sound one can hear, comma, a comforting noise whose effect is not unlike the rhythmic crashing of ocean waves back home, period. The ship-hire agency was kind enough to include a basket of locally-produced cheeses and baked goods, comma, and a hydroponic claret from the first vintage grown, comma, fermented, comma, and bottled under completely artificial conditions, period. This is in itself an amazing achievement, comma, since both wine making and proper cellaring depend so much on the precise force of gravity, period. Here, comma, viniculture is as much a product of pioneering and creativity as of craft, period. Processes which have been relied on for millennia must constantly be adjusted and reinvented, period, paragraph.

Gazing around aboard ship, comma, I notice another amenity, comma, the loveliest decanter I have ever seen, comma, a handsome silver flask-shaped receptacle, comma, no doubt rendered opaque to protect the color and body of the fragile wine against the long-term ravages of light rays made especially harsh in the open air of this only partially terraformed environment, period. Note, recheck sentence for run-on, end note. Herein lies the most difficult task of an otherwise carefree excursion, period. I must confess that my technological skills are sadly lacking, since my best efforts to unstopper the bottle have proved futile, period. We pay a price for the remarkable transformation of this orb and the onward march of society, comma, and mine is that the use of a simple decanter in this place on this day evidently requires an instruction manual, period, paragraph.

I run up the rotation of the fans with a simple motion on the console, period. The sail billows beautifully and the ship's pace increases slightly, period. I savor an unusually sharp slice of superbly aged Jack as I cut the foil and push down on the pullscrew, period. The downward pressure soothes the plastic cork up and out, comma, a fascinating bottle design also attributable to the ingenuity of these artisans, period. What a glorious moment, period. The wine shows a brilliant ruby color against the white sand aglow with the soft starlight, period. I tilt the nosepiece to enjoy the aroma of cassis and black cherry, semicolon, it can be removed safely for up to two minutes at a time, comma, and this is most definitely the time, period, paragraph.

I look again at the pullscrew and realized that I have solved my problem, period. The decanter design must match the bottle, period. I center the screw and push down the lips retracting into itself pulls me in t e r

Let us be timid for a moment. In a continuum of limitless possibilities, the likelihood of random disaster is also infinite. How can one hope to predict the effect of a quantum inference into a singularity, or an encounter with antimatter? Learned ladies and gentlemen, the only thing of

which we can be positive is that we cannot be positive. And since the indeterminants are unstable even in the best of circumstances, the consequences would be as subtle, and as profound, as that of an ounce of thrust used against a moving object in space, or on the waters. In such a scenario, the behavior of a theoretical malfunctioning device is something of which we can only speculate. Once again, the theoretical risks, being known to us, would certainly also be known by the issuing technology, which would doubtless have built in critical safeguards to prevent, or at least circumscribe, potential cataclysmic events.

face down in the galley, babe. You call it a galley. Down there. It's all gone now. But check out the coffee can.

's up with that? You hiding it or something?

From the man, yeah. From you, come here, babe.

Mmm.

Mmm.

Dude tried to mess with me at the airport. I'm like, officer, I have a plane to catch, so if you want a body search, it's gonna cost you, plus the plane ticket.

Ek ek ek ek. What he say?

She. She said look like it might be worth it.

I'd pay it.

Mmm.

Mmm.

I'm gonna check out that coffee can. You want something?

Red Stripe.

Here ya go, main man. Twist it up real nice, too.

What took you so long?

Had to twist one! Plus find a church key for your ice-cold Stripe. How long you had this boat anyway? Can't find anything down there.

Got it in April, last run to Cayman.

Had it long enough to screw up everything down there, though. Needs a woman's touch, sugar.

I need that, too.

Mmm.

Mmmaah.

Now ain't that better?

Damn. I'm taking you downstairs, woman.

Think you better rest up a little first. I want you in top condition before we go down there.

Where's that twist?

You want me to wet it up?

Damn.

Taste better this way.

Hold the tiller. Pppph. That is some sweet shit, babe. They're gonna be running for me when they hear this shit is coming.

Pppph. Where we headed?

East. Down to Antigua, Martinique. Barbados if we still got some left. Big man in Barbados. Got a place at Crane Beach. Wants to talk about a whole shipload, me to him.

I wish you'd find some sugar daddy like that and stick with him. Stop all this small-time shit. It's dangerous, honey. The more times you make land, the more chances you'll get caught.

Yeah, well, nobody gonna catch us today. We got all the blue ocean to run in. I swear, I never ever get tired of my sweet Carib.

Yeah, pppph, this shit makes me look real close at it. Huh.

While you're looking, mama, gimme that tiller and get me another Stripe. And put on Billy Ocean or some shit.

Aye aye, captain lover man.

What took you so long?

Look at this.

What's that?

I thought it was yours. It's not yours?

Hell, no. Where was it?

Sitting out on the counter.

I never saw it before. Must be the last guy who owned this boat.

You clean up some, you might see a lot more things around here. It's beautiful.

I repeat, what is it?

Look like something on *Babylon 5*.

I didn't know you were a Rastawoman. Or whatever they call it.

No, *Babylon 5* the space show. God damn, there's other things in this world besides a twist. I'm talkin' about all chrome and shit, like space stuff.

Okay, okay, Babylon's in space now, I repeat again: what is that thing?

Well, Captain Kirk-my-ass, it is some kind of silvery bottle, and we will find out exactly what is inside it when we open it, I mean, duh.

What's wrong?

Can't get it open.

Come on, pull.

Unhh. Won't come.

Give it to me. Unhh. Damn.

Maybe we just need to get a hole started. Got an ice pick?

Nope.

Wait—the church key.

Okay.

Okay. Now hold it tight, let me get a grip, and I'll just get it started. Ready?

Ugh. Sounds like a beehive.

Baby, stop! You're bleeding re

There are those who would assign religious significance to the sudden appearance of this object, since it materialized aboard a merchant vessel whose cargo included consecrated items bound for an offworld settlement. The council acknowledges the holy starsailors who acted promptly and properly in referring this matter to its authority, and to this SkyLab, where research may be carried on under the strictest quarantine conditions. The fact that we do not understand the origin or purpose of the device is incontestable, but that certainly does not make it extra-natural. Quasi-*natural might be a more fitting descriptor. At any rate, science must assume that an explanation exists, even if we cannot apprehend it today.*

set for meat. Meat run fast. Some meat swim. Meat swim, man swim. Swim on top. Me man make swim thing. On top. Some man say no man swim on top. No. Me man on top. Me man take meat that swim. Some man no swim on top. Man go down. Not me man. Me man have swim thing. Make from land. Stay on top. Make more swim things. Take meat that swim. Eat meat that swim. Ha!—shine thing! Take shine thing. Me man eat sh

The positing of such unusual scenarios may seem unnecessarily reckless, but the fact remains that, as stated, some explanation must exist for the baffling condition of this object. Repeated tests conducted by the council, yielding data that has withstood our most rigorous cross-checking and redundancy procedures, have affirmed the anomaly again and again. In simple language, this object's volume appears to be greater than its outside dimensions would permit. In fact, the differential is so astonishingly large that it defies the tenets of logic. These data indicate that inside this vessel is a theoretically infinite capacity for storage. But theory can only bring us so far.

ut down! Perfect! It's back!"

"You're kidding!"

"No, no, it worked!"

"How long? What? A microsecond?"

"If that. I just barely saw a flutter, and I'm not even sure I didn't imagine it."

"I missed it completely."

"Get the temperature. Is it hot?"

"No change. No change."

"Okay, then. How do we know it went anywhere at all?"

"What did you set it for again?"

"First thing I could think of. I just entered the word 'ship.' "

"Ha, that's the swashbuckler in you. I tell you the truth, man, a couple hundred years on and Robert Louis Stevenson's still got to be the most influential author in the Valley. A generation of nerds with swords, right? Geocoordinates?"

"Free float. Slice and dice."

"So it could have been anywhere."

"And any time."

"Past and future?"

"Unknown, but in theory, yepper. In theory, it could have been *everywhere*. Everywhere there's a ship. Or was a ship. Or will be a ship. And very nice range, too."

"Hope you typed very carefully when you set the control sequence, my friend."

"Vox, man. Get real."

"Then I hope you really popped your P, know what I'm sayin'? Something smell around here?"

"Ha. Nobody types any more except newszappers. For the solid-mail packets. So last century. This thing's got thought recog, too, but I decided to play it safe. Let's see, it can't have had an infinite ride, else it'd still be gone. Or would it? Is infinity ever over? I guess it could be, in a finite but expanding universe."

"Too deep, too deep. You're starting to hurt my head. I blew off physics in school. I'm just in marketing, man."

"Well, get ready to market your ass off. This is the most outrageous bot anybody ever saw."

"You got that right. New rules from now on. This is the hottest patent ever. This is the future, sitting right here on this beautiful little counter, and people are gonna be killing themselves to get at it."

"Pop the Dom. We're rich, my little demographics-running chickadee. We are stone cold rich. Roaring drunk rich. Private yacht rich. Private *island* rich! We are now the Microdiz of information retrieval."

"It's badder than that. We just put every search engine on the net out of business, man. Microdiz got nothing on this. It's the ultimate selling proposition: everybody wants it, and only we have it. This is a company-maker. A dynasty-maker."

"Okay, let's see what we've got."

"Great touch, making it fold inward to open."

"Just makes it a bit tougher for accidents to happen."

"Hey. Feels like static electricity, man."

"No sweat, I've got gloves."

"Hey, it hurts."

"Me, too . . . get it over with. Okay, little baby, spit it all out. Play

This council has been assembled to address one simple question at the heart of the matter: how are the two physical states—within and without—able to coexist? To that end, and you may follow me on your monitors, we now enter the stasis chamber where the object has been stored since its arrival at this laboratory. Omnalysis reveals that the vessel has no fracture points, that it is evidently one solid construction. Now we probe the device for possible entry vectors. It has already been demonstrated that it is built to resist all the lateral force we can bring to bear on the neck versus the bowl. Of course, learned colleagues, physics gives us another option, which we will now explore. To pull has been heretofore futile. Therefore, as may have become obvious by now, we will push—attempt to collapse the subject item in upon itself, and hope that we may thus expose the nature of its construction and use.

Please assume your protective position and wear the goggles that have been assigned to you. You may begin the pressure sequence no

back from Good Hope, that was a damn deep dive all right, but it still wasn't as dark as this. Not nearly. Get the whole thing, Willy. That's right, hold, hold on the stern as we drop. Try not to shake. Perfect. Jeez, look at the fish down here. Way underwater is like going to Mars. Same thing. Watch it, Willy. Don't get antsy. Cool and calm. Keep it focused, focused, get the phosphor patch, now zoom in, nice, nice. David, take us in very slowly, and . . . wonderful. Lovely. What a pilot, Dave . . . very sexy moves. Okay, out again and once more, like we're entering the wreck. Move the sphere in like a dolly, David. Fantastic. Willy, great work. Get some cutaways now. Beautiful. Beautiful. God, she's a handsome ship. How long ago did you say? Hundred and fifty? What in the world could have made that mess? Me, too, but they just didn't have that kind of explosive back then, did they? I mean, cannon shot can't do that. Poor bastards. What's that, Willy? No, back, back. That's no fish. What is that? How close can you get, David? Can you use the arm? Easy, easy. Hold it up. My God. Jesus. A bottle, you think? It looks brand new. Can't be from this wreck, can it? How come it isn't covered with shit like everything else? Get it aboard, David. Tight on it, Willy. God, what a piece of work. Man. Great dive, gentlemen, thank you very much. David, put it in the compartment with the rest of the stuff. We'll open it upstairs.

PYRATS!

BY JODY LYNN NYE

"PINK one, hear me!" the captain shrilled, loud enough to break glass. "Come out at once!"

Tobie Marley started, knocking her head on the ceiling of the maintenance duct. It was just barely high enough and wide enough to accommodate a big-boned woman 170 centimeters tall. The telekythe interface that had been painfully attached into her skull didn't hurt anymore, but voices seemed to be loud because they were carried by bone conduction. She pulled herself out from underneath the captain's bathtub (swimming pool, really, since the captain was a white lab rat only the size of her shoe). His fur was ruffed up, a sure sign of bad temper. She stayed on her hands and knees, eye level to the rat perched on the edge of the tub.

"What'd I do?" she asked.

"It looks like you have done nothing!" he screamed. She winced. "Does it work?"

Marley flipped on the taps using her little finger. Water, clean water, gushed out of the spout. "Yes, it works. But don't use it in zero gee."

The captain's fur settled down immediately, and his pink-rimmed eyes slitted with pleasure. He trotted over to test the temperature of the water on his tiny hand-like paw.

"Good," he squeaked, and the interface translated it. "Leave me. Go eat. The bell rang a while ago."

Marley held up her wrists, showing him the sensor bracelets. She needed him to deactivate them for this zone. If she tried to pass outside the allowable area, powerful electrical shocks would bring her to her knees with pain. It had happened too many times during her early captivity for her to leave without making sure.

Impatiently he scurried to a control panel a few inches square at the foot of the door, fiddled with the controls for a moment, then scampered back to the steadily filling tub.

Marley didn't wait for dismissal. She stood up and strode out. Food was the only reason she was putting up with the rats at all.

She walked as quietly as she could through the maze of auxiliary tunnels and corridors leading to the workers' mess hall. She sniffed the air. The scrubbers were working again. The one thing that had been hardest for her to stand at first was the smell of ammonia produced in the rats' urine. They didn't mind, but Marley's eyes watered for weeks. She thought she would never get used to it, but between improvements in the ventilation system and the passage of time, she'd stopped smelling it unless it got really bad. Amazing, when she stopped to think, there must have been a few hundred thousand rats on the freighter.

All the primary passages, the direct ones, had been roofed over at about knee height, for their exclusive use. The area above them had been divided into warrens, complex, multichambered living quarters for rat nurseries, as had almost all of the comfortable cabins. The few sleeping quarters that remained intact were kept for the exclusive use of the captain and ship's officers, all rats, as a sign of high status. Marley envied them the room to stretch out. The enslaved human work force lived miserably by comparison, stuffed together four to a cabin. It was adequate; the workers weren't supposed to be in them except to sleep and groom.

The conditions were meant to make the humans want to move on as soon as possible, or die.

The rats really didn't dare, once they'd gotten a decent amount of work out of them.

That wasn't completely true, Marley had to admit. The rats treated her reasonably well, except when she stepped out of line. Their discipline was brutal. She had bite marks all over her body from massed attacks she had suffered while she was being "trained," for being defiant. In spite of her fear and distrust, she was fed, housed, allowed to be clean, given work to do, and—above all—kept alive. When she fell sick with an internal complaint in the early days of her captivity, they allowed a human medic, a fellow prisoner-of-war, to tend her. And they fed her good food.

Humanity really had brought this on itself, Marley thought, passing the elevator station, where a monitor broadcast constant images of Earth. The rats wanted a ready reminder of their mission, their goal, and their enemy.

Over the last few hundred years, the human population had spread out so much that superior pest control became necessary to safeguard health and protect precious food supplies. Storage facilities were robotized, complex facilities that attacked intruders of any size with poison, electricity, or worse. In order to survive, parasites and scavengers had had to evolve beyond animal cunning into intelligence.

The first species to break through the barrier into sentience was raccoons, but they were too large and too obvious to avoid detection. Humans caught up with them within mere years of their breakthrough. Some were put into zoos. The rest were wiped out. Coyotes made a try, but they were even easier to round up than the raccoons.

Next came the real survivors: rats.

Having been bred to almost human intelligence in laboratories over the course of centuries, it only remained for a bored and motivated population of captive animals to observe the observers, to understand their speech, to learn how processes and systems worked, and to create a viable language of their own so they could communicate these behaviors to one another. Enough escaped, by dint of their own efforts (or through the assistance of animal-rights groups made up of humans), and settled down to breed a superior species.

The suspected "Lucy-rat," the first rodent to achieve speech, was never found, but her daughters, sons, and billions of grandchildren soon started an underclass, stealing food supplies and counteracting nearly every trap set for them. Human beings did their best to eradicate the new rat, but they had waited too long. The race had been preparing for survival. Out of arrogance, humanity had assumed no other creature, except cute ones like dolphins and elephants, could achieve intelligence, let alone become a dominant species.

The rats now took the initiative. Having determined that the best way to survive was to wipe out humanity so they could have Earth all to themselves, a few brave and persevering rats swarmed aboard a spaceship that was outward bound to strip out useful equipment from an abandoned space station in the Sol system. Once outside the defense grid of Earth, they took the human crew prisoner, and established the first pirate colony in the orbiting hulk.

Within a short time they figured out how to make the food machines work, how to fire the weapons, and how to work the environmental controls. What they could not do, with their superior intelligence, watchfulness, and above all, ability to breed quickly to fill the ranks of their troops, was perform ship maintenance. For that they needed human slaves.

The first group, survivors from the coup, was unsatisfactory. The workers kept trying to escape or dying inconveniently. The rats figured out they needed to convince their slaves that their cause was just—or maintain a credible threat that kept them from attempting a counterattack.

Marley and her shipmates were from the second wave. They had been the crew of a mining ship on its way back into Earth orbit from the asteroid belts. They were tricked by a distress call. The young female engineering tech who had made it had apologized ever since. Her distress was real. Unfortunately, now so was theirs.

The mining ship *Sophia* had not been a random choice. Highly maneuverable and with backup systems on its backups, it was intended for long-term missions away from the facilities of Earth. Once it had docked at the space station, a few rats crept aboard while the crew went looking for the humans who had made the call. Before the captives could explain, the rescuers were overwhelmed by hordes of rats. Marley and a few of the others fought their way loose and tried to get back to the ship, but by the time they did, the hatch wouldn't open for them. The rats had taken control of the systems.

A spectacular explosion consisting of rocket fuel and all the metallic and plastic garbage aboard the space station made it seem as though the *Sophia* had been destroyed by an internal fault in the drives, so no one would ever come looking for them. Marley had lost hope after that. Her parents had undoubtedly arranged for a plaque on the wall of the main neighborhood corridor in their section, where busy passersby could ignore it on their way to or from work, Marley thought, cynically. Since then, the rats had taken over a gigantic long-range freighter, the *Mary Sue,* and two more mining ships, the *Crowbar* and the *Simpson* (perfect for their intentions of halting and diverting food shipments coming in to Earth). When it sounded like the Terran governments were going to get it together and attack the space station, the rats and their captives had abandoned it and gone to live aboard the freighter. Going back over the vids in their collection, they'd named it the *Avast Ye.*

"It is something real pirates say," the captain had

explained. (He fancied himself a cross between Kidd and Drake.)

The converted ships preyed upon food supply ships coming to Earth from the many agricultural colony worlds throughout the galaxy. After taking what they needed, the rats diverted megashipment after megashipment of vegetables, fruit, livestock, and grain to other pastoral planets, often along with the crew members who wouldn't cooperate in the rats' efforts.

The loss of the vessels had been put down to space pirates.

"Who knew it was pi-*rats*?" Marley had said, ironically, changing the emphasis of the syllables. The rats overheard her. They liked the sound of the word, and officially designated themselves pyrats. Marley was upset with herself. She didn't want to do anything they liked.

Marley knew the rats saw themselves as the liberators of Earth. Their intention was to starve out the humans, and make them all go away. If humanity died off, that would suit the rats' purposes, but all they really wanted was to get them off the planet so it could return to a natural condition.

But she found herself wondering if they *could* restore Earth to its original state. All that green openness she saw in the history vids scared her at first, but soon she began to find it attractive. Her fellow human beings weren't going to do it any time soon. Why waste room in the megaloburbs for farmland when you can ship in all the food you want from colony worlds? (Not that it was recognizable by the time it reached the people.) She had been raised on cityswill, and shipswill was exactly the same with an added tinny taste from the storage vats.

Earth was no paradise, she admitted that. Living conditions were miserable no matter how you looked at it. People starved there, she thought with a fleeting pang of sympathy that quickly faded as she entered the mess hall.

The enamel walls of the room had been tinted screaming orange, no doubt a bright thought to instill cheery moods in diners by some psychologist who had never set foot off Earth. The curved chairs were unbreakable plastic in a blue so dull it looked like a mistake. The captives had been allowed to keep them only because the rats couldn't think of anything to use them for.

All fifteen of her fellow human workers were already eating. Marley mentally cursed the captain for keeping her past the beginning of meal break. Had they left her enough food? She hurried to the steel serving table and flung open the hatches one after another. Plenty. Whew! She grabbed a steel tray and began to scoop food into the six compartments. Slices of some kind of brown-red meat. Green things like little trees. Peas; she had tried peas before. They were good. Potatoes. Lots of potatoes. She loved the texture on her tongue. Some little cubes of pale gold fruit in gooey sauce. Milk in a round squeeze bulb. She took three of those.

The other survivors of the *Sophia* watched her warily as she came to sit by them, curling their arms protectively around their own trays. Marley kept her own food just out of leaping distance. Bell, a small man with leathery brown skin who had been a senior mining tech, nodded to her. His job was to keep the drives and life support running. Iverson, a slim blonde woman with pale turquoise eyes, had been the hydrophonics chief. Now she was seconded to a huge brown sewer rat who treated her with kindness, but acted as though she had the intelligence of a sentient watering can.

Marley nodded at them, and fell on her meal voraciously, sawing chunks of meat small enough to stuff in her mouth in between bites of the vegetables. She could remember when she'd been repulsed by the neon-bright redness of precooked meat, for example. And the different textures of real, fresh vegetables. She had never, ever seen anything like that that hadn't been reprocessed and re-formed into absolutely uniform segments. The remembered flavor of cityswill came back, almost making her gag. The paste consumed by all workers of a certain level contained all the nutrients needed for life. It tasted horrible. She gulped down some of those sweet-bitter treestalks to cover the memory. They were delicious. She had to go back for more.

Only when she'd gotten to the sweet fruit compote did she become aware of Bell's voice. He must have been talking the whole time.

". . . Going to be too fat to escape, if we ever manage it." Marley looked up at him in alarm.

"You can't talk that way," she whispered. "They're always listening."

"Sorry," he said, with a sheepish shrug. No one wanted to be overheard talking mutiny. "Just joking around. You get the tub running?"

"Yes," Marley said, gulping down the second bulb of milk. "I can't understand why the crew sabotaged the plumbing." She glanced at the next table where the six men and women who had originally been assigned to *Avast ye* sat alone, under guard by a dozen rats, each almost a meter long. They weren't permitted near any sensitive or vital installations. Ironically, the shock bracelets had once been collars worn by live animals the freighters sometimes carried. Who'd know the system could be changed to keep humans themselves out of their own control rooms?

"Wish we had some entertainment," Bell continued. "I'm getting bored out of my skull. I never watched the news before, and you can only look at Earth so long without going crazy." He shrugged at the monitor embedded in the wall, on which the blue planet revolved serenely.

"Can't," Thomas said wistfully. The lanky young man had been their computer systems specialist. "Everything's on the hard drives, and we can't get near it."

No books, no music, no art programs. No cultural enrichment. No gossip. No newsgroups. Marley knew what the others were thinking. They were all suffering from withdrawal symptoms.

"Remember?" Bell asked fondly. "Solitaire. King of the Mountain. Fate. Bomb Shelter."

". . . Space Invaders," offered Iverson, then tittered nervously as the others groaned. "Well, maybe not."

"I know *I'll* never play it again," Bell insisted.

"I just wish I could, y'know, get close to the computers again," Thomas said, flexing his long fingers. "I wouldn't mess with the control programs. I just want to . . . connect again. I'm so twitchy. It's all there, and I can't touch it."

"You could become a trusty," Marley said, her mouth twisting in a sour grimace. The others barked out deprecating laughs.

"Yeah, right," Iverson said, with heavy irony. "Turn rat. Sure. Like Orcas."

They glanced over to a table set apart from the rest. A small, thin woman ate by herself. She never looked back at her fellow humans, if you could call them that any longer. She'd gone over to the rats' point of view, coming to believe that humankind no longer deserved Earth. Marley blamed the brainwashing they'd all gone through when they'd arrived on board. Unlike the rest of them, Orcas wore no bracelets. She didn't need physical compulsion to stay in line. She'd done it to herself.

One of the guard rats, a huge male, leaped up on their table, ears flattened, black-brown fur bristling, ugly, naked tail lashing. They all cowered back from him. He bared his long front teeth at Marley and seized her third bulb of milk. She watched, terrified, as he tore open the flimsy plastic and swallowed down the contents, all the while keeping a beady black eye on her. He kicked away the empty, then jumped down again to join his fellows.

"Why did it do that?" Iverson whispered. "There's plenty more in the hatches."

"Because it can," Bell said. "Because it wants to remind us not to get cocky. They're in charge, and we're not."

Marley was still thirsty. Keeping an eye on the band

of guards, she edged her way around to the hatches and picked out a couple more bulbs of milk.

A klaxon blared, making her drop them.

The proximity alarm! A ship! The warning lights around the doorway began to glow red. Humans had to stay where they were. Any trying to pass the check stations to either side would get shocked. Marley and the others stared at the screen.

The view of Earth was replaced by the image in one of the ship's long-range sensors. As it came closer to the freighter—close being a relative term—Marley could have jumped up and down with glee. It was another mining vessel, this one heavily armed. They were coming to save her!

The screen scrambled briefly. A swarthy, muscular man's face appeared.

"I am Captain Lichtman of the World Government ship *Delos,*" he said. "We heard your distress call, *Mary Sue,* and we are coming to help. Anyone in need of medical help? Respond?"

Distress call? Marley thought. Oh, no! The *Delos* was flying right into a trap. If Marley could have, she'd have jumped right through the screen, waving them off.

As it was, she had no choice but to watch as the ship came into near visual range. As it approached, the glow around it of meteor shields gradually died. *Don't do that,* Marley pleaded with it mentally. *Why aren't you more suspicious?*

As though the captain could hear her thoughts, the *Delos* slowed, and its exterior started to luminesce again. Marley let out a heartfelt sigh, echoed by Bell and the others. But the ship's response had been too slow. Red tracer lines lanced through space toward its hull. Two missed, but one tiny white-hot dot appeared, etching a glowing gash in the metal.

The *Delos* juddered as its internal stabilizers fought to keep it steady. Three more red lines came from other directions as the conscripted mining ships swung out from behind the hulk of the wrecked space station. *Delos* rotated and fired its engines to cut and run. Red lines shot out from its mining lasers toward its pursuers. *Crowbar* took a solid hit in the nose. It spun wildly as hull sections tumbled away. *Simpson* veered off to avoid the debris, and took a wide angle up and out of sight.

Sophia appeared in the bottom right of the viewscreen, its cutters on full force. It fired again and again. Beside Marley, her shipmates cringed. Those lasers were only supposed to cut through asteroids in search of ore, not to kill other humans. *Delos* was quite a distance out by now. Marley could only see the dot provided by the computer to indicate its whereabouts.

But the shots had been aimed precisely. A bubble of white power expanded, as the explosion consumed the ship's store of liquid oxygen, then winked out. The dot that was *Delos* began to spin end over end, hurtling back toward the *Avast Ye*. By the time Marley could see it again, its exterior glow was gone. Green tracers took the place of red, as the *Avast Ye* stretched out tractors to draw the helpless ship in.

The captain's image reappeared on the screen. In the background Marley could see crew members frantically working over their boards, trying to reestablish control.

"What in hell are you doing, *Mary Sue*?" he demanded. "Who the hell is running things over there? What are all these ships? Mayday, may . . ."

The screen fizzled into blankness as Marley's heart sank. For a moment, she'd thought she was going to be freed. She knew the others felt the same despair.

The whole ship boomed as the *Delos* was dragged close against the *Avast ye*. Marley felt the telltale vibration humming in her feet as the lasers taxed the freighter's engines for enough power to breach the captive ship's hull.

Suddenly, the red lights around the doorframes

winked out. The huge rats moved toward Marley and the other humans, gnashing their long, yellow teeth. They lifted their hands and marched toward their cabins.

The door slid open, and guard rats nipped at Marley's heels to make her jump in.

Six men and women in shipsuits seated on the featureless benches at one end of the room looked up at her. The burly man, Captain Lichtman, stood up as if to catch her when she stumbled, but he withdrew, arms folded.

"Hi," she said. "My name's Tobie Marley. I'm here to . . . interpret."

"What the hell is going on here?" Lichtman demanded. "You grabbed us, tore a hole through our hull, threw a million vermin at us to get us off our guards . . ."

"We . . . I mean, humans didn't do it, sir. It's the rats. They did it all."

The humans sneered their skepticism in her face. "Yeah, right," Lichtman said, belligerently. "This is an act of piracy! I demand to see your captain."

Marley glanced at the army of rats at the opposite end of the room. "He's over there, sir. The white one in the middle."

Lichtman looked at the captain, who pulled himself upright to his full ten inches. For a moment the human seemed incredulous, then burst out laughing. "All right, I've had enough of the trained animal act. Bring me an officer I can deal with."

The captain was offended. He let out a screech that nearly sent Marley to her knees with pain.

"I demand respect!" he shrilled through the telekythe. His temper had a short fuse. "Tell them!"

Marley gulped. She knew the drill. She'd had to do this before.

"He's offering you a choice. Three choices. He needs human crew, to do maintenance. You can stay here, or transfer to . . . a nontechnological planet . . ."

"Or you can give me back my ship and stop screwing around," Lichtman interrupted her. "I want to get out of this stench and back to a nice, clean deck before . . ."

The captain had lost patience. He leaped at Marley, who immediately lay down on her back and exposed her throat. The two-foot-long guard rats were close behind, roiling around her feet like piranha. The captain stopped just short of biting her neck. She could smell his musk.

The captives jumped to their feet. A couple plastered themselves against the far bulkhead as the rats swarmed around them, baring their yellow fangs.

"Tell them!" the captain screamed.

She kept an eye on him as she addressed the newcomers. "Or they'll make you walk the plank."

"Yeah, right."

"I mean it!" Marley shuddered. "I've seen it happen more than once. If you don't surrender and cooperate, they'll put you into an escape pod. It's aimed square at the middle of the Washington-Baltimore megaloburb defense grid. If the grid recognizes the pod as an unarmed vessel, it captures it with tractors. If not . . ." she paused and swallowed. "At least it's over quickly."

One of the newcomers, a thin man in his early twenties, collapsed in a faint without making a sound. The others went ashen. Lichtman still held himself erect.

"This is bull," he said.

The captain leaped off Marley's chest and ran up the man's jumpsuit to his shoulder. Lichtman shuddered and batted him off. In nothing flat, the big man was covered with guard rats, nipping and screeching. He killed a few by breaking their necks with his boot, but the remaining mass bore him to the ground. He yelled wildly. Marley wished she could help him, but she didn't dare.

The captain picked himself up and ran up the man's body to stare down into his face.

"You think I do not understand you," he squeaked, in perfect Standard. "I do. Both ways."

Lichtman looked shocked. "It can talk."

"They all can," Marley said. "At least, they can all understand Standard. You have to watch what you say."

Lichtman looked at his terrified crew. His face was covered with bleeding cuts and bites, and his shipsuit had tears in it. "All right," he said. "We surrender—for now."

Surrounded by an army of guards, Marley escorted them to a couple of cabins still fitted out for human occupation. Lichtman looked at the room he was expected to share with two of his crew and stopped short, baring his teeth.

"I demand a cabin of my own. I am a senior officer. According to the Geneva Convention . . ."

The white-furred captain, riding on Marley's shoulder, bared his. "We did not sign it."

Marley braced herself, expecting another fight. To her relief, the dinner bell rang. The rats stirred among themselves. They hated to be late for meals.

"Can we settle this after we eat?" she asked.

The furry white face looked up into hers. The captain's eyes were slitted as though he was amused.

"Humans are always more amenable with increase in blood sugar," he squeaked.

Lichtman sat at the table with his arms crossed. With barely controlled disgust he and his shipmates watched the human workers eat. Marley thought the elder female ensign was going to be sick.

"Don't you want your bread?" Iverson asked. Her eyes were wary as she snaked out a hand for the roll sitting on the edge of the tray. Marley reached out and slapped it away.

"Stop it," she said. "They don't know the rules yet."

"You can't like eating that . . . obscenity," the thin ensign said.

Marley glanced down at the piece of roast beef she'd just stabbed with her fork.

"You mean this?" she asked. "It took me a while to get used to meat, but I like it now."

The newcomers were aghast. "That horrible red!" the female ensign exclaimed. "It looks like an open wound."

"It's really good," Marley insisted. She glanced back over her shoulder, worried that they were taking too long. "You ought to eat your meal. The rats don't like it when you waste food."

"You do what they say?" Lichtman said, more of a statement than a question.

"With all respect, sir, we eat a lot better here than we ever did, on ship or at home," Bell said.

"You are letting your stomachs make you traitors to your own kind," the human captain stated, his face an ashen mask as Marley ate the offending bite and followed it with a big forkful of spinach. It was fresh out of the hydroponics section, and Iverson was justly proud of it. Her boss rat had been full of praise. "Unprocessed?"

"It's sweet this way," Iverson said. "Want to try it?"

That did set off the ensign's gag reflex. She went running, followed by a contingent of guards.

During the distraction Lichtman leaned close. "We have to get out of here. It's your duty as free citizens of Earth to aid and abet us. When you return, you'll have a hero's welcome. I can see to it that you have improved rations, maybe even an increase in the size of your living quarters."

Iverson, Bell, Thomas, and Marley exchanged glances.

"We're outnumbered by about half a million," Bell said. "Besides, there's no escape pods."

"But my ship—"

"—Is currently being refitted with controls for paws about the size of your pinky," Bell said. "It's going to be part of the pyrat fleet from now on. They'll have fixed the engines as soon as they got you off the ship. You aren't going back to Earth, not just yet."

"You're traitors!" Lichtman snarled.

The tone of his voice alerted another gang of guards who looked angry to be disturbed from their meal.

"What do you expect us to do?" Lichtman asked.

Lichtman slammed his fist down on the table, making their trays jump. While Marley and the others put protective arms around their food, giant rats surrounded the newcomers.

"You'd better go with them," she said.

The next time she saw Lichtman and his crew, they were cleaning fur out of the air filtration system with hand brushes. It was a sign the rats must already have decided not to keep them on board the *Avast Ye.* All of them had bites on faces, hands, and throats from "training." Tears were rolling down their cheeks, as much from frustration as from the heavy concentration of ammonia in the air. Even Marley, who was acclimated, felt the characteristic burning at the back of her throat. She was sorry for them. They looked terrible. A couple of the men had obviously stopped bathing. They stared at her, red-eyed.

"Hi," she said. "I've got to go. Hydroponics."

"Don't go," Lichtman whispered, when she passed close to them. "I want to talk to you. Please."

"I've got an errand," Marley said. She thought quickly. "Mealtime is soon. Go toward the mess hall through hydroponics. I'll wait for you there."

"How long?" the rat in charge of the garden room asked.

Marley looked at the tanks and consulted the plan in her hands. "At least three work periods. One to clean out the fallow tanks, and two to set them up and plumb them, attach the lights. Maybe longer."

"Two," the brown rat said. She sat up as high as Marley's thigh. Her ancestors had come from New-York-Jersey. In spite of her city origins, she loved plants, and had a fierce pride in the hydroponics system. The working tanks were full to bursting with burgeoning green that spilled out and over the edges, hiding the utilitarian containers from view. The chamber had the freshest air on the ship. Two corridors ran alongside the section. Passersby, rat and human alike, stopped when they could, just to breathe.

"I'll need help," Marley said.

"You'll have it. Iverson!"

The blonde woman shoved her way past a forest of potato leaves. "Ma'am?"

"Work for her. She will show you what we need done. It will be good."

Marley gave her an apologetic grimace. Iverson grinned.

The two women worked in silence. The brown rat came by from time to time to chuckle possessively over the tanks they were scrubbing. She muttered to herself in her own language about onions and raspberries. Marley got the translation through the telekythe.

Toward the end of the shift, Lichtman and his crew came trudging wearily past the far edge of the growth lights' halo.

"We need help!" Marley exclaimed suddenly. "Chief? What about them?" She pointed.

The brown rat, standing on the edge of a tank picking green beans, looked up. "Yes, yes, if you want those. You six, please come in." The *Delos'* crew shuffled into the room, blinking at the bright lights. Marley almost smiled as they started to sniff, then take deep breaths of the fragrant air.

"We're cleaning out these vats to set up," Marley explained.

She was shocked at their condition. Lichtman and his people were almost reeling on their feet. They looked gaunt. All of the men had stopped shaving, and the pink of half-healed bites showed through their beards.

"Chop chop!" the brown rat exclaimed, patting her

little paws together. She jumped down from her perch and ran away toward the seed storage facility, chuckling, and the telekythe in Marley's skull picked up her glee at the Standard phrase. "Hurry (colloquial)."

Marley showed the newcomers what to do. She divided the group up into three teams. She and Iverson took Lichtman to the far side of the area.

"I'm so tired I can hardly see straight," Lichtman said, propping the tank up so the women could wash it out. "We have to get back to Earth and raise the word about what's going on out here."

"We can't get away," Marley said, industriously scraping away at mineral deposits.

"Stop thinking like a rat," Lichtman hissed. "You're a human being. You ought to want to be free."

"I *do,* but . . ."

"Then do something about it. I want my ship. I'll take all of you with me."

Marley felt almost giddy with hope, then her heart sank. "There's probably ten thousand rats on board. We have no weapons."

"I have," Lichtman said proudly. "They might have built themselves into better mice, but we built a better mousetrap. I've got a state-of-the-art vermin control system in there."

"Poison?" Marley asked, in distaste.

"No. It's a box, set to give off waves that disrupt the cells of specific gene patterns. Built into the hull. Independent power source. Wipe 'em out." Lichtman's teeth gleamed in the scruffy growth of his beard. "if you can get it for me, we can kill every rat on these ships."

"Oh, no!" Iverson said, glancing around for her chief. "It's too dangerous. They'll tear us to pieces!"

"Not even to get home?"

"No! I can't kill them all like that."

Lichtman abandoned her and eyed Marley. "You showed some initiative, getting us in here where we could talk. I bet you could get on board *Delos*. What's your price?"

"Make sure I can get back into space," Marley said promptly. "If they condemn me as a collaborator, I'll be stuck groundbound forever. I can't live like that. I'll do anything if I don't have to go back to New-York-Jersey. Get me a berth on anything spacegoing."

"I understand," Lichtman said.

"And one more condition," Marley said. "I'm with Iverson. I don't want to kill all the rats. I just want to get away from them." Iverson looked surprised for a moment, then nodded vigorously. Lichtman looked from one to the other.

"Are you crazy?"

"No!" Marley said. She let go of the spray handle to clutch Lichtman's arm. "I've had a lot of time to hate them, but when you just said it like that, 'wipe 'em out,' it made me feel sick. Don't you see? They're sentient. They've *evolved*. You can't destroy a whole civilization. That's what they are now."

Lichtman was astonished. "After the way they've treated you?"

"They've treated us a whole lot better than we would have treated them under the same circumstances," Iverson said. "Maybe we can just disable the ships, or . . ."

A small figure bounded up out of the mass of potato leaves and closed its jaws around Iverson's wrist. She shrieked with fear. The hydroponics chief took the human's hand from her mouth, and patted it with her little paws.

"I do not see how you survived as a species," the brown rat said, surveying them all with her beady eyes. "You do not survey the terrain to make certain it is free of predators. Arrogance."

"Aren't you going to call the guards?" Lichtman sneered. "Starve us? Chew on us?"

The brown rat snorted. "I, too, am growing weary of this vengeance toward humans. We set out to prove we are better, but we are proving the same. It is annoying. All the universe is before us, and we must look back upon one planet that is nearly depleted. Let me help you to go away. Do not kill us all. We are not all like the captain. We want peace and a good life for our young."

"You'll *help* us?" Lichtman asked.

"Not to kill my species. You want your ship. You want to leave. So be it. Give the device to *me*. If I can control the others, take command, we will go to one of the worlds where we are diverting foodstuffs, and live there. Most of the others will follow once they hear my plan. We can start over, prove that we will be good stewards, without humans. You will never see us again. She," the rat nosed Iverson, "is a good little sister, but I can't stand the smell of you humans."

"The feeling is mutual," Lichtman said. He looked at Marley. "Do I trust her?"

"She *didn't* call the guards," Marley pointed out.

"I will help," the brown rat promised. "You need me to disable the punishment bracelets, or you will never make it through to the ship. But at least finish my hydroponics tanks before you go."

Iverson funked it. She just wasn't brave enough to bull her way onto the *Delos* in search of the pest-control box. Marley had to go all by herself. She tried to whistle as she strolled toward the air lock, but she was so nervous she was just puffing air. The way through was open. Rats came and went onto the captive ship, bringing in equipment to adapt the controls. A few human workers carried hull plates and structural braces, for converting the cabins to rat use. They glanced toward her, then looked away again. No one wanted to attract attention. They were excited.

By the end of the second shift word had spread among the human population that an escape attempt was under way. The rats were suspicious, but since their workers had no advantages they knew of, they had no target for their suspicion. Lichtman's people had lost their hopeless look and were making plans for a hasty departure as soon as the kill box was in their hands. All the humans had to be in position to get aboard *Delos*. Their ally promised to do the rest. Lichtman didn't like relying upon one of the enemy, but even he saw they had no choice. Everyone was poised to move when they heard the word "go."

The guards at the opening surrounded Marley immediately.

"What are you doing?"

"Hydroponics," Marley said. "The chief wants me to get whatever tubing and control circuits are in there for her." She held out her tool kit. The rats nosed through it, then withdrew. One of them crawled over to the air lock controls and adjusted them to let her through.

Marley stepped through the hole. The *Avast Ye* had drilled the *Delos'* hull in the middle of the cargo bay. She was aware that this was the most important moment of her life. For months she had been living as a terrified drone. She'd lost sight of her humanity.

Lichtman was right.

The rats had brainwashed her.

She could get away. She could *do* something to help herself and the others.

Gray conduit snaked all over the walls where the deck plates had been removed and stacked to one side. Half a dozen humans were at work rerouting the power conduits. The hydroponics/food-processing center was just beyond.

She'd almost forgotten what an ordinary ship's food system looked like. The tanks were behind plexiglass, untouched by human hands. Under the glare of lights robot sensor hands identified ripe produce, plucked it, and shoved it into a hopper leading to a processing chamber that filled a tank with freshly made shipswill. Marley wrinkled her nose.

She identified the pillar that Lichtman told her about. The kill box was off. Swiftly, she undid the bolts and removed the device. It looked too small to be that powerful, but Lichtman assured her that hooked up to full power it was sufficient to clear a whole ship. Marley glanced around. Guards had come in behind her, making sure she was doing her job. She tossed the box lightly into her carrier, and went on to disconnect as much of the redundant hoses as she could to make it look good.

Arms full of tubing, Marley staggered toward the hatch. Every moment she expected to be stopped and searched. Ten more steps. Eight more steps. Her foot caught on something and she stumbled.

A loud screech erupted. Marley backed up hastily. She'd stepped on a rat's tail!

The offended guard swarmed up her body and began to bite her cheeks and ears. Marley dropped everything and huddled, protecting her face with her arms. The other workers glanced at her briefly, never daring to come to her rescue. Marley let herself drop backward and lay on the deck with her throat up.

I will never have to do this again. She held onto the thought while the guards scratched and bit her. *Never.*

When at last they let her up, she piled the hoses on top of her tool kit, and left the *Delos,* head hanging in shame. In her secret heart, though, she rejoiced that she could—would—strike back at last.

Lichtman was waiting for her in the hydroponics section. He received the kill box with joy.

"Now," he growled. He snapped a battery to the frame and lashed it in place with strapping. "This'll work in a small radius. It'll be enough to get us all on board *Delos*. Spread the word. One hour until lunch. We'll gather in the mess hall."

That was the longest hour of Marley's life. As soon as the bell rang, she headed in and gathered up the largest meal she could fit on the tray. Most of her co-workers were too excited to eat. With her mind firmly on the shipswill vats, she began to eat. Bell sat down across from her, and set to his meal with a dogged expression. Thomas arrived, then Iverson. Twenty minutes. Fifteen. Marley slewed her eyes around, counting. Only twenty humans had arrived so far. Where was Orcas?

Marley gulped the contents of a milk bulb and popped open her third.

Just as she did, Orcas burst into the mess hall. For a change the little woman didn't look mousy or terrified. She was triumphant. She pointed dramatically at Lichtman.

"He's the one!" she cried. "He has it." Around her feet, a sea of rats swarmed, heading for Lichtman.

Lichtman sprang to his feet. Marley and the others leaped up. "We've got to go *now*!" From the sleeve of his ragged shipsuit, he yanked the kill box and turned it on.

The little device emitted a *wow* that steadily rose into a whine. The first rats to reach him managed to climb halfway up his clothing before they fell to the floor. Lichtman struggled with the controls. The whine dropped slightly, then got louder.

"Stop him!" The captain's voice carried over the telekythes of every human in the room. Marley had to stop herself from instantly hurrying to obey. The whine of the kill box grew louder still. The captain and his guards retreated, but too late. Most of them fell to the floor, twitching.

The humans stared at them. Marley found she had squeezed the milk bulb until it burst.

"Hurry," she said. "The alarm will go in a moment." Too late, she saw the red glow rise around the hatchway.

"Move it out!" Lichtman shouted. He pointed at Orcas, who stood over the bodies of the dead rats, screaming. "Bring her along! Carry her if you have to!" A couple of the larger crew hurried to grab Orcas' arms.

The rats cowered away from the door as he rushed toward them with the kill box in his outstretched hand.

"Yeah, you little monsters," he said, grinning ferociously. "You all die."

He reached the archway when the metal bracelets on his wrists arced with blue light. Lichtman dropped to his knees. The kill box went flying. The rats, seeing their enemy disarmed, scurried toward him, gnashing their teeth. Marley threw herself across the heaving bodies to the box lying against the bulkhead. She picked it up and brandished it. The ones that didn't die scurried to the far end of the room.

"The battery won't last forever," Lichtman said, clutching his wounded arms to his chest.

"She'll keep her promise," Marley said. "I hope."

Abruptly, the red light died away. Marley almost collapsed with relief, then cowered. In the hallway beyond, hundreds of thousands of rats waited outside the range of the kill box. They were going to block the humans' escape bodily if they had to. They had the numbers. All of them screamed threats that made Marley cringe. They were going to punish her again.

"Come on," Lichtman said, face contorted with pain. "They can't stop you anymore. Go!"

Marley held the box up as the huddle of humanity forced its way along toward the *Delos*. Wave after wave of the yellow-toothed menace rushed at them, and fell over dead. The humans had to walk over heaps of furry bodies all the way to the ship. Orcas was weeping as her escort pulled her along.

The air lock was sealed when they reached it. Within the protective circle of his companions, Thomas went to work on the coded control panel.

"We'll have to bond panels in place on a temporary basis to cover the hole in the hull," Lichtman said, no longer the pathetic captive. "Sealing tools are in the hatches. Everyone get ready to move as soon as the door opens."

"There!" Thomas said, rocking back on his heels in triumph.

The air lock door slid open. With deafening shrieks, thousands of rats that had been hidden inside launched themselves at the humans. Marley stood in the midst of a nightmare as bodies rained down on her. A few hardy ones managed to bite or scratch her just once before they died. Lichtman grabbed the box from her, turned it on high, and held it at arm's length into his ship.

Horrible shrieks erupted, rising to the highest pitch. Marley found herself on her knees holding her ears. Tears burned down her cheeks, not from pain, but from grief. The loss of all those lives, even if they were the enemy, tore a hole in her. They were all dying so that she could go back to living like a human being.

The noise didn't last long. Lichtman withdrew his arm and turned the kill box down. Its whine was fading. The battery had only a little power left.

"More of them!" At the far end of the hallway, Marley saw another cluster of rats. Lichtman reached for the control again, to turn it on full.

"No, don't!" Marley cried, grabbing his arm. It was the hydroponics chief and a cluster of guard rats. The brown rat kept her distance but held out a paw.

"Why not?" Lichtman asked, turning toward her, his eyes wild. "We can't let this species continue. They'll destroy humanity!"

"Keep your promise," she begged him. "We're free. Let her try."

Lichtman looked disgusted, but he nodded. "We got what we wanted. Everyone! On board!"

He signaled to his crew to start sealing in hull plates. When there was only enough room for his hand left, he switched the box off and flipped it out into the corridor.

Marley's last sight of the *Avast Ye* was of the hydroponics chief swooping down on the kill box. She shot them a bright-eyed look before the air lock snapped shut.

"We're lifting as soon as we can get the engines heated up," Lichtman said. "My crew, to stations! Anyone not *Delos* personnel, go wait in the mess hall. You, there! Shut up!"

Orcas had had to be carried on bodily, weeping and trying to get back onto the *Avast Ye*. When she saw there was no way out, she collapsed in a corner of the cargo bay.

"That woman needs serious help," *Delos'* engineer clanked his bracelets together, and grinned at his guests. "I can have these things off us in no time."

The crew of the *Sophia* followed their guide to the bright orange room. It was spartan but clean, fitted out with a food dispenser, entertainment facilities, and monitor screens. The newly freed captives didn't know what to do first.

"Look at that," Marley said. "All the seats are human-sized."

"We're free," Bell said, rapturously flinging himself down. "No more rats."

"No more bites," Thomas said. "No more pee-stench. No more fur in the ventilators."

"No more carrots," Iverson said sadly. "No more potatoes. No more pears. Shipswill from now on until we die."

Marley heaved a sigh. "No more roast beef."

They settled down in front of the vidscreen in the *Delos'* mess hall, to catch up on the news after so many months of being incommunicado. Thomas immediately disabled the miniaturized controls and plunked his hands onto the touchpad like a maestro rediscovering his favorite keyboard. The all-day, all-night *World News* channel popped up.

"Ah!" he crowed.

"I'm going to miss eating like a rat," Bell said. "But I won't miss living like one."

The news announcer's voice interrupted them. "In the headlines today, food riots in Madreas-Bangalore broke out again. At issue also is living space for the protesters. . . ."

"No," said Marley wryly. "We live worse."

NO STARS TO STEER BY

BY ED GREENWOOD

ALL his life, Ben had been looking up at the Ocean. He never grew tired of gazing at its starry glow overhead—though it seemed more as if it was *around* him, now, like a welcoming cloak. Welcoming . . . and deadly.

It'd taken years to get upside, but at last here he was, the *Emreldon*'s youngest drifthand, in the midst of learning that some things his parents had told him were pure wild-tongued fancy might just be true after all. The pirates who sailed the stars, for example. Yet it still seemed that no one could *feel* the Ocean sliding past like Ben Telgryon.

Did that make him some sort of . . . freak?

The "awake hands" had been deep in excited pirate gossip when he'd emerged from one shift, so it'd been easy to ask what he wanted to know. He caught a sip bulb of kava someone had tossed his way, gave that someone a grin of thanks, found a perch, and just listened.

"They clamp their own rockets on," Yarlo was saying, his florid mustache bristling with a life of its own as he leaned forward to tap the table with one stubby finger for emphasis, "and blast the ship off course, to some planetoid where they've a ship waiting. There they blow their capture, killing everyone aboard, strip it of everything worthwhile, and just leave it to drift."

"Well, *I* heard they take slaves, for some world the Constellar won't tell us about yet," Marrakis said, and nods around the table told Ben that others had heard that, too.

"Bah!" Hendrock said, looking up from the egg he was always writing a new tale into; under another name he was famous in three worlds for torrid romances of the spaceways, but the egg was coded to him alone, and they'd all given up trying to sneak peeks at his latest yarn. "Ever used clamp-on rockets? I have, when we were mining Go-be-long's asteroids. A little better than half the time, when you go to shut them down, they blow up on you! So these pirates couldn't help but lose a lot of ships—theirs *and* the ones they're taking. Any of you hear of a lot of ships going missing?"

"Well, there was the *Shiftrift,* out of Gulder, and the *Martian Crown Jewels,* and . . . and . . ."

"Aha!" Hendrock said triumphantly, "there you are. Two, maybe three more. Not a 'lot,' hmm? And just where would they hide this slave-world?"

"In the Ocean?" Ben asked excitedly. Three heads turned to give him scornful looks, and he hastily tried to look wide-eyed and eager.

"Boy, *no one* hides in the Ocean and comes back out again! No stars to steer by! Oh, I know there's always talk of that—after all, it's so blamed big and it's *right there,* in the middle of the Constellar! It'd be a good place to hide a lot of things, and I'm sure it holds more'n one thing someone wanted lost forever—but I've never heard of anyone managing to get in there and find their way out again quickly and easily. They still lose three or four scout ships every Turn, on little test trips in and out. They've mastered the 'in,' all right . . . but near as no one comes out."

"The *Wulvert* came out, last Turn," Pasker said suddenly, abandoning his attempt to peer at what Hendrock was writing.

"So it did, at—what?—thirty Turns after going in,

with everyone aboard sitting there dead, starved hollow! What use is that?"

What use, indeed? So here he was, days later, back in the tank, staring at the endless Ocean and wondering. He could feel it now, tugging at, and . . . well, *caressing* the unlovely hull of the speeding *Emreldon,* as they slowed and began to veer away from the beautiful glow. The starship must be nearing Sarkon, which meant they hadn't told him the truth about how long he'd been asleep in the medpod. Hmm. Just how suspicious of his greenest drifthand had Brender become? Or . . . some-one higher ranking?

He turned away from frowning soberly at the port in the rear tank wall, and back to face the glowing thing that filled and lit all the other walls: the glorious, sparkling Ocean. Here in the tank, it felt like you were hanging in the midst of it. It had been magic at home dirtside, a glorious glowing arc across the night sky that winked and sparkled just for him, all those years—but out here in the Great Empty, it was breathtaking. Men called it "the Ocean," though it was really a whirlpool of gases and dust, a vast racing pinwheel of deadly murk spinning at the heart of the Constellar. It glowed royal purple in a few places, and greeny-gold elsewhere, because of the stars blazing at its heart. All the star systems humankind had spread to encircled the starry Ocean like a circlet of tiny gems.

And so did ships like the *Emreldon.* Unless something went seriously wrong, starships never entered planetary atmospheres. They skimmed the whirling edges of the Ocean at the right angle to ride along and around—and then fired their rockets at just the right time to be flung away from the Ocean to the right "star well," to loop and brake and settle into planetary orbit. "Straight shots" directly between a planetary surface and the Ocean were far rarer and more fuel-expensive . . . and rarer still were interstellar voyages that didn't make use of the Ocean. As for heading into its murk . . . well, nobody even tried that anymore. A few lucky "gasfarers" had blundered out again, nowhere near where they'd been trying for and with the hulls of their ships scoured rough and dull and dangerously thin. The others had simply not been heard from again.

Because it was his first voyage, the older hands had taken great delight in telling their new audience all the best horror stories of lost ships and "bone voyages" of the dead found drifting out of the Ocean . . . as well as their tired old jokes, superstitions ("Never face away from Lowball when leaving it, lad, or that voyage'll be one Murphy after another."), and other tales of space, from the great drifting beasts called "dragons" that many spacefarers swore lurked in the dusty depths of the Ocean but scientists refused to believe in, to drifthands who'd burst like squashed fruit when they did this or that dirt-headed thing, to the new peril of the spaceways: the Manderock pirates.

Ben didn't quite believe the stories of boardings and needle-gun battles—where would the pirates take a ship, once they snatched it? The only worlds that hadn't joined the Constellar yet were the Wild Colonies, and everyone could see what ships went to and from them, bulging like hard-rind fruit with their own shuttles bolted around their middles. But the needler drills had been serious enough, with even gruff old Brender leaping around and looking grimmer than usual until they were all panting and dripping with sweat.

Manderock was supposed to be a planetoid not in any voyage tank, a sunless world behind a shield of tumbling asteroids. No one lived there, the tales whispered, not even the pirates.

So where did they live, then? Some invisible world that swallowed starships? Or had someone finally found a way to hide in the whirling Ocean, and get back out again alive?

Well, someone named Ben Telgryon just might have.

Three days out from home (no, he had to break the habit of thinking of Dargonith as "home"). Brender had warned him about that. All the Constellar was his "home" now, with scout ships whirling away from the racing Ocean farther and farther out all the time, seeking new worlds to mine for their metals—or even better, to farm and live on and make the Constellar a little bigger.

How big was the Great Empty, now? *There* was a question. Brender had just laughed when he'd—

Scarm it! Lying here in the tank, drifting ever so slightly with nothing to do, certainly made the mind wander . . .

There was always at least one drifthand suited and in the tank, at the ready for whatever bot assists might be necessary. Most folks thought drifthands worked in orbit and slept or did nothing for the rest of a voyage, but the truth was far different. Things fell off starships or shifted to undesirable locations all the time.

Three days out from home, Ben had been caught in the tank during a storm, when the ship had flashed through one of the moving, ever changing arms of the Ocean that spacefarers called "waves." Sometimes ships hit planetoids in the grinding dust and blew apart, almost always they wrapped themselves in spectacular, crawling lightnings . . . and sometimes they raced through fierce stellar radiation.

It had been just his luck to be training in the old, cannibalized, unarmored suit when they'd hit the wave—and even with Brender roaring curses and thrusting the great waldoes at his novice drifthand with terrifying speed, it had been a long time before Ben Telgryon had tumbled out of the lock and been pounced on by a grim crew of hands, racing under Olm Brender's shouts.

He'd been sick for days, pitching onto his face right after he'd proudly told Brender he was fine. Falling into suddenly waiting flames, for five burning days before he woke, feeling cold and weak, in the medpod. He might never be able to have children—or normal children, Kulkutt had told him, looking more bored than sad—but in a day he'd felt right again, and he'd been doing regular shifts in the tank for eight days now. The other hands had even stopped looking at him like he was some sort of monster itching to grow tentacles the moment they turned their backs.

But he *was* different, though it hadn't taken more than one look at Brender's coldly suspicious face to tell Ben that he dared not say anything about it, or do anything to betray to the other crew what he could now feel.

Radiation. Yes, he could *feel* radiation—the intense, localized power sources of the *Emreldon* like sharp, ever present noise, and beyond them, outside the ship, endless flows: the currents of radiation swirling along in the Ocean that the ship was riding. He could almost *see* where this stream curved, and that one broke away . . .

Maybe, just maybe, he could navigate *inside* the Ocean, if he didn't go in deep! Oh, any ship doing that would get scoured down to is innards if it went the wrong places, and everyone aboard would bathe in more radiation than he'd tasted, so it might all be an impractical dream, but still . . .

Still something to think about . . . *later*. Soon now, he'd be seeing another system than his own for the first time in his life, awakening without Dargonith's familiar tired gold overhead. They said Sardon was green, far greener than its tiny holo floating in the crew-cabin voyage thank. Not that he'd come anywhere near setting foot on the dirt of New Hope. The occasional starcrew might ride a shuttle down—but not drifthands, unless heading for a sick-stay.

He and his fellow hands had work to do whenever the ship was orbiting a planet. Their movements, encased in their ungainly armored suits in the telefactoring tanks, operated the loading bots. Lifting, stacking, shifting . . . all in drifting silence. In emergencies, drifthands even put on spacesuits and went out into the Great Empty themselves, to do things the old way.

And whenever one of the "clowns" or "idiot monkeys" wasn't deft enough, things got broken or lost, spinning away forever into space. Wherefore starcaptains spent a lot of time cursing said clowns and blaming them for every last ill of a voyage.

The first time a furious voice had snarled into his ear, erupting tinnily in his helmet, Ben Telgryon had cringed inside his suit, making warning lights wink into life up and down the telelink. It had been a long and sweating hour later before he'd unsuited, expecting dismissal, only to see Brender shaking his head incredulously and muttering, "The Old Lady must like you, Telgryon. She was almost flirting, there."

Recalling graphic promises of slow disembowelment and hide flayings, it had been Telgryon's turn to look incredulous. *That* had been "almost flirting"?

Ben sighed at the memory. So he was a lowly drifthand. For now. By the way Multer Strarver—the navigator, and a man even older than Brender—frowned over his tank as he repeatedly punched up the voyage log and called up checks on the astro beacons, Ben knew *he* couldn't feel the currents of the Ocean.

And Strarver was supposed to be one of Halsion's best, staying aboard the last few voyages of an extra Turn to make sure his younger replacements wouldn't get the *Emreldon* and the *Jastipher* and the *Schend* lost, or shattered against something too solid to ignore.

So feeling the flows must be som—

His helm came to life with the flat, harsh alarm *blat* that was meant to awaken. Ben stiffened and rolled over to reach for his suit cable. He didn't want to get caught out in the tank again, if—

"Strarver to the deck," said the captain's voice, and Ben took hold of the cable and started to pull himself in, as fast as he dared. The Old Lady, her voice usually equal parts ice-cold command and flat boredom, sounded scared—even out of breath!

What, by all the blazing Ocean, could be happening?

Ben reached the port and palmed it open. The usual light flooded out of the lock, but as he stepped inside, the *Emreldon* shuddered around him.

What could make a starship *shudder*? Had they hit something?

"Strarver!" Starcaptain Narnyk's voice came again, strident, almost a shout. This must be bad. Ben watched the lock lights cycle impatiently, as the seconds seemed to drag on forever, and—

The heavy door hissed open—revealing darkness. Ben blinked in astonishment, stopped himself in mid-snatch at his helmet catches, and peered into the room that should have been flooded with light from the suiting bay.

All he could see was something dull red, down low and moving . . .

His helmet com made a confused sound, and the lock trembled around him.

There was a heavy thump from the darkness, and wet sounds, then flashes of reflection as unseen tumbling things caught the light streaming from the lock behind Ben.

And then, without any fuss, the pressure and air composition lights on the bay side of the lock winked out.

There was no pressure in the bay!

Ben found himself panting as if he'd run for miles, staring into the darkness and wondering just what to do *now*. Those wet sounds . . . he clicked on his suitbelt light, just for a moment, and by its beam saw what was spattered all over the suiting bay. His fellow drifthands. All of them.

Then the moving redness turned, and he saw it was the light inside the old Noron suit's helm. Brender's head was inside it, glaring at Ben as if he'd been personally responsible for this.

The head hand lurched forward, throwing himself from side to side in the wallowing that passed for hurrying in the old, stiff-jointed Noron suit. Ben backed away uncertainly, finding one of the handholds in the lock frame with one hand and wondering what he could find with the other to use as a weapon, before—

Brender's gauntlets came up and tugged at the side of Ben's helmet.

He screamed—he knew he had—and shook himself desperately, trying to get away, slapping awkwardly with his web gloves at the old man's armored suit, at the gauntlets that must be reaching for his helmet catches. Brender must have gone spacecrazed, must've—

There was a brief shriek in Ben's ears, and then silence. His own breath echoed around him now, sounding different.

Then Brender's helm clicked against his, and he heard the gruff, familiar old voice say, "That sounded convincing. Good. They'll think you're dead, so long as we don't power up any locks and you don't reconnect that com lead. Stay still, lad. We can talk while our helms are touching."

"W–what happened?" Ben managed not to shout, or babble too much. He hoped.

"Pressure blown—deliberately. Someone aboard changed our course, taking us away from the Ocean."

"Pirates?"

"Must be," Brender said grimly. "Or someone gone spacecrazed. It could even be someone wanting to kill someone else aboard—though they'll never be able to claim an accident, not with needler burns all down the long tube. I'm in this suit because I found Strarver there, with two holes burned through his head, even before the captain missed him."

"I thought only the captain could issue needlers!"

Brender's laugh was a short, bitter bark. "You'd need her thumb and the codes to open the command locker, yes, but I've never known a ship yet that wasn't carrying more little hidden things than it had crew aboard! Why, when we needed to do some cutting, we'd have to carry away enough mystery packages to fill the spare bay, as often as not! We'd leave them, without a word, for their owners to sidle in and collect and find new hiding places for. There's not a crewhand in space that doesn't have a little something riding along with him!"

"So what do we do now?"

Brender laughed again, sounding—if that was possible—even more bitter. "We sit here and wait to die, lad. This suit'll stop a needler for perhaps a minute, yours about long enough to throw your hands up and strike a pose. We're dead men, Telgryon."

Ben found himself panting again. "Why?"

Brender snorted. "Either something went wrong updeck—the captain managed to strike back, say—and our pirate's dead and the whole ship's blown, thundering along into nothing with no air and no crew . . . or the pirate'll get where he's going soon enough, and they'll come through salvaging, and find us then. Either way—"

He broke off, and turned more swiftly than Ben would have thought anyone could in the old suit, to slap at a panel. The bay around them was suddenly flooded with sound.

"—Aid! Aid! Aid!" came the voice of the chief medic. "*Emreldon,* nineteen days out, blown and outbound! Aid! Aid! Aid!"

"We're here," an unfamiliar voice crackled, overriding the chant. "Sing no more!"

There was a brief crackling and clicking, and then silence. The head hand turned and touched his helmet to Ben's, his face like stone.

"Piracy. That was no distress call; Kulkutt's our traitor—or one of them. We must be right in their laps already."

"A pirate ship, you mean, like Yarlo was talking about?"

Brender nodded inside his helmet, scowling at Ben in the Noron's dim ruby light. "Close, too. We'll feel the grapples when they clamp on."

Ben nodded. The shuttle that had brought him up into the Great Empty had thrust out huge round disks on long, snaking cables. One by one their magnets had clunked against the *Emreldon,* and then the cables had been winched in.

"Brender," he heard himself asking calmly, "what if we could steer the ship? Will the pirates be able to . . . blow us up? Fire anything at us?"

The head hand stared at him. "Not unless they've learned to do things with a cutting laser that the best scientists in the Constellar can't do. If they're clamped on, yes, but otherwise they'd just have to chase us and *try* to grapple." He grinned suddenly. "I can steer a starship—or rather, I can *aim* one for as long as I have to. You want to die fighting?"

Ben shrugged. "I don't want to just stand here waiting, *knowing* that they're coming. . . ."

A gauntlet clapped his shoulder cable hard, almost turning him around.

"Good lad!" Brender growled. "Go down with glory it is!" He hesitated for a moment, and then added, "Come!"

Before Ben could reply, Brender spun away, and the tiny red lights that marked the widest part of the Noron suit's shoulders winked on.

Ben reached quickly for Brender's helmet, and when his web gloves tapped against it, asked, "We're going for needlers?"

The head hand didn't bother to turn his head. His bitter laugh came back to Ben faintly through the metal web of the telefactoring gloves. "Ben, I don't *have* any needlers. My little packages are on the outside of the ship, and you drink what's inside them."

(Like every starship, the *Emreldon* was a great ungainly thing of storage tanks and crossbeams and docking pods that looked like a junk pile against the sleek, streamlined atmospheric shuttles that soared up to meet it. Navigation rockets, cupped in their blast shields like satellite dishes, were clamped to outrigger beams on all sides of the ship, making the *Emreldon* look like it'd once been covered with scales, and since lost most of them somewhere. Ben had clambered over most of those shields already, securing cargo. All sorts of large and bulky pods rode clamped and netted to the outside of every starship hull, in the nooks and crannies between beams and hull bulges. A lot of them, Ben had begun to suspect long since, were highly unofficial in nature.)

"Oh," was all Ben could think of to say, now, as he stumbled after the little red lights, his feet slipping in what it was probably best he couldn't see.

Brender set a punishing pace. Out through the suiting bay to the loading lock, and then opening the tight door with its handwheel, down into the cargo chute.

Of course! The old spacefarer was taking them forward through the bulk hold, where no one but loading bots went, under the long tube where Kulkutt or another pirate had killed Strarver and would probably be waiting with a needler for anyone who might have survived to come creeping forward to the nav deck.

Abruptly the ruby light turned, and Brender's grim face leaned forward. Ben understood, and cautiously thrust his own helmet forward until the plexes touched. I'm going to turn off my helmet light now," the head hand growled, "in case Kulkutt has the hold viewplate on. It'll be dark—and I mean *dark*. Don't go spacecrazed on me. I'll let out my clip line—here—you hold on to it. We'll crawl to the front, and then I'll pass you a tangler. Don't hit me or show light when you feel it—don't worry, if pirates attack you, you'll get to see lots of fire and suchlike!"

A tangler. The guns that fired rubbery webs that caught and held loose cargo from tumbling into space or smashing into other cargo, holding everything in a clinging goo. It could blind men, or strangle them, or choke them if the web got down a throat. You could breathe through web, but you couldn't get free—not for days, anyway, until it dried out enough to become brittle.

"Now, this tangler . . ." Ben tried to remember Brender's

rasping words of instruction, on the second day out when his head had been reeling from far too much shiplore already. Oh, yes: "can fire perhaps twenty feet." Oh, well. One could go into battle with worse.

No real spacefaring experience, for instance.

Ben swallowed a bitter curse and devoted himself to keeping hold of Brender's line, knowing the old spacehand would move fast. A mag strip ran down the center of the hold; with power gone, they'd not be able to anchor to it, but they could move knowing that it was a clear path.

All too soon the tangler slapped into Ben's glove—how could the old man *see* in this?—and the line tugged in Ben's grasp . . . oh, he knew where Ben was by the line, of course . . . and they were moving forward again.

A little amber light winked into being out of the darkness, then vanished again. Winked on, and went out again. And agai— oh. Of course, it was the hatch light, blotted out by Brender's suit.

A scrambling moment later, or so it seemed, they were touching helmets right underneath the amber light. Ben could just see Brender's savage grin.

"Here's where we die for sure, if Kulkutt has friends," the head hand growled. "If he's alone, we just *might* die."

"Heartening to know," Ben said, through teeth that had begun to chatter. Well, he'd never deliberately stepped forward to his own likely execution before.

"Sure you did, lad," Brender's rough voice came at him cheerfully. Ocean above, he'd said that last sentence aloud! "You did just that when you left your home dirt. We all do. The trick is to make the 'when' wait for years before the Great Empty reaches out with a cold hand and gathers you in."

By all the blazing Ocean, Brender was turning poet!

"Haven't you heard the song?" The old spacehand's voice was incredulous. "Scarm it, *what* do they teach young hands these day?"

Ben opened his mouth to reply, and the old man shook him a little. "Think of something clever later," he growled. "Right now, I need you to wait here for my belt flash—and when you see it, shove that hatch up fast and be ready to fire even faster, at anyone you see that isn't me!"

Noron gauntlets moved in a deft pattern over half-seen studs, something clicked, and the light went out. Ben felt firm hands on his shoulders, turning him and moving him to one side, until he was directly under the hatch. Holding the tangler in both hands as he crouched, he swung the safety cup off its muzzle, and clicked back the fire catch. An unseen gauntlet patted his arm, and then was gone.

Ben sat alone in the darkness and listened to his own racing breathing. It was fast, but not the panting he'd been doing earlier—not quite. He was probably going to die. He *was* going to die. We all die, spacehands sooner than most.

The old man had spent years in space, riding the Ocean, and was going to his death cheerfully. *Cheerfully,* scarm it.

Right now, Brender would be undogging the strong-bay hatch so they could thrust themselves up in unison, giving Kulkutt two targets to put a needle ray through. They both had tanglers, but Brender would probably be facing the pirate, and would be dead before he could even aim.

The flash came out of the darkness, and Ben's life was up.

He swung up his hand angrily, touched metal, and stood up, raising his tangler. The light was blinding, but he didn't wait to see anything—he just fired the moment the hatch was up far enough.

There was a startled oath—he heard it even through the roaring of air racing past him, streaming down into the hold—and something crashed into him, tangled in his web and struggling feebly. Ben turned awkwardly in the telefactoring suit, feeling cables rip away, and flung Kulkutt or whoever it was away over his shoulder, straining in the same movement to get a leg up out of the hatch, and climb up into the ready room. He had to get the hatch closed, and keep some air, or all he'd manage to do was share a tomb with Brender and Kulkutt.

Heavy boots clunked up to him, and gauntlets were tugging him upward. Brender grinned into Ben's face and threw him aside, slamming down the hatch and punching studs almost before Ben knew what was happening—and long before the son of Belormo and Astra Telgryon had found his balance and stopped reeling wildly across the ready room.

Ben fetched up against the edge of the hatch that led into the nav deck, and saw the open hatch into the strong bay next to it. Brender was already turning back, with Kulkutt thrashing feebly in a tangle of web against the far bulkhead. A needler glinted on the floor plates at the base of the pillar that carried the power feeds up through the ready room.

The opening of the hatch must have snatched Kulkutt off his feet and sucked him back into Ben's web before the pirate could fire at Brender.

"I think he's alone!" Brender yelled, slamming his helmet against Ben's. "Get the needler, web him proper, and then get in here! I can fly this thing, but I can't look into the tank and pick out more'n a dozen stars—you're going to have to play at being navigator!"

The head hand didn't have to add the words: *And hurry*. The pirate ship must be drifting up to them right now, its grapples curling out. . . .

Kulkutt was white and gape-mouthed, his eyes staring at nothing and blood trickling out of his ears. Ben didn't wait to see if he was still alive.

The youngest drifthand was panting again, harder than ever, by the time he lurched into the nav deck. Brender slammed a pair of switches flat to the board, and Ben almost fell as the *Emreldon* leaped forward.

The old spacehand did something else, and then reached up to a red blister above Ben's head and tapped it with his gauntlets. A tangle of wires spilled out, and he deftly snared a handful of them, clipped one lead into his helmet and held the other out to Ben, and then reached up again to punch a stud.

Ben fitted the lead to the port Brender had ripped his com lead out of, earlier, and could suddenly hear the crackle of the head hand's breathing.

"We're on the command loop, lad; talk freely. They were right on top of us," Brender growled. "There's still air in the foredeck, but no signs of life; I flashed the lights and sent an all-call through the com . . . so we're running from pirates, somewhere in space, and we can doff suits if we have to—but let's not have to, hey?"

"How long do we have?" Ben asked, looking back over his shoulder as if starships had rear windows to show pursuing pirates to nav-deck crew.

Brender grinned. "A while," he said gruffly. "They had their grapples out and were drifting slow through spacedrift and some larger rocks. So, whither?"

Ben looked down into the voyage tank—the real one, with beacons and projected-path arcs and holos twice the size of the one back in the crew cabin—and found the winking light that was the *Emreldon*. Even a child would have known the great wheel of radiance, off to its left, was the edge of the Ocean.

He looked up at Brender, pointed with a firm finger, and grinned. "Turn her into there," he said.

The old spacehand frowned. "Lad, that's madness!"

Ben shook his head. "No," he said softly, "I don't think so." He tapped the other winking light in the tank, the one that marked the pirate ship, and added, "Now trying to outrun that—look how far they've gained on us already—*that's* madness."

Brender looked at him for a long, silent moment and then growled reluctantly, "Into the Ocean it is. We can't hide there for long, mind, but it'll win us some time to think of something to greet them with, when we have to come out."

Ben nodded, wondering how best to tell Brender. "Show me Sarkon," he said, reaching for a plas-pad and stylus.

The old spacehand gave him a curious look, and then pointed.

Ben peered, and plotted an arc, and wrote things. He was just finishing, intent over the tank, when Brender made a little sound deep in his throat. It sounded almost like a whimper.

Ben shot him a look. The veteran spacefarer was staring fixedly at the scudding brilliance of the Ocean, dead ahead, and clutching the back of the nearest command chair. His knuckles were white and trembling.

And then they plunged into the Ocean, and the nightmare began.

Aboard a starship in the Ocean, there's a constant hissing and snarling as dust and the tiny floating rocks spacers call spacedrift grind away at the hell of a ship. Without the tarse fields, they'd punch through rather than shrieking along, and voyages would end swiftly. So long as the *Emreldon* had power, the fields would keep them safe for months—unless they blundered into something too big to brush aside, too quickly to turn the ship. And Ben, unsure of his calculations, had told Brender to throttle back and run slowly.

He punched up another bearing, nodded as curtly as any starcaptain, and said, "Turn to that."

Brender gave him another strange look—one of many in the last few hours—and even as he engaged thrusters with deliberate care, muttered, "This isn't a *Space Glory* episode, son, no matter how much you play at being captain. We're never going to get out."

Ben shook his head and allowed himself a smile. "I'm not playing at anything. We should be out very soon."

"How can you know that, lad? We're flying blind! Oh,

you've done the figures, and as well as I've seen any plotter do it, too—but we're just fooling ourselves if we think we're following them!"

"Not so," Ben told him, looking hard into the head hand's eyes. "I can feel the currents. *I can steer in the Ocean!*"

Brender stared back at him in open disbelief. A little wild hope was creeping into his eyes when the clanging began.

It was coming from the ready room. They hurried around the corner together, Ben snatching up the needler as he went and slapping it into Brender's hands as they rounded the bulkhead.

Kulkutt was managing to beat his belt buckle repeatedly against the floor plates, but he was still securely webbed. He looked white and weak—but he also looked terrified.

"You're mad!" he husked, as the two spacesuits loomed up over him. The hissing of the passing dust was somehow louder back here. "We're in the Ocean!"

"Not for much longer," Ben told him—and as he spoke, the hissing died away.

Brender reached up to the nearest viewplate and punched a stud. The Great Empty stretched before them, aglitter with a thousand thousand stars—and Sarkon, blazing emerald-green in front of them.

"Right where you said it would be, lad," Brender said roughly. "We rode inside the Ocean, with no stars to steer by, and got here, just as you said."

He shook his head slowly, looking at the glorious view with as much wonder as if he'd never seen it before, and then shot Ben a look. "You're going to be the most valuable man in the Constellar, lad."

"Or the most deadly pirate," Kulkutt added from inside the web, "if you've the guts for it. Any of us could near bury you in credits, and still make more than we ever have before. You could *really* be the most valuable man in the Constellar, Telgryon, not just grow old working every moment for starcaptains who tell you how vital you are, and then keep the credits for themselves. You could be a king among pirates!"

"For a voyage or two," Brender snarled, "until one of them chased you down and blew your ship to shards! They'd gather together to do it, even the worst rivals, to be rid of you! Don't listen to him!"

"No," Kulkutt grinned, "don't listen to *him*. He's all duty and growing old slaving for someone else. Don't you want to taste a little adventure? A little . . . glory?"

Ben smiled down at him, and then looked over at the furious face of the old spacehand with the needler in his hand. Turning away to look to punch a stud that would replace emerald Sarkon with the glow of the Ocean, he said to them both, "I suppose so. We'll just have to see, won't we?"

SALVOR'S PEARLS

BY JEAN RABE

ONE hundred and twenty meters down the alien sea looked like an unending blanket of fog—a green-gray murkiness that extended away from the broken spaceship. There was a hint of brightness directly overhead, a faint cerulean blue that registered on the salvors' visors and that was cut through by a black wedge, the *Mary Carleton* that hovered above the waves. But where the salvors worked in the thermocline against the shattered asteroid reef, where the spaceship had tightly wedged itself, was a place filled with shadows. It was eerie and still.

Worlds differed more on the surface, the salvors knew. The oceans and the wrecks they contained tended to be much the same.

"Captain Kilian." (The tenor voice belonged to Pug Willum, the latest addition to the crew who was picked up on the Neptune colony four months back.) "I've found somethin' a bit unusual ma'am. *Captain.* You might want to come take a look."

Willum was the farthest from the crashed ship, capturing images of the entire scene. It was standard practice for the *Mary Carleton* to keep a visual log, and Willum was trying to document the angle from which the wounded vessel had entered the sea and where it broke up against the reef. This allowed them the option to retrace the spaceship's path, determine where it entered the planet's atmosphere, and discern if anything valuable was jettisoned along the way.

A dozen salvors crawled about the wreck in yellow skintight suits that managed to keep them dry, warm, and easy to spot against their dark and murky surroundings. Their slightly bulbous helmets, and the small turtle shell-shaped rebreather tanks on their backs, made them look like overlarge crustaceans.

One figure separated itself from the back and moved silently toward Willum, propelled by the small thrusters on her belt (these were the same thrusters they used when working on repairs on the *Mary Carleton*'s hull in space, just fixed to different settings; the captain was economical where equipment was concerned).

"This better be good, Rook," came the whisper-hoarse voice over the com. Rix Kilian referred to anyone who served under her for less than a year as a rookie.

Willum was pointing to something at his feet.

It was a humanoid skull, though obviously not *human,* coral growths thick around its long, pointed jaw and under its double-ridged eye sockets. There were other bones nearby, amid rotted planks of wood and a twisted fluke anchor, and looking closely, almost an entire skeleton could be seen half buried in the silt. The being who had died here would have been a little more than eight feet tall in life and would have had feet resembling horse hooves.

"I figure, ma'am, that when that ship hit the asteroid reef over there," Willum was now pointing back at the spaceship lodged in the fissure it had created, his eyes following the form of a slight yellow-suited salvor who slipped inside the hull breach, "I figure the impact stirred up the silt all the way over here and exposed this old wreck and these bones. Should I get some sifters over her, ma'am? *Captain?*" He returned his attention to her, trying to pick through the lights on her helmet to get a good look at her face and read her reaction. But the water and the lights distorted everything, and he all he caught was his own gawky reflection in her visor.

She didn't answer him, as she was studying the skeleton.

"Ma'am," he risked repeating. "Captain? Should I get some men over here? See if there's somethin' valuable? Might be ancient. A real sailing vessel. Rigging and all. Maybe better'n what you sent us down here after. 'Sides, ma'am, the land above ain't inhabited anymore. Records say the beings who lived here blew themselves up in a fusion war a few decades back. This ship's gotta predate that war. By a lot. Really ancient."

Rix was still staring at the skeleton.

"Not ancient, Rook," she said finally. "Definitely worth taking a look at, though. Old, quite a bit before the war certainly. But not *that* old. Can't be. Pearls for eyes."

"Captain?"

She knelt and ran a gloved finger around an eye socket.

"Full fathom five thy father lies;
Of his bones are coral made
Those are pearls that were his eyes;
Nothing of his that doth fade
But doth suffer a sea change.
Into something rich and strange."

Willum glided over to stand even with her. "That's pretty, ma'am. *Captain.*" He corrected himself again. "Did you write that?"

She shook her head, the light from her helmet bouncing off a half-buried bell and making the shadows dance wildly. "It's from *The Tempest*. Shakespeare wrote it, Rook."

"Who?"

"Someone truly ancient. Someone who lived on Earth more than a thousand years ago." She stood and faced him, stared through his visor at eyes that seemed too small for his wide, boyish face. "I'd say what you found maybe goes back six or seven decades." She gestured at the bits of wood and the anchor. "You don't find remains on wrecks that are much older than six or seven decades."

Willum cocked his head.

"The sea eats them, Rook. The fish. The scavengers. The only creatures that survived this planet's war. What are they teaching in the science academies these days?" She let out a sigh, a fine stream of bubbles escaping from a thin tube at the back of her neck, catching the light from her helmet and looking like sparkling gems rising to the surface. "But we might have gotten lucky. It is *cold* here, and the cold tends to preserve things. Maybe what you found is older than I first thought, near a century dead maybe. Or more. We finish with the spaceship over there, and we'll take a look around here. In the meantime, disturb nothing." Rix was looking at the coral-encrusted skull again. "On second thought."

Then she was gliding toward the downed spaceship, directing her people to stop what they were doing and to move to the older wooden wreck, calling her own ship. The *Mary Carleton* eased into the water above Willum, moving slowly so as to carefully displace the water and stir up as little silt as possible, its sleek lines making it look like a huge Earth reef ray. Sound reached the salvors through their helmets, a groaning noise the ship always made in dives, but one that the crew never seemed to hear in space. Rix jokingly told her men it was ghosts in the hull. They were protesting the change in environment, fearing the ship might become one of the undersea wrecks that its crew sought and salvaged for a living.

At least this wasn't a deep dive. The gravity around objects in space was one thing, but the pressure of various worlds' oceans was often times worse. *Mary Carleton*'s hull, though specifically designed to withstand all the rigors of underwater work, was still suffering some of the effects from last week's deep salvaging foray into the Antarean Cluster ocean worlds.

"We'll take the old sailing ship first," Rix decided. "Be careful around it, you picaroons. It's a fragile one."

Minutes later, her crew was swarming over the find, collecting brass decorations from old firearms, the wood of which had long since rotted away, gold finger bars, neck chains, and pottery jars—one containing a trace of mercury, an intact fragile goblet, the pale color of which was impossible to visually determine at the moment, a large cylinder that Rix pronounced was a wrought-iron breech-loading gun, and more. They were all things reminiscent of Old Earth, from the sixteen to seventeen hundreds when pirates sailed the seas.

Willum swam above it all. An underwater archaeologist who specialized in primitive rim would surface cultures, he made meticulous recordings of what little of the exposed structure of the sailing ship they found—aided by a network of frames and underpinned strakes offloaded from the *Mary Carleton*. The purpose was to gather information, which in some circles was as valuable a commodity as the objects that were being floated into the *Mary Carleton's* hold.

The information would show how the sailing ship had been constructed and what its purpose had been. They didn't need to go to such elaborate work on the wrecks they normally sought—those wrecks were space-going vessels and computer logs provided all of that information.

Tubes were dropped so silt could be uplifted, revealing more of the old vessel, and in the process stirring up the sand and making everything seem murkier.

"Rix?" A salvor swam from the *Mary Carleton*'s hold, straightlining toward the captain. "Rix?"

"What is it, Dalan?"

"What are we doing here, Rix? We should be working

the Leerkan vessel that plowed into that asteroid reef. You were damn lucky to pick this system and by chance make the find. We should be working it."

"I'm always lucky, Dalan. And we will work it."

"Look at it over there. Couldn't have crashed more than a month ago in a cold sea on a backwater world where nobody lives and where probably no one on any nearby worlds noticed. No record of any other salvor activity here. It was a fast freighter, and that means she was probably carrying something important. Should be a good haul. All ours."

"She might have been a pirate ship." Rix was staring instead at the scattered remains of the old sailing ship the crew continued to pick its way around, her eyes locked onto what might have been part of a mast, a line still intact and now floating free when more of the silt was moved. "I named the *Mary Carleton* after a pirate, you know, one of the most famous female swashbucklers ever to sail the Carribean back on Old Earth. Sixteen or seventeen hundreds, if I recall my ancient history correctly. Mary might have had a ship like this one."

Her first mate rolled his eyes.

"I fancy myself a pirate sometimes. Dalan. We're stealing from the rim worlds' seas and from the dead, plundering their riches and making them our own. What treasures will we find here?"

"Treasures? Ha! Broken trinkets of a dead planet." Dalan shook his head. "And this work's for what? Only a few eccentric historians will buy whatever we dredge up from here, Rix. You know that. Or maybe you can get some antiquated spacer to pick up a couple of baubles to set on his desk. We'll get more money from that Leerkan vessel. Worlds more."

"I imagine she was a pirate ship." Rix was still staring at the mast, as if she hadn't heard Dalan. A pin-striped fish swam by, intrigued by the floating line. It made a strike at it, then finding it inedible, streaked away. "Had the weapons for it, she did. See? So primitive. There's another breechloader. But we'll know for sure what the ship was in the weeks to come, when we carefully study the evidence we're taking into the hold and piece together the past." She let out a deep sign, more bubble-gems floating to the surface.

A pair of salvors freed the bell, turning it and noticing the engraving. The words were in an alien script, but Rix's microcomputer zoomed in and translated some of it, displaying it on the inside of her helmet. The *Dauntless*. A press of a button and her visor was clear again.

"You can tell quite a lot about the people and the time from a ship. It's all frozen here in front of us. The ship, the crew, fashions, politics, what they considered valuable, what they loved, the whole of their lives and their alien culture—everything held in stasis by this cold, cold sea, frozen at the moment of its sinking. A salvor's dream, Dalan. The skeletons will tell us if the beings of the time were healthy, if their teeth were intact, if their bones were straight and strong. The armaments, how advanced they were. Did a fight bring them to the sea floor, as if did the Leerkan spaceship? A storm? It's all a window."

"Rix?"

"This wreck, Dalan. It's a window to the past (another sigh). The Leerkan ship is too recent to be a window. It's simply a door to wealth, and one that we'll open when we're done here."

Dalan returned to the *Mary Carleton,* knowing the captain had made up her mind. Twice before in the five years he'd sailed the space lanes with Rix Kilian, she'd accidentally came across old wrecks and lost herself in them. "You're mad, Rix," he breathed. "Always knew you were."

Eight days later he returned with the rotated crew, this time to work on the Leerkan spaceship, all that had been practical to salvage from the wooden vessel locked away in the *Mary Carleton*'s reserve hold. Dalan was pleased that at least Rix had a smattering of sense to keep the large hold for the space vessel's cache. He watched her float into the lower hatch of the *Mary Carleton,* the black wedge swallowing her along with the last of the crated antiques and eight crewmen.

"Yo ho ho. At least she had the presence to let me take over on this one," he mused.

The muscular salvor moved to the recent wreck, the numbers TRG-237 barely discernible because of the color used—blue, black, or green likely—against a hull that was also one of those shades. In water, certain colors were almost indistinguishable from each other and hard to see in anything but the most crystal-clear of seas.

He could tell that the spaceship had been under power when it made planetfall, but not under control, or else the crew would have brought it down on one of the large land masses and not smashed it against the submerged asteroid reef. He pictured the vessel slicing into the water, ramming into this asteroid reef and embedding itself there, offering the crew little chance of escape and at the same time ruining what was left of this dead world's ecosystem in the immediate vicinity. The fuel tanks had ruptured and spilled whatever they had left inside along the reef. Most of the coral was dead as a result, no creatures crawled over the ridge, and only an occasional fish swam by.

The hull was beached in two places from the impact, but as he looked more closely he spotted three other areas where the hull was ripped open from weapons' fire.

"No chance of escape," he whispered.

As he floated along the ship, he saw traces of scoring at the bottom of the mid and aft sections and a spot where a plate had buckled, not from water pressure and not by dropping from space unexpectedly into the planet's gravity, but from a sanz-torpedo.

"Pirates," he chuckled. Only privateer ships skirting the rim's merchant lanes carried those kinds of torpedoes anymore. They were unavailable in most mercenary circles and largely unwanted because they were not always precise. But they were cheap and the staple of black market weapons' dealers who operated in the far reaches, and when they hit, they did their job.

"So you didn't run afoul of some interplanetary government. You probably didn't steal your cargo and find yourselves chased across half of known space by its former owners. Pirates came after you, TRG-two three seven. But you fell into the water before the pirates could plunder you." Another chuckle as he headed toward the largest breach. "Yo ho ho. All the better for us."

His com crackled, interrupting his musings.

"Twenty-eight bodies, no survivors. All of them Entirians."

"Leave them for the fish," Dalan cut back. Had Rix been here, she would have told the Salvors to lash the corpses together and weight them down—her version of a burial at sea, and she would have demanded their records be pulled from the computer so their kin could be tracked down on whatever world they lived and properly notified. That still might happen, Dalan thought, if the records were in the chips that were being pulled from the bridge.

"Captain's log recovered."

"Good work," he replied over his com. He was about to slip into the breach for a look himself.

"Debris cleared away. We're at the main hold, opening it now."

Dalan growled from deep in his throat. In some respects he was like Rix, caught up in the discovery of something, wanting to be the first to see it—before the crew had a chance to disturb anything. He'd told them to wait. Why hadn't they listened?

"I told you to . . ."

An explosion rocked the vessel, propelling Dalan away from the breach and into the asteroid reef. The wind rushed from his lungs, and he gasped for air, instantly sputtering when he inhaled water. The impact had cracked his rebreather, and dead coral had sliced through his suit. He felt the warmth of blood along the back of his leg and the icy cold of the alien sea.

Without a second thought, he pushed away from the ridge, flicking on his thrusters and aiming for the *Mary Carleton*. He didn't look back to check on the crew, he didn't have to. His com crackled with a half-dozen voices, some of them screaming, all of them in a panic. Dalan heard Mitchell trying to restore calm, assess the damage, but Mitchell's voice cut out, only to be replaced by rapid breathing. At least two were dead, the hysterical voices told him that, another two injured—one with a vent pipe lanced through his gut by the concussive force of the blast.

Dalan balled his fists in frustration. He couldn't do anything about them—couldn't help them, couldn't even reply to the cries over the com, couldn't risk expelling his last precious breath. He kicked his feet, hoping the added momentum might get him to the ship faster. Then he could do something, after he put on a new suit. His teeth chattered, and he felt his fingers grow numb. There was nothing to keep out the terrible cold of the sea now. How cold were his fellow salvors in the wreck below?

Dalan reached the hatch, just as he felt himself blacking out, his body involuntarily inhaling and drawing more of the icy water inside his lungs. It was several moments later before he came to, the *Mary Carleton*'s lone medic working over him. Around him a half dozen salvors from the previous shift were scrambling into suits, attaching rebreathers to each others' backs, not bothering to check their instruments before setting their weight belts and dropping through the hatch.

"I need a new suit," he told the medic. Dalan tugged his belt off and tossed it near his helmet. He stared—the back of the helmet was covered with spiderweb fine cracks. He was lucky it hadn't shattered. "Gotta go back."

"You're not going anywhere," the medic corrected. She pointed a doughy finger at Dalan's leg, which was stretched out in a pool of blood. "You got yourself cut up good." Then without another word she was running a pack over the wound, sealing the flesh while at the same time cleaning and disinfecting it.

"Have to see Rix."

The medic shook her head. "Missed her. She just went down."

"There was an explosion."

"No kidding, Dalan." Then she was helping him up and gesturing. "Move. To your quarters. In a minute I'm going to have seriously injured people to deal with—one of them a Rizer, and I don't have any of his blood cloned for a transfusion. I'll check on you later."

Dalan knocked before entering the captain's cabin.

She looked old, outside of her yellow diving suit, and small—not more than five feet tall. The soft light of the cabin revealed a myriad of wrinkles around her watery-blue eyes and her lips, wisps of gray-tinged brown hair that danced in the breeze of the air recycler. Rix was sixty-eight, and she had done nothing with cosmetics or nanites to ease the years. She'd never had surgery and she resisted cloning technology. She believed her age gave her a visual edge on the younger crew.

Dalan, who was a little less than half her age, believed the alcohol and the hard life she'd chosen made her appear a decade older.

"Mum?" she asked.

He shook his head, and ran his fingers through his close-cropped black hair. Dalan detested the stuff, a mix of wheat and barley malts flavored with herbs and sweetened, brewed by the chef to Rix's precise instructions, approximating a seventeenth century strong ale favored by pirates and the men who hunted them.

She poured him a mug anyway. He noticed she was drinking form the goblet they'd recovered from the old wreck. It was pale blue etched glass, looking like a piece of carved ice and fitting perfectly in her small, age-spotted hand. He discovered that he was admiring it in spite of himself.

"Thanks," he said, as he uncomfortably settled his bulky frame into a narrow chair across the table from her and took a sip of the stuff. At least mum was better than the captain's other drink of choice—flip, this also a seventeenth century concoction made of watered beer and flavored brandy. She was born about fifteen hundred years too late, he thought. "Mitchell?" he asked.

"Still dicey. Doc says not much brain activity, but she hasn't given up yet. Cameron and Juth reported back to duty this morning. And our Rizer's coming along."

"Three dead."

Rix nodded.

"The cargo hatch on the spaceship was booby-trapped."

Another nod.

"My fault," Dalan said after a moment, drawing his lips into a thin line. "I didn't have them use sensors on it, even though I saw the sanz-torpedo evidence. Didn't think the Leerkan crew would do something like that to their own ship."

"The Entirian captain feared they would be boarded by the pirates." She nudged a green chip across the table until it touched his fingers. "It's in his log, already translated. He was ready to destroy the whole ship to keep them from taking it and the cargo. A proud man."

"A foolish one," Dalan breathed.

She shrugged. "Everything logged?"

Dalan shook his head, his dark eyes dancing. "Took only one day to recover what we could of the cargo, a fraction of the time you spent on that old sailing ship. But we're still inventorying everything."

Rix raised an eyebrow.

"Despite what was lost to the explosion, it's still quite a haul. The ansally-sealed crates to the back weren't harmed, just knocked clear. I told the men to double-check everything. I want them to be exact.

"And . . ."

Dalan offered her a rare smile. "So far we've logged irichium ore capsules, two thousand of them, all nice and labeled and packaged. Bet they were destined for a rim energy weapons' plant. Maybe the planet Delkin or Rauk. Bolts of natural fabric, figured we could keep a few of those. A ton of dehydrated orinthris roots from the Ordis Colony, and half that much again of Rel spices—which will bring a small fortune if we unload them in the right port. Here's the partial inventory." He dropped a small black chip next to her goblet. "Yo ho ho. We should celebrate."

"After we mourn our fallen."

It was Dalan's turn to nod. "Still, you should be pleased."

Rix raised the goblet and offered a silent toast, then ran her index finger around the edge of the glass until it hummed. "Real crystal. I am pleased."

"Best haul we've made in the past four months." Despite the loss of men, Dalan couldn't hide his enthusiasm.

"Indeed. A marvelous haul."

It took Dalan a moment to realize they were talking about two different ships.

She nodded to a shelf above her narrow bed. On it were a few of the objects taken from the *Dauntless*. Dalan recognized a sextant, a piece that might actually bring some money if it was sold at a military space station. He knew the rest of the objects were still in the smaller hold, in containers of seawater. Incomplete or damaged by barnacles and other alien growths, they would have to be restored or preserved before they could be brought into the open air.

Dalan took a long pull from the mug, the liquid stinging his throat. "You've a port in mind? I have all the documentation from the frigate, TRG-two three seven is the call number. It's a clean find. No one will contest us. And it crashed on an open space planet. Any relatives and creditors are out of luck."

She was staring at her reflection in the liquid. "A few minutes ago I gave the coordinates to the helmsman. We'll sell in the Wauk Colonies. Another few days and our holds will be empty again. And we'll be richer." She paused, clinking her nails against the goblet stem. "We'll take on some crew replacements, and then we'll head for the Dener System. I've a strange feeling we'll find another wreck or two there."

"Somehow, I've a feeling you'll be right." Dalan rose and left his half-finished mug on the table. He hadn't quite made it to the door when the claxon sounded. The *Mary Carleton* rocked, and Dalan grabbed the edge of the doorframe.

"No!" Rix's goblet jangled against the table, and she tried to snatch it. But it slipped through her fingers and struck the tile floor, shattering and sending mum flying. Behind her, the sextant slipped off the shelf and fell harmlessly onto her bed. She steadied herself against the table and then impatiently waved Dalan into the hall.

Moments later both were on what amounted to the *Mary Carleton*'s bridge. It was a small room, wedge-shaped like the ship. Rix settled herself in the chair at the point and peered out a viewscreen that wrapped itself around half the room and displayed nothing but winking stars and a distant comet.

"They're behind us." This from her helmsman, who Dalan was leaning over. Both men's fingers flew over switches and panels. "One large ship. A smaller trailing it."

"No markings. They're not responding to the hail." Dalan let out a deep breath, the air whistling through his clenched teeth.

The *Mary Carleton* shook again, and the main grid lit up with damage reports.

"Sanz-torpedo strike! Rear crew quarters. No one

there. No casualties," Dalan reported with some measure of relief in his voice. "Damn it all. We're being chased by pirates."

"Again," the helmsman said softly.

The *Mary Carleton* was built for deep space and oceans, not speed. And despite the best efforts of the helmsman and Dalan, she couldn't outrun the unnamed pirate vessel. Laser fire scored her outer hull, but did not breach it.

"Either we're lucky, or they're lousy shots," the helmsman muttered.

"I'd say neither," Dalan quietly returned.

The air crackled with a burst of static, then a tinny voice cut through. "*Mary Carleton,* this is the cruiser *Sabrewind,* Commander Ormane. Prepare to be boarded. Or prepare to die." There was another burst of static, then silence. The handful of men looked to Captain Kilian.

Rix was leaning forward, punching rapidly at an instrument panel. "Slow to a third," she snapped. "Swing her around. We'll let them through the aft docking hatch." Her shoulders slumped, and she ran the back of her hand across her sweat-slicked forehead. Her fingers trembled in time with her lower lip.

"If only we had some decent explosives," Dalan said, his voice barely above a whisper. "I'd rig the cargo doors and give them a taste of what TRG gave us. I've plenty of pride, too."

Rix brushed by him. "Take my chair. I'm going to greet our . . . guests."

She was sipping mum again, this time from a mug. Dalan was glad there wasn't a spare mug in sight for her to offer him some.

Rix looked up as he entered, Willum was behind him, furtively peering around. She raised an eyebrow at the rookie's presence.

"They didn't take everything we had," Dalan began, "the pirates."

She shook her head and stirred her drink with a slender finger. "No. Half the irichium, all of the spice. It could have been worse. Much."

"Odd that it wasn't."

"Seems their hold was already pretty full," she sharply returned. "They didn't have room to take on anymore."

"Just like the last time," Dalan cut in. "You know, Rix, you're pretty convincing. Going through the motions, trying to elude the pirates, sweating, looking all frazzled. Letting them damage our ship—but not damage it too much. My compliments."

She pushed the mug away and steepled her fingers.

"Rix . . . why?" Dalan's angular faced was etched with bewilderment. "Why are you in bed with pirates?"

She laughed softly, the sound of wind chimes filling the small cabin. "You're smart, Dalan. More wits than I gave you credit for."

"That's why you hired me. For the big brain inside the big body, you told me."

A pout overtook her lips. "Still, I thought things—the raids—were spaced far enough apart that even you wouldn't be suspicious."

"It was the same ship that came after us two months ago." Dalan edged closer. "Why?" he repeated.

She looked up, the lines on her face more pronounced, the gray in her hair shining in the cabin's muted light. "It was a charte-partie I signed."

He cocked his head.

"A charter party, a freebooter covenant. It was drawn up years ago between their pirate commander and myself. It delineates the division of spoils from the ships they notify us of."

"Yo ho ho." Dalan whistled and shifted back and forth on the balls of his feet. "TRG. The pirates told you where it was? Didn't they?"

A nod. "And several others in recent years. The ship that they downed and that went into the seas."

"Where they couldn't get them, because their own ships weren't equipped for oceans."

"But the *Mary Carleton* could. And could do it legally. I guess I'm fortunate you didn't figure it out before now." She paused. "Not a bad arrangement, actually. We both come out ahead—we 'found' wrecks we likely wouldn't have otherwise, getting a share of them, and the pirates getting part of the booty they went after. I'll have to cut you in now, it seems."

Dalan paced in a tight line, the cabin too small for him to move much. "But why, Rix? We didn't need to. We've been making a good living salvaging legitimate wrecks." He stopped and met her stare. "Just how many of them have been legitimate finds?"

She smiled. "About half."

"A living. A good one. Better than most salvors, in fact."

She shrugged. "But not a fine living. And not an exciting one. Besides, Dalan, I told you I considered myself a pirate at heart."

"Then why not tell the crew about your . . . charter party? Most of 'em would've gone along with you. They're mercenary enough."

She wrinkled her nose. "Then I'd have no secrets. Besides, would you have gone along with it?"

He didn't answer.

Rix reached for her mug of mum and he moved quickly, catching her off guard. Dalan grabbed her arm, knocking the mug from it and spinning her around, clamping her hands behind her back. He expected her to struggle; she was a fit woman despite her age. She should have at least cried out. But she didn't put up a fight and she didn't offer an argument. Not even as he and Willum led her through an empty hallway and to the aft docking hatch air lock.

"A mutiny, Dalan? Rook?"

Dalan didn't answer at first. "I guess you could call it that."

"Fitting," she judged. "So you'll have me walk the plank, then return the *Mary Carleton* to strictly honest work."

"Ah, the *Mary Carelton*. The ship you named after a famous woman pirate." Dalan chuckled. "Mary Carleton wasn't a pirate, Rix. I know my Earth history, too. But Mary Carelton knew more than a few of the pirates. She was undoubtedly the most celebrated whore in Old Port, Jamaica. Some called her the German Princess. They hanged her in sixteen seventy-three in Tyburn, I looked it up."

He opened the hatch and shoved her into the air lock, swinging the door shut and flipping the lever that jettisoned her into space.

"Pearls for your eyes, Rix," he said.

"Sorry ma'am," Willum offered.

Willum followed Dalan silently back to the captain's cabin. "Should I bring your things here?" he asked after Dalan had settled himself at the table.

"Yes, First Mate Willum," Dalan answered. "But not till tomorrow."

He returned to the bridge, finding the captain's wide chair comfortable and to his liking. The stars spread out before him, winking at him. He wasn't sure how long he'd sat staring before a gentle tap on his shoulder interrupted his thoughts.

It was the crew's only Rizer, a being who looked wholly human save for his pale green skin.

"Sir?"

Dalan nodded, pleased that the ship's medic had patched the Rizer up like new. He was a good salvor.

"Some bad news, sir." The Rizer's voice was halting.

"Go on."

"It seems there was an accident in the reserve cargo hold. Captain Kilian must have been restoring some of the things recovered from that old sailing ship. She hadn't properly secured the air lock when she flushed the seawater from a couple of the crates."

Dalan stared incredulously.

"She's gone, sir."

He swallowed hard, forcing tears to his eyes as the Rizer explained that Dalan was the captain now, the ship his as Kilian had no relatives and no will.

Dalan wiped at the tear and took a deep breath. He looked suitably sad and made his lower lip tremble.

"Sir?" the Rizer seemed to need direction.

"Notify the officials in the Marsh system," Dalan instructed him. It was his first order as captain of the *Mary Carleton*. "Rix might not have had any family, but she had friends there, and an ex-husband if I recall. But first notify the crew. We'll have a service for her at the end of this shift."

"Yessir."

Then the Rizer was padding away and Dalan was staring at the stars again. He was silent for several long minutes, squeezing the bridge of his nose and shaking his head in feigned grief. It was an act he thought Rix would have been proud of.

"Helmsman," he said finally, his voice a gasp, "take us to the Galitor Quadrant. I've a hunch we'll find some choice wrecks to salvage there."

He leaned back in the chair and tugged a red chip from his pocket. It was his own charter party.

In a secret communique from Commander Ormane a few days ago, the pirate told Dalan he'd downed two merchant haulers in that quadrant, both slipping into a deep ocean. "There will be others, too," Ormane had said. "This is just the beginning."

Fifty-fifty on everything, the arrangement between the two had been sealed, a little better than what Rix had offered Ormane. But it was more than enough to please Dalan. At least for now.

"And this is just the beginning," Dalan whispered. "Yo ho ho."

THE WAKE OF THE CRIMSON HAWK

BY RON GOULART

HE'D been on the planet slightly less than five hours when the initial attempt on his life took place.

About thirty feet ahead of him three burly catmen came splashing up out of the vast azure exhibition pool, armed with antique harpoon guns. Dripping and snarling, they took wide-legged positions on the poolside tiles and aimed their weapons at him.

Jose Silvera, who'd been walking along poolside and discussing modifications of his ghostwriting contract with the diminutive owner of *Billy Laguna's Aquacade,* shoved the short, pudgy human aside and dropped to the turquoise tiling.

Rolling evasively, Silvera yanked the stungun out of his shoulder holster and, pausing in his rotation, fired a crackling beam of purplish light at the nearest catman, a shaggy ginger-colored fellow in candy-striped trunks.

The beam dug into the soggy fur of the catman's chest just as he'd squeezed the trigger of his weapon. The gun made a *thung* sound and the harpoon went shooting up toward the distant plastidome ceiling of the swimming arena.

While the stunned and stiffening lead assassin was toppling over, Silvera rolled to a new location on the tiles. He fired at the second and third catmen.

One harpoon whirred over his head, less than two feet above it, and the other, its aim spoiled, knifed into the pool and was followed by one of the freshly stunned attackers.

The third catman swayed from booted paw to booted paw twice, produced a mewling yowl, and then fell straight through a holographic decorative shrub to sprawl out on the plyoturf.

Carefully, Silvera got himself upright. "Were you expecting any assassins, Billy?" he asked the aquatic entrepreneur.

Laguna was hunched, breathing in a panting way, on a neowood seat in the first tier of bleachers. "I'm well liked on this planet, Jose," he assured him. "Fact, very well thought of on all the many planets in the Barnum System." A bit shaky, he stood up. "These louts must've wanted you."

"I haven't been on Murdstone for four a half years, not since I was here ghosting five sea novels," said Silvera thoughtfully.

"True, but you have a way of annoying a lot of people," Laguna pointed out. "You're pretty damn aggressive for a freelance writer. On more than one planet people resent your policy of always getting paid all the money that's owed you."

"Possibly, but the editors, publishers, and writers who attempt to cheat me out of advances and royalties rarely try to do me in with harpoons." He genuflected beside one of the unconscious catmen and frisked him. "Nope, no ID packet, no skycar license tag, nothing at all."

"That guy who fell back into the pool hasn't come up yet," mentioned the showman.

"And?"

"Well, I don't like to have people drowning in my pool," he said, moving closer to the edge and crouching down, squinting at the blue water. "Especially a couple of hours prior to a matinee performance of my swim extravaganza." He pulled his phone out of the pocket of his sea-blue blazer. "Get a rescue crew out to the pool pronto, fellas."

"Nothing to identify this other lunk either." Silvera stood up and moved away from the second sprawled catman. "Not that I expected to find a pamphlet entitled *Six Reasons Why I'm Going to Knock Off Jose Silvera,* but some small clue would've been a help."

"Keep in mind why you came out here to Murdstone, Jose, and why I advanced you first class spaceliner fare," reminded Laguna. "I'm hiring you to help me write a series of three *Aquacade* mystery novels in the old-fashioned paperback format. Unlike on the Earth planets, paperbacks are still darn popular on Murdstone. They still sell better than demand books, virtual disks, or brainplants."

"Billy, I can find out who's trying to kill me *and* ghost your mysteries," the tall, wide-shouldered writer assured him.

Laguna chuckled. "You hacks," he said admiringly. "I don't see how you do it. About how many books have you turned out so far in your career?"

"In which planet system?"

"Just give me the figures for the Barnum System, I guess."

"I lost count after 1500," admitted Silvera, watching two white-enameled guardbots hauling the waterlogged assassin from the pool.

"These goons'll be out for at least six hours, won't they?" asked Laguna. "But after that the Territorial Police can question them and discover who hired them. So you won't have to waste your own time trying to—"

"More than likely, Billy, they're freelance goons, brought in for this specific job," said Silvera. "They won't know a damn thing about who hired them, even if the cops use truth disks on them. Nope, I'm going to have to do some digging on my own."

"Don't forget that my first mystery novel, *Murder At The Aquacade,* has to be delivered to the publishers in just three months."

Silvera, very briefly, grinned. "I never miss a deadline," he assured his client.

Silvera was on the eighteenth level pedestrian ramp when he achieved possible enlightenment.

Deciding to walk the two miles from the Aquacade Pavilion to his hotel, he noticed an eighteenth level tri-op billboard that he hadn't spotted on the skycab ride earlier.

The floating sign showed a sailing ship on a storm-tossed sea. Stirring music was blaring from the multiple floating voxboxes and a deep, pleasant human voice announced, "Live again the romance and adventure that you've loved in Runyon Kamargo's stirring, immensely popular *Crimson Hawk* sea novels in all their many best-selling forms. Yes, now you can experience all that first-hand—not just virtual sea journeys, not just brainstim pirate raids, not just vidisk naval battles. Now you can come to the new Captain Hawk theme park here in Agualera Territory—you can actually sail on the *Crimson Hawk* with the captain, rent a room at the Smugglers Inn Hotel, and visit all the exciting, romantic ports of call that you first encountered in the brilliant Runyon Kamargo's multiform seafaring yarns. Don't delay, friends. Fax your travelbot today or contact us directly at crimhawk.biz."

Silvera had halted at ramp edge to take all this in. "Bingo, a motive," he said, smiling thinly. He had ghosted the first five *Crimson Hawk* novels for Kamargo and the multimedia contract he'd insisted on gave him twenty-five percent of all income from any source.

"Multimedia, theme parks, three-dimensional ads," he muttered. "Crimhawk.biz ought to owe me several hundred thousand Earthbucks."

But in the four and a half years since he'd last been on Murdstone no additional money had ever found its way to him. It could well be that somebody thought having him knocked off was a good deal cheaper than paying him all those accumulated royalties.

The dogman desk clerk at the Regatta Hotel said, "Oh, yes, the *Crimson Hawk* novels have done sensationally well in the last three or four years, Mr. Silvera. While I also enjoy the vidwall *Crimson Hawk* films, the skycar vidisks, the brainstim chips and the holodramas, for real excitement give me the novels themselves in their pure paperback form."

Elbow leaning on the neomarble counter, Silvera said, "I hear the first four or five novels in the series are the best."

The clerk scratched his shaggy ear, thinking. "Yes, I believe that's so," he agreed after a few seconds. "Although there's something to be said for *The Crimson Hawk and the Treasure of the Lost Lagoon,* and that's eighth in the series. But *The Crimson Hawk and the Haunted Galleon* and *The Crimson Hawk and the Peg Leg Pirates* are much more exciting. And they're third and fourth."

"Fourth and fifth," corrected Silvera. "This Crimhawk outfit controls the whole setup, huh?"

"Yes, with Runyon Kamargo as the CEO and whatever children of his he's not feuding with at the moment as executives," answered the clerk. "There was a report in the Murdstone Edition of the *Galactic Wall Street Journal* only last month stating that the company had netted $14,000,000 in the last quarter."

"That's impressive," said Silvera. "Hell, even twenty-five percent of that would be impressive."

"There is money to be made in writing, Mr. Silvera. You ought to think about attempting a best-seller yourself," the dogman clerk advised.

"I just might. But first I think I'd like to visit this *Crimson Hawk* theme park. It'll probably inspire me to do better work."

"This might not be the most opportune time for that,"

confided the clerk, lowering his voice. "There's a small civil war going on in the jungle territory near the park, the workers in the bordering sweatshop that turns out the Captain Hawk tricorn hats, plaz swords, and embroidered T-shirts are in the midst of a violent struggle to organize into a union and some of Kamargo's more disgruntled offspring are acrimoniously building another rival theme park in the vicinity."

"Even so," said Silvera. "What's the simplest way to get there?"

"I'd use the maglev bullet train," said the clerk, scratching his ear again. "The skytram is faster or you can rent a skycar, but there you run the risk of getting shot out of the sky by some warring faction." He pointed a paw in the direction of the revolving glaz doors. "You can catch the train at the Level thirteen station, every two hours on the hour. The trip's about two and a half hours"

"Thanks for the information, and the warnings." Silvera took the airtube up to his suite.

When he got there, he found a pretty red-haired young woman sitting, cross-legged, on his bed.

Her left leg, from knee to ankle, vanished. "Darn," observed the red-haired young woman, "I keep telling them this holoprojector needs a tune-up, but they—"

"Be that as it may," cut in Silvera, frowning down at the incomplete image of the seated woman. "Who the hell are you and how come you've intruded into my suite?"

"You're still alive, Joe, that's the most important thing," she said, smiling. "Although you're looking even more battered and weather-beaten than the last time we met. Of course, I suppose that's to be expected when a man's near fifty and has led—"

"Forty-two is nowhere near fifty," Silvera pointed out. "And when did you see me last?"

"Admittedly I was a gawky kid four and a half years ago, Joe, but I thought you'd remember me."

"How could you be a gawky kid four and a half years ago? You look to be in your late twenties now."

"Well, my gawky stage was pretty protracted. I'm Amanda Kirkyard."

"Means nothing. Why are you—"

"I didn't always have red hair and I used to be Mindy Kamargo. One of Runyon Kamargo's daughters," she amplified. "I changed my name to Amanda Kirkyard when I started writing my own seafaring series. Haven't you heard of my *Admiral Betsy* novels?"

"Nope, never," he told her. "But let's talk about the money your father owes me for—"

"We can talk about that in a while, yes," said Amanda. "What's more important is . . . Oh, nice, my leg's back. The main reason I pulled strings and got a permit to do an intrusion projection on you, Joe, is so I could rush over and warn you."

"That was thoughtful. About what? That you and your dad and his many offspring had screwed me out of an immense sum of money?"

"Well, the money is part of it," she said. "But more importantly—they're going to try to kill you. When I found out about it, I rushed over to warn you to be awfully darn careful, Joe."

He said, "They've already tried."

"Darn, I knew I should've come before I took my Hot Yoga class," the redheaded young woman said. "I'm glad they didn't succeed. Did you catch the would-be assassins?"

"Yep, but I imagine they're just hired hands who don't know who they're actually working for."

"Exactly, yes."

"So who specifically hired them, Amanda?" He took a step closer to the projected image.

"My father's the mastermind behind it," answered Kamargo's daughter. "He really doesn't want to pay you the $806,000 in royalties that Crimhawk owes you. He was hoping you'd never come back to the Barnum System or to Murdstone and, hence, would probably never learn what a success those five novels you ghosted had become. But then he saw an item on the *LitNews* channel that'd you'd arrived to assist Billy Laguna and he decided he'd better resort to murder. He and two of my nastier brothers—Avner and Nigel to be exact—plotted the whole thing. If the initial attempt failed, they'll probably—"

"What do you mean $806,000?" he asked. "Twenty-five percent of $14,000,000 is over $3,000,000."

"Oh, you must've seen that puff piece in the *Galactic Wall Street Journal*. That was mostly PR baloney and the profits are nowhere near that," she said. "But $806,000 isn't bad, is it?"

"If I had it."

"That's the other reason I dropped in on you," she said. "My ogre of a father doesn't know this, but I'm chummy with the Head Accountant android at Crimhawk. I can cut you a check for the entire—"

"I don't trust a check from you people."

"This'll be a stop-proof check, Joe," she promised. "Can you get out here tomorrow?"

"Where are you?"

"I'll meet you at the *Admiral Betsy* Hotel in Portown," she said. "That's a place I built about a mile from the *Crimson Hawk* park. Eventually, when my stuff is a bit more popular, I'll be putting up a park of my own. It'll be a lot nicer than the dippy Mr. Midshipman Strongfort theme park that my dumb brother Jim is building."

"What time?"

"Let's say 2:00 p.m. in the Cutlass Cocktail Lounge," she suggested. "Oops, my nose is starting to fade. I'll be signing off, Joe. Nice seeing you again." Her image flickered and was gone.

Silvera nodded at the spot where she'd appeared to be sitting. "Let's hope this isn't a trap," he said.

*   *   *

The rented skycar headed through the gathering dusk toward the coast of Agualera Territory. Using the tap-proof vidphone, Silvera called a number.

A freckled human of about thirty-five answered. "Harry the Tipster here."

"You're not the Harry the Tipster I patronized when I was ghosting *The Coffee Table Book of Organized Crime* some years back."

"Ah, you must be Jose Silvera, the hard-boiled hack," realized the information provider. "The Harry the Tipster who tapped info sources for you turned the franchise over to me about three years ago. I've built up the service considerably since then and we've got five other Harry the Tipsters operating on Murdstone now with two more planned for Barnum by next—"

"Where's the old Harry the Tipster?"

"He was compelled to lie low somewhat suddenly, Jose, and at the moment he's in a witness protection program in another planet system," explained the new Harry. "Fact is, they've got him playing trombone in an all-girl dance band that entertains starship troopers. At first Harry didn't like hiding out in drag, but now it's become second nature to the guy."

"Next time you communicate with him, give him my best."

"I will, Jose. He always spoke highly of you and your work. Harry was especially fond of those *Crimson Hawk* books you ghostwrote. Myself I'm partial to Young Adult equestrian adventure tales, but the original Harry—"

"I need some information on a member of the Kamargo family," Silvera said. "She's now calling herself Amanda Kirkyard, but she's actually Mindy Kamargo."

"The madcap heiress," said the current Harry the Tipster. "You planning on writing more sea yarns for—"

"I'm planning on collecting what's owed me for the books I already did."

"That's right. You're known for always getting what's—"

"How soon can you get me information on her relationships with the rest of that family, what she's up to lately, any scuttlebutt you can pick up?"

"Call me back tonight around about midnight," said the information merchant. "Speaking of collecting money—the fee's now $250 in front."

Silvera thrust his Banx card into the slot on the skycar dash panel. "Talk to you again at midnight," he said, and ended the call.

Silvera arrived in Portown safely, but an hour later than he'd anticipated. While piloting his skycar over the Selva Grande jungle, he'd got involved in a dogfight with two rebel fightercars. He tried to explain over his carfone that he was an offplanet neutral and the author of five books on pacifism over in the Hellquad System of planets. Furthermore, not being familiar with the neon insignia glowing on the bellies of the craft, he wasn't even sure what cause they represented. The odds were, if he knew what the hell it was, he'd be sympathetic.

Ignoring all that, the two cars started firing at his rental with the kilcannons mounted in their noses.

Fortunately, Silvera remembered most of the basics of air combat he'd picked up while researching *The Boys' Big Book of RAF Dogfights* that he ghosted for a retired wing commander some years ago in the Earth System. Unarmed, and in a slower craft, he managed to outfly and outfox both ships. However, that took, nearly an hour.

He landed on the rooftop parking pad of the Flying Dutchman Inn in Portown, rode an escalator that played sea chanteys down to the lobby and registered as James Perry Willis of Carson's Landing, Venus. While writing *Counterfeiting for Dummies* he'd picked up a knack for producing whatever spurious documents he needed. This close to the Kamargo clan's headquarters he felt it was unwise to use his real name.

According to all the information Harry the Tipster

was able to provide when Silvera contacted him on his tap-proof room phone. Amanda Kirkyard was the maverick of the Kamargo family and had a reputation for being trustworthy and relatively honest. "She's got a second-rate prose style and is forever splitting infinitives," Harry had reported, "but there's nothing linking her with any of the dirty deeds, kidnappings, and assassinations that Runyon Kamargo and his kids have indulged in since he struck it rich."

"That's gratifying to hear," said Silvera, and he wished the informant a good night.

Being on the outskirts of the vast *Crimson Hawk* theme park, the town was much given over to things nautical. Fog was also pumped in from the direction of the sea. On the next afternoon, as Silvera started walking to his meeting with Amanda Kirkyard at her *Admiral Betsy* Hotel, several of the fog machines were malfunctioning somewhat and the mist shrouding Portown was tinted pink and smelled strongly of cinnamon.

Several of the tourists who'd stopped to watch the android midshipman in front of a ship chandler's shop dance a hornpipe were sneezing and rubbing their eyes. The outdoor tables at a grog shop were attracting few customers.

A gray-furred catman hailed Silvera from the doorway of a souvenir shop. "Special sale of scrimshaw, mate," he said, making an inviting gesture with his right forepaw.

"My wife says I've got too much of it around the house already."

"How's about a ship in a bottle? We've got scale models, exact in every detail, of many of the handsome ships you see anchored in yonder harbor."

Silvera glanced into the thick fog. "I can't even see the harbor from here."

After sneezing, the proprietor shook his head. "I keep telling them they're overdoing the darn fog, but they never listen," he said. "If you could see through this muck, mate, you'd see, among others, the *H.M.S. Betsy,* a handsome three-masted sloop like the one Admiral Betsy uses. You'd also view frigates, corvettes, and ships of the line."

"Actually what I'm hoping to see is the *Admiral Betsy* Hotel, where—"

"I can offer you a model of Admiral Betsy's ship in a bottle. Or you might prefer a miniature of the *Crimson Hawk,*" continued the shopkeeper. "Standing next to the taffrail is a tiny redheaded Captain Hawk. As you no doubt know, because of his fiery red thatch the captain is also known as the Crimson Hawk. So the ship and the—"

"Being a great *Crimson Hawk* fan, I could talk about him for hours on end," said Silvera. "Today, though, I have an appointment, and so—"

"How about you buy the *Crimson Hawk* and I'll throw in the *H.M.S. Betsy* for half price?"

"Tempting, but I'll pass." Silvera continued on his way.

When he entered the domed lobby of the *Admiral Betsy* Hotel, he was confronted with a large scattering of guests who were shouting, screaming, and making other signs of unease.

The source of the agitation was the five peg legged pirates, armed with cutlasses and kilpistols, who were dragging a struggling, screaming Amanda Kirkyard off toward a side exit.

"That poor child," exclaimed a nearby matronly bird-woman.

Taking a step forward, Silvera tugged out his stungun and took aim at the limping pirate who had both arms wrapped tight around Amanda's legs.

"Not today, sonny," suggested the matronly bird-woman. She yanked an electosap from the bosom of her flowered dress and whapped Silvera on the side of the head.

A strong electric shock went zigzagging through his

body and, dropping his gun, Silvera thunked to his knees. He tipped over, hit the holocarpet, and passed into unconsciousness.

"C'mon, kiddo, off your ox. Rise and shine, huh?"

Very slowly and cautiously, Silvera opened his eyes. There was an imitation antique hurricane lamp dangling from the low, beamed ceiling. His teeth felt fuzzy, most of the bones in his skeleton seemed to itch. When the big author hunched his shoulders, his bed swayed and he realized he was lying in a neocanvas hammock.

"Time's-a-wasting, Joe. Wake up so we can get rolling."

Perched on the back of a plaz chair was a large green and yellow parrot. He was eyeing Silvera with a gaze that mingled impatience and disappointment.

Beyond the bird's feathery head Silvera saw a porthole. "Have I been shanghaied?"

"Naw, this is part of Amanda's suite at the *Betsy* hotel, chum," answered the parrot. "Get up."

"And you're?"

"I told her you were basically illiterate, despite all the crapola you've written. Here you don't even recognize one of the more famous literary characters in the universe."

Silvera, feeling briefly woozy, managed to swing his legs over the edge of the hammock. "Oskar the parrot," he guessed as his feet touched the planks of the hotel room floor. "The nitwit bird who accompanies Admiral Betsy on all her voyages."

"A guy who's written all the garbage you have, Joe, is not in a position to hang such critical judgments as *nitwit* on—"

"I only read one of Amanda's *Admiral Betsy* books, after she intruded on me yesterday. Maybe the parrot isn't such a halfwit in the others." He stopped still beside the hammock, waiting out another spell of dizziness. "So what are you, Oskar, a toy her merchandising people cooked up?"

"Do I look like a toy?" inquired the bird in his reedy voice, spreading his bright wings wide. "I happen to be, chum, a state of the art robotic parrot. When Amanda gets her park up and running, similar, though obviously inferior, parrots will act as lecturers and guides in the Maritime Museum and the gallery of—"

"Who'd sit through a lecture by a parrot?"

"You seem to be, jocko."

Silvera asked, "How long have I been out?"

"Two hours. The old dame had her sap on the lowest setting," said Oskar. "Now then, Joe's let's get a move on."

"Did they catch the birdwoman who bopped me?"

"Nope, she scrammed along with the kidnappers," said the robot parrot disdainfully. "The hotel has a half dozen big clunky security bots, but all you have to do to incapacitate them is shoot them with a cheap disabler."

"Where were you when Amanda was grabbed?"

Oskar gazed at the beamed ceiling. "Well, I have to admit they used a stunner on me, too," he said quietly. "I was only out for a half hour, though. Soon as I came to, I asked if you'd showed up."

"You knew I was supposed to—"

"Hey, I'm more than a pet or a mascot to Amanda," cut in Oskar. "I'm her pal and also her mentor."

"You'd have to be pretty dopey to accept a robot parrot as a mentor," observed Silvera. "Did those peg leg pirates abduct her out of this suite?"

"Nope, she was in the Crossbones Cocktail Lounge, awaiting your arrival."

Silvera nodded. "And why are *you* so eager to have me up and around again?"

"I'm exceptional in a great many ways," explained Oskar. "But I'm not much good when it comes to roughhousing. I've been planning to install a stunbeam in my left claw, but thus far . . . Anyway, pal, I need a big muscle-bound lunk to help me rescue Amanda. Admittedly you're not much of a writer, but you've got a reputation of being handy with your dukes and a variety of weapons."

"I'm enough of a writer to have won Pulitzer Prizes on three different planets and—"

"But not one Nobel so far, huh?" When the parrot shrugged, the feathers on his back fluttered. "So are you up to helping me track down the goons who abducted Amanda?"

"You know who they are?"

"Not specifically, but Amanda's scoundrel of a father has to be behind the whole—"

"I did some research on the *Crimson Hawk* park," cut in Silvera, starting, carefully, to pace the cabinlike room. "There's a Peg Leg Pirate Academy that trains actors to impersonate one-legged buccaneers. Runyon Kamargo insists on having peg legged pirates in all his novels and just about every attraction in his park uses them, too."

"By Jove, I believe you've hit on something, Joe."

"It seems likely that the peg leg pirates who pulled off this job are associated with the academy," continued Silvera, feeling steadier on his feet now. "It'd be a good place to start asking questions about where she was taken."

Oskar left his perch, flew over to a table that held a computer terminal. "I tapped some Crimhawk files and got hold of the maps for the underground tunnel system and all the passcodes needed. We can sneak up on the academy from below and—"

"I'm assuming that they found out Amanda was going to pay me off and want to stop her."

"Yep, they must have. I advised the kid to use the dough for herself, but she insisted on—"

"She has the stop-proof check with her?"

"Had it when they snatched her."

Silvera said, "Okay, let's see the maps."

The parrot leaned, tapping the keyboard with his beak. "Coming right up."

Following in the wake of the *Crimson Hawk* proved to be more difficult than anticipated. Particularly after the commandeered three-masted frigate struck a reef off Skull Island and commenced, albeit slowly at first, to sink.

Silvera was amidships when the ship hit, produced immense grating noises, and then floundered. Using a powerful brass telescope, he'd been following the course of the *Crimson Hawk,* a massive ship of the line warship. They were closing on the craft as it sailed across the large artificial ocean that lay at the heart of the theme park.

As the gurgling of the seawater spouting into the hold increased, Silvera went running across the neowood planks of the deck to the fo'c'sle. "This may well delay our pursuit, Oskar," he mentioned.

The electronic parrot was standing on the padded seat that faced the open-air control panel for the ship. "That's darn odd, Joe," he remarked. "This particular reef wasn't on the charts at all." He pointed his beak at one of the monitor screens.

"Are the pumps automatic?"

"You'd think so, wouldn't you?" The bird opened his wings, shut them. "It could be the reason this particular re-created frigate was in dry dock and relatively easy to swipe was because it's still in need of a heck of a lot of basic and essential repairs."

"What about lifeboats, Oskar?"

The frigate was sinking at a more rapid rate now.

"There ought to be a couple of those around here someplace."

"Let's locate at least one and abandon ship," Silvera suggested.

Things had gone relatively smoothly until they'd struck the unexpected reef. The journey through the plaz-walled underground passway had brought them, with Oskar as guide, directly to the lower level of the Peg Leg Pirates Academy.

"We're nearly there," the robot parrot had announced as they neared the facility. "Hearken, chum, and give a listen."

A multiple thumping could be heard now echoing in the tunnel.

"Practicing walking, are they?" inquired the big free-lancer.

"Righto. After they learn how to bend one leg up behind them and attach the neowood peg, they have to undergo several sessions of learning to stomp around."

"So I hear."

"They've got several things to consider," amplified the parrot. "They've got to keep their balance and not trip over their keisters, *and* at the same time they've got to look menacing. It also helps if you can growl, 'Ar, shiver me timbers!' in a forceful, piratical fashion."

"Let's slip inside."

Within the academy, after Silvera had stungunned two staff members, they located the Dean of the training school. A plump humanoid former actor with his curly hair dyed *Crimson Hawk* red, he knew quite a bit about the fate of Amanda Kirkyard.

Applying a truthdisk—left over from research he'd done on *The Interplanetary Oxford Companion to Interrogation*—to the red-haired dean's right arm, Silvera got him to provide considerable information. After delivering some negative opinions about Amanda's prose style and syntax, he told Silvera and Oskar that Runyon Kamargo had indeed had his daughter abducted. She was now aboard the replica of the *Crimson Hawk* ship and being conveyed to Dead Man's Isle. The senior Kamargo maintained a small sanitarium there with, among other things, a staff expert in applying mind wipes and other neurological applications.

Amanda was due to be processed and converted into

a more cooperative member of the Kamargo family. Something that, frankly, should've been done long ago. Her plan to pay Silvera an outrageously large sum of money was, when he got wind of it, what prompted her father to have her hauled back to the theme park for modifications.

Because aircraft and skycars didn't fit in with the historical Earth look of the park, they were restricted. The young woman was, therefore, being taken to the brain lab by ship.

Leaving the dean in a stupefied state, Silvera borrowed a frigate from a nearby shipyard and set off in pursuit of the *Crimson Hawk.*

Now, as twilight closed in one the artificial ocean, they located a lifeboat and lowered it.

"We're in luck, kiddo," observed Oskar as the small craft smacked the water. "This is one of those anachronistic jobs with a fuel cell-propulsion system."

"Then we ought to be able to catch up with them." Silvera settled down at the controls.

They were still some distance from the *Crimson Hawk* when an enormous explosion sounded and one of the ship's masts shattered. The main topsail went winging away into the gathering darkness.

"That's what did it, buster," pointed out Oskar as they came drifting, motor off and lights out, into the cove at Dead Man's Isle.

"The sloop that's anchoring over there, you mean?" inquired Silvera. "The one with the two-dozen-some smoking cannons mounted on her and bearing the slogan *For The Best in Maritime Fiction Read the* Mr. Midshipman Strongfort *novels by James M. Kamargo!* emblazoned in foot-high litestrip letters on its side? That ship perhaps?"

"There's no harm, if it doesn't become too frequent a habit, in pointing out the obvious," observed the robot bird in a slightly miffed tone. "Jim and his pop have been feuding for weeks and he's finally decided to assert himself."

"These Kamargos are a terrific family," observed Silvera as they moved quietly closer to shore. "On two of the planets in the Trinidad System five-act tragedies dealing with fratricide and patricide are very popular. Next time I get hired to knock out a couple, I can use this clan for inspiration."

"Typical of the mercenary hack mentality," remarked Oskar, "taking the troubles of others and converting them into cheap—"

"Help, help," cried a faint feminine voice off their portside.

"That's Amanda," exclaimed the bird, feathers fluttering.

"Yeah, there she is over there trying to swim to shore," Silvera pointed into the thickening twilight.

He guided their craft over to the struggling young author, leaned out and caught hold of her soggy singlet. He hauled her into the safety of the lifeboat. "Welcome aboard, Amanda."

"Jose, how providential," she gasped, as, with his help, she got herself seated. "Of course, I got into this whole mess because of trying to help you out, and so it's only fair that—"

"Are you all right, hon?" The anxious parrot had risen up and was circling her head.

"Yes, I'm in pretty fair shape," she told the robot bird. "Jose, it's wonderful that you came to rescue me."

"You *and* the check," he corrected. "Do you still have it?"

"As a matter of fact, yes." She tapped her left ankle. "It's in my boot in a plyo envelope. They never got around to searching me."

"Splendid," he said, smiling.

"My father is still aboard the *Crimson Hawk,*" she informed him. "I managed to jump overboard when my dippy brother Jim attacked us, but my father is still out there on the ship."

"That's interesting," said Silvera.

"I imagine he and Jim will be fighting it out for a while," she added. "A perfect time for you to sneak aboard unobserved."

"Why the hell would I want to do that?"

"Well, darn, wouldn't revenge be a sufficient motive?"

"Revenge for what?"

"The way he treated you, not to mention what he had in mind for me."

He pointed at her boot. "Could you hand over the check, Amanda? Then we'll make an unobtrusive departure from hereabouts."

Sighing, she tugged off her soggy boot and drew out the waterproof envelope. "I must say, Jose, this isn't my idea of the way to end a romantic adventure."

He opened the envelope, determining that the stop-proof check was within. "This isn't fiction, Amanda," he reminded her. "This is, more or less, real life."

SARGASSO

BY SIMON HAWKE

IT filled the viewport of the lounge, looking like some vast, interstellar wrecking yard. A veritable mothball fleet of ships in various stages of reconstruction or destruction lay docked in scores of improvised work bays, often little more than bare steel girders held together by spit and baling wire. Just about everyone in the lounge gathered to stare as we came within sight of the least glamorous destination in the Belt.

"Ladies and gentlemen, we are now approaching Sargasso," the captain announced over the PA. "It will be visible through the viewports on our left, or you can tune in to our external cameras on Channel 3. Passengers taking the shuttle to Sargasso may begin reporting to the docking area in about five minutes."

The comments from some of my fellow passengers were as familiar as they were predictable.

"My God, *look* at that! It's huge!"

"And ugly, too. Looks like a giant floating junk pile."

"It's hard to believe that anybody actually lives out there."

"Yeah, if you can call that living."

The habitats had never been known for their aesthetic exterior design, but the man certainly had a point. Even though it was inhabited, Sargasso was not a habitat in any traditional sense. It was never designed as a closed, self-contained, and perfectly balanced ecosystem. It didn't even *have* an ecosystem. Sargasso just sort of evolved. Or perhaps accumulated would have been a better word. Some people compared it to a gigantic salvage yard, but to me, it had always looked like the scores of floating junks and sampans all yoked together with planks and ropes out on the quays of Hong Kong. It kept changing constantly, like some sort of mad kinetic sculpture that had hundreds of demented welders working on it, without one of them possessed of a defining vision.

"Well, I think it's a disgrace," another passenger remarked, an elegant looking woman in her forties, fashionably dressed for travel, very sleek, stylish, and well-coifed, undoubtedly en route to one of the resort habitats. "It's a hideous eyesore. I simply don't understand why they would allow it. And I'm sure it's environmentally unsound."

I snorted and she must have heard me, for she turned and fixed me with an icy glare. "Lady, it's space," I said, from my stool behind her at the bar. "Just what exactly do you suppose is out here to pollute?"

She sniffed, contemptuously. "Space is the final frontier," she said, with the smug air of someone who repeated politically correct clichés as if they were holy writ. "It should be kept pristine and pure for future generations, not cluttered up with all of our waste products."

"If you had any idea what you were talking about, then maybe you wouldn't sound so ludicrous," I replied. "Sargasso does not produce any waste products. The people in Sargasso have refined recycling to an art. Their livelihood depends on it. The people who live on Earth are the only ones who send their waste products into space." I paused to take a sip of my drink. "And I suppose that includes tourists, too."

She gave a little gasp and her jaw dropped open. It took her a moment to recover, then she turned away from me with a gravely offended air. "Lord, what an insufferably rude man!" she said, to everyone and no one in particular.

Well, she was right, I guess. Not that I cared. I wouldn't have said anything, ordinarily, but I was in a surly mood and I felt like venting some of it. I got sour looks from a few of the other passengers, but I got some smiles, as well. The smiles came from the Regs, the ones who lived and worked out in the Belt and tended to share my feelings about tourists. Not everybody felt that way, of course. The economy of the resorts depended on the tourists, but the corporate habitats were out here first and there was little love lost between the Regs, the Belters who worked for the industrial corporations, and the Neos who came out to work at the resorts.

They were different types of people, really, who lived in different types of worlds. Superficially, they seemed the same, but only superficially. The Regs were more liable to be fourth, fifth, or even sixth or seventh generation Belters, while the Neos were, with rare exceptions, fairly recent arrivals. A fair number came out from the Luna domes and the orbital, Earth-based habitats, because the resort companies found it easier to reorient those recruits to the perspectives they would encounter when they came out to the Belt, but they couldn't always make their employment quotas that way. A lot of Neos coming up from Earth had to have extended periods of orientation on arrival. Often, they needed therapy, as well.

To a surface dweller from Earth, accustomed to a life of seeing a horizon in the distance and a blue sky up above, looking up and seeing buildings hanging ten miles overhead could be a bit upsetting. A habitat constructed on the curved inner surface of a hollowed out asteroid, spun so that Coriolis force could produce the effect of gravity, took some getting used to. The resorts used VR simulations in their orientation training, but there was a psychological effect to virtual reality that was inescapable . . . it simply wasn't real, and everybody knew it. It was one thing to experience an asteroid habitat in a VR simulation and entirely another to be there in real life.

Neos invariably experienced serious bouts of vertigo that, at best, resulted in dizziness and nausea and, at worst, produced a constant sense of falling that induced paralyzing fear. Tourists, of course, were no exception, but then their brief habitat experiences were usually carefully controlled, their itineraries specially arranged so that the shockingly unfamiliar perspectives of an "inside-out" world were relatively brief and balanced with familiar and settling interior perspectives that allowed them to reorient themselves. And, of course, there were drugs available to help with the experience. It was a little like getting your seasickness in small doses.

It was one thing, however, to visit the habitats as a tourist and have a vicarious vertiginous experience, but it was something else entirely to come out as a new inhabitant and try to get your sea legs when you weren't born to the life. A lot of people never made it and had to be shipped out, which often put them into debt for damn near the rest of their lives, because the resorts didn't give free rides to anybody. It was an expensive way to find out that space wasn't for you. However, when it came to Sargasso . . . well, Sargasso took the concept to a whole new level.

Unlike the corporate habitats, or the resorts that followed them, Sargasso wasn't planned. It just sort of happened. And by the time anyone thought to do anything about it, Sargasso had grown and spread like some surreal, floating coral reef. It was already pretty big when I came out, and that was some twenty years ago. Now, it covered almost three hundred square miles, an area roughly the size of New York City. And it was still growing.

However, that three hundred square miles was a misleading figure, because to properly calculate the size of a space habitat, it had to be done in cubic feet. And with

Sargasso, that was practically impossible. The habitable volume of Sargasso was interspersed with empty space and uninhabitable volume, and the parameters kept shifting.

No one seemed sure exactly when Sargasso came into existence, but everyone agreed it started out as a salvage operation and pretty much remained just that, although it had diversified somewhat and grown much more elaborate over the years. The corporate habitats had been preceded by the space stations, which in turn were preceded by the ships that built them to house the workers who came out to mine the Belt and whose descendants participated in the construction of the habitats. By the time the first of the habitats were built and ready for people to move in, there had been a human presence in the Belt for nearly a hundred years. That left a lot of space junk to be recycled. And since it was cost prohibitive to return most of the old ships and outdated stations to Earth, many of them were simply cannibalized and just left floating. Many weren't even cannibalized, because of old technology, but simply abandoned.

When there were enough new habitats constructed, with enough traffic between them to make the old ships and empty space stations a navigation hazard, the hulks were simply yoked together into a sort of floating boneyard, a spaceborne "mothballed fleet," as the old expression went. And every now and then, some independent operator would go out to look for parts or recyclable material. After a while, it became evident that there were people actually *living* out there.

No one was certain exactly when that started, either. Most people weren't even sure *why* anyone would want to live out there, much less how they managed it. When they first found out about it, the corporations sent out some engineers and they returned to report that the "salvage rats" who lived out in the wrecks had done some pretty creative engineering of their own to cobble together jury-rigged life-support systems from a plethora of parts, some new and some recycled, and they managed to do without many of the comforts of the habitats. They were, the engineers reported with some admiration, hardy and creative nonconformist types who were able to get by quite nicely and had even developed their own idiosyncratic subculture. They were not poaching on any corporate claims or otherwise bothering anybody, and since they had started to do their own salvage and recycling business with the habitats, which served a useful purpose, the corporations left them pretty much alone.

At some point, someone made an analogy between the stories that inevitably began to circulate about the strange goings-on among the Rats out in the boneyard and the old Earth-based myths of the Sargasso Sea and the name just sort of stuck. The original Sargasso was located between the Azores and the West Indies, in the Bermuda Triangle, where the currents followed a peculiar, rotational pattern, rather like a gigantic, lazy whirlpool. The area was marked by the proliferation of a peculiar type of footless seaweed and the name came from the Portuguese "sargaco," which meant grape, because the Portuguese sailors of the old days thought the bulb-shaped floats of the seaweed resembled wine grapes. The area was known for the unique marine lifeforms that could be found there, curious aquatic species which had symbiotic relationships with the seaweed, and it was also a spawning ground for eels of every type from all over the world. As such, it became a natural focal point for myths, and there were many legends that sprang up about sea serpents and seaweed that would trap sailing ships and prevent them from escaping. There were stories of ghost ships that were trapped forever in the Sargasso, the spirits of their crews haunting the old hulks, much like the self-exiled outcasts of the habitats haunted the hulks of the old ships out in the boneyard. So Sargasso it became, and Sargasso it remained. Mysterious and peculiar and forever outside of the mainstream of life out in the Belt.

By the time I got there, Sargasso was a thriving colony

of salvagers, ex-miners, engineers, bohemians, and crazies who had hammered out a lifestyle built around recycling junk and light manufacturing with occasional small-scale piracy, a sort of spaceborne, floating Dry Tortugas where the attitude was pretty much anything goes, so long as it did not jeopardize the infrastructure. I came there because I had grown tired of my life and just wanted to go away and be somebody else for a while. Anybody. It didn't much matter at the time.

"Ladies and gentlemen, we have contact with the Sargasso shuttle," the captain announced, interrupting my reverie. "It should be docking in approximately five minutes. All passengers for the shuttle to Sargasso please report to the docking area at this time. On behalf of the entire crew, I'd like to say that it has been our pleasure having you aboard Omega Starlines; please enjoy your stay out in the Belt and do come fly with us again."

I finished off my drink, retrieved my flight bag from the storage compartment, and made my way down the companionway, past the seats and toward the elevator and the docking area. I could almost feel that female passenger's gaze boring into my back with angry indignation as I was leaving. I didn't care. It felt good to be coming home again.

The shuttle attendant gave me a big smile as I boarded, along with the handful of other passengers going out to Sargasso. It wasn't exactly the most popular of travel destinations. The resorts definitely had it outclassed six ways from Sunday. More comfortable, more luxurious, more things to do, and overall, a better class of people, I guess, depending on your perspective. But Sargasso did have a certain attraction for a certain type of tourist . . . the same type who, in the previous century or so, would have been attracted to the rough trade seaports such as Marseilles, Hong Kong, or Singapore. There were fewer rules, and with fewer rules came more diverse entertainments. There were people in Sargasso who catered to those kinds of tastes, as well. If there was money in it, someone in Sargasso eventually figured out how to make it or otherwise provide it.

"Good to have you back with us, Mr. Logan," the young attendant said, as she greeted the passengers coming aboard. It took a second to recall her name.

"Good to be back, Beth."

Her smile grew warmer. "I'll have your usual ready for you as soon as we undock."

My usual. I had become a creature of habit. Perhaps I always was, only I simply hadn't noticed it before. Beth brought me a mineral water with a slice of lemon. Out in the Belt, it was the equivalent of fine wine on Earth. In space, getting booze was easy. Mineral water with fresh lemon was a more costly commodity.

"Thanks, Beth." I smiled at her.

She smiled back. "Successful trip?" she asked.

"It had its ups and downs. But, yeah, I guess you could say it was successful."

"Good. Welcome back."

There were a little over half a dozen other passengers with me on the shuttle, a few of whom I recognized from the ship, and it did not escape their notice that I was getting slightly special treatment. As soon as she had brought my drink, Beth went around getting orders from the rest of them. Most of them were males. But not all. I counted at least two women and a couple I really wasn't sure about. A guy sitting across the aisle from me leaned over slightly.

"Come out here often?" he asked.

I wasn't especially in the mood for conversation, but then I seemed to have left my casual rudeness back aboard the ship, with that snooty female passenger. Not that this guy was going to be much of an improvement. I was pretty sure I knew what was coming, but I figured what the hell. These people were coming into my port. I supposed the least I could do was be polite. "I live here," I said.

His eyebrows went up. "You don't say?" Several of

the others overheard and glanced toward me with interest. "Well, then I guess you're the man who knows, huh?"

"I guess." I awaited the inevitable question.

"So . . . what would you recommend?"

There it was. His eyes were practically glittering with anticipation. "I suppose it would more or less depend on what you were looking for. Could you be a little more specific?"

His voice dropped about an octave. "Intensity," he said, moistening his lips.

"Ah. I see."

It hardly came as a surprise. There were not many things one could do out in the Belt that one couldn't do on Earth more cheaply, except have the experience of being in the Belt. And the habitats provided that experience in spades, a lot more comfortably, and with a great deal more variety and luxury. Sargasso could not, and did not try to compete. It was not, after all, a resort. Far from it. But there were a few areas in which a few hardy independents from Sargasso *could* compete.

The chief one, perhaps, was in providing a reasonably authentic experience of what life in space might have been like back in the old days, before the habitats, with their well-appointed ecosystems, with lush parks and well-stocked lakes and, near the central axis points, zero-g aquatic recreation centers, complete with talking dolphins. Sargasso could provide the experience of a much more primitive space environment, with all the risks that sort of life entailed, and all the interesting sorts of people a life like that attracted. Sargasso also had fewer laws than any of the habitats, which was to say, essentially none, to speak of. And, largely because of that, Sargasso could also provide the ultimate in designer drugs.

There was no genetic engineering lab on Earth whose clean rooms could compete with what could be built in space. And in Sargasso, they could be built quite cheaply. After all, the raw materials for the construction were all free, part of the floating real estate, so to speak. All you had to do was salvage what you needed and then import anything you could not salvage. The corporate habitats were more than happy to oblige when it came to doing business, so long as what they sold was not illegal. What you chose to *make* with what they sold you was your own business. So long as you did not export anything illegal back to them. But there were always ways around those kinds of concerns.

Most of the tourists who came out to Sargasso—and it was only a small percentage of those who went out to the habitat resorts—came for the adventure. A little bit of roughing it in outer space. Next year, maybe they'd go camping in the Rockies . . . assuming there was still any part of the Rockies that hadn't been developed. But of that small percentage, there was a smaller percentage still who came to Sargasso to indulge tastes that had become so jaded and exotic that nothing left on Earth could satisfy them. For them, there was Intensity.

There was something about the look of glittering desperation, the manic yearning in his eyes that gave me the creeps. I'd seen it a few times before, and the experience did not improve with repeated exposure. It made my skin crawl. I noticed that the other passengers were all watching me intently. Not just a few of them, *all* of them. And the realization struck me . . . it was a tour. I wondered what devilish entrepreneur came up with this one. Intensity tours to Sargasso. What a hellacious concept. And in all of Sargasso's outlaw nonconformity, I could think of only one place that could be involved in such a thing.

"I wouldn't know much about anything like that," I replied to the tourist with the hungry eyes, "but if you went to a place called 'Floaters' and asked around, chances are you could probably get a line on what you're looking for."

"Yes, 'Floaters,' I'd heard that," the man said. I saw several of the others nodding. They were satisfied, apparently.

It was confirmation from a local that what they had been told was accurate. How nice. I made a mental note to mention it to the Committee. There was no further conversation with any of the passengers, which was just as well. Something in the tone of my response must have revealed my disapproval. The remainder of the trip was short, which was just as well, because nobody seemed in any mood to talk.

By now, we were making our final approach, passing underneath Sargasso—or beside it, or over it, I guess, depending on your point of view. From our point of view aboard the shuttle, it was above us, visible through the canopy as the pilot skimmed below and threaded through the various projections that made up the perimeter. Everyone was watching with rapt fascination, and so was I. No matter how many times I experienced it, the close flyby and docking approach to Sargasso always got to me. It was a bit like looking into one of those kaleidoscopes kids used to play with back in the old days before they had computers. They had mirrors and little pieces of cut crystal in them and each time you turned one and looked through it, an intricate new pattern appeared.

Up close, the uniqueness of Sargasso became apparent in a way that could not be fully appreciated from a distance. Much of Sargasso was a gravity-free environment, but parts of it achieved the effect of gravity through Coriolis force. From a distance, Sargasso's mass was primarily what registered, looking like a huge agglomeration of space junk. It was not until you got closer that it became evident that large parts of it were moving, independently of other parts, which often moved in opposite directions, like a gigantic mobile floating out in space. It was like watching a huge construction project over a period of time; you kept seeing it change. Only with Sargasso, the construction—and the gyroscopic movement—never stopped.

When I had left, the old starship that the Hugo brothers had started to refit had looked like little more than an old space derelict, with most of its outer hull removed, cannibalized over the years by scavengers until little more than the ship's skeleton remained. It made one think of some kind of mutant beached whale. Nobody even remembered what the ship was called now. But the Hugo brothers had decided to perform a total restoration, maybe not exactly concourse quality, because they were making all sorts of changes to the original design, but it was an impressive undertaking nonetheless. Now, it looked almost complete, at least from the exterior. Doubtless, there was still a ton of work left to do on the inside. Nobody was really sure why the Hugos had taken on anything quite so ambitious, except to demonstrate that they could. I had no idea what they were going to do with it once it was finished. I assumed they did, but they weren't talking.

As the massive project loomed over us, we could see dozens of pressure suited workers with lifelines, jet packs, and welders scurrying around and over the ship and the massive girders of the drydock superstructure like ants floating in a still, black pool. The Hugos had a large labor force working on this one, but then they could afford it. As we flew past the drydock, their last really big construction project majestically came into view. This one was finished. At least, for now. I'd seen it before, of course, because it had been completed long before I left, but it still looked impressive as all hell. As for the tourists, it just took their breath away.

Most people had seen at least one space station, and many had been aboard one, but few people outside of Sargasso had ever seen anything like this. It looked as if some crazy, suicidal pilot had gotten behind the controls and flown the damn thing right into Sargasso. The closest analogy I could think of was taking an old twentieth century aircraft carrier and ramming it full speed into a marina. At least thirty percent or more of the space station looked as if it were embedded into Sargasso, permanently welded into it.

It was, of course, the way most of Sargasso had been

built, piecemeal, one salvaged hulk welded to another over a period of time, with new constructions springing up out of those amalgamations of salvaged material as the need arose, like some kind of cross between a coral reef and an erector set. But no one had ever attempted anything on so grand a scale before.

You don't just salvage an entire space station. It's not like some outdated ship that's too expensive to return to Earth, where you'd have to pay exorbitant geosynchronous mooring taxes in an already crowded orbit, meaning you could easily bankrupt yourself just putting the thing in mothballs. It was a lot cheaper to strip and abandon it. But a space station, no matter how old or outdated, was still viable real estate. There weren't that many of them left out in the Belt anymore. They had largely been supplanted by the habitats, but every once in a great while, the corporations decided to divest themselves of one to raise some venture capital or pay off some corporate debt. Usually, most of them were stripped first, but not this one.

The Hugos had bought it—lock, stock, and docking facilities—for what had to be a fortune. The specifications of the deal had never been disclosed, but it had to be of Byzantine complexity, because I was quite sure the Hugos hadn't paid it all in cash. Not even they were that well fixed. It always made me wonder just what kind of deal with the devil had been signed, because the corporations never gave anybody any deals. In any case, once Hugo Station was completed, it became Sargasso's spaceport terminal. There were a lot of other docking facilities around the perimeter—most any dry dock construction mooring would do—but nothing could compare to the facilities of Hugo Station, which was also where the Hugos had their headquarters. They never called it their corporate headquarters or their company headquarters, just their headquarters—or, more frequently, their "offices." They did not want any confusion between them and the corporations. They defined themselves strictly as a limited partnership, a family business. It was just that some families were more interesting than others.

The docking was performed routinely and within moments, we were exiting the shuttle and passing through what the Hugos rather charmingly referred to as "Customs." For anyone accustomed to visiting the habitats, this was nothing out of the ordinary. It made perfect sense in closed and ecologically controlled environments to keep careful track of what could be brought in. Sargasso, on the other hand, did not have any ecology to speak of, much less a controlled one. Each independent docking facility had its own rules, and some had no rules at all. But the Hugos liked to have firm control of what went on within their private sector, in part because they were protective of it and because putting everyone through "Customs" as they arrived gave them an excuse to have everybody stopped and searched, so that they knew not only who was coming aboard, but everything that they were bringing with them . . . especially in terms of cash and available credit.

As everyone lined up to check in before passing through the scanning station, I started to go around. Immediately, I felt someone grab my arm.

"Excuse me, sir, but you'll have to get in line and check in with the others."

I turned and saw a young, well-built, and very serious looking gentleman in the black uniform of Hugo Security standing right behind me, holding onto my upper arm. Someone I'd never seen before, not that I knew everybody in Sargasso, not by a long shot. However, before either of us could say another word, a senior officer approached, glanced at me quickly, and whispered in the young man's ear. My arm was released at once.

"I'm sorry, Mr. Logan," the young man said. "I didn't realize who you were."

"That's quite all right . . ." I glanced down at his name tag, ". . . Mr. Knight. No problem." I nodded at the other officer.

He nodded back. "Welcome back, Mr. Logan."

"Thank you, Cy."

The interchange was not lost on the other passengers, who by now must have been convinced that I was somebody important. Nothing could have been farther from the truth. I was so unimportant that the Hugos didn't need to concern themselves about me, though they found me useful on occasion, which meant, of course, that it did not work the same the other way around. The Hugos were probably the most important people in Sargasso. They didn't need their security at Customs to tell them I was back. They knew from the moment I stepped aboard the shuttle. And if they had wanted me to check in with them before I made my report to the Committee, then Cy would certainly have told me. But then, Vox Hugo was on the Committee, and for political reasons, he probably didn't want to look as if he wanted to get a jump on any of the others. Not that it mattered very much, but Vox liked to be polite. Ric Hugo was another story, but then Ric was not on the Committee, which was just as well. His talents could be best employed in other areas.

Before I did anything else, I wanted to go home and freshen up, then get a bite to eat. What passed for food on Earth these days was downright unpalatable, not to mention unhealthy, and I was dying for a decent meal. I took the circulator around the Ring, then made my way out of the station and into the floating warren that was the main part of Sargasso. I could have lived in the Ring if I had chosen, though it would have cost me. The accommodations there were the best Sargasso had to offer, and because Hugo Station spun through its massive moorings, firmly anchored to Sargasso at its poles, the Ring afforded the luxury of "gravity." However, I found that working for the Hugos on occasion was enough of a threat to my sense of independence without also having them for landlords.

I decided to take a gyp back to my spartan quarters.

It wasn't much of an expense, and it was the fastest way to get around Sargasso, unless you were a tourist, in which case the pilot would make sure you'd see every foot of the exterior before you arrived at your destination. Most of the passengers who used the small, independently operated taxis were locals, because Sargasso still didn't get too many tourists. However, that was changing. And a lot of people did not think it was a change for the better.

My taxi, like all the rest of them, was a reflection of Sargasso itself in microcosm, a battered little four-seater cobbled together out of salvaged parts. It looked like a bunch of tin cans welded to an eggbeater, but it worked and, in Sargasso, that was all that mattered. The pilot was a Gypsy Rat, one of the many locals who didn't have a fixed abode, but anchored for the night wherever they could find a space. They had a style all their own. They had few possessions, and usually wore most of them, often clipped to various piercings in their bodies without the disadvantage of being weighted down by gravity. Like their taxis, the Gypsy Rats were themselves often an agglomeration of salvaged parts, festooned with tattoos and mechanicals. They preferred to hang around the weightless sections of Sargasso and stayed away from the more modern areas like Hugo Station, which they regarded as insufferably "Neo."

I chipped my fare to him in barter points, which told him I was local and made him happy. I wasn't paying in tourist creds, which could only be redeemed at a handful of locations in Sargasso, most of them directly controlled or indirectly affiliated with the Hugos. And since the exchanges all took a percentage for every tourist cred they redeemed, the tourists usually got soaked to make up for the difference.

"Been out?" the pilot asked, as we skimmed over the rugged exterior of Sargasso, winding our way around and through as if navigating an underwater canyon.

"How'd you guess?"

"Got that Heavy look about you."

"I didn't think it showed." I must have looked as tired as I felt.

"Not as much as on the Heavies," he replied, meaning the tourists. He had elaborate, swirling black and blue tribals tattooed on his face. The design was bold and striking. "I've seen enough of them lately that I notice. Been away long?"

"To Earth and back."

"Long trip." He glanced at me again. "You'd be that Committee rep?"

"I'd be."

"Just got back, uh? Lotta people be waitin' to hear how it went."

"I suppose."

He grinned. "Not gonna tell me, uh?"

"Why not? It'll be news soon enough. We got a deal."

"Hey. Good terms?"

"Good enough."

"Well, in that case, the ride's free."

"But I already paid."

"So you don't havta tip me."

I smiled. "Fair enough."

He gave a snort. "I hope you negotiated a better deal than that on earth."

"I don't know. Maybe you should've gone instead of me."

"Not on your life. And they can keep their Heavies, too. Or else just send 'em to the habitats."

"But that would cut into your fares, wouldn't it?"

He snorted again. "Redemption cuts into my fares. And if we increase the fares on passengers who pay with creds, the Hugos just increase the redemption charges."

"Well, they pretty much have to do that to keep the credit accounts in balance and maintain the tourist economy," I said.

"If you think they don't make a profit off redemptions, then you're kidding yourself. It's just not worth it. Only ones who make out on Heavy creds are the damn Hugos."

"They do good business," I agreed.

"They do *Neo* business."

"They create new jobs and markets," I said, playing devil's advocate as much to pass the time as anything else. I didn't feel any pressing need to champion the Hugos. I was the Committee's representative, not theirs, even if Vox Hugo did swing a lot of weight on the Committee.

"Not all the growth is good growth," the gypsy replied, repeating what had practically become a mantra among the Rats who could trace their lineage back several generations. "They also create rules and restrictions. Leave it to them and they'd make all of Sargasso just like the damn habitats. Then we might as well all get jobs working for the corporations."

I listened to him grouse about the Hugos and the state that things were coming to for the remainder of the trip, which didn't take very long, fortunately. Part of my mind was taking a side trip, anyway. I was thinking about cycles.

When I got home to my small cabin in the Crow's Nest, a large, multi-level structure that jutted out from the main body of Sargasso rather like an abstract sculpted mast rising from a ship, I thought some more about how the place had changed just in the years since I'd arrived. The gypsy had a point. The Hugos and other enterprising types were doing a lot of good things for Sargasso, but in the process, they were also changing the character of the place. Most of them were Neos who would not wind up staying very long, if they remained true to the pattern. They'd make their money and move on to more comfortable surroundings in the habitats, so it really made no difference to them how Sargasso changed. I wasn't sure if it made much difference to me either. I had moved around a lot in my life, but I seemed to be running out of new places to go. However, the trip had taught me one thing for sure—I had no desire whatsoever to return to Earth.

There was a message from the Committee in the form of the personable and avuncular Vox Hugo. I keyed in, and his personable and avuncular face appeared on the monitor.

"Welcome back, Logan," he said, smiling and sounding warm, friendly, and sincere. "Everything went well, I trust. The Committee is anxious to hear your report. We're meeting at 0900 in the boardroom and we've got you scheduled first on the agenda. If that proves inconvenient, please give my office a call as soon as you get in and we'll reschedule. Good to have you back. Be seeing you soon."

I wondered briefly what he'd do if I called back and told his office to reschedule. It would've been a bit like getting an audience with God, then calling up and saying you couldn't make it because it was "inconvenient." One did not keep Vox Hugo waiting, much less the whole Committee. I stuck a meal into the nuker, warmed it up, sucked it down, and tossed the pack into the recycler. Delicious, no muss, no fuss, and vastly preferable to Earth food. I recalled a time when I never would have thought that I'd prefer bioengineered and predigested food paste to "real" food that you could chew. I had made many concessions, it had seemed back then, in order to live in Sargasso. Now, I didn't see it that way at all, especially after a trip to Earth.

As I tethered myself for sleep, I thought about the strangeness of it all. There was an old saying about how you couldn't go home again. Well, I had, but it no longer seemed like home, which was the whole point. The gravity had made me feel tired and heavy, in spite of all the exercise I'd done to keep in shape. The food had made me feel heavy and bloated, and it tasted funny, and despite choosing what I ate as carefully as possible, I knew I was taking poisons into my system that could cause me serious problems down the line. Even the air had an oppressive, heavy taste and feel. I'd been born and lived most of my life there, but for the life of me, I had no idea how on Earth—pun sarcastically intended—I had ever been able to stand it. As I literally drifted off to sleep, I though about how things had changed for me in just a few short years. I was arguably still a Neo, though I'd been around long enough to see a new generation of Neos arrive at Sargasso, bringing a new generation of changes with them. In a way, I was now part of that. And I didn't like the way it felt.

"Now wait a minute, let me get this straight," said Chairman Kruse. "We've just concluded a ten-year deal with a renewable option to take not only their trash, but their *recycled* trash, as well?"

I nodded. "In essence, that's right."

"What the hell kind of negotiating was that?"

"Well, they didn't really give me any choice. Leaving out their recycled raw material would have been a deal breaker."

"But we're *sending* them recycled raw material," said Kruse, staring at me with bewilderment. He was a fifth-generation Rat and chairman of the Trade Committee, the closest thing Sargasso had to a central government.

"Yes, that's right," I said again.

"That's totally absurd!" said Gregg Harris, the representative from Sargasso's Sector Twenty-five. "We're selling them recycled product and they're turning around and selling it right back to us? Where's the sense in that?"

"Well, we're selling them *our* recycled product, and they, in turn, are selling us *theirs*. However, we do profit on both ends."

"Okay, so then what's the catch?" asked Vice-Chairman Tom Foy, frowning suspiciously.

"We take a cut in profit on the front end of the deal," I explained, summarizing what was spelled out in much greater detail in my report. "As you'll see, it's a significantly smaller profit margin than before, but still a profit, nonetheless, and we essentially make it up on the back end, because they'll be letting us have their recycled product at below market price."

Foy tossed aside the report. "So for this we needed to send a representative all the way to Earth?" He snorted. "From what I can see, we're no better off than we were before. This is basically the same deal we had last time, once you wade through all the bullshit."

"No, not quite," said Lisa Muratori, from Sector Three. She'd been studying the figures thoughtfully while the others spoke. "They're manipulating the market conditions. They're forcing us to buy back some of the same type of product that we're selling them. It'll create a growing surplus on our end, forcing us in the long run to drop our prices and keep right on dropping them if we want to stay in business. And at that rate, eventually, we'll be out of business."

Harris pointed an accusatory finger at me. "You've screwed us, you son of a bitch! You completely exceeded your authority! How much did they pay you?"

I wasn't about to rise to that bait. Harris was half my age, a third-generation drydocker who could frankly break me in half. I was about to protest calmly that I hadn't been bought off and that it would've been easy enough for them to check that if they did not believe me, but before I could reply, Vox Hugo spoke up for the first time during the meeting in his usual, calmly modulated tones.

"I believe we are doing Mr. Logan an injustice," he said. "He was neither paid off nor did he exceed his authority. As a matter of fact, I expressly gave him that authority."

All eyes turned to him. There was a moment of stunned silence.

"You did *what?*" asked Harris.

"I gave him the authority to conclude the deal under those terms," Vox repeated.

"How could you possibly do that?" asked Kruse, frowning. "The time lag for communication—"

"He did it in advance," said Muratori dryly. "He anticipated the situation before Logan even left and cleared him to conclude the deal under those terms if that was what they put on the table."

"Is that right?" asked Kruse, with disbelief.

Vox nodded. "It is. I saw this coming. It was inevitable, really. They're choking on their own garbage. They recycle it, then just wind up throwing most of it away again because there's not enough market on Earth for all of their recycled goods. The only thing they can do to avoid drowning in their own garbage is send it out to space. But of course, there are strict environmental laws governing that sort of thing. They can't just use space as a dumping ground for their garbage, so they have to export it. We are the logical market."

"Leaving aside for the moment the question of why we have to be the ones to buy their problem," said Jeff Martin, the rep from Sector One, "what gave you the authority to speak for the entire Committee and make that decision?"

Vox merely shrugged. "I never said I spoke for the entire Committee. If you read the agreement carefully, you will note that the language specifies the Sargasso Trade Committee and/or their members and affiliates. The Hugo Brothers are very much members and affiliates. If the rest of you don't like the terms, then you don't have to accept and honor them. The Hugo Brothers will take that burden from your shoulders."

"I see," said Martin tersely. "We just have to buy you out, is that it?"

Vox raised his eyebrows. "Not at all. There is nothing in the agreement that binds you to anything of the sort. If you don't like it, walk away. It's as simple as that. The Hugo Brothers will accept all the risk and liability for the agreement."

"And all the profit, too," said Muratori.

Vox shrugged. "Is that unreasonable? If we are going to accept full responsibility—and all the risk—then why shouldn't we be entitled to the full potential profits?"

"Why do I have the feeling we're being had?" asked Harris.

The debate went on for quite a while. I stayed to answer questions, but I soon became superfluous to the proceedings and was dismissed while the argument continued. I was dismissed not only from the meeting, but from my job, as well. Nobody fired me; the job was merely over. At least, that particular job was over. I had little doubt that Vox Hugo would have another one for me before too long.

As things turned out, it took less time than I thought. I received another call from him within twenty-four hours—about two hours after three of the tourists who came out on the shuttle with me were found dead.

"We don't know what became of the others," Vox Hugo said, pacing slowly back and forth behind the desk in his office. The desk alone was almost as big as my entire apartment. It was carved out of a single piece of amethyst crystal mined from an asteroid. It was meant to be impressive, and it was. "It was possible the rest of them are drugged out of their minds somewhere, or else they were jettisoned and the three that were found didn't make it through the air lock only because whoever was disposing of the bodies was interrupted before they could complete the task."

Just hearing that made me feel queasy. People had been killed in Sargasso before; it was not the safest of environments by any means. But these tourists hadn't even been in Sargasso for more than seventy-two hours. That had to be some kind of record. "Was this an overdose, or are we talking about murder?" I asked.

"Well, I would not use the word 'murder,' " Vox replied carefully. He stopped his pacing for a moment and gazed at me pointedly. "Murder is a word with strongly negative connotations."

I had to laugh. "No shit."

Vox managed to smile. "Yes, I realized how foolish that sounded even as I said it. However, my point is that we've got a highly sensitive and highly volatile situation on our hands here. We have to be extremely careful about the words we use even in talking about it, much less how we go about dealing with it."

"Sure. This kind of thing could put a serious dent in the blossoming tourist industry," I said.

Vox gave me a wry half smile. "You don't think very much of us, do you, Logan?"

I shrugged. "Well, I think you're a shark, but at least you seem honest and up front about it. Your brother, however, I don't think very much of."

"Don't worry, he doesn't think much of you either," said Ric Hugo, entering the office behind me.

"Although he does have a grudging respect for your abilities," Vox added, with a smile.

"Yeah, he'd just be a lot happier if my abilities were totally under his control," I said, without turning around.

"And you don't think I'd want the same thing?" Vox asked.

I shook my head. "No, you're capable of understanding that you don't get the best performance out of people when you own them. That's the main reason I can work for you."

"And the fact that we pay better than anyone else doesn't hurt either," Ric added dryly.

"No, it doesn't hurt," I said, glancing at him as he came around from behind me and stepped into my field of view.

Every time I saw them together, it struck me how little they resembled one another. Vox Hugo was the very image of the solidly built, avuncular corporate executive, from his conservatively coifed white hair and sparkling blue eyes with kindly crow's-feet at the corners to the toes of his soft, synthetic leather shoes, with the trouser legs of his charcoal gray suit breaking on the tops just so. Ric Hugo, on the other hand, was whipcord lean and snakelike, from the fluid and graceful way he moved to the anthracite hard gaze of his dark, piercing, hooded eyes, made all the more pronounced by his shaved head.

"There has to be an investigation," Vox replied as he resumed his pacing while Ric leaned back against the wall with his arms folded across his chest. It struck me that with such an impressive desk in the office, it seemed a shame no one wanted to sit behind it. "We do not have a police force," Vox continued, "just our own security here in the Ring. Those unfortunate tourists had families back on earth, or in the Lunar colonies. There are going to be a lot of questions asked, demands made. Somebody is going to have to take point on this. We'd like that to be you."

"Who's 'we'?" I asked. "The Committee or the Hugo Brothers?"

"Both, actually," said Vox. "There were a few people on the Committee who were a bit lukewarm about the idea of your being tasked to handle this, but the majority were overwhelmingly in favor of it."

"Nice to know I have so much support. Who will be paying me? You or the Committee?"

"Officially, you'll be working for the Committee, as before," Vox said. "But if there are any resources you require on this job, you may come straight to me."

"If I take this job, I'll follow it up wherever it leads," I replied.

"I would expect nothing less," Vox said.

"Even if it leads to Ric?" I asked.

Ric stiffened abruptly and came away from the wall. "What's *that* supposed to mean?"

"Somebody in Sargasso is manufacturing Intensity," I said, keeping my tone neutral, "or else having it brought in from one of the habitats. That's what those tourists came here looking for. My guess is that it's being made right here, and whoever's producing it has got a connection to the tourist trade from Earth. That would take resources most Rats just don't have."

"But the Hugo Brothers do, is that it?" Ric said flatly.

I nodded. "That's exactly it." I glanced at Vox. "And that's what a lot of people are going to say. Even if they don't have the guts to say it, you know they'll think it."

"Are you going to take this crap?" asked Ric.

"If it was crap, I wouldn't take it," Vox replied. "But Logan has a point. If, indeed, someone back on Earth is arranging exotic drug junkets to Sargasso, I can see where we might be the logical suspects."

"That's absurd!" said Ric.

"Is it?" I replied. "I just got back from a trade mission to Earth. I went as the Committee's official representative, but in practice, everybody knows that means I went as the Hugo Brothers' representative. You swing a lot of weight with the Committee, and sometimes you ride herd over them. And you're not shy about the way you do it. You get things done, no argument, but they don't like it. To most of them, you're just a couple of well-heeled Neo bullies and they're not disposed to think well of you."

"Without us, this place would be nothing but a boneyard with a bunch of freaks and outcasts living hand to mouth on drifting piles of junk," Ric replied.

"That's right," I said. "And there are a lot of people here who *liked* it that way."

"A minority, I suspect," said Vox, "but your point is well taken, nonetheless. I don't want any talk about us being involved in something as unsavory as drugs, if I can help it. I don't know very much about this Intensity business. What sort of drug is it?"

"Not that I'm an expert," I replied, "but from what I understand, it's a designer drug, engineered to a degree of purity that would be almost impossible to achieve in atmospheric conditions. On Earth, it would require a clean room on the level of a biogen conglomerate. Out here, you could probably set up to manufacture in a closet, with little more equipment than a high school chemistry lab. The perfect vacuum of space makes for very cost effective production."

"What does it do?" asked Vox.

"It supercharges the nerve receptors to a degree previously unheard of," I replied. "The least physical sensation becomes magnified something like a hundredfold. Hence, Intensity. The lightest touch of a finger on your palm can give you an orgasm. A light smack on the fanny can feel like a whack with a hi-voltage cattle prod."

"Really?" Vox chuckled. "What's the down side?"

"The down side is the effects are cumulative," I said.

Vox frowned. "What does that mean?"

"It means the more Intensity you take, the more intense it gets. Eventually, the only way you can survive is to seal yourself off completely from all sensation, live inside a plastic isolation bubble and hope some stray molecule doesn't brush against your skin."

"Can people actually live that way?" asked Vox.

"No, not really," I replied.

"Why the hell would anybody want to take the stuff?"

"Because the first few times, the intensity of the experience is supposed to be incredibly powerful and addicting. People do lots of things that aren't good for them, just because they feel good. People like to feel good . . . even if it kills them."

"Well, if they want to kill themselves, then let them stay on Earth and do it," Vox replied. "We don't need them doing it here and causing trouble."

I glanced at Ric. He was watching me, but he wasn't saying very much. He wasn't naturally very talkative to begin with. But he was the kind of person whose silence made you nervous.

"Find out what's going on, Logan," Vox said. "Find out as quickly as you can. We need some answers."

"And when you get 'em, what happens then?"

"I'm not sure. I suppose that will depend on what the questions are. And who's going to be asking them."

I caught a gyp to a docking facility in Sector Ten, then used the traverse tubes to get to the area known as "Little Shanghai." As I pulled myself along the tube, occasionally using handholds mounted on the bulkheads to propel myself along, I wondered what I was getting myself into.

This was not a trade mission or some business meeting with corporate officials in the habitats. This was messing around with drug dealers, who usually did not take kindly to people who stuck their noses in their business. There was, I realized, a very real possibility that *my* body might be the one to be discovered next. Under the circumstances, I thought it best to carry some protection.

I strapped on my fighting Bowie, because firearms and space habitats do not mix very well. If anyone in Sargasso was lunatic enough to own a firearm, they kept it to themselves, because if it got out that they had one, they'd very quickly wind up taking one small step for man and one giant leap into the void right through the nearest air lock. Projectile weapons, especially those powered by explosives, were definitely frowned upon as an environmental hazard. Edged weapons, on the other hand, were perfectly permissible, as were contact stunners, clubs, and chuks and knuckle-dusters, anything that required you to get up close and personal. And there were certain areas of Sargasso where it was highly inadvisable to travel without some form of personal protection. Little Shanghai was certainly one of them.

I drifted into Floaters at about 1800 hours. The time did not particularly matter; the place was always busy. Sargasso ran on a twenty-four-hour clock, but there was really no such thing as a so-called "normal" day. Nothing in Sargasso ever closed. The only light Sargasso had was artificial, and except for those few places that had observation ports, there was usually no view to the outside.

Floaters neither had any view to the outside, nor much in the way of light. And since there was no gravity, it had no up or down either.

As I came floating in through the entrance, which had once been the hatchway of a ship, I came upon a scene that had no counterpart anywhere on Earth, because on Earth, it would have been impossible. All four walls, in addition to the floor and ceiling, had tables and chairs bolted to them, as well as steel railing constructions that resembled the monkeybars I used to play on as a child back on Earth. Strictly speaking, there was neither a floor nor a ceiling, because in Floaters, as in most of Sargasso's gravity-free zones, those concepts were completely relative. The floor was wherever you happened to be sitting at the time; the ceiling was what you saw when you looked up.

For tourists, this sort of thing could be upsetting. They always felt like they were falling, except where there was no gravity, obviously, you didn't fall. You floated, much like the dancers who moved to the music without any need of a floor, or of any up or down perspectives, for that matter. Your dance partner could be sideways relative to you, or upside down in front of you, which could—and in Floaters, often did—make for an intriguing *pas de deux*. Zero-g dancing, like anything done in zero-g, took some practice, but once you got the hang of it, you could pull off moves even Baryshnikov could have only dreamed of.

"Hey, long time no see, Logan," said Brooklyn Dave, handing me a chilled bulb as I drifted over to the bar and hooked onto the railing. Tiny crystals of frozen water vapor sparkled off the bulb and drifted off into all directions. "How ya been, man?"

"Okay. Just got back from Earth."

"Yeah, I heard that," Dave said, hooking a leg around the rail on his side of the bar, to keep from drifting off. He was a second-generation rat, born and raised in

Sargasso, yet somehow no one in his family had ever managed to lose their Brooklyn accent.

I sucked on the bulb. Lemon-flavored mineral water. He remembered. And it had been a while, too. "Did you also hear about the tourists who got killed?" I asked, not wasting any time.

He nodded. "Yeah, I heard about that, too. Shame. Damn shame."

"They were here just before they died, weren't they?"

He rubbed his dark stubbled chin. "Yeah, they were here. Hell, you knew that; you sent 'em."

"You mean they used my name?" I tried to remember if I gave it to them. I didn't think I had, but then I realized the attendant on the shuttle used it when she greeted me.

"Yeah, they said it as if they thought you were somebody important. Can you imagine that?" He grinned.

"I think I've learned to imagine almost anything," I told him. "I need to find out where those people went, Dave."

Dave shrugged. "Damned if I know. I don't really remember."

"You remembered they were here; you remembered that they used my name; you remembered my drink, and I can't even remember the last time I was in here. Come on, Dave, don't bullshit me."

"Hey, come on yourself. What do you care about some Heavies who came out here lookin' for trouble and got in over their heads? It's none of your concern. Stay out of it."

"I can't stay out of it, because it's *become* my concern. Officially. I've been hired to look into this on behalf of the Committee."

Dave sighed. "Man. . . . What do you want to get involved in this for? They don't care about you. You're gonna wind up gettin' yourself hurt."

"I know what those people were looking for," I said.

"I sent them here, and they wound up dead. I guess I feel at least partly responsible. Just tell me where they went, Dave, or who they spoke to while they were here. That's all I'm asking. It's not so much, is it?"

Dave just stared at me for a moment with a mournful look. He shook his head. "You could wind up gettin' shoved out of an air lock. You know that, don't you?"

"I know that you know just about everything that goes down in Little Shanghai. And if there's something you *don't* know, then you know who does. Just tell me who you sent them to. Please."

There was a long pause. Then Dave took a deep breath and let it out in a sigh. "I sent 'em to see Frankie."

"Frankie Cocklereece?"

He nodded. "Yeah."

It was my turn to sigh. "So Frankie's into Intensity now, too?"

Dave merely shrugged. "I ain't sayin'. But it's like you said, if I don't know something, I usually know who does."

"Right. Has Frankie been around lately?"

Dave merely pointed over his head. I craned my neck back and saw Frankie Cocklereece upside down above me, seated at a table in a corner with her entourage. I thanked Dave, waited for a break in traffic among the dancers, and kicked off from my perch. I did a slow and lazy cartwheel in midair about halfway across, reversing my orientation so that I'd come drifting in feet first.

One of Frankie's boys grabbed me around my right ankle as I came drifting in, and the other grabbed the left, arresting my forward momentum. One of them chuckled and said, "Hey, Tony, make a wish."

"*Yeah!*" said Tony, and for a second, I wasn't sure if they were serious or not.

"Leave the nice man alone, boys," Frankie said. "He's all right. Slide over, Thomas. Mr. Logan's going to join us."

They pulled me into the table between them and I

hooked my feet and knees under the rungs. "Thanks for not breaking me," I said.

"Any time, pal," Thomas said. He didn't take his eyes off me as he said to Frankie, "He's packin' a blade."

I had no idea how he knew. I was wearing it in a concealment sheath and was pretty sure it didn't show. If that was case, then logic dictated that he must have given me a quick frisk as he pulled me into the table, but I hadn't felt a thing.

"It's not a problem," Frankie told him. She looked at me. "Hello, Logan. It's been a while, hasn't it?"

"Yeah, I guess it has. How are you, Frankie?"

"I'm good," she replied, gazing at me thoughtfully. "I'm real good. Hear you're doing pretty well, yourself. Official trade envoy to Earth, no less. That's a long way from that wet-behind-the-ears Neo you were when we first met."

"I suppose. Seems we've both come a long way since then. But it hasn't been that long since we've seen each other, Frankie."

She shook her head. "No, it hasn't. But it's been long enough. Long enough for me to know that this isn't a social call. It's about those dead Heavies, isn't it? The Committee's all bent out of shape about it, and they sent you to find out what happened."

I nodded. "Exactly."

"Well, I didn't kill them."

"I didn't say you did."

"But you *were* wondering."

I shook my head. "Not really."

"Yeah? Not even just a little?"

"Well, I suppose it's possible, but there wouldn't have been any profit in it for you, so far as I can see. On the other hand, you might have made it easier for them to kill themselves, if they made it worth your while."

She smiled faintly. "You're such a charming bastard, Logan. So what are you asking me? Did they make it worth my while? Did I help them kill themselves?"

"Yeah. Did you?"

"I suppose that depends on your perspective," she replied. "You'll have to be more specific." Thomas chuckled. She shot him a quick glance, and the chuckle died instantly in his throat.

I took a deep breath. "Did you sell them Intensity, Frankie?"

She shook her head. "No." She watched me for my reaction.

"Okay, so you're telling me that Intensity is *not* a commodity you handle, is that it?"

"That's right."

"But you sent them somewhere. In exchange for certain considerations, of course. And they wound up dead, so in a sense, I suppose one could say that you *did* make it easier for them to kill themselves."

"Like I said, it depends on your perspective. But I didn't kill them, Logan."

"Do you know who did?"

She shrugged.

"Let me put it this way: if you *did* know, would you tell me?"

She thought about it for a second. "Maybe. But then you'd owe me."

It was my turn to think about it. I wasn't sure I wanted to owe Frankie any favors. That could get real complicated. But the trail led to her, and I seemed to have no other options. "Okay. I'll owe you."

She smiled like a cat about to gobble a canary. "Why don't you go and have a little talk with Mike Hocherl?"

That name brought me up short. *"Vox Hugo's Chief of Security?"*

She chuckled at the expression on my face. Thomas and Tony seemed to find it pretty funny, too. Only I wasn't laughing. Instead, I was thinking about cycles once again.

Mike Hocherl didn't look like a guy who would kill anybody. He was creeping up on thirty, but he looked about ten years younger. Even in the black uniform and ball cap of Hugo Security, he still looked like a fit and clean-cut college athlete who always played by the rules.

"You asked to see me, sir?" he said softly, as he came into the office.

"Yes, Mike. Have a seat," Vox Hugo said.

The security chief quickly glanced at me and Ric, then looked back at Vox. "That's all right, sir, I'll stand."

"I said have a seat, Mike," Vox repeated, without altering his tone at all, but Hocherl sat down as if he'd cracked a whip. He did not glance at either Ric or me again.

Vox looked down at his big amethyst crystal desk for a moment, as if deep in thought, then looked up at the security chief, sitting across from him. "Tell me about those tourists, Mike," he said.

I had to give Hocherl credit. He didn't even blink. Nor did he try to play dumb or finesse his way out of it. "They weren't really tourists, sir," he said. "They were here as representatives of several major Earth-based drug cartels. There was no question about that, sir; my intelligence was excellent. They came here looking to negotiate the export of Intensity to Earth. That would have had very serious consequences, especially after Mr. Logan had just successfully concluded negotiations for a new trade agreement." He gave me a quick glance, then looked back at Vox Hugo. "I felt I had to make a decision, sir, and I accept full responsibility."

For a moment, no one spoke. Then Vox said, very softly, "I see. Well, I appreciate your frankness, Mike." He put his elbows on the desk and clasped his hands together tightly. He compressed his lips into a tight grimace, took a deep breath, and said, "Damn it," very softly.

"You going to just sit there and let him take the blame all by himself, Ric?" I said.

Vox Hugo jerked his head around so sharply I thought his neck was going to snap.

Ric could not pull it off as coolly as the security chief

did. He blinked several times and paused just a shade too long before replying. "Am I supposed to know what you're talking about?" he asked, a bit too offhandedly.

"Yeah, you are," I said, "because Mike's a pro and he's not going to admit that Hugo Security doesn't do anything unless a Hugo tells them to. Usually, it's Vox who gives the orders, but in this case, it was you, Ric."

Ric snorted. "You've got a lot of balls, Logan, I have to give you that. I always knew—"

"Be quiet, Ric," said Vox. He glanced at Hocherl briefly, then turned to Ric and me. "I know you two have never liked each other," he said, "but I find it difficult to believe you'd make an accusation like that out of simple animosity. So let's hear it."

"It's all about business," I said. "Recycling, to be exact. It's a political necessity for Earth-based governments and corporations to recycle, only they can't do anything with the stuff they recycle because there's just too much of it. They can't use it for landfill anymore or dump it in the oceans, all they can do is export it. So on paper, they send us their recycled garbage and we send them ours. Of course, we produce much less, and our process is more cost efficient and much cleaner. They're getting a better grade of recycled product, supposedly, and we get their recycled product, which we can then reprocess more efficiently and use in construction or else in trade with the habitats.

"Except in practice," I continued, "and correct me if I'm wrong, Vox, what's going to happen is the product we receive from them will get mixed right back in with the product that we sent them. So they get back a little more each time, but then they turn right around and fire it back to us. It's a neat little cycle that allows them to claim they're recycling and exporting their recycled product when in fact all they're doing is putting it into a continuous massdriver-powered loop that's going to have a big snowball effect a few years down the line. But that's all right, because by then it'll be someone else's problem, which is how they got into this whole situation in the first place. Everybody passes the buck down to the next generation. Only in our case, we don't mind so much, because we turn a nice profit on the deal. Except there's one small problem. . . .

"With everything all set to work so smoothly and profitably for the next decade or two, the last thing anybody needs is the added complication of a brand new drug trade between Sargasso and the Earth cartels. Sooner or later—most likely sooner, because you cannot mass manufacture Intensity on Earth—someone's bound to notice this new little import/export business and that would lead to investigations. But we don't want investigations, do we? Because then somebody would probably figure out that this whole trade deal was nothing more than a political snow job. And, coincidentally, it would also hurt our tourism, because why should well-heeled tourists shell out all that money for exotic drug junkets to Sargasso when they can just conveniently pick up the stuff at home at a considerably cheaper dealer markup?"

Ric gave a derisive snort. "Are you seriously accusing me of being a drug dealer?"

"No, Ric, nothing so dramatic as all that," I replied. "I'm just accusing you of being a travel agent who books cruises. The Heavies come here for the exotic, rough trade thrill of it all and drugs aren't the only things they spend their tourist creds on. Creds, which you are in the business of redeeming, after all, since we work on barter points that are meaningless to tourists. I don't really think you have anything to do with the manufacture of Intensity and I'd be willing to bet that you don't know who does, either, because you want plausible deniability or else because you simply don't care. Frankie Cocklereece probably knows where the stuff comes from, but she wouldn't tell me and I didn't want to force the issue, because I wasn't in any position to try."

I glanced at the youthful-looking security chief, whose face betrayed no emotion. "I don't know if you did the job yourself, Mike, or else had some of your people do it for you. Either way, I figure you had no real problem with it because a) they were just scumbag drug dealers and b) Ric gave the order. It wasn't hard to figure that they'd go to Floaters or that Dave would hook them up with Frankie. Maybe you just picked them up from there, or else had Frankie set them up for you. Maybe you made sure that they OD'd. I don't know the details of how it went down and I don't really want to. I just hope your intelligence was as good as you say, because it would be a shame if any of those dealers you spaced turned out to be innocent tourists who only came out in search of a new high. But then maybe you think that doesn't make them so innocent. Bottom line? It wasn't really about drugs. It was about protecting a somewhat shady trade agreement and the Hugo Brothers' stake in the growing Sargasso tourist industry."

"It's a very nice theory, Logan," Ric replied, dryly, "but you can't prove any of it, can you?"

I shrugged. "Who says I have to? It's not as if anyone is going to get arrested, is it? This whole thing was just a show for the Committee and anyone from Earth who might start asking questions about a bunch of missing tourists. 'Hey, we tried. We appointed a special investigator, the same guy who was our trade envoy, that's how much we thought of this. But you know, Sargasso can be a dangerous place to visit.' The truth is, I don't think anyone's going to ask too many questions, because that would not be very good for business, would it?"

"No, I don't suppose it would," said Vox. He leaned back in his chair, folded his arms, and glanced from me to Ric and back again. "One of you is a bit too smart and the other isn't nearly smart enough," he said. Ric's mouth tightened, but he said nothing. "I like you, Logan," Vox continued, "and I respect you. A lot of people here do. And that's part of the problem. Even if you did choose to work for me full-time, and I know better than to ask, it just would not work out. I'll have your fee and a sixty percent bonus credited to your account. You can use it to relocate to any habitat you like. Mike will escort you home and help you pack."

"No, don't bother, Mike," I said. "I think I'll just leave straight from here and catch the next shuttle out." I checked my watch. "There should be one in about twenty minutes."

Mike looked at me and held my gaze for a second, then nodded. "Whatever you say, Mr. Logan."

I looked back at the Hugo Brothers. "I'll just see myself out, guys," I said.

Twenty minutes later, I was shipping out and leaving Sargasso behind for the last time. I'd grown accustomed to the place and I would miss it. I wasn't sure I'd like life in the habitats. But I wasn't going home again. All I had were the clothes on my back and some barter points in my account. As an ancient Chinese named Confucius said once, "In the course of a long life, a wise man learns to abandon his baggage many times." I hadn't left behind very much in the way of baggage, but I was sure it wouldn't go to waste. Someone would probably find a use for it. And if not, it could always be recycled.

COMMODORES AND COMMANDERS OF THE COSMOS

The high seas whether on Earth or in space are always dangerous and in dispute whether it be between humans and aliens, officers and crews, or men and machines.

Nautical engagements, shipboard mutinies, and tales of glory and combat of the past, all have their place in the annals of the cosmos.

A MATTER OF FAITH

BY ROBERT GREENBERGER

FROM the Captain's Log of the starship *Sojourner*:

We're just about a year away from Arcadia and I find myself faced with an unexpected and most unpleasant turn of events. While on the Bridge, I made a decision to abort a rendezvous with an asteroid belt to collect needed raw material. From all the projections it looked too dicey to risk the crew. As I was giving the order . . . order, an interesting concept.

Society is built around order. Without it we would never have made it from Earth to find Arcadia. It was order and adherence to same that allowed us to take the world and make it our own. And now, generations hence, following our orders from Earth, we're on our way to another star, another planet to spread humanity's seed. Order, they say, inhibits creativity. Chaos is what allows true artistic genius to surface or to allow a scientist to make a leap of faith and find something new and extraordinary. Those philosophers I studied . . . none seemed to feel it was possible to house both order and chaos within one's mind. And yet, that's expected of a captain—to follow orders and protect the crew. Still, when the unexpected arrives, he must harness the chaos and channel it, forced it to help provide a solution.

My life is ruled by order. As I was giving the command, Midshipman Nicole Wright tried to countermand it. She tried to convince the crew that I was in error, had lost the nerve to command and therefore should not be followed. Some of the duty personnel were her friends, and they hesitated. Our words escalated to shouts, and I finally called security to escort her off the Bridge. Wright is a woman of much conviction, and she is to be admired for such passion. Sadly, though, her actions have consequences and now those convictions may, in turn, convict her of mutiny. I am about to head below to our first court-martial. It is not an experience I am particularly looking forward to.

"Prosecution calls MP Chief Suzuki."

"Do you swear to present the truth, the entire truth, and nothing but the truth, so help you God?"

"I do."

"Proceed, Lieutenant Mahomes."

"Chief, walk us through your preliminary investigation."

"Yes, sir. When Lieutenant Wright first made her accusations, I spoke with our chief engineer, our chief medical officer, our first officer, the morale officer, and Wright's bunkmate. Wright had specific concerns, and I checked each of those with the above-named officers. At that time, I made a report, as you know, to the first officer."

"And how did the first officer react to the facts, as you presented them?"

"Well, sir, it all seemed spurious to him. The first officer wanted to give Wright a fair hearing but ultimately reached the disposition decision to take no action."

"When did things change?"

"When Midshipman Wright refused a direct order on the Bridge, and tried to incite a riot."

"Object to the term 'riot.' "

"So noted, Lieutenant Kobayan."

"The captain had her removed from the Bridge?"

"Yes, sir. My men took her to the crew bunks and remained with her until I arrived. At that time, the captain wanted her arrested and charged with mutiny. He preferred charges, and we began the trial proceedings. Again, I interviewed the people Wright spoke with and once again made a report to the first officer."

"And then . . . ?"

"Well . . . he finally decided there was little choice but to have this hearing."

"Thank you. Your witness."

"Chief, do you like Midshipman Nicole Wright?"

"I suppose so. I don't really know her, Lieutenant."

"Did it seem in character for her to raise these concerns you investigated?"

"I may not know her well enough to guess."

"What did you think when the captain changed duty shifts?"

"It was certainly odd. Made me do some mental gymnastics to switch from a three-shift day to a four-shift day."

"And when we did not launch the probes on schedule?"

"I'm not an astrophysicist. I don't know why the captain made that decision, so I don't have an opinion."

"Okay, moving to something you have more expertise on, what do you think, in your official role, of the captain censoring the communiqués?"

"Objection. We have no proof the captain censored a single message."

"Objection sustained. Continue, please."

"We have had occasion to need a review of messages between encampments back on Arcadia. I presumed the captain had a good reason to order the message review."

"But you never questioned the decision?"

"I usually don't see a need to question the captain's commands."

"I see. We're done."

"Prosecution calls Dr. Walker Erdel."

"Doctor, did you perform a psychiatric evaluation of Midshipman Wright?"

"You know I did."

"And your findings?"

"Wright's psych profile was within normal limits, but clearly she was stressed over the captain, almost obsessed."

"Obsessed, I see. Did this impair her ability to do her job?"

"No, she performed her duties well, always received good evaluations."

"Then why the concerns over the captain?"

"I wish I knew. Nicole, I mean Midshipman Wright, saw little things that bothered her, started making connections and concluded the captain was working against the crew. She was bordering on the delusional."

"Is she a threat to herself?"

"No."

"Is she a threat to the ship or crew?"

"Stirring up all this talk of the captain being crazy doesn't do the crew's morale any good. We're a small enough vessel so people will be concerned about working alongside her, wondering how she'll react toward them if she's this outspoken against the captain. It won't help us for the next decade or so. Nicole means well, but what she says and does has an impact on all of us."

"Your witness."

"Doctor, if she did her job well, good evaluations, and has no history of mental disorder, why do you conclude her questions about the captain's competency are bordering on the delusional?"

"Well, I know the captain, served with him for seven years before we left Arcadia. What she says doesn't match what I know about him."

"So rather than consider circumstances might have changed, given the strain of deep space command, you conclude Midshipman Wright is wrong."

"If there's a question in there, I think you're asking about the captain."

"Okay, say I am. Did you examine the captain on the off chance she was correct?"

"No, no, I did not. Saw no need for it."

"I see. We're done."

"Prosecution calls Chief Engineer Jennifer Ringley."

"Chief, did Midshipman Nicole Wright complain to you about the captain?"

"Complain sounds strong, Lieutenant. Nic did come to me on several occasions, asking fairly innocent questions about what the *Sojourner* was up to. Of course, she wasn't the only one to ask about the ship. This deep space assignment has a few people concerned."

"What sort of questions did she ask?"

"Well, let's see . . . she wanted to know more about the satellite relays that powered the sails as we left the solar system. Wright also asked about the need for collecting raw material in the asteroid belt. Lots of technical questions."

"Anything about the captain?"

"Sure. Every time the captain gave an order regarding the ship's operation, she ran it by me for an opinion. Just figured she was the nervous type. But the questions got awful technical as time went by. She knew the specs, but it seemed she was looking for something very specific."

"Would you know what that was?"

"No, but it did involve each decision. There was the time we launched the probes against specs or the week we had a red alert drill every afternoon at 1500 hours. Nic wanted to know more about our course heading, how close we were to the other five ships, what the communications relay time would be. When we'd be too far to get same-day communications from Arcadia. Things of that nature."

"Did she come out and suggest you challenge the captain's commands?"

"Nope, wasn't on the Bridge that time. She kinda came close when asking some of the questions. Made me uncomfortable to think we had someone aboard who was that unhappy with the CO."

"Your witness."

"Lieutenant Ringley, in your professional opinion, why did we launch the probe off schedule?"

"Captain had a thought about the telemetry, wanted a different set of readouts to compare with the other vessels. Didn't harm the mission."

"What about the decision to avoid the asteroid belt?"

"It was always gonna be a dicey op. We had to use the scoops to pick up the raw ore without shedding momentum. It's one thing to run sims on it; it's another to actually do it in the vacuum. Captain knew we had another option a year out."

"The option meant hardship for the crew, right?"

"Well, yeah. Supplies are being rationed now and will be until that ore is collected and refined."

"Do you feel the captain put the needs of the crew ahead of the comfort level to perform this proscribed mission?"

"Aw, hell, it's risky one way or another. If we calculate wrong, we could lose trajectory and fall behind the other ships—which isn't smart. If the projections are wrong, we may run out of energy before hitting the next opportunity. Captain had to make a choice, that's why he's the captain."

"Were these projections and options discussed with the Command Crew before the captain reached his decision?"

"No."

"Any idea why not?"

"It was all covered during the preflight meetings. I guess . . . I guess the captain didn't want to waste time rehashing the same data."

"When did the captain reach the decision to abort?"

"On the Bridge, just at the point of no return."

"Which is when Midshipman Wright questioned the decision?"

"That's my understanding, sir. I was nursing the scoops, ready to act. Nic was up there, arguing."

"We're done here."

"Prosecution calls Morale Officer Tokemeh Thupten. Please tell us how Midshipman Wright fits into the crew."

"She's bright, funny, and gets along well with everyone. She had an exemplary psych profile, which made her desirable for the mission."

"Then why would she commit mutiny?"

"In her eyes, it was for the safety of the ship and crew. The mission is to extend our reach to another world. We've all agreed to give up two decades of our lives traveling to make that contact. People who are that convinced of their path usually think in absolutes. Wright was no different. Being bright, she can add two plus two and conclude four. In her case, she added two plus two plus two and came to a conclusion the rest of us do not agree with. While rash, her actions demonstrate her conviction and her desire for the crew to survive the mission."

"Sounds reasonable, but you haven't told us about breaking regulations and inciting a near riot . . . excuse me, incident."

"Wright had been adding her twos, explaining her sum to a select few officers. Not one agreed with the conclusion. As word began to spread, as it would in any small community, whispering began. Wright began to feel isolated, so she needed to hold on to her conclusion for moral support. She reached a decision on the Bridge on the day in question and rather than explain once more what the sum was, she chose instead to act. The pressure had been building within her, and Wright felt it was time to do something different. Again, calculated. She weighed the consequences of breaking the regulations against the possibility her sum was correct and the crew was being endangered by the captain."

"Interesting. So, you're saying she had a breakdown?"

"No. I am saying she chose a course of action that allowed her to continue believing her equation made sense."

"You do the math. Add up all her twos and what do you conclude?"

"The captain continues to act in an unorthodox manner, consistent with his psych profile from Arcadia. He was chosen to captain this vessel because he had the kind of creative thinking necessary to ensure the mission was completed and he could reach independent solutions to achieve that goal."

"Okay. So, you don't agree with Wright's sum?"

"I do not."

"Your witness."

"Did you ever discuss this with Midshipman Wright before the alleged mutiny?"

"No."

"Had you heard these whisperings?"

"I had."

"Where?"

"It was discussed during at least one staff meeting. And I heard something about it in the rec room."

"Did any of this prompt you to seek Wright out and hear things for yourself?"

"No."

"Why not?"

"Because what was being said was of no great consequence to the smooth running of the ship or crew. We had other people grumbling about things, especially after the rationing began."

"Were you involved in the captain's decision to avoid the asteroid field, knowing it would impose a hardship on the crew?"

"No. The captain made that decision on his own."

"Shouldn't he, by regulation, at least consult with the morale officer before something that dramatic happened to the ship's complement?"

"Yes, but this was a last-moment decision, and the regulations give him a great deal of latitude in these matters."

"We had been approaching the asteroid field since we left Arcadia, it was on the mission plan. What changed in all that time?"

"I do not know."

"And such a last-minute decision, doesn't that strike you as a little strange?"

"I really didn't consider it."

"When the captain changed duty shifts to four a day, was that done with your input?"

"No."

"When the captain held drills above and beyond what's called for in the mission specs, was that done in consultation with you?"

"No."

"All of these things have a direct impact on the crew's morale. Did you not once talk to the captain about these things?"

"No."

"Why not, Officer Thupten?"

"In each instance, the crew adapted and handled their jobs fine. I saw no change in the tension level, medical reports indicated no adverse affects on their physical well-being, and not a single crewmember came to me to either complain or question it. Including Wright."

"To the untrained person, change after change, two plus two, starts to add up, doesn't it?"

"I suppose so."

"And still you didn't see these changes through the crew's eyes; didn't step back and imagine what was going through their heads. Didn't once take a proactive position to help them through these changes, until rationing began. . . ."

"I object. She's badgering the witness."

"We agree. Lieutenant Kobayan."

"Sorry. I'm done with the witness anyway."

"The prosecution rests. We think we have made our case."

"We'll adjourn for today. Defense may begin in the morning."

"You may begin, Lieutenant Kobayan."

"Thank you. Defense calls crewman Neil Mutumbu. Crewman, you have bunked with Midshipman Wright since the beginning of our voyage, right?"

"Yes."

"And did she strike you as a troublemaker?"

"Not at all. She was pretty levelheaded."

"Did she talk to you about her concerns?"

"Sure. Not until she thought there was something more than a few isolated incidents. Nikki was convinced there was something amiss. She never asked us to rebel."

"As you listened to her concerns, what was your opinion?"

"She might be reading too much into the captain's actions. Didn't seem to bother the crew as much as it bothered her."

"Did any of the captain's actions bother you?"

"Well, I didn't like all the drilling."

"Why didn't you report Nicole's concerns to your direct commander?"

"Nikki's a big girl and could bring them up when she was ready."

"Given all that has transpired, have you changed your opinion?"

"Now that's a good question. Guess you could say I think Nikki spotted the problem earlier than the rest of us."

"So you agree we have a problem with ship's command?"

"Oh, yeah. Every time Nikki did talk to someone, they closed ranks around the captain and ignored her."

"Did she talk to the captain about her concerns?"

"Actually, she tried to. There was one night, Nikki had pulled the dead dog shift and she found the captain just watching the maintenance guys replace a fuse relay. She went to ask him something, but he just started on about something else entirely. Wouldn't hear her out."

"Thank you. Your witness."

"Crewman, if you felt Midshipman Wright had an issue, wasn't it incumbent upon you to bring this to your CO's attention?"

"Guess so."

"She talked about her concerns to many people?"

"I know she discussed it with me, Tatiana, Ayana, those of us in the bunk. Maybe a few others."

"None of you saw this as seditious?"

"Seditious? Because Nikki thought the captain was not commanding us properly? Girl's entitled to an opinion."

"You say she tried to speak with the commanding officers of this vessel. Why do you feel they 'closed ranks around the captain'?"

"Maybe because they saw it, too, but like Nic, refused to acknowledge it."

"I think we're done here."

"Defense calls Engineer's Mate Donald Agbayani. Can you tell us what happened two months ago?"

"We were cleaning the deck after a spill, and I looked up and saw the captain watching us. Didn't say a word. Just watched."

"Was the chief engineer also present?"

"No, just the captain. He watched us and left."

"Your witness."

"Seeing as there's no point to this witness, I have no questions."

"Defense calls Nurse Roger Adderly. Nurse, describe for us your encounter with the captain six weeks ago."

"Yes, sir. Communications Officer Nichols burned himself when a relay overloaded. I was treating the wound when I saw the captain watching from the doorway. He just watched and walked away."

"What time of the day was this incident?"

"According to my logs, I treated him at 0230 hours."

"Thank you. Your witness."

"Again, I see no reason for this and have no questions."

"We are inclined to agree that the court does not follow your direction, Lieutenant."

"I have a long list of crewmen who will testify that the captain was watching them perform their duties, in silence, at all hours of the day and night. We can trace these visitations from about three weeks after we left the solar system until last week. It all goes to substantiate Nicole Wright's assertion that the captain is acting in a questionable manner."

"Watching the crew perform their duties is within the captain's prerogative."

"Actually, Lieutenant Mahomes, the fact that the captain watched is within his job description. However, not a single one of these visitations led to a single log entry, not a single agenda point at the Command Crew meetings. Using our morale officer's terminology, that's adding lots of twos and coming up with a big, fat question mark. Exactly what is our captain doing?"

"To keep these proceedings moving, will Prosecution stipulate to all these visitations?"

"We have no problem with the captain doing his job."

"So stipulated. Proceed with your next witness."

"We call the captain."

"Once again, we object to this."

"Lieutenant Mahomes, the captain made the accusation, and our regulations allow for the accused to face their accuser. Everything we've heard involves the Captain and his actions. We'd like him on the record."

"Agreed. The captain will testify."

"Captain, can you tell us your opinion of Midshipman Nicole Wright?"

"Wonderful girl, good crewman."

"How can you say that if she's been accused by you of mutiny?"

"Good question. Let me put it this way. Wright is officer material, keeps her eyes open, not unwilling to speak her mind. Wish I had more crewmen who would do that."

"Even if it meant a chance for mutiny?"

"I had her removed from the Bridge to avoid a nasty confrontation that would hurt the crew's morale. Unfortunately, in so doing, I triggered our judicial mechanisms which gave me little choice but to have her so charged."

"You've watched our proceedings, what's your opinion of the testimony given?"

"That I haven't done a very good job communicating my decisions with the crew. Fortunately, we've got at least a decade of travel to go, so I get plenty of opportunities to correct that. For this mission to succeed, we need to be comfortable with one another, comfortable enough to speak our minds."

"Yet, Wright did just that and is on trial for mutiny."

"Poor Nicole went beyond speaking her mind, and actively tried to prevent the crew from carrying out my orders."

"We've just stipulated to you silently watching the crew at all hours. Can you tell us why?"

"Captains have a lot on their mind, so I like to take exercise walks. Rather than disturb the crew, I watch, let my mind wander, and move on. No one is put out by having the Old Man around."

"You've been accused of censoring communiqués, not letting the crew talk with the other ships. Care to explain?"

"We have a long way to go, and I'd rather not use up precious power with idle chatter. I've looked over messages before transmission to gauge their worthiness. We're at the beginning of a long flight. If we don't correct poor behavior now, very bad habits will be created and at a later time, if I had to cut off the transmissions it would seem that I was acting capriciously."

"I see. Our engineer has already explained away the probe matter, so we don't need to review that."

"Thank you."

"Captain, we have carefully covered how the senior officers on the ship ignored Midshipman Wright's questions and concerns. Were they right in doing so?"

"This is a handpicked command crew. All excel at their particular functions so if they ignored her, they did so after careful consideration."

"Nice answer. If you handpicked these men, would you say this ship's Command Crew is close-knit?"

"Extremely."

"Talk with them often?"

"As often as necessary."

"Interesting. In that case, why did you not discuss your shift changes with morale officer Thupten?"

"It was a command decision."

"Yes, but one with a direct affect on morale. What about the extra drilling? Cover that with the first officer?"

"Didn't see the point."

"Tell me, do you consider them loyal?"

"Extremely."

"Would it be possible, then, that loyalty could blind them to a problem with their commanding officer?"

"Not likely."

"Could such loyalty lead them to shield the crew, to protect their captain from close scrutiny?"

"Never."

"Never. I see. You didn't talk much with your Command Crew, nor did you talk to the crew when wanderng at all hours. But what about your long conversation with Midshipman Wright?"

"Which one would that be? I've made it a point to talk with all of my crew."

"I think we've established just the opposite, Captain. Do you recall the conversation or not? Think back to the time she found you in the chapel. It was at night. Do you recall the substance of the conversation?"

"Not especially. She seemed interested in matters of faith, I believe."

"Exactly, Captain. Matters of faith, of whether or not she believed that other races exist in the universe. Her concern was that after all these centuries of searching; mankind has found no evidence of any other intelligent life. In fact, the theory of our existing as the result of some form of accident has gained as a religious tenent. Did you offer her words of comfort?"

"I don't believe so. I try not to meddle in such personal issues."

"You didn't comfort her at all, because Wright was surprised to hear you shared those beliefs. In fact, you hold to them dearly, don't you, Captain?"

"Those beliefs do not have a bearing on Wright's conduct, do they?"

"Actually, they do. She was shocked to hear her captain worry aloud that the entire mission was in question. You told her you thought finding Arcadia was more luck than science, didn't you?"

"I . . . might have used the word providence, not luck."

"But you doubt we'll have such fortune again?"

"Again, Lieutenant, those personal beliefs do not have a bearing on her actions."

"Oh, but they do, Captain. Please tell this court, do you believe this mission will end in success?"

"I have every hope."

"Not hope, sir, but belief. Do you believe this will succeed?"

"Badgering, your honor!"

"Lieutenant Kobayan, please redirect your questioning."

"Of course, your honor. Captain, how do you gauge crew morale?"

"I think morale is mixed, to be honest. The rationing was not well received."

"Rationing you insisted upon because we missed the scheduled supply pickup. Tell me, sir, why did we miss the asteroid belt?"

"In studying the final mission specs, in comparing our data with the telemetery collected by the other ships, I deemed it a prudent action."

"Was this a conversation you had with your fellow captains? I believe mission protocols call for all captains to agree on any major change in the mission."

"I don't recall."

"Did you, by chance, discuss this with your senior staff? Weigh the effects this would have on both the mission and the crew?"

"Probably not."

"May I ask why?"

"May I ask what this has to do with the charge of mutiny?"

"Captain, it's likely you did not discuss any of this with your Command Crew because you knew they would object. They, in turn, saw you making the mission harder for all, not easier. But out of loyalty, they rallied around you, kept the crew from seeing what Wright so clearly saw."

"Your Honor . . ."

"Lieutenant, save it for the closing. Another question, if you have any."

"Do you recall what Midshipman Wright accused you of on the Bridge?"

"No."

"She said you lost your nerve, didn't she? She said you were so convinced the mission would end in failure you were out to sabotage every effort to reach its conclusion."

"I don't recall that."

"You don't recall her pointing out to the Bridge officers how you were trying to force us to return to Arcadia through your every move? That you suppressed the telemetery from the probe, that you isolated us from the other ships in an attempt to avoid completing the mission?"

"No, that's not . . ."

"Nicole Wright insisted the crew follow their orders, not miss the asteroid rendezvous, so we could complete the mission. She felt you had a crisis of faith, that you . . ."

"Objection! Where's the question?"

"That's not what she said. . . ."

"Lieutenant Kobayan!"

"Captain, you threw Wright off the bridge because you knew she would force you to finish the mission, finish a mission you had no desire to complete! You lost your faith in the goals of our people!"

"Objection!"

"You let personal fears replace command training. Your handpicked Command Crew chose to close their eyes out of loyalty, further harming the mission. As a result, this entire ship is now suffering both rationing and isolation. You deliberately want us cut off from the other ships, knowing they can't simply turn around and find out what's wrong. The engineering specs call for going in one direction to maintain precious momentum. You wanted us cut off so you don't have your fears justified!"

"I did it to protect this crew! Everything I did was to protect the crew! If it's a total void, better we know it now than later, when we're old and useless."

"You admit to losing your faith?"

"If faith is what you call it, Lieutenant, then yes. Out here, with nothing surrounding us but vacuum, you see things differently. You understand how unique we are, how precious life is. I saw the crew working and playing. I saw them with their full lives ahead and realized I was wasting those lives. Better they return to Arcadia and do something that will succeed. I owed them that as their captain."

"No, sir. They signed on to this mission, knowing full well what the risks and odds were. This is how they wanted to spend their time, their years. To repeat what their ancestors had done, to seek out some new world, some new place to hopefully expand our reach and maybe, just maybe find that elusive life out here. You were robbing people of those dreams for your own selfish fears."

". . . yes . . ."

"Midshipman Nicole Wright acted in the best interest of the crew and of the mission, didn't she?"

"She . . . did . . . she saw my own fear better than I did."

"Your Honor, I submit the charges be dropped against Nicole Wright and the Command Crew convene to determine this crew's best course of action. On behalf of the crew, I further submit that the captain be relieved of duty and a new commanding officer be placed in charge. Finally, I insist the Command Crew put aside loyalty to the captain and act, for a change, in the interest of the crew."

"Your Honor, this is highly irregular!"

"Lieutenant Mahomes, everything has been highly irregular since we left Arcadia. Clearly, we have to review the testimony just submitted against the charges as well as the captain's own admission of malfeasance. For the moment, this court relieves the captain of the burden of command until such time as this court and senior staff can review all data and information pertinent to our collective future. At such time, we will make a general announcement to the crew. I suspect, Lieutenant Kobayan, you may get your wish. We stand adjourned."

"Begging your pardon, but what of Midshipman Wright?"

"I see. Nicole Wright, you are returned to your duties effective immediately. Your charges of mutiny are suspended until this court rules further. Dismissed."

From the Captain's Log of the starship *Sojourner*:

I find the crew to be handling the changes in command fairly well. I have taken possession of the captain's cabin and have been holding several meetings. If I've learned anything from presiding over the court-martial, it is that we're not communicating enough. Our Command Crew was isolated from the rest of the ship's complement and maybe this ugly incident precipitated by Nicole Wright will improve matters over time.

Still, the damage is done both physically and spiritually. We remain on rations until our next supply opportunity. Our Morale Officer has already started working on programs to keep people from turning this into a larger negative than it has to be. The captain is now working on sensor analysis, one of his true loves. If there's something out there, I want him to be the first one to confirm it. He needs that show of faith, needs to know he did not leave his crew in a dire situation. Instead of watching the crew like a phantom, he has sought some of them out and awkwardly, they are responding. It gives me some hope.

Wright has been returned to her former duties, all charges dismissed. It was an extraordinary set of circumstances that brought about our court-martial. I don't want them to happen again, and I will need to remain vigilant to prevent that. Order will be maintained.

But still, he raised the specter of failure, which, coupled with the rationing, put a serious dent in our optimism that this next phase of mankind's reach for the stars will result in success. It has forced me to address the crew and remind them that we plotted a course for a star system that has proved to have planets, at least two that should be able to sustain life. Arcadia was no fluke, I reminded them; it took years of study and preparation and even more years to make the planet a home. I don't know what's happening back on Earth—it was left by our ancestors and is now a legend like Heaven. I don't know what's happening on the planets before us and word from Arcadia comes more infrequently. But with Earth and Arcadia as our testament, we know there's life in this universe and with that to draw inspiration from, we're going forward. I want the people that are now my crew to hold out the hope that one of those two worlds will become our new home, our latest step forward.

The above fragmentary documentation was found in a routine marker buoy left by the *Sojourner* and found seventeen years after its departure from Arcadia by a solar system patrol. No word had been received on the ultimate fate of the *Sojourner* and the other ships on that colonization mission.

—Arcadia Space Exploration Committee report

THE OLD WAY

by Bill Fawcett

THE drop of sweat stung as it clung to the brow of one of Harry's deep blue eyes. He was more than two thousand miles away from where he could wipe it without removing his space suit. His light brown hair was plastered against his forehead and even working full on, after eleven hours a day for almost thirty days in a row, even a custom-fit suit chafed under his arms and against his thigh.

But at the moment these minor discomforts were the last of Lieutenant Harrison Coronet's concerns, because all his attention was focused on the explosive bolt he was attempting to fix on the half completed hull of DDS 11, the newest and still incomplete orbital in the Allies' distant orbit defensive ring of missile platforms.

The bolts were there to break off the covers of the launch tubes in seconds (which, considering how sophisticated electronic countermeasures were getting, might be all the warning they might have of any attack) and there was enough high explosive in the small, flat cylinder he was attaching electrodes to the side of to easily blow both his hands off (though in the vacuum of space any breach in his suit would be instantly fatal, which would actually be a merciful death compared to his fate if his suit held and the blast propelled him away from the station as their picket ship had been withdrawn days ago).

If he lost contact with the incomplete DDS 11, there was nothing to do but to wait for his air to run out.

In a more peaceful time, standard procedure would have required a ship capable of rescuing any lost man or shuttling the injured back to Earth, not to mention keeping the Connies away, on standby at all times, but with the orbital war escalating and threatening to move down the gravity well onto the planet itself, everything that could fly had higher priorities than babysitting forty-three naval Construction Battalion roughnecks and Harry, their very young and currently very nervous commander.

Finally the last connection was made without triggering the explosives, and Harry's concern shifted from the unit he had successfully attached to the three dozen or so in the insulated container on his belt. They were, he knew on an intellectual level, inert unless triggered by a specific electrical charge, but the assurance didn't make carrying so much explosive in an environment as unforgiving as vacuum any less nerve-racking. He did take time to shake his head and almost dislodge the pesky drops of sweat.

The young officer took a moment to look over his "command." The half-built station was still a mass of round, hollow titanium alloy struts. The struts' round shape gave them incredible strength, but made the half-complete Defense Station resemble a bad Escher painting. Moving amid the jumble were "his" men, visible mostly by the lights on their space suits or the abrupt glare of welding torches.

Harry sighed as he surveyed the incomplete station.

As a sixth-generation navy officer, there had been expectations. His great-granddad-to-the-third had served in the American Civil War on ships with wooden hulls. His great great grandfather had been on the *Maine* when it went down in Havana Harbor. Those were the days his own father had often spoken of from the time Harry was able to understand, and his enthusiasm had been infectious. Among the few personal items Harry had taken with him into orbit was a complete set of Forrester's *Hornblower* novels. The adventures of the nineteenth century Royal Navy officer never failed to thrill Harry. Those were the days when the man on the bridge made a difference.

Now most officers were engineers with management skills.

It had been hard to explain to his father why he wasn't serving on a combat ship. When his father had completed the academy, there had been no space navy. The few military personnel who got into space were called astronauts and they shared those primitive shuttles with civilians. There were only so many berths and every new officer wanted them. He had made it into space, even though he had to transfer to the Construction Corp to accomplish it. Better yet, even though he was a very junior officer, he had his own command, inglorious as it was, and in space at that. When he eventually applied to transfer back to the real navy, it would help.

"Lieutenant, you might want to come back in . . . sir," the voice of his master chief startled the young officer.

"After eleven hours out here, you are right about that, Chief," Harry agreed.

"It's not that, sir. You had better get in here now," the voice insisted.

Those two sirs in a row alerted the officer that something was very wrong. Things tended to be very casual in space. There wasn't much of an option about that.

"Here" was the half-finished core of the Distant Defense Station, currently three large rooms and the life support and power dome. This meant there was no real privacy and little personal space. Any officer who tried to stay aloof from his men was doomed to failure. There was no "apart." His separate quarters were divided from the common room by a blanket. All that accomplished was not letting the men see him scratch himself when he first woke up. It wasn't like on the line ships, where the CO had his own room and office. Picturing the long, elegant combat ships that roamed the lower orbits gave Lieutenant Coronet a twinge of regret. When he had originally applied to the Point, he had expected to serve on one of the Alliance of Nations' growing fleet of warships. But there were always too many good, more experienced officers who wanted those jobs. Taking this slot hadn't been much of a choice; he was serving in space and that was a very big something, not that he hadn't sometimes regretted the decision.

Those inside the environment knew something was wrong. The almost constant sounds of grinding and drilling were missing. The men, veterans with years of space time, watched as the young officer tried to look unruffled as he hurried past them. From the expression on the chief's face as he entered the communication's center, this was going to be one of the days he regretted being here.

The communications room and the waste center were the only areas separated from the large, open cylinder that served as barracks and workshop for the construction crew. Normally there would be a man on duty and two or three more waiting to speak with family on the surface. Today the chief, a twenty-year veteran of space service, was alone, manning the radio and radar himself, and the curtain across the entrance was closed. Harry had long understood that part of the jumpsuit-clad man's job was to continue training the baby officer, him, or reporting to some admiral that Harry was hopeless, but today the occasionally solicitious air the veteran often took around Lieutenant Coronet was replaced by apparent concern.

"I got an alert from the *Mauprin,*" the older man began without even turning from the screen in front of him. "They think they spotted something that tracked as if it was heading our way. No way to be sure."

Lieutenant Coronet understood the ambiguity. Space was empty, except for a few thousand satellites . . . but that didn't mean a warship was easy to find. Electronic Counter Measures and radar absorbing hulls gave "fog of war" an extra relevance to orbital warfare. If a ship from the Confederation of Republics had snuck past the low orbit picket line, they were lucky to have gotten any warning at all.

"How likely is this to be real?" he asked the older man.

"I served under Captain Aubrey on the *Mauprin.* He doesn't tend to panic," the chief assured his young commander, "nor would he report a wisp just to cover his rear."

"Which means?"

The master chief turned and faced Harry for the first time. "That there is a very good chance that we will have some unwanted company in the next few minutes."

"Have you sent out a call for assistance. Is the *Mauprin* nearby?"

"Nothing is getting out. Maybe it's solar storms, maybe we are being jammed. *Mauprin* was on her way down. No help there. Hard to tell." The chief turned back to the console. "Nothin' here. They would have to be pretty close before this unit would crack their ECM.

Coronet watched the radar screen over the older noncommisioned officer's shoulder. It seemed to be a very long time. Should he call in the men working outside? What good would that do? They were a sitting duck if a Connie ship appeared.

As if on cue the screen suddenly came alive with a rapidly growing shape.

"Shit," the chief muttered.

Harry said nothing, just staring as the blip slowly grew and grew until it filled the local range radar's screen. They were matching the DDS 11's orbit. No IFF signal. It was a Connie and a large one.

What they wanted was obvious.

This station, once armed, would be a tough nut to

crack, but until then they were defenseless. The only question was whether the Connies wanted prisoners or would just blow them apart.

Time passed, and slowly the two men began to breathe again. The Connie ship continued to approach. It appeared they wanted prisoners.

"We had better alert the men," the chief reminded Harry. "That ship is getting so close it will soon be visible to the work crews outside."

"Call everyone in," the lieutenant agreed. "We'll need to talk once they make contact." He tried not to sound as flat as he felt. His first command—his career was about to end.

"This is the Confederation ship *Spirit of Deng,*" the speaker said in heavily accented English. "This is Captain Lee Bo Tho. Who is the senior officer there?"

Before opening the channel to reply, Harry's mind raced. "Chief, trigger the destruct on the codebooks now," he ordered. Within seconds, the chief had thrown every paper in the room and one particularly sensitive board from the radio into a thin-walled aluminum case, triggering the attached magnesium flare. Only after he opened the now painfully hot case and they could see nothing remained but ashes, did the young officer reply.

"This is Lieutenant Coronet of the Alliance Navy, Captain Lee."

"Your station is unarmed and unguarded," the Connie began by stating the obvious. "There is no loss of face in your surrender. Another ship will arrive in two hours. All of you will embark on that ship into the hospitality of the Confederation."

He didn't even ask for our surrender, confident bastard, Harry noted . . . but then Lee *was* sitting inside a destroyer armed with half a dozen nuclear missiles. The Confederation hospitality he promised was notorious and occasionally fatal. The Connies had a policy of never freeing trained spacemen. Men such as Harry were simply too valuable a tool in the undeclared shooting war over who would control space to return to the enemy.

"Captain Lee, you leave me no choice," was all that he could respond in a very flat voice. They were unarmed and defenseless. Knowing this didn't make the fact he had to surrender without even a gesture palatable. Even in Nelson's day, a ship's officers were allowed to retain their pride with a single broadside aimed wide. The total armament available was the .45 automatic sitting unloaded in the lieutenant's locker (not that he could even fire the side arm without the near certainty of breaching the environment's hull).

"If there is any problem, I will not hesitate to stand off and send a missile into the station you *were* building," came back the threat.

The next hour was spent in near silence by all of the men aboard the incomplete DDS 11. Some wrote letters that might not get delivered and others simply sat staring at the metal walls. Twice Lee Bo Tho radioed, seemingly to do no more than to remind Harry how helpless he was. When the second call ended, the young officer simply sat alone in the radio room and stared for long minutes. Finally, rising from his funk, Harry listened for what sounds the men were making.

The silence was ominous.

All knew that they were going into a captivity none were like to escape from. Many of the men had families and worked in space because of the massive bonuses offered for hazardous duty. Harry also began to realize he was *the* officer in charge and the men were waiting for him to take the lead, to do something. But what could forty men on an unarmed and incomplete station do against a Connie destroyer?

The young officer considered and rejected half a dozen plans, each more ludicrous than the last. If they tried to attack the destroyer, Lee needed only start his engines for a short burst and the ship would move safely away from the station, and be far enough away to then allow the Connie commander to blow them all to hell. Finally, simply out of habit, Harry reached for his reader and activated the *Horatio Hornblower* novel he had been rereading. It was tempting to just pass his last hour of freedom ignoring an unfair world. He stared at the reader without seeing the words on it. He was the one in command of DDS 11, unfinished or not, and he had to do something. Hornblower never accepted defeat, no matter what the odds—but life was simpler in those days; you could improvise a broadside and then storm over the enemy's gunwales cutlass in hand. The only way to get out of this mess was to be as resourceful as C. S. Forrester's character, somehow reversing the odds by doing the unexpected. For a moment the image of smoke and fire spraying from the end of thick iron guns soothed Harry and filled him with regret. . . .

Then Lieutenant Harrison Coronet snapped out of his personal fog of defeat, and his mind raced. It was a chance, a thin one, but a chance. He opened the curtain and looked across the large room they worked and slept in. Harry's eyes strayed to the pouch of explosive bolts still attached to his suit and the cases of similar small explosive charges carefully stacked against one wall. All around the room were sections of the tubing used for the station's frame, and even some scrap metal in two large bins.

Like Hornblower, indeed, like him for sure.

The men in the environment were surprised to hear his sharp, short laugh. Eyes turned and watched him as the young officer glided into the middle of the cloud of hovering men.

Then he set to work saving the day in the same way as his favorite hero would.

The first thing, Harry realized, was to get Lee on the *Deng* to cooperate, if unknowingly. Then he had to ask the men. The whole thing was crazy, but even if they failed, it would be glorious.

It only took seconds for the Connie radio operator to summon his captain.

"Captain Lee, this is Lieutenant Coronet. We were in the middle of structural changes when you, um, arrived. If we do not complete the reinforcements, there is a good chance this station will collapse at any time," Harry explained. Now if they only wanted the station, not just to destroy it . . .

"You have my permission to complete the reinforcements on the Confederation's newest station, but any sabotage will be severely punished." Connie Captain's tone was harsh. "You have one hour and eight minutes left. Can this be completed in that time?"

"We can try," the young officer replied, trying to keep the triumph from his voice. "I like to leave things neat," he finished, offering some explanation as to why they would repair a station about to fall into enemy hands.

"Very well, begin," Lee conceded, "but I will be watching closely."

When Harry explained his plan to the men, they were at first filled with skepticism. For what seemed a long time Harry hung in zero gravity in front of them, explaining just how his plan would work. As he went into details, he could see the smile on the chief's face grow. Then the chief spoke up, pointing out what the alternatives were and agreeing that the crazy scheme might just work. As the young lieutenant began giving them details and assignments as if they had already accepted his idea, enthusiasm grew. At least the morale would be good for the next hour, he reassured himself. Soon the room was busy with men and machines screaming as they rushed to complete their preparations in the hour that remained.

Trying to look useful, the lieutenant moved along their thrown together assembly line. Near the start the chief was welding closed one end of a three-foot length of hollow titanium strut he was being given by the two men who were cutting them. He walked carefully past the men who were wiring the explosive bolts into the bottom of the half-sealed cylinders, giving each a word of gentle encouragement that they probably didn't need. Still it made him feel, well, *officerly.* Eventually Harry pitched in, helping the men who were creating round blobs from the scrap in the bins. Zero gravity made that job surprisingly easy. In one corner the sound of the grinder putting an edge on some of the longer pieces of metal was reassuring.

When the first of the outside crew went into vacuum to install the struts, he joined them. It was soon apparent that there wasn't much he could do there, but this was where things would go wrong, if they did. Listening for Lee's voice with fearful anticipation, Harry clung to the hull and watched as the men welded and strung wires with frantic urgency. Eventually, he simply floated along with a strut facing the Confederation destroyer. The ship itself had settled into a stationary position less than fifty meters from the larger DDS 11, its hull paralleling the station. That had taken a good piece of flying, Harry realized. It also allowed Lee to watch them closely, but would the Connie understand what he was seeing?

It was a beautiful ship, he had to admit, designed only for use in space. Not streamlined, but elegant with its angular, radar negative hull and bulging missile launcher. That hull was mostly ceramic and plastic like their station's own living quarters with only a thin lining of the same alloy as in the struts, put there to absorb micrometeor hits. With every ounce of weight being allocated to fuel or missiles, the men from both sides who ventured into space these days did so protected only by their stealth electronics. He was counting on the Confederation ship staying just where it sat. If it moved even a few meters, their efforts would have been wasted.

"Ten minutes," the sudden sound of the chief's voice over the radio almost caused the young officer to lose his grip.

"Have all of the men get into space suits . . . to prepare for the transfer," Lieutenant Coronet radioed back.

"An intelligent preparation," agreed the haughty voice

of Captain Lee Bo Tho. He had, as Harry had expected, been monitoring their transmissions. Then, in a less demanding tone, the Confederation officer asked, "Have you finished the repairs?"

Looking toward the men, Harry realized he no longer could see the glare of welding. Everything must be in place.

"It appears so," he answered in a noncommittal tone while watching the rest of the men under his command, except the chief who remained inside, pouring out of the environment's main lock. Best they act now, before Lee realized what was in most of the men's heavily gloved hands. When he gave the command, it felt good.

"Chief, fire!" Lieutenant Harry Coronet of the Alliance Space Navy ordered.

Suddenly the two dozen cylinders attached to the hull were filled with gas and energy as the shaped charges inside them were triggered. With one end open, there was only one place for all this energy and exhaust gas to go, out to where they were pointed and ahead of that gas was pushed the carefully fitted balls and foot-long bolts. In all, they were a fair, if higher technology, version of the cannon, well—more like cannonades, used by Nelson to defeat Napoleon's navy.

In a matter of seconds the metal balls propelled out of Harry's cannon slammed into the destroyer's side. While the curved hull deflected a few off into space, most smashed their way through the ceramic hull and created satisfying, jagged holes all through the engine compartment of the enemy ship. Almost instantly fuel and bits of metal emerged from the meter-wide gaps the "cannonballs" had made.

That did it! Several of the metal balls had broken through into the engine compartment. Sensitive equipment would be smashed. The *Deng* was crippled. Now they had to complete their attack. Firearms might be too dangerous to use in space, but that didn't mean they would be attacking unarmed.

From beside his suit, where he had been hiding it along a hull strut, Harry raised his cutlass, a carefully shaped section of straight steel with the tip and one edge ground sharp. Against a space suited, or unsuited man, it would be deadly. Each of the construction crew carried a similar weapon. He wondered if the Connies had anything like them on board their destroyer. He doubted it. If their admirals were as stodgy as his, like him they would have a few pistols they were forbidden to fire. He was going to enjoy this. So Lieutenant Coronet gave the one command he had always wanted to, but never expected, to give.

"Boarders away!"

THE ADMIRAL'S RECKONING

BY J. ROBERT KING

As he watched his gunboat drift in stately majesty across the dat screen, Admiral Davies had only one thought: *I've got a bunch of good boys and girls.*

Davies snorted. He'd always hated it when a ranking officer called him a boy. Now, at thirty-five, Davies outranked everybody, and he committed the same offense. He shrugged. It was true. With these good girls and boys, he'd won the Vangosian War.

Davies took a long draw from his maduro cigar. Tobacco was outlawed in space, of course, but war heroes were allowed their excesses, especially here in the admirals' room. The Scotch, too, was an excess—single malt and deep, here eight hundred million miles from any pool of peat. Even the chamber's artificial gravity was needlessly grave, adding weight to the overstuffed chairs and helping velvet drapes properly pool across mahogany floors. Such luxuries repaid Davies for his sacrifice, and he appreciated the cigar and the Scotch, if not the extra gravity. The last was only a reminder of legs that could no longer stand.

Davies wheeled closer to the wide window. It was in fact a dat screen, pixilated so tightly that its images seemed more real than real. Just now, Saturn dominated the view, its surface draped in bunting of purple and pink. The gas giant reached out icy arms as if to grasp Space Station Roosevelt and the Solar Armada. A thousand ships had gathered to celebrate the annual Saturnine Regatta, and this year's regatta was special, commemorating the end of a bloody war by reenacting it in bloodless panoply.

Gunboats paraded past the dat screen. Every last blast point had been patched, every fire-blackened crystal replaced. Even the laminar scoring of space dust had been polished away. No longer war craft, the gunboats were now showpieces. They sported ancillary fins and false bridges. Five-man fighters had been refitted to look like thousand-man cruisers. Each crew member represented twenty of his or her fellows. In miniature, they would reenact the glorious victory of the Solar Armada over the Vangosians. It would be a glad regatta. . . .

Especially for Admiral Davies. At last, he would get the recognition he deserved. Though he'd won the Battle of Delgoth and the Vangosian War, only he and his folk knew it. Admiral Belius had taken the credit. Davies had led his squadron on a suicide attack of the enemy base, had destroyed it, had forced an unconditional surrender, and in the bargain had sacrificed the use of his legs. He would have willingly sacrificed his life. No one seemed to care. Belius wore the medals. He hadn't even flown at Delgoth. He hadn't fought. His legs worked just fine, though his breathing was a little labored under all those medals—Admiral Belius, the Hero of Delgoth.

That title would not last long once the other admirals saw what happened today. Davies' boys and girls would make sure the whole fleet knew how the battle had truly gone, and who was the real hero of Delgoth.

"Hello, Davies," said the old bastard himself, appearing out of the crowd of admirals who filled the room. Belius carried a file folder next to his chest—paperwork was his shield—and he slapped his supposed protégé between the shoulder blades. "Damned glorious day, what?" The man was the quintessential old guard admiral—white mustachioed and pompous. His generation and their imperialism had begun the Vangosian War. Davies' generation—clean-shaven and black-haired—had had to put an end to it. Still, Belius and his cronies took credit for the whole damned thing.

"A glorious day, yes," answered Davies. His hands clenched into fists within the wide sleeves of his dress uniform. "Just like the last. It'll be just like it was last time."

Belius studied the dat screen and his nostrils flared. His mustache began an easy inch up those monstrous cavities. "You've not fielded all your gunboats," he said, blinking beneath flocculent brows. "You've twice the complement present here."

"*Now,* I do, yes, sir. But not then," replied Davies. He stared proudly at his gunboats. Twelve ships, decked out with miniatures of the precise arms and armaments of his twelve cruisers—plasma cannonades, temporal repulsers, titanium rams, and flack countermeasures. Antique stuff. With that ancient equipment, the Seventh Fleet had battered the Vangosians into defeat—with antique equipment and sheer guts. Admiral Belius' ships had had sixth-dimension guns and time-slip armor. It did them little good. His crew had no guts aside from Belius' own infamous paunch. His fifty battleships had lingered on the verges of the dogfight, all twisted metal and bluster, while the true heroes won the day. "Or don't you remember the fight?"

"Of course I remember it," Belius replied. "I won it."

That was almost more than Davies could bear. Yes, at the Battle of Delgoth, Belius had commanded Davies. And, yes, Belius himself had advocated the promotion. But neither fact gave him the right to steal his protégé's glory. The old skydog had left him dangling in the breech, left him to die. When Davies had in fact prevailed, Belius robbed him of the victory. . . . Davies' fists almost rose from their sleeves, but this was neither the time nor the way to teach Belius his lesson. The regatta would do that, in front of the whole armada.

"Take a seat," suggested Davies, gesturing to a brocade chair nearby, "so we can be on the same level."

Nodding, the old man pulled the chair toward the dat screen and its swarming ships. He set his file folder on a nearby side table. Cocking an eyebrow at Davies, the old man said, "These days, the cybergeneticists have engineered gams that could stop a cruiser. How long before you get your new legs?"

"Never," Davies replied.

"Never?" spluttered Belius. "Don't you want to walk again?"

"I don't miss walking. I miss flying," Davies said flatly.

There seemed nothing more to say after that. While the other admirals mingled, Davies and Belius watched the gathering ships. They glowed beautifully before Saturn, massive and languid. It was the perfect backdrop for the reenactment. Its pink and purple clouds were so bright, its rings so vibrant; they dimmed the stars, which shone everywhere else like the lights of an endless city. To those who had not been at Delgoth, Saturn might have seemed a gaudy prop, but for Davies, the planet looked eerily like the home world of the Vangosians.

They were a species spawned in oceans of liquid hydrogen, pieced together under pressures and temperatures utterly beyond the predictions of terrestrial science. As it turned out, life hadn't merely a single, carbonic path into being, but thousands of routes through hundreds of elements. Life was the overwhelming organizing principle of the universe. The reason that quantum mechanists had never found the Unified Field Theory was that they had approached the problem from the standpoint of physics. Instead, they should have used biology.

Vangosians were a perfect example of biological diversity. They had no eyes, for their very skin was retinal, absorbing liquid hydrogen vibrations more precise than any reflection of light. They had no arms except those they willed from their protoplasmic forms—pseudopods large enough to grasp and digest ten humans. They had no need for instrumentation, for EVA suits, for thrusters. Their interstellar craft were merely extensions of their own all-seeing skin. Vangosians swam through space like carp through water. They ate human spacecraft as though they were hard-shelled prawns.

Even now, their part in the regatta was taken by great balloons of mercury, shimmering and silvery, able to break upon a Solar craft and course eagerly along its every conduit. For ten years, the Vangosians had done just that, overwhelming the fleet.

. . . Until Delgoth.

From that single, massive base, they had launched all their attacks. They had hidden the station well among the icy rings of their home world. The Solar Armada had pounded site after site on Vangosia only to be repeatedly trounced by swarms from Delgoth. When at last the station was discovered, Admirals Belius and Davies had been sent to destroy it. They had. It was that very battle, in miniature, that would play itself out today.

In place of Vangosians, mercury balloons hovered in a vast cloud at the center of the dat screen, mirror bubbles that wore the black of space on their glowing hides. To either side waited Belius' gunboats, menacing and beautiful with their bristling arms. Directly before the Vangosians, though, hovered Davies' ships—small, few, but tenacious. It was so familiar a scene, it took him back to that horrible, glorious day.

He was not supposed to command from here, from within a flack ship, but Davies was a new admiral, not about to fight this battle from some coffee-sipping command chair. Besides, the aching sky beyond, the reeling stars, and the gas giant Vangosia called to him. This would not be battle, so much as festival.

No command chair fit Davies like this piloting harness. At his literal fingertips were fire controls for antimatter torpedoes, lightning salvos, and beam cannonades. His arms defined the attitude of wings, his legs the throttle of thrusters that propelled him across the sky. No human could be closer to flying than the pilot of a flack ship, and though Davies had been promoted, he was not about to give it up.

"Keep the ring tight," Davies instructed over the com line. He sensed the presence of his squadron in a warm buzz around his ship. "Target the center. The cross fire will rip apart any Vangosians near enough to strike and open a corridor up the middle." He led the way, his ship skipping out across the icy rings of the gas giant.

"Aye, Admiral," came the response from a number of voices. Davies' wingman, Lieutenant Jenkins, went on, "What do we do once the middle's open?"

"Keep it that way. We've got to make a corridor for Cruiser *Gigliousi* to get near enough to blast Delgoth Station. Once it's gone, the Vangosians will be stranded in the rings, and we'll mop them up."

Davies sent his flack ship into a light dive. He pulled out, strafing along the icy lanes. His approach drew out Vangosian sentries like schooling piranhas. From amid tumbling ice chunks, they rose.

The beasts came like amoeba, formless and fierce. They flooded up as if on a single wave. Light from the gas giant poured through their translucent bodies and gave them a peptic hue. Their skin, forged in furnace heat and impossible pressure, was proof against cold and vacuity. The gelid beasts swarmed toward him.

Davies was ready. Ring fingers depressed the pressure pads on their tips. With a thump, a pair of net capsules sprang from the ship. The pods hurtled out and split open. Titanium mesh spread across two square miles of space. Nets enmeshed the nearest Vangosians. The metal filaments themselves could not have contained the beasts, but the lightning pulses within the fibers scrambled neural impulses. Wobbling piteously, the Vangosians were dragged away by the nets.

More titanium mesh ripped from the rest of the squadron. The devices spread in a wide circle of destruction before the slanting ships. One square mile at a time, they opened the way toward Delgoth Station.

It was a spiny structure, seeming almost a sea urchin as it clutched one of the largest and most ferrous of the ring's asteroids. Any Vangosian who brushed against the needle-sharp spines could be absorbed into the inner sphere, to rest and replenish in the well of a shared essence. Any Solar ship that approached too near these spines would be ripped apart. Once Cruiser *Gigliousi* could draw a bead on that urchin, though, it would be gone, and the Vangosians would be obliterated.

Davies ignited his rocket cannons and watched as Vangosians before him spattered like water droplets.

"Clear the way," he shouted to the others. "Here comes my cruiser."

"There goes my cruiser," Admiral Belius announced with satisfaction.

He and Davies had been watching the regatta progress. Tiny disarmed heat bombs had jittered among the silvery balloons in imitation of Davies and his flack ship brigade. Now the way was open for Davies' cruiser to punch through—only it wasn't Davies' cruiser that advanced, but Belius'.

The old admiral watched gleefully as the gunboat that represented his counsel ship penetrated the wall of gasbags. "There goes my cruiser!"

"Yes," Davies replied, fairly hissing, "*your* cruiser. You ignored the battle plan we had laid out."

Belius puckered his face, eyebrows and mustache almost meeting in a scowl. "No, I did not ignore the plan. I modified it on the field."

Heat entered Davies' voice. "It was to be my flagship—*Gigliousi*—that took the lead, not yours. I had left strict orders. You pulled rank on *Gigliousi*'s captain so that your ship could steal the glory."

"The moment was too critical to be handled by a mere captain," Belius replied offhandedly. "It needed a ship with an admiral—"

"*Gigliousi* had an admiral—me!"

"No, *Gigliousi* had a captain. Your flack ship had an admiral."

"Yes, and with those flack ships, we won the battle!" Davies shot back, wheeling so near the dat screen that the chrome of his seat rattled on the glass. He jabbed his finger toward the images. "See!"

The heat bomb that represented Davies' flack ship took on a sudden, amazing life. It and its squadron whirled through space like spinning fireworks, circling and protecting Belius' cruiser—in fact, a massively armed and armored gunboat. In their midst, the huge ship seemed dark, inert—like a giant stopper shoved in the center of the sky. It was Davies' squad that pierced the quicksilver balloons, that slew Vangosians in their gleaming hundreds—just as it had been in the real Battle of Delgoth.

"What the hell is he doing?" Davies raged into his com line. With the precise motion of a man standing to peer out over a crowd, Davies extended his legs and triggered a massive afterburn from his flack ship. The vessel leaped across the sky, a lightning jag following an ion trail. Davies' squadron charged in his wake. They lanced toward a new swarm of Vangosians that threatened Belius' cruiser. "That idiot! What the hell is he doing?"

Belius had forgotten how to fight. He had never known how to fight Vangosians. If it had been *Gigliousi* in the breach, Davies would have taken the battle to Delgoth Station. With Belius' cruiser, he'd have to fight sheer defense.

Davies' flack ship roared down an aerial canyon of mercurial droplets—the drifting protoplasm left by the Vangosians he'd already killed. He angled toward a huge sphere of mercury. In that ball, he saw his ship's own reflection. It was as bright and sharp and fast as flame. All around the image loomed the black shadow of Belius' cruiser. Davies attacked the Vangosians as if he attacked Belius himself.

His fists clenched.

Fingertips depressed the fire controls of antimatter torpedoes. With mechanical glee, fat canisters chucked free of their barrels. They tore across empty space and ripped into the mirror face of the Vangosian. It was just like shattering a Christmas ornament. The silvery orb cracked. The warped image of the flack ship and the cruiser splintered. Within lay darkness, the syrupy heart of these horrid beasts. The antimatter torpedoes had opened a door into blackness, and through that door soared Davies.

His flack ship plunged into the meat of the monster. Muscle like mercury parted before the prow. The blood of the beast, plasmic stuff somewhere between metal and electricity, coursed across the lines of the flack ship. This was how Vangosians killed. They swarmed their foes amoebically—surrounding, absorbing, digesting. Davies' flack ship was just another meal, except that it had been shot into the beast's mouth with the momentum of a rocket.

There was a moment in blackness—while acids etched the screens and Vangosian neurology synapsed through the flack ship's conduits—when Davies wondered if he would live or die. There, in his piloting harness, cinched into the heart of his ship, Davies was in one-to-one contact with his foe. He sensed its hatred of him and of all things human, and then its shock that this microbe was tearing its way through, and then the thrilled agony of a mortal creature glimpsing its end.

This was why Davies flew. This was why he would always fly. This was when he was truly alive.

Shrieking like steel on glass, Davies' flack ship cracked out the other side of the Vangosian. He roared across the emptiness and dragged the shimmering guts of the monster in his wake. All around him, more flack ships tore from the bellies of more Vangosians. They smeared the things through space like slugs on cement.

Davies whooped, "Great flying, kids! Belius won't have to fight after this. He'll just take aim and shoot!"

The moment the words skated away across the com line, Davies knew they were wrong. His aft view ports showed the admiral's cruiser retreating back through the hole that Davies had carved.

"You coward!" Davies hissed under his breath. He stared in disbelief at the aft screens, watching the huge ships retreat. "*Gigliousi* would have destroyed the thing by now, and you withdraw. Coward!"

Mercury balloons disintegrated spectacularly under the assault of heat bombs. Meanwhile, the gun ship that represented Belius' cruiser made a slow retreat. The regatta painted a giant eye upon the looming blackness of space. Davies' flack ships spattered Vangosians into a spreading iris, and Belius' cruiser formed the empty pupil at the center.

"I'm surprised you had the courage to let them see what happened," Davies said, the giant eye reflected doubly in his own. "To let the whole fleet see how the battle played out."

Admiral Belius had obviously had enough. He was done allowing his honor to be so often, so completely impugned. "Everyone knows what happened. Everyone here knows. Only you seem to be surprised."

"You blocked *Gigliousi*'s entrance into combat, only to withdraw yourself—" raged Davies.

"We had received a surrender signal. You could not have known it in your flack ship, but my cruiser had received a signal suing for peace."

"Peace!" growled Davies. "What did Vangosians ever know of peace? You didn't feel their hearts. You didn't sense their hatred—"

"Nor did you feel their hearts. You felt *one* heart. It

was one warrior, one whom you slew, that felt that way—not the leaders. Not the nation."

"The surrender was a ruse. A feint. You fell for it, and I didn't. You withdrew, and I completed our objective. Watch!"

The men no longer masked their rancor from their fellow admirals. They were fighting a public battle. Each wanted to be believed by his fellows.

The heat bombs that represented Davies and his crew converged in spinning fury on a new figure.

It was a mercury balloon, as had been all the others, but this one was different—twenty times the diameter of the rest, bloated and spiked like a blowfish. The giant sac loomed up with such sudden malevolence from behind the shattered Vangosian balloons that all conversation in the admirals' room fell silent. Every eye turned to the dat screens, every mind considered the brave line cut by one flaring heat bomb.

"If Belius won't finish the job, we will," Davies shouted over the com line. It crackled furiously. Streamers of dead Vangosians ripped apart the electromagnetic field. Even now, Davies' flack ship dragged what was left of his slain foe across the sky. "We destroy Delgoth just as we destroyed its defenders."

"What do you mean—" shrieked his wingman, Lieutenant Jenkins, only belatedly adding, "—Admiral? You mean a ramming assault?"

"This is the Vangosians' Pearl Harbor, except that the destruction of Delgoth will end the war, not start it. And what did the Japanese do at Pearl Harbor? They made their planes into bombs."

"Admiral, you can't command us to do this," Jenkins replied. "You can't order a suicide strike."

"I'm not ordering anything," the admiral said, keeping his eyes on the station that swelled out before him. "I'm not back in some cruiser somewhere telling you to die.

I'm out here. I'm flying. I'm fighting, and I'm asking you to fly and fight beside me. If we die, we die together, but the world lives."

There was a long silence after that. Space scrolled by. Stars stared in avid disbelief at the surging flack ships. They seemed as small and furious as gnats before a giant.

"I'm with you, Admiral," came Jenkins' response. "You're one of us."

Davies did not even smile. He only nodded in appreciation. He'd expected no less from his wingman.

One by one, the others in his squad added their assent. Every last one. What a good batch of boys and girls.

There was time for no more. Delgoth had swelled outward to eclipse Vangosia. There were no stars anymore, no chunks of ice or spinning rock—only that huge station, echinodermatum and iron.

Davies' fists clenched, unleashing every last payload. Antimatter bombs blazed away first. They pocked the mirror edge of the station and ripped holes through its fuselage. Then beam weapons stabbed out, reflected along the shimmering spikes, and slammed, multifarious, into the blackened holes left by the bombs. Pure energy gashed them wider. Next, lightning reached craggy hands toward the station. White-hot energy leaped gladly to the metallic spikes and mantled them. Millions of gigawatts of electricity fried what would fry and scrambled the rest.

The last and most brutal weapons of all were the ships. Davies' flack ship struck the station like a dagger. His nose cone augured through living metal. Delgoth gave way, as soft as flesh, as hot as blood. Davies' fighter plunged through protoplasm. Beams glowed through the dark heat of the station and boiled the goo. Lightning strikes rolled out in eerie pathways of red, like the blood vessel in an egg. Heat bombs jagged to detonate nearby with a sucking roar. Davies' fingernails cut through the control gloves and into his own palms. He emptied his arsenal into these murderous beasts.

That was what the liquid was, incubating Vangosians—some fetal, some wounded, some resting. Soon, all were dead.

Davies killed them with fury, not just because he remembered the massacres at Titan and Europa, not just because of the Martian atrocities, but also because he now knew what this station was. He couldn't help knowing. The beasts he killed screamed the truth through the piloting harness. Their dying flesh clove to the outside of his ship, telling him who he was killing.

Delgoth was no mere station. She as the fecund queen of the Vangosian hive. She was no military base, but a huge entity, the mother that gave birth to all the others, that healed their wounds and succored their weaknesses. She was their goddess, their only hope for survival, and Davies was killing her—Davies and his good girls and boys.

Through the dying body of the Great Vangosian, Davies glimpsed his squad. They chopped their way through the goddess' flesh, just as he did. They burrowed, chiggers through muscle. They were the worst parasites—voracious and relentless. Their beams and bolts and bombs riddled the heart of the goddess. Just like Davies, every last flier knew what he or she did.

This was worse than a suicide mission. They would all live through this. They would all have to live with what they had done.

Beyond the dat screen, the spiny balloon collapsed upon itself. Fires flared fitfully where there was oxygen to fuel them. Mercury gushed like blood from the shattered form. From the far side of the deflating figure burst heat bombs—one after another. They represented Davies and his squad, hurtling out of the dying goddess.

In his wheelchair, Davies jabbed an emphatic finger toward the dat screen. "Look at that, Belius. Get an eyeful! Did you have any idea what that station was?" he raged. Every admiral in the room listened to him. This was his moment. This was when he could nail Belius to the wall. "Did you have even the faintest notion why the Vangosians had hidden that station so well, why they had fought tooth and nail to keep us away from it, why they had surrendered the moment we approached it? It was no station, Admiral. It was a being, a goddess, forever creating the Vangosian race. Do you realize what we did in destroying that creature? We committed genocide. We destroyed the future of an entire sentient species! Without her, they could not reproduce. But you couldn't have known that. You came nowhere near them. You never fought them. You never felt their minds crawling through yours. You never engaged. Of course you didn't know what Delgoth was."

"Of course I did know," replied Belius flatly, interrupting the rant. It was not the shuttering response Davies had expected. The old admiral was stern-eyed and utterly sober. Gone was the lint-haired dolt that Davies had so despised. Beneath the softness of age shone a steel-edged warrior, who had once been no different from Davies. "Of course I knew what that station was. I read the confidential reports filed by the scout ships."

Davies stared in bald-faced disbelief at the old admiral. "What?"

"I knew Delgoth was the Vangosian breeding mother, their goddess. I knew that once we had her cornered, the Vangosians would surrender. Our attack was never meant to go to completion. It was meant to be a checkmate, stopping short of taking the final piece. We wanted to end the war with the Vangosians, not to wipe out their species." From beneath stormy brows, Admiral Belius glared at his protégé. "But this was what you did, wasn't it, Davies?"

The younger admiral's jaw hung open. "If you knew all of this, why didn't you tell me—?"

"I *did* tell you, but you didn't listen. I said that Delgoth was the key. I said they would never allow us to fire a shot on her. I said we wanted to force a surrender, to drive them to their knees."

"You said nothing about a goddess—"

"You received the same reports I did. Why didn't you read them? And the word goddess appeared countless times in my briefings. But you care nothing for reports and briefings. You think bureaucracy is a waste of time. You weren't even in your command seat when I signaled the rest of the fleet to cease fire. You were out flying, out fighting, so mantled in Vangosian dead you couldn't hear the order to retreat. Even if you had, though, I'm sure you would have ignored it."

Admiral Belius dragged Davies' wheelchair to face him. He stared levelly into the younger man's eyes. "You think you should be the Hero of Delgoth—I know you do. But let me tell you why you are not. You didn't fight like an admiral at Delgoth. Not even like a captain. You fought like a gunner. You wanted to feel every bolt leave your fingertips. You wanted to sense Vangosian claws through your piloting harness. Unless you killed it with your own little ship, it wasn't dead. And, look what you killed with your own little ship, Davies. Look!

"Admirals cannot fight that way. We must consider our whole fleet, and the enemy's whole fleet, and the nations that send these fleets. We cannot afford to attack every planet and fight every foe. Memos, reports, meetings, maps, rosters, schedules—these are our eyes and ears. Without them and the distance to interpret them, we fly blind and deaf and dumb. That's how you fought at Delgoth. Blind and deaf and dumb. Yes, Davies, you had courage. Yes, you had will. And look what they brought you." He gestured at the dat screen.

Davies stared at the great, burning balloon. It flailed piteously in its death throes—what once had been a goddess and now was but a collapsing membrane. Vertigo laid hold of him. The stars spun violently. Davies had arrived in the admirals' room hoping for recognition from his peers, from his nation. He had thought he needed to educate them about the sacrifice he and his boys and girls had made at Delgoth. Now he realized that they needed no education. They recognized all too clearly what had happened.

Davies looked beyond Belius to the silent room of admirals. One by one, they nodded grimly. Their eyes were not accusing. It seemed each man and woman there had made similar mistakes. It was part of the rite of passage from captain to admiral. It was equally obvious that no man or woman there had made the mistake of slaying a species and its god.

Davies began a retort. His voice was low, like the growl of a dog. He wasn't sure what he would say until he opened his mouth. "I have made mistakes, surely—most grievous mistakes. I recognize that. But they were honest mistakes, made out of courage, honor, and self-sacrifice—the virtues of a warrior. I've lived by those virtues all my life. Yes, sometimes, they have led me down destructive paths, but all in all, they are the best counselors of my soul. I cannot for one moment believe that paperwork can replace courage, that meetings can replace honor, that bean-counting is better than self-sacrifice. Bureaucracy does not win wars, does not protect freedom, does not save lives. Warriors do that. I cannot believe the best admiral is not a fighter but a bureaucrat—"

Belius replied in a firm voice. "Yes, you can believe it, and you do believe it." Deep sadness filled his tone.

Davies' face swelled with blood. "How can you know what I believe?"

Belius reached to the table beside him and lifted the folder he had brought. "Paperwork—my eyes and ears. It is how I know." From the folder, he slid two slim reports. The first had been dictated by the fleet neurosurgeon and signed with his voice imprint. The second was a longhand note from the imperial cyberpsychologist, Frank Gheist. "These reports indicate there is nothing wrong with your legs . . . except that you are unwilling to use them."

Davies snatched the pages from the man's hand. "These are confidential! Where did you get these?"

Ignoring the question, Belius said, "And the reason you are unwilling to use them is that you know, as an admiral, you cannot fly, cannot fight like you once did."

"God damn you, Belius!" hissed Davies, lunging for him.

Belius retreated, just as he had at Delgoth.

Davies landed, panting, in a heap on the floor.

Belius continued, "It's why I didn't have you demoted, because you knew you needed to change—"

"God damn you!" Davies barked again. He lunged at his tormenter and brutally swung his fists.

The old man stooped and caught both strikes. "I didn't demote you, Davies, because you are a good man, and because I knew it was only a matter of time before you stood up and joined us." Gritting his teeth, Belius lifted Davies slowly to his feet.

Once-dead legs twitched with pain. Flesh shuddered. Bone engaged bone.

On limbs that creaked like old timber, Davies stood. His hands were still clenched within the grip of his mentor. His face was still swollen with blood. But now, the fury—and even the humiliation— were gone. His eyes were filled with a look of strange triumph.

"Yes," said Admiral Davies as he stared at his shaking, living legs. "It was only a matter of time . . . till I stood up . . . and joined you."

STRINGS

A Story of the Starworld Federation

BY ROLAND J. GREEN

ABOARD F. S. S. *Trollstep*:
0135

Brigitte Tachin forced what wanted to be a colossal yawn to settle for being a modest one (a big yawn, Petty Officer Cuenco at the other Weapons board might notice). If the yawn was really big, she might swallow her throat mike.

Instead, she stretched, wishing that she was home. When she stretched like that, her husband always pretended that she was a cat and started stroking her back. She usually pretended to purr. Sometimes the pleasure went on from there.

She switched to PERSONAL RECORD and began subvocalizing in her birth French.

"Cher Rafael,

Nous ne sommes plus au cul de rien . . ."

"Dear Rafael,

"We are no longer up the arse end of nowhere. We are nearly out of it, and a courier ship should have this letter in no more than eight days, when we finish our transit to Euclid. Meanwhile, however, the G-74CF-2 system is still a dreary place for anything except the kind of serious planetologist who collects exotic rocks, and is willing to turn over hundreds of ordinary ones in search of that elusive rarity.

"Sentiment aboard is that if the Baernoi are interested

in the system, that interest raises doubts about their sapience. Some people suggest that we put the system on that secret list of places the Baernoi have to keep if they ever do win the Big Brawl. Or maybe we should try to peddle it to the Merishi—except that the cliff-climbers have probably catalogued this system a long time ago without telling anybody else.

"At the moment I'm Combat Center duty officer, with Chief Cuenco on the other board, being his usual dour self—"

—although nothing a newly-promoted lieutenant commander really needed to notice, even if she was also a department head.

That wasn't quite the compliment it might have been, since *Trollstep* had the reputation of being one of Eighth Zone's holding files for odd personnel specimens and obsolete equipment, but big enough. But apart from what was riding in the holds, the transport had twelve hull-mounted weapons, forty missiles supported by three buses, and two close-support attackers—enough to keep a battle cruiser like Tachin's old *Shenandoah* busy for a whole ten minutes, but a larger responsibility than the Fleet usually handed to a junior two-and-a-half striper.

"The screens show two views of Kiggle's Planet, one from the ship, one from the recon drone four hours ago. In both, it looks a dismal blue-gray—more blue than gray on our side, more gray than blue on the other. I looked up the other five planets of the system, wondering why this one is classified as 'Marginally habitable.' The others are even worse. I found no record of biosampling, so I don't know if the place has ever been probed for life signs. We certainly won't be doing the job, unless we've embarked a probe I don't know about.

"Which we might, for all I know. Captain Schneewind once faced a court-martial for leaks to the media, and barely made his fourth stripe. Now he talks as if God gave him a strict quota of words to use in his lifetime, and will take him the moment he uses it up. That's rubbed

off on the rest of the crew, so that you can hear a dust mote fall on the tablecloth in the wardroom at most meals. The food is barely worth eating, let alone talking about, but—"

Cuenco's voice intruded. "Commander, we have a trailing contact."

Tachin switched back to operational channels and studied her board.

"So we do. Passive scan, IFF on standby."

Hitting a contact with a ship's whole sensor suite told you more about the other party, and the other party more about you. IFF was the second step, if the contact didn't ID as unequivocally friendly or hostile—

"Full range of Baernoi emissions," Tachin said. Cuenco looked peeved at not having said it first. Then he reached under his console and thumbed the alarm switch.

Sirens wailed and whooped. Near and far, feet thudded on decks, and doors hissed shut, or opened for crew running to their battle stations.

"Interrogate recon bus," Tachin called over the din.

The ship's central AI was already doing that without orders—*definitely brighter than some of the crew,* Tachin decided. The recon bus was already on the fringes of the asteroid cluster on the far side of the planet, and was now switching its sensors from a planetary scan to probing the asteroids.

"Four signatures." This time it was Cuenco who spoke first. "Powered down but not blacked down."

Cuenco had to be more on edge than he ought to be, Tachin realized. The bus' sensors wouldn't be able to detect a blacked-down ship, and you had to be desperate to black down a ship in an asteroid belt or any other kind of junk space.

Conclusion: the local Baernoi are not desperate.

Brilliant, Tachin. That leaves only about forty other mental states. Would you like to refine your hypothesis until it's useful?

Tachin was about to obey her inner voice, when the

Combat Center door slid open and Captain Schneewind sidled in, followed by the rest of the CC crew.

0145

"All right. I want to collect information and then bring it safely to Euclid or someplace else the Federation has ears," Schneewind said. "We need to confirm Baernoi activity in the system, not a space-to-space battle."

A laudable goal, if the Baernoi cooperate.

"We'll put the drone into a sling shot maneuver around the planet, letting it fly back out at our trailer. Consider it expendable— Brigitte, does it have a weapons load?"

Tachin frowned, thinking the captain should have been able to read that off his own board. Then she saw that the data wasn't showing on hers, which meant she hadn't called it up on his either. She muttered the commands and the data came up, not fast enough to keep the captain from glaring at her.

"Letting promotion go to our head?"

"No, sir." *Regulation phrase, for use in the face of unanswerable questions.*

Schneewind contemplated his board. "Flares and a self-destruct charge only. Can't see why we waste space with an S-D charge in those junkyard refugees. The Baernoi must have one in every trophy hangar in the Khudrigate."

There's another one listening to his nerves tinkling like a wind chime. For Schneewind, three sentences was the equivalent of a ten-minute speech from somebody else.

The drone would go sailing back toward the Baernoi trailer, which was roughly the equivalent of a Federation heavy cruiser. Meanwhile, *Trollstep* would make a low-altitude pass over the north temperate zone of Kiggle's Planet, just above the atmosphere. That low, the background emissions of almost any planet would confuse sensors having to look out from junk space.

Climbing out, *Trollstep* would back down, then track,

choose, and launch at the nearest asteroid. Half a dozen warheads would reduce one large cold rock to many small hot ones. Inside this cluster of sensor-fuddling fragments, *Trollstep* would ride through the asteroid cluster and the Baernoi attack radius, then accelerate beyond hope of being overtaken.

The Seguridad maneuver. John Kishi had threatened to haunt anyone who named it after him, even though he'd invented it in the Starworld Federation's war of Independence. For nearly five centuries the consensus had been that John Kishi's ghost was not one you wanted to have visiting.

But under any name, making a ship or ships just one blip out of several hundred on a sensor display was still effective. At longer range no fire control suite yet made could pick out one ship from amid fifty rocks. At shorter range, they could—but short range meant the other side had to be down and dirty among the rocks, and if they didn't get bopped by one, they were in range of *your* sensors and weapons. Even if you were an attack transport sent to do a cruiser's job. . . .

"Rendezvous and grapple to any of the rocks?" That was the XO, Commander Lal, raising a point Tachin was glad to hear from somebody else. She was suddenly the most important officer aboard, and she thought she could hear *her* nerves joining the chorus of the stress-ridden.

"No,' Schneewind said. "No time. If our trailer ignores the drone, or just blasts it, they could be scanning us as we climb out and have a solution for buggering us before we launch."

The more graceful term for striking your opponent from the rear was "up-the-kilt shot," but Schneewind would probably think being called graceful was a mortal insult. Tachin was in any case sufficiently busy talking and punching in commands to the drone, initiating launcher activation and weapons selection, and doing half a dozen other preliminaries to actual shooting. Her hands weren't quite steady, but she thought her voice was when she said:

"Request permission for Weapons Free?"

There. Five words and every one clear as a bell—she hoped.

"Authorizing Weapons Free, at 0146," Schneewind said. His voice also came out like a bell—a large one, tolling earnestly for the dead.

Three hands flourished red cards. Schneewind and Lal inserted theirs into the Weapons Free slots on their boards. Tachin suddenly found herself sweating so that she was afraid of not getting her card in the first time, or even of dropping it.

"Inserting third card . . . Mark! Weapons Free at 0146.25. Initiating bus maneuver and arming of eight Mark 56s."

0150

The Mark 56s launched on two buses, to give them an initial boost to within their optimum range of the target. They were short-range missiles, although "short" in this case meant as far as from Earth to Luna or even Charlemagne to Alcuin; *Trollstep* lacked the system-scanning sensor suite of a capital ship. Adjustable-yield warheads meant that they could be set to blow up a single mountain or lay waste to the entire coastline of a good-sized continent.

Tachin set the yield for single-figure megatons, which should be enough to thoroughly fragment the target asteroid—and thoroughly fry any organic forms unlucky enough to be too close.

She hoped the Baernoi had sense to stay clear from the beginning, and not wait until loose rocks started coming their way.

Meanwhile, Communications was dumping data from the drone, Navigation was tweaking the figures for the optimum course, and the AI was doing a thorough scan of Kiggle's Planet's surface as *Trollstep* raced over it less than four hundred kilometers up. The low-altitude junk and vapor laden atmosphere would be a formidable barrier to space-based sensors, active or passive. Missiles coming down from the high ground would face the same barriers, and lasers attenuated quickly shooting through formations of orbiting icebergs.

Trollstep wasn't risking much, even if she might not learn very much either.

Tachin had a moment's attention to spare for Cuenco, who seemed to be half asleep. The only sign of wakefulness was the toe of one shoe scratching the ankle of the other foot, in a steady rhythm that Tachin was afraid to look at for too long or she would be the one falling asleep.

The CC team seemed to be up to its job, even though *Trollstep* wasn't doing anything half as challenging as some of *Shenandoah*'s maneuvers. Tachin remembered particularly the night the battle cruiser came in low over Linak'h, to attack the Merishi cruisers supporting the attack on the Ptercha's Confraternity from *underneath*.

The buses had reached maximum acceleration now, then eight displays showed exotic light dances as the Mark 56s ejected and boosted independently. Tracking was nominal, hits were seven out of eight guaranteed (barring too much fratricide as the earlier explosions irradiated the following warheads—hardened, but not invulnerable), the asteroid doomed, the trajectories of its fragments certain to form a spreading, ship-screening cloud even if some of them might fall into orbits that would eventually decay and let them hit Kiggle's Planet—

The light dances turned dazzling. The screens blacked and then translated the eye-searing glare from the fuser bursts into graphics. At the same time the acceleration gauges showed *Trollstep* leaping up from low altitude, more light blazed as the Baernoi trailer fired at the approaching drone—and an alarm chimed softly and insistently in Tachin's earplugs.

She wasn't the only one who sat up and stared at the screen displaying readings from the surface of Kiggle's Planet. It was as if everybody had suddenly grown eyestalks, because even those with faces toward their own displays seemed to be staring at the surface readings.

Unmistakable heat sources and metallic signatures showed on the screen, from below the heavy chill clouds, probably from below the surface of the half-frozen oceans. Heat sources too small and too regular to be volcanic vents or hot springs, metallic signatures of too high a purity to be ore concentrations.

In short, artifacts.

Kiggle's Planet had been settled.

"Those dirty Tuskers!" somebody muttered. "*They're* the ones who pushed for the 'No secret settlements' clause."

Outlaw colonies or settlements established by private parties without informing the central governments decreased everybody's security—if only by raising the level of tension—and increased nobody's wealth—except the rogue entrepreneurs', who were behind so many such efforts. No race was innocent of trying to snatch a planet out from under a rival's nose, but nobody was willing to openly encourage it either, and the Baernoi less than some.

Which meant that if the Baernoi were here defending a new settlement that was legitimate but not in *Trollstep*'s files, the Federation transport had just committed what might be called an act of war. If the Baernoi were here circling an illegal colony, then they had no rights—but lack of rights wouldn't stop them from blowing *Trollstep* into her component molecules to cover their tracks.

Tachin shifted uneasily in her seat, her hand straying toward the button for activating the environmental capsule for her seat. She felt the horns of a dilemma prickling her in the rear. Be court-martialed for participating in an act of war brought about by incomplete data, or be virtuously atomized by Baernoi whose illegality would not affect the accuracy of their missiles or lasers?

If I had known how many situations I'd face, where the only way to be innocent is to be dead, would I have joined the forces? Although it was a bit late to ask that now, with the missiles only a hundred-odd seconds from impact.

The clock flashed the missile's rapid closing, Cuenco stared at his displays as if sheer willpower could make them even faster, and Tachin smelled sweat, not all of it her own.

"First impact!" she called out, as graphics again translated events no human eye could witness and survive into images quite vivid enough for all practical purposes. *At least when we're shooting at rocks. With people on the target, maybe a display of flesh peeling off bones and melted eyes running down cheeks would keep fingers from getting itchy for the firing cards.*

Cuenco shifted in his seat, suddenly confronting her with an open mouth and eyes squeezed so nearly shut that he looked even more piglike than usual. Tachin had opened her mouth and raised a hand when her own display began a silent shriek of alarm:

"Anomaly! Anomaly! Anomaly!"

—with the AI's origin code.

"Peste!" What sort of anomaly, and where, and a few other unanswered questions on the same order made her curse the AI's discretionary features.

Then between one breath and the next, the questions were no longer unanswered.

No one traveled to the home world of the octopoidal K'thressh, to seek the experience of receiving one of their mass telepathic projections. Not everyone who approached that world (known only as Home) survived such an experience. Those who did had left vivid accounts of what it felt like—and Tachin had not only read those accounts, she had watched the visual recordings of people in the grip of K'thressh projections, including some of the nonsurvivors.

All of which counted for exactly nothing, or maybe a little less, with her brain actually gripped by K'thressh mind twisting. She tried to concentrate on visual surveillance of the displays in front of her, not looking to either side, trying to shut her ears to the sounds from elsewhere in the CC. At least one person was trying to scream, another had succeeded in vomiting, and Cuenco's voice was reciting with implausible steadiness a list of trajectories that the disintegrating asteroid's pieces were following, or would follow, or had followed—

In Tachin's case, the physical aspect of K'thressh projection was comparatively mild. She merely felt that all the convolutions of her brain were filled with itching powder, and that she needed to unzip her scalp, unscrew the top of her skull, and scratch vigorously. Compared with some she'd heard described and probably some she was hearing close at hand, this was almost endurable. She retained enough free will and power of concentration to study her displays as they confirmed Cuenco's list of trajectories.

Some of those trajectories would bring pieces of asteroid the size of small mountains flaming down through the chill air of Kiggle's Planet, to impact with cataclysmic force on the surface. Fireballs, shock waves, seismic convulsions, massive disruption of a marginal environment, probably the annihilation of the settlement on the planet—bad enough with a new Baernoi settlement, or possibly even an unmanned scientific station.

What would happen with the destruction of the first interstellar colony of the K'thressh (and never mind that it had no business existing)? Their collective gifts as projective telepaths made the K'thressh adept at keeping secrets—including how many other planets they might have (never mind *how*) colonized.

Someone was shouting into Tachin's ear—no, over the audio net. She would have recognized Captain Schneewind's voice even if she hadn't managed to turn her head. Her neck felt so stiff that the movement sent pain blasting up her jawline and both cheeks to her ears.

"Target the Tuskers!" he was shouting (gabbling, rather). She understood about one word in three, but he was repeating himself so often and so loudly that the message came through. Tachin had the sensation of hull, bulkheads, and clothing suddenly vanishing, leaving her body as naked to space as her mind already was to the K'thressh.

0155

The Seguridad maneuver was actually working, as irrelevant as this might be. Even with most of her attention on working out the firing solution for hitting the Baernoi, Tachin could follow from the same set of data the spreading cloud of rock, gas, and debris that was screening *Trollstep* from the sensors of all Baernoi ships within range.

Of course, this cut both ways. The salvo would have to ride the last bus into sensor-friendly space, then target the—she could not say "enemy"—ships from the bus' own data. Enough margin for error that if one or two missiles hit plummeting rocks, nobody would ask awkward questions.

Enough margin for errors the other way, too. And killing a Baernoi ship would be a lethal error—possibly not one that the Khudrigate would be willing to write off as an accident either.

"Captain?"

"Eh?"

Schneewind looked as if he had just crawled up his front steps after a night's drinking. Bloodshot eyes, blotchy complexion, a trickle of drool at the corner of his mouth, and, slurred speech all combined to make Tachin speak strictly for the record.

"Preparing to launch, but under protest." *What's the least unconvincing argument I can push through that mental haze?*

"Protest. . . ."

"This is the first encounter between Baernoi and humans under K'thressh observation. Do we want to appear more dangerous than we are—or than they are?" The last seemed to come off her tongue of its own volition, without passing through her mind. K'thressh influence or her long-standing conviction that even at their worst, the Baernoi were hardly more ferocious than humanity at *its* worst?

Bloodshot eyes or not, Schneewind was staring at her as if the intensity of his gaze could move her hands to the switches.

"Initiating launch sequence," she said, barely above a whisper. The pain in jaw and cheeks was now flowing around to her throat, so that it was an effort to speak. She wondered if it would become an effort to breathe before she saw the results of her changes in the targeting plan.

A bus with twelve missiles plunged out into the junk space surrounding *Trollstep,* accelerated, then raised its shield to ride through the debris into launching range. Tachin's throat was so tight now that she did not try to speak, only tapped out an order to the Cargo Department to start breaking missiles out of the freight containers and prepping them for loading. If she had anything to say about it, *Trollstep* would put up a long, even epic fight, without harming a single bristle on a Baernoi nose unless they started firing back with lethal intent.

0202

Seven minutes from launch, the bus cleared the debris cloud. Tachin bit her lip hard enough to draw blood. Missiles set to hit could miss. Missiles set to miss could hit. She tried to speak, to ask the cargo handlers how they were coming with the reloads, that would surely be needed if this salvo flew wide, doing nothing either good or bad.

Tiny hot daggers seemed to thrust into her neck from all sides. The pain leaped down her spine, so that she twisted convulsively against the retaining harness. She forced herself to key in the message about the new missiles, to keep her mind off the prospect of the bone-breaking convulsions that usually came on after the pain reached the spine. Convulsions that left three out of four victims dead—

Baernoi defensive missiles swarmed into the path of the bus, just as it dropped shields and launched its load. That was one of those vulnerable moments that every Weapons Officer of every spacefaring race dreamed of finding, and that the Baernoi had found against Tachin's launch.

Tears of pain and frustration dribbled messily down her cheeks as she watched *Trollstep*'s salvo swallowed by a series of overlapping fireballs. The Baernoi must be using high-yield weapons; any Federation missiles not turned into gas would be turned into harmless chunks of metallic slag.

Either the pain of her consciousness was fading. Tachin watched with a detachment and clarity she ought to have found incredible, as the Baernoi ships spread out. They were accelerating, so their shields had to be down, in space so loaded with junk that they would surely take a hit that even a massive Khudrigate-built hull could not survive.

And they were launching as they accelerated, to give their missiles an even larger initial boost than the buses had given *Trollstep*'s salvo. Tachin hoped no one saw her face in the moment when she realized that the Baernoi missiles were pursuing the asteroid debris on meteoric trajectories.

Kiggle's Planet—or whatever the K'thressh called it—was safe from the by-blows of *Trollstep*'s Seguridad maneuver . . . Baernoi targeting was up to its usual standard, and no one in the Fleet ever bet against that. Some of the Tuskers might be lousy shots, but if so they were a closely guarded secret, probably kept chained in the cellars of the Khudr's palace to entertain the court at wild parties—

One by one, the plummeting rocks whiffed into gas or fragments too small to be dangerous even when they weren't flying off on escape trajectories at nearly escape velocity.

Tachin smelled worse things than vomit, and from so close that she was afraid to think where they came from. Out of the corner of one blurred eye, she saw Cuenco unsnapping his harness, which violated about six regulations. She didn't care. She wanted to unstrap, too, lean forward, and rest her forehead against the cool ceramic and metal of the Weapons board. Even better, she could lie down on it, sink into it, become part of it while the AI healed her itching brain and twisted nerves. . . .

A hand touched her shoulder.

"Ah—ma'am?"

She thought she recognized Cuenco's voice. She knew she recognized Schneewind's, in spite of a rasp that made him sound like a man dying of lung-mites.

She also knew that she was going to pass out, for the two or three seconds before she actually did so.

0840:

Tachin awoke in her own bunk, which gave her a moment's uneasiness. She had vomited, her stomach felt as if she might do it again, and her neck and head had a theme of steady throbbing, with variations of hot stabs of outright pain. If Sick Bay couldn't take her, then what were the people it had taken like?

In the early days of human-K'thressh contact, before the Federation established the Sensitive Corps and the K'thressh apparently did somewhat the same, major contacts had been known to kill twenty or thirty humans. Some Sensitives claimed that K'thressh Contact Masters had also died in the encounters.

Tachin wouldn't wish that on the K'thressh, who had done more good than harm—far more, during the Hive Wars. But she could console herself a little, with the thought of a Contact Master sprawled on his/her/its platform, tentacles too sore to wiggle and head aching as if it had been battered against rocks.

More consolation came a few minutes (she thought) later, when a medic came in and changed the nursepak that Tachin hadn't noticed hanging from the bunk head. She recognized one of the models from the cargo—apparently the hold gang had gone right on turning cargo into ship's assets.

She wondered if there was a case of champagne among the cargo. She was probably loaded with things that interacted badly with ethanol, but was sure she would be in bed long enough to sleep off any nonlethal reactions.

Then she snapped to full alert as Captain Schneewind came in. One look told her that the CO was possibly even less fit to be out of bed than she was.

So she pitched her voice low, and chose her words carefully.

"If anyone came out ahead, who was it?"

Schneewind licked lips that showed cracks and specks of dried blood, and rubbed the back of one hand over both cheeks. "I—I think it was a three-way tie. One rock did get through to the surface, which ought to balance all the missiles and sick bay time we and the Tuskers have spent. But—ah, Lieutenant Commander . . . ?

He would get somewhere eventually, and prompting him was the one sure way of arousing suspicion. Tachin snuggled down under the covers until only her head was free. That pain in her head briefly made her want to reach up and hold it in place with both hands so it wouldn't roll out of bed and shatter on the deck.

"Do you think the K'thressh got into our AI, to affect the targeting of our last salvo?" Scheewind asked. "The Tuskers hit it far too easily, far too fast."

"I—why would you ask me?"

"You and Cuenco were in the closest contact with it during our period under K'thressh influence. He said he didn't detect anything, but the K'thressh could probably prevent him. Your psych profile suggests that you might have more resistance."

If this is what I get for resistance, Lord spare me ever having to surrender to the K'thressh.

Schneewind rambled on, while Tachin tried to hold on to a few more productive thoughts and turn them into words. She was ready to reply when the captain interrupted himself with a fit of coughing.

"Here, sir." She handed over the water carafe from the bunk's side clip-on table. Rather to her surprise, her hand didn't tremble.

"Thank you. I'm trying to get some preliminary data for our report. Because if the K'thressh have *any* capability for touching an AI—"

If Tachin hadn't known the answer, she would have gone at the question, as no doubt everyone else aboard had when it occurred to them during her convalescent nap. K'thressh-proofing ships' AIs would be appallingly expensive, if it could be done at all—but it might have to be done, if the K'thressh were starting interstellar colonization and might turn up the Lord knew where. . . .

Nice to find a question I can answer.

"Eh?"

"I aimed the last busload to miss," Tachin said, laying each word down as if it were made of finespun crystal. "They might not have hit any of the falling rocks, but they certainly wouldn't have hit the Baernoi."

Scheewind cocked his head to one side, at such an angle that Tachin wondered if his neck would survive. He looked like a rooster who'd just recognized a rival's challenge.

"I gave a direct order. Which you appear to have disobeyed."

"Was it intended to supersede your previous order, about not getting into a space battle with the Baernoi?"

"Did I give that one?"

"I remember hearing it."

"What about K'thressh influence on your memory?"

"What about K'thressh influence on your second order, to silence the Baernoi? They had us all wrapped up and ready to deliver by then!"

She realized that her tone was a trifle sharp for addressing her commanding officer, but if he was going to go around with regulations up his—

"Not impossible," Schneewind said, which Tachin recognized as conceding her point, at least for now. "The CC record should have it, and we'll be doing a thorough study of that before we transmit it."

"Have we jumped?" If they had, she'd been asleep much longer than she realized, and—

"Transmit it to Inmar su-Deiz. The Baernoi squadron—commodore, roughly."

"The K'thressh hit them?"

Schneewind nodded and stood up. Not being quite normally coordinated, he banged his head on the nursepak. "Those damned octopussies were pulling *both* our strings and watching what happened."

He lurched out, leaving Tachin alone and glad to have the rank that gave her a single cabin. She not only didn't want human company, right now the company of her own thoughts wasn't much more agreeable. And Raphael was at least two hundred light-years away.

The least disagreeable thought seemed to be finishing the letter.

"PERSONAL RECORD file, Tachin, this date," she said, and started rearranging the pillows behind her as the bunkside display lit up.

LAST SHIP TO HAEFDON

BY BILL BALDWIN

COMMANDER Leroy Spangenberg, Imperial Fleet, accepted the KA'PPA-COM message in the wardroom of *I.F.S. Revenge* (DD 783) about Dawn plus three. It ruined his breakfast:

HKJG47037655 GROUP: 70 191/52068

Emergency Unclassified

TO: ALL STARSHIPS
FROM: I.F.S. AVALON CITY

EMERGENCY * EMERGENCY * EMERGENCY

FORCED DOWN ON ABANDONED GIMMAS-HAEFDON STARBASE. SHIP DAMAGED BEYOND REPAIR. STAR GIMMAS DISPLAYING SIGNS OF IMPENDING TERMINAL IMPLOSION. IMMEDIATE RESCUE REQUESTED FOR SINGLE PASSENGER, 35 CREW.

EMERGENCY * EMERGENCY * EMERGENCY

END EMERGENCY UNCLASSIFIED

HKJG47037655 GROUP: 70

Spangenberg didn't need to inquire about *I.F.S. Avalon City*; everybody knew the royal yacht—which made that "single passenger" none other than the elderly Onrad V, Grand Galactic Emperor, Prince of the Reggio Star Cluster, and Rightful Protector of the Heavens. How in the name of Xaxt his ship could have been forced down *anywhere* was beyond imagination, much less on frozen Gimmas-Haefdon. He shrugged. *How* didn't matter anymore; even royal yachts suffered occasional malfunctions. And unluckily—at least for himself—*Revenge* could well be passing close enough to the star Gimmas that he wouldn't be able to ignore the distress signal.

Quickly brushing the odd crumb from his perfect uniform, he climbed briskly to the bridge, threaded his way forward among the control consoles, and settled into the right-hand helm. When its displays came alive, he called up a NAV summary, then grimaced. Sure enough, he was within half a parsec of the dying star. Once he knew where to look, he could see its glow clearly through the side hyperscreens. He sat staring, listening to the slow, muted beat of the drive, and damning his luck. Only eight days out of Avalon—eight days short of finishing the only deep space command he would ever have to endure—and now *this*. How he *hated* starships!

"Shall I order *Revenge* to change course, Skipper?" Chief Rimer asked as he sat at the left helm, propped comfortably against the arm of his recliner with his jacket unbuttoned to reveal a none-too-clean sweater.

Spangenberg snorted irritably; no matter how the man dressed, you simply *knew* he was a real StarSailor. "Very well," he grumbled without turning—he disliked Rimer intensely, but needed his expertise to run the ship. His own reflection appeared momentarily in a darkened display panel, and for the millionth time he acknowledged that he really didn't belong here on the bridge. His place was back on Avalon at the Admiralty, commanding a room full of engineers. Of course, there wasn't much he could do about that now. "Tell KA'PPA-COM to send the yacht a message saying we're on our way," he continued, "then have *Revenge* set a direct course for the old base at Gimmas-Haefdon; coordinates are still in the Fleet database."

"A little more speed, perhaps, Skipper?" Rimer asked. "Looks like every cycle's going to count."

"I'll let you know," Spangenberg snapped irritably.

"But, Skipper," Rimer began, "that star's about to implode. . . ."

"I said I'd let you know," Spangenberg warned, avoiding Rimer's eyes. What he *really* wanted to do was slow down. *Revenge* couldn't possibly be the only starship in a busy space lane like this. Someone else out there was certain to get the message, too, beat him to the rescue (as well as the glory), and that would be that. No trouble—so long as he kept his head.

"Setting course for Gimmas-Haefdon Base at current speed," Rimer acknowledged in a voice dripping with resignation. "*Revenge,* you will redirect your heading to Gimmas-Haefdon Starbase."

"Modifying course for Gimmas Haefdon Base, coordinates 41214fo-sgw423480-312f," *Revenge* intoned.

Like the talented engineer he was, Spangenberg matched the spoken coordinates with those on his own display. They checked. Outside, the starscape smoothly skidded left, then steadied.

"From the way she's blurred, Gimmas could be jumping to the next energy level any moment," Rimer grumbled—*just* under his breath. "Bet things are lively on the surface of Haefdon."

"That will be enough, Rimer," Spangenberg snapped. He didn't even want to think about Haefdon's surface—or the storm-roiled atmosphere that was certain to go with it. The fact was that nobody aboard *Revenge*—certainly not himself—had the skill to even navigate in that kind of maelstrom, much less attempt a ship to ship rescue. They'd all be killed, including his two civilian charges who were merely cadging a lift back to Avalon!

Some thirty clicks later, a horrified Spangenberg watched Gimmas—now centered in the forward hyperscreens—shift color rapidly from white to purple: the Psi-8 event. He checked his timepiece. Very bad news. It meant there were barely two metacycles remaining before the star collapsed on itself—and still no replies to *Avalon City* from any other ship. Frowning, he ran some figures at his console, then ground his teeth. *Revenge* and everybody aboard her could easily end up being sucked into the black hole that remained. Now it was suicidal to even linger this close to the dying star, much less attempt the rescue of a downed starship on its only planet.

Soon he would have to sheer off and run for safety: otherwise . . . well, he didn't even want to *think* about being caught in a black hole. On the other hand, he considered with a grimace, if he left the Emperor to die without even attempting a rescue, he might well find himself in a kind of *personal* trouble that was a lot worse than mere death. He gripped the sides of his console in near panic. Right now, both he and the Emperor badly needed a miracle. . . .

A second message from the crippled royal yacht came some fifteen cycles after the Psi-8 event:

HKJG47037655 GROUP: 70 191/52068

EMERGENCY UNCLASSIFIED

TO: ALL STARSHIPS
FROM: I.F.S. AVALON CITY

EMERGENCY * EMERGENCY * EMERGENCY

DUE TO THE PROXIMATE NATURE OF THE GIMMAS IMPLOSION AND THE CLEAR, PRESENT DANGER IT PRESENTS, I, ONRAD V, PERSONALLY FORBID ANY ATTEMPT TO RESCUE MYSELF OR MY CREW FROM THE GIMMAS-HAEFDON STARBASE. REPEAT. I

FORBID ANY ATTEMPT AT RESCUE. ALL SHIPS ARE TO STAND CLEAR OF GIMMAS.

EMERGENCY * EMERGENCY * EMERGENCY

END EMERGENCY UNCLASSIFIED

HKJG47037655 GROUP: 70

Spangenberg closed his eyes and took a deep breath; he could hardly believe his good fortune. The message was salvation, pure and simple: for his crew, his ship, and especially for himself. Now, nobody was going to learn the ugly little secret he'd kept so well all these years. He felt a certain sympathy for Onrad, but what the Xaxt, the old boy had enjoyed a long, comfy life and a successful reign—not bad in anybody's book. Almost faint with relief, he ordered Chief Rimer to have *Revenge* sheer off and return to her original homeward course.

At that moment he sensed a hand on his shoulder. "You're altering course, Commander?" a quiet voice demanded.

Spangenberg glanced up to see the two elderly civilian passengers standing beside his console: the Earl of Grayson—a Wilf Brim, if he remembered correctly—and his huge manservant, Barbousse, or something like that. Both wore the blue cloaks reserved for Imperial Fleet veterans; he hadn't remembered *that* about them, although he'd paid the two men little attention at all since liftoff. "What was that?" he demanded; he didn't approve of civilians riding on military starships, especially civilians like Brim, who—it was rumored—had endured a courtmartial years ago.

"We wondered why you ordered the ship to change course, Commander," the one named Brim declared impassively. "We understood that we were on our way to rescue Emperor Onrad."

"How in Xaxt did you learn that?" Spangenberg demanded.

"*How* we came to know, Commander, has little significance," Brim replied firmly. "The important fact is that you have altered course from Haefdon while each click is crucial to Onrad's rescue." He frowned. "When, sir, do you intend to return to that course?"

Spangenberg felt his temper rise. "How *dare* you question me?" he growled. "I am Captain of this ship, and don't you forget it!"

"I am well aware of your position aboard *Revenge*, Commander," Brim replied, looking Spangenberg directly in the eye. "And every moment we remain on this vector, you make rescuing our Emperor more and more difficult."

"No longer," Spangenberg declared with what he hoped was a dismissive wave of his hand. "The Emperor has just warned off all rescue attempts—personally. He feels the risk is too great, and I agree."

"Commander Spangenberg," Brim replied with a look of disbelief, "do you intend to just . . . fly away when there's still a good chance of saving everyone aboard that ship? I can't believe you'd do such a thing."

"Listen, Brim," Spangenberg snarled with exasperation, "another word from you and I'll have you thrown off the bridge. Keep in mind that you're only a passenger on this ship—and subject to my commands."

"In the name of Voot's greasy beard, Commander," Brim protested, "you can't just let those men die when there's still a good chance of pulling off a rescue. You're committing *murder,* pure and simple—and you know it."

"I am completely within my legal rights, Brim," Spangenberg growled. "It is the Emperor's wish that I do not risk my ship."

Suddenly, Brim's countenance took on a look of concern. "Is it possible that neither you nor anyone on your crew *can* take the ship off automatic mode, Commander?" he demanded in a quiet voice. "Is that what's bothering you?"

Spangenberg felt ghostly, icy fingers tighten around

his throat. Just what did this Brim know? Had the old bastard somehow discovered the truth about his Helmsman's rating: that he wore the coveted Winged Comet of a military Helmsman when he'd really washed out of spaceflight school—that he'd hacked bogus passing scores into the Academy's computers after graduation? And now . . . he cursed his luck. He'd only signed up for this single, milk-run deployment, because he needed time *in command* to earn his next promotion. So far, the ship had flown the whole route herself— as planned—and he wasn't about to change things this close to the end, even for the Emperor. "Brim," he warned through clenched teeth, "I shall brook no more of your insults. I order you off the bridge immediately. Consider both yourself and your manservant confined to quarters until I personally release you. Understand?"

Brim stood his ground and glared, his grizzled eyes suddenly blazing with a fire that Spangenberg found terrifying. "Commander Spangenberg," he ordered with authority. "We *are* going forward with the rescue. Now!"

At that moment, Spangenberg felt what he strongly suspected was fast-rising panic. "A-are you threatening to take over the controls yourself?" he demanded in a voice that cracked in spite of himself.

"Precisely," Brim said quietly, starting toward the left-hand Helmsman's console. "We both know the ship can't do her own flying in the kind of environment we'll meet in the vicinity of planet Haefdon. So either you will take the controls—or I will."

At that moment, it became apparent that Brim actually *did* intend to commandeer the bridge. It was too much for Spangenberg. He panicked. "Mutiny!" he bleated and mashed the internal security alarm. "Guards! Help! The bridge is being attacked."

As sirens filled the bridge with deafening clamor, members of the Security Watch raced into the bridge drawing their blasters. "Where? Who?" one of them demanded in confusion.

"These, er, civilians!" Spangenberg shouted, pointin to Brim and Barbousse with a shaking finger. "Marc them to the brig immediately. They tried to take ov the helm!"

"Commander!" a chief exclaimed as he reset th alarm on Spangenberg's console. "You're pointing a Admiral Brim and Chief Barbousse!"

"I don't care who they are!" Spangenberg screame "Get them off the bridge before that giant of his a tacks someone."

"But, *Commander* . . ." the chief began.

"It's all right, Chief," Brim interrupted calml "You've got to obey orders." Then he turned t Spangenberg. "*You,* however, will live to regret thi Commander," he said, raising his hands in surrender bu never taking his angry gaze from Spangenberg's eye "That's our Emperor out there."

"Take them to the brig. Now!" Spangenberg shoute averting his eyes and clenching his fists. "And thro away the Xaxt-damned key!" Not until the two men ha been ushered down the aft companionway did his breath ing return to anything he considered normal. But eve then, he found himself ceaselessly grinding his teeth, n matter how he tried to stop.

Afterward, Spangenberg helplessly watched his con sole clock counting off cycles that passed like Standar years on the shocked, silent bridge. His worst anxietie had come true: *Revenge* was unquestionably alone in th vicinity of Gimmas-Haefdon, and probably would b until sometime after the star imploded. Before Brim ha come onto the bridge, he'd been well within his right by prudently continuing on to Avalon in automati mode. But now that same prudence would *also* smack o the worst cowardice imaginable. He shook his head i disgust. If he could—if he had any talent at a helm— he'd actually be glad to take the ship off automatic an try the rescue himself, if only to escape the burden o guilt he felt. But he couldn't—literally; he was helpless. What was he going to do?

"Er, Captain . . . ?"

Startled, Spangenberg glanced to his left, where Rimer was regarding him from the helm as if he were a half-triggered space mine. "Yes?" he asked.

"Captain," Rimer said hesitantly, "Admiral Brim probably *could* pull off the rescue . . . if you'd let him, of course."

"Brim?" Spangenberg demanded.

"Yessir," Rimer replied quickly. "I flew more than once under his command years ago—during the last war. He was the Empire's greatest Helmsman at the time."

"The last war was nearly a generation ago, Rimer," Spangenberg growled. "Skills that old can have little meaning today."

"I doubt if you looked at his manifest when he came aboard, Commander," Rimer said quietly. "If you had, you'd have seen that he's on his way home from flying an experimental starship exhibition at the Sherrington Plant on Rhodor. Natural skills like his don't diminish much with age."

"He *is* good," Lieutenant Jarvis Fahid asserted from the Navigator's console. "My mother served with him aboard *I.F.S. Truculent*; swears he was a great Helmsman even then."

"Aye, Captain," an engineering officer seconded from the Systems console, "I was aboard a Sherrington Star-Fury when he . . . ?"

"Enough!" Spangenberg shouted, his head spinning. "Silence on the bridge!" Suddenly, his whole universe seemed to be caving in. Though he was *legally* within his rights to continue on course for Avalon, after his tiff with this nettlesome Brim character, someone probably *would* start asking questions. And when that happened, his illegal Winged Comet would not only be unearthed, it would end his career and probably earn him time in an Imperial prison, as well. In short, he was finished, one way or the other. On top of that, the thought of th doomed Emperor and his crew trapped on a planet th: was about to be destroyed was really more than he coul take. He might be a bogus Helmsman, but *not* a mu derer, in spite of what Brim said! He checked the consol clock again, reviewed his fast disappearing options, an made a decision. *He was wasting time!* "Guards!" h roared. "Escort Admiral Brim to the bridge—on th double!" Then he turned to Rimer. "Chief," he sai "have *Revenge* return to a course for Gimmas-Haefdo then you'd better prepare to turn over the helm."

A hard-faced Brim appeared on the bridge almost in mediately, leaving Spangenberg with the strong suspicio that he'd never been more than a few steps from th bottom of the companionway. "Give your seat to Chie Rimer, Commander," he ordered. "On the double."

"B–but where will I . . ." Spangenberg began.

"Sit in that jump seat behind you, if you must," Brir growled. "Just stay out of the way."

For a moment, Spangenberg bristled, then quickl changed his mind. *Revenge* was his starship no longe: and—one way or another—never would be again. H moved meekly to the jump seat behind the right-han helm and watched Brim with growing fascination.

"Action Stations," the old admiral ordered over th intercom. "All hands to action stations immediately! Spe cial duty spacemen to your posts. Close all airtight door and scuttles. Down all deadlights; this is no exercise. Re peat, this is no exercise."

Instantly, the deck vibrated to scores of thudding fee Dull of airtight doors and hatches echoed from belo while figures ran haphazardly among the consoles. Hu miliated, Spangenberg shrank from the slipshod confu sion everywhere he looked. It was quickly dawning o him that commanding a starship required a great de: more than merely the helmsmanship he lacked.

"*Revenge,*" he heard Brim order in a steady voice,, "I
m immediately taking control of your flight and propul-
ion controls. Acknowledge."

"Your serial number, please?" *Revenge* asked from a
onsole speaker.

Brim pronounced a sequence of numbers and letters.

"Are you Admiral Wilf Brim?"

"The same," Brim replied.

"Your password, Admiral?"

Brim quickly pronounced another series of letters and
umbers from memory.

Spangenberg grimaced. The Admiralty had issued him
list of one-use passwords, too, but he kept them in the
hip's safe—unread.

"That is a valid password, Admiral," *Revenge* intoned.
'I relinquish flight and propulsion controls."

"Acknowledged," Brim replied, then, "I'll also need
he whole suite of attitude readouts on my console here
lus some sort of 'to target' indicator. Got that?"

"Acknowledged, Admiral."

While the console reconfigured itself, Spangenberg
ould identify only a few of the new readouts and instru-
nents that appeared. Cheeks burning from mortification,
e watched Brim's hands begin to move rapidly over the
ontrols. Soon, the deck began to throb more insistently
inder his boots, and he listened to the mounting thunder
f the drive with surprise. It occurred to him that he had
ever heard a starship exerting any more effort than the
recise amount necessary to achieving economical transit
etween two points in space.

Suddenly, the whole starscape outside skidded to the
ight at a tremendous rate and from deep below came
he clatter of dislodged tinware and crockery—the crash
f lockers torn from their weldings. Spangenberg found
imself hanging on to the seat for dear life while bewil-
lered shouts filled the bridge.

"Gravity limits exceeded! Gravity limits exceeded!"

the voice of *Revenge* warned in emergency inflection– another phenomenon Spangenberg had never e perienced.

"*Revenge,* you will raise your warning limits twen percent," Brim ordered as he brought the ship back o course.

"Doing so will permit maneuvers that exceed spac frame structural limits," the starship objected.

"Acknowledged," Brim grunted, putting the ship in a wild roll that turned the forward starscape into whirling, one-dimensional disk of concentric circle "And while you're at it, disable all warnings on propu sion output—from either system. I don't want to he them at all."

"Done," *Revenge* acknowledged as the gyrations su denly ceased, then recommenced the other way.

Brim tested the flight systems in all axes for near ten cycles before he appeared satisfied that he had th ship's controls mastered. By this time, *Revenge*'s velocit had increased considerably, and the planet Haefdon wa visibly growing against the huge, wobbly disk that wa its star, Gimmas. Also growing was a wicked gravity tu bulence that was throwing the ship around like a r caught in a terrier's teeth.

"KA'PPA-COMM Center: put me in touch with *Av lon City,*" Spangenberg heard Brim order.

"*Avalon City,* here," a voice crackled present through waves of static. "You are ordered to sheer o immediately. The star Gimmas is about to implode. R peat: sheer off immediately."

"Belay that," Brim growled. "This is starcruiser *I.F. Revenge*; we're on our way to pick you up."

"*I.F.S. Revenge,* you're to sheer off immediately!" th voice repeated with an indignant inflection that was clea despite rapidly increasing static.

"Xax-damnit," Brim growled as he fought the co trols. "Stow the dramatics and tell me what kind of shap you're in. We're coming to take you off."

"Who is this, anyway?" the voice demanded. "Identify yourself."

"The name's Brim, StarSailor—Wilf Brim, and if you're planning to give me trouble, you'd better get Onrad on the thraggling horn right away!"

"The Emperor?"

"Yes, our stubborn Emperor. If you have any hopes of seeing Avalon again, get the old guy on the horn—now! And while you're at it, start a homing beacon I can follow to where you are."

Long moments of relative silence went by as *Revenge* smashed her way through successions of gravity rollers that hazed the outside view like great ocean waves. Finally the KA'PPA-COMM crackled to life. "Brim, you thraggling lunatic," a deep voice resonated through the static, "I don't know how you got there, but it has to be you because anyone else in the Known Universe would have the good sense to head the other way at top speed. Now turn around and get out of here while you still can—otherwise you're going to kill everybody on your Xax-damned ship. That's an Imperial order!"

"Sorry, Your Highness," Brim said, dodging *Revenge* around a huge asteroid that appeared out of nowhere, "I can't seem to hear you. Now—with all due respects—don't waste any more of our time; I'm coming for you. Tell me what the crash site is like and help me figure the best way to make an approach."

As Spangenberg eavesdropped, it became apparent that *Avalon City*'s Helmsman had managed to crash-land on the abandoned Gimmas-Haefdon Starbase itself, coming to rest near the old Eorian Starwharves in the lea of a half-ruined starship hangar. The wreck was temporarily safe from the full effects of Gimmgas' last throes because it was on the night side of the planet; however, Haefdon's normal rotation would deny that shelter within less than a metacycle.

By the time they switched from hyperdrive to the ship's three powerful gravity engines, Brim was flying

Revenge through the kind of swirling energy storm tha
Spangenberg only heard about when old Helmsme
swapped "Iron-Man" stories at retirement banquets. Th
deck kicked as splinters torn from the planet's edge
smashed against the hull with savage crashes. For fe
cycles, the pounding eased as they entered Haefdon
shadow, then resumed with a vengeance when the fir
traces of Haefdon's maddened atmosphere began to bu
fet the ship. From that point on, conditions outsid
worsened at a terrifying rate. Soon, they were bein
bounced around through swirling, pitch-black gales, whil
great arcs of lightning flashed through glowing, roilin
clouds that were racing to meet them faster tha
Spangenberg's mind could accept. The gravity engine
surged and roared while the spaceframe protested wit
great creaks and shudders.

Through it all, Brim piloted with such calm authorit
that he seemed to be from some other time and age–
one that Spangenberg couldn't even divine. The ol
man's sense of the ship was absolute. Mere artifice coul
survive no more than a moment in such a cosmic whir
pool; anything less than perfection—for even an in
stant—would quickly end in disaster. "Chief Rimer," h
commanded without turning, "better pipe your bes
boarding party aft to the main hatch. Tell 'em we'll b
at the wreck in about twelve cycles."

"Aye, Admiral," Rimer acknowledged and busie
himself at his console.

They were now descending into the clouds surrounde
by a constant fusillade of intense lightning flashes—ac
companied by crashing discharges of concussion an
thunder that hurt Spangenberg's ears even through th
hullmetal sides of the starship. Suddenly, a great clangin
blow rang through the ship, sending a shudder throug
every plate and frame.

"Impact at Station one-thirty-nine! Impact at Statio
one-thirty-nine!" *Revenge* warned.

Startled, Spangenberg glanced around the bridge, the

noticed Brim struggling with the controls. "What's happened?" he blurted out in terror.

"She won't answer the helm!" Brim gasped through clenched teeth. "Feels like the link to the steering engine's gone."

Spangenberg froze in his seat; he knew what was wrong with *Revenge*; any good engineer could figure it out. Steering impulses were carried aft from the helms to the steering engine by light beams traveling in wave guides that ran along the belly of the starship. Flying debris must have smashed into the hull crushing—or even breaking—both of the wave guides; it was the only explanation. He took an appalled look through the hyperscreens as the ship plummeted toward the surface; from this altitude, he guessed they had no more than ten cycles before impact—if that. Suddenly, he knew exactly what he needed to do—he might not be able to fly the starship, but he could fix what was wrong. A little-known quirk in *Revenge*'s design provided an emergency path for the steering beams—directly along the belly stringers. But to rig it, he'd have to crawl outside the hull to one of the forward inspection hatches, then enter the space within the double hull. He couldn't do it himself; he would need someone of supreme strength with him—and he knew *just* who that might be. "Chief Barbousse," he cried out. "I think I can fix the steering, but I'll need your help."

The huge man exchanged glances with Brim for a moment, then rose to his feet and narrowed his eyes. "I'm ready, Commander," he said in a voice that matched his size. "Tell me what I can do to help."

"Follow me," Spangenberg ordered, dodging into the narrow forward companionway that led to a tiny docking chamber in the very nose of the starship. There, sturdy harnesses and lengths of stout line permitted a suited-up boatswain's mate to be streamed out to another starship in case of an emergency. But instead of floating forward in the tranquillity of outer space, he was about to let the giant Barbousse pay out tether while he crawled aft through the howling slipstream. And very little time remained before *Revenge* bored a large, deep hole in Haefdon's snowy, soon-to-be-vaporized surface.

Outside in the roaring wind, things were even more dicey than Spangenberg had imagined. Moving through the boundary layer at the very surface of the starship's skin, he found his chest crushed against the harness that kept him from being swept aft in the terrific gale; he could only imagine the strain on Barbousse's arms and hands as he paid out tether a few thumb-lengths at a time. Twice, the raging storm managed to double the pressure on his back, making it all but impossible to draw breath. Through it all, he kept wriggling aft; he had no choice. Ahead, he could see the huge gouge in the ship's belly just forward of the gravity-engine pylons—his diagnosis had been correct.

After clicks that passed like centuries, he reached the hatch, prized it open and . . . it tore free, then went flying off into the murky darkness. Somehow, he managed to struggle inside, nearly collapsing in the low, curving space between the two hulls—no place for claustrophobia! But he couldn't rest. Panting in the rarefied air, he unclipped the tether and secured it to a stringer, then switched on lights in the fingertips of his gloves. Luck was with him. immediately he located the two red-and-yellow-striped wave guides and followed them hand over hand to the first circular repeater box—that was the key. Boxes like that could send or receive steering signals from anywhere. All he had to do was cut the wave guide downstream, then bend the forward part outward so the box sent the steering beams aft. The first circular box past the stove-in section would pick up the signals—even reflections would do in an emergency—and pass them on to the steering engine almost as well as if they arrived along the wave guide itself.

After his struggle along the hull, Spangenberg was running on nervous energy, but feelings didn't matter anymore. He had a single task to accomplish—nothing else mattered beyond that. Keeping one hand for himself and one for the ship, he groped at his waist until his fingers grasped the regulation pfizo-knife attached to his harness. He pressed the actuator, then waited until the blade glowed white hot. Carefully, he cut through the wave guide itself, then slit about two irals of the micro-weld that kept it in place against the starship's outer skin; abruptly, the dark chamber filled with a wavering blue glow—Brim's now-useless control inputs. This done, he braced himself and bent the freed section out into the 'tween-hulls cavity at about thirty degrees and waited . . . and waited.

Nothing happened!

Literally terror-stricken, he glanced around to see what was preventing the beam from going aft. Everything *looked* clear. What had gone wrong? There couldn't be more than a few moments left before the ship crashed into the surface. In angry frustration, he smashed his fist against the wave guide, bending it farther into the chamber and . . .

Immediately, Spangenberg was thrown from his feet, then plastered against the curved floor as the gravity engines howled in what was surely emergency military overload. Too late? Trembling, he braced himself for impact—the moment of violent, searing pain that would end his life. He ground his teeth and waited. And waited . . . Cycles later, he felt his weight begin to level off, then realized he'd been holding his breath so long he was seeing flashes before his eyes. Rolling over cautiously, he pushed himself to his knees and crawled to the hatch where wind and snow were howling in with the force of a hurricane. When he peered out, he had to stifle a shout of terror. Even now, the ship wasn't more than a hundred irals above the surface—and slowing as she smashed her way through the obviously worsening storm! Only Xaxt knew how Brim was managing to keep the ship under control. Down below, in the glare of the ship's searchlights, he could see the wrecked star yacht coming up quickly through the driving snow and debris—had to be that; everything else was buried in white. How in Xaxt Brim was going to get close enough to board the people down there was a pure mystery—but then, that was clearly what he was trying to do. Somehow, universe knew how, he was positioning the ship alongside the wreck and . . . there went *Revenge*'s boarding tube. Heart in his mouth, Spangenberg watched it extend downward to match *Avalon City*'s main hatch and connect, just as if they'd been back at Grand Imperial Terminal in Avalon. From his vantage point in the belly, he watched people begin hurrying up through the tube toward *Revenge.* Incredulous, he wondered how Brim could keep the ship so utterly motionless in the raging storm, then decided he'd never understand, even if someone tried to explain.

As the flow of survivors through the tube began to thin, Spangenberg saw a hand grip the hatch sill, then another. The next moment, Barbousse appeared at the opening. "Time to go, Commander," he shouted over the howling wind. "We have only a few cycles."

"H–how did you get here?" Spangenberg demanded. "Without the slipstream, there's no way you could have walked the bottom of the ship."

"The tether," Barbousse said "I used it for support."

Spangenberg swallowed his gorge imagining Barbousse making his way hand over hand as he dangled from the tether. "I can't go back that way," he shouted. "I don't have the strength."

"Then I'll take both of us," the giant said indifferently. "But hurry—the Admiral will lift as soon as all survivors are aboard."

"W–what do you want me to . . . ?"

"Hurry, Commander; lock your arms around my neck. Now."

Frightened almost beyond fear, Spangenberg climbed tremulously through the hatch, glanced down during a moment of absolute terror, then locked his arms around the giant's neck and consigned himself to Lady Fate. His stomach nearly gave up breakfast when the tether stretched to its limit and they fell at least ten irals into the driving snow. But through it all Barbousse held on and began to move forward—hand over hand—toward the starship's nose.

After an eternity of near madness to Spangenberg—during which his fast-tiring hands continually threatened to lose their grip on each other—Barbousse reached the hatch, then literally dragged both of them inside and slammed the cover shut. Immediately, Spangenberg's legs went limp, and he fell to the deck gasping for enough air to fill his lungs. But no sooner did he feel Barbousse helping him to his feet than the two of them were brutally smashed against the aft bulkhead by acceleration that immediately exceeded the ship's internal gravity. As he ground his teeth in agony, Spangenberg pictured the bridge a few levels above them where an old man hunched over the left-hand Helmsman's console—fighting to save everyone aboard. One way or another, Wilf Brim was doing all he could to take them home—and Spangenberg could only hope he'd succeed.

During the next cycles the two reached the bridge mostly on hands and knees, emerging from the forward companionway just as the hyperscreens went ablaze with lurid, purple haze generated by Gimmas' final demise. By that time, however, *Revenge* was well into hyperspace and safe from the expanding gravity wave that only scant cycles earlier would have carried them to their doom. Improbably, they were safe—*everyone* was safe—in spite of how close they'd come to disaster. Weakly, Spangenberg slumped into an empty Navigation console and tried to regain control of his runaway emotions.

During the next clicks, Brim moderated the ship's acceleration until local gravity took effect again, then set the ship back to automatic operation. Finally, he turned the helm over to Chief Rimer and headed for the aft companionway.

Spangenberg watched his every move, waiting for the retribution he knew he'd earned.

Instead, when Brim came abreast of the Navigation console, he stopped and smiled. "A brave thing you did in the belly of the ship, Spangenberg," he said, putting an age-mottled hand on the man's shoulder. "If you hadn't had the guts to go fix the steering, we'd all be riding Haefdon into that black hole back there.

"Thanks, Admiral," Spangenberg said, avoiding the old man's eyes. "But I can't take much credit for what I did; I couldn't have pulled it off without Chief Barbousse."

"Without the chief, I couldn't have done a lot of the things I did either," the admiral said with a chuckle. "You've vindicated yourself in my eyes, Spangenberg, no matter who helped you. You may or may not be a Helmsman, but you're a brave man, and don't ever forget it, no matter what the future holds in store."

A short time after Brim disappeared along the companionway, Spangenberg started aft himself. Better, he thought, to spend the remainder of the voyage in his stateroom than face the unspoken ridicule of the people who once were under his command. He'd hardly cleared the third bank of consoles when a heavyset man wearing a head bandage—a man who looked a lot like the Emperor—appeared at the top of the moving stairway. He was followed by Brim.

"That him?" the man asked, nodding his head at Spangenberg.

"Yes, Your Majesty," Brim replied. "Emperor Onrad—may I present Commander Spangenberg of Your Imperial Fleet?"

"Pleased to meet you," Onrad said, extending a hand that clasped Spangenberg's in a warm, friendly grip.

"I am . . . h–honored," Spangenberg stumbled dazedly.

"Yes, you probably are," Onrad replied with a chuckle. "Especially since I'll be awarding you the Imperial Medal for Bravery after we arrive in Avalon. And you'd better have someone sew a fourth stripe on your cuffs immediately, *Captain,*" he added with a little smile. "Brim lost no time telling me that you're the man who managed to fix the steering gear."

Spangenberg tried to speak, but the Emperor stopped him with a warning hand.

"We all owe you our lives, Spangenberg," Onrad said quietly. "That's why I've promised Brim I'll inquire no farther about the scuttlebutt concerning certain occurrences on your bridge earlier today. But understand this, Captain," he continued as his face darkened. "At some convenient time following our arrival in Avalon, you *will* permanently remove that winged Comet from your uniform. And if you ever wear it again, I shall personally instruct my Palace Guard to have you shot. Do I make myself clear?"

Sangenberg didn't know whether to laugh or cry, but he did understand he'd been handed his life again, at a time when he was certain he'd lost it forever. "I understand," he managed to stammer. "T–thank you, Your Majesty."

"Don't thank me," Onrad said, "Thank Brim for refusing to tell me any more about today's rescue." Then he pursed his lips and peered into the Bridge dismissively. "All right, Captain," he said, "how about taking us home?"

"I'll get right at that, Your Majesty," Spangenberg said. "Immediately." Then turning on his heel, he made his way forward to his accustomed seat at the right-hand helm. He had only a few more days in command of a starship, and he intended to make the most of them.

Fragment of the Log of Captain Amasa Delano
(as retrieved from the asteroid belt several years after the events described herein)

BY BRIAN M. THOMSEN

YOU can call me Delano, for I am as much of a fool as my newly acquired namesake, and when you are a captain of a ship it is up to you to assume full responsibility for your actions even if—as the fates would have it—you are not allowed to survive long enough to receive proper exactitude in penalty for your actions.

Let he who reads this, even if it is long after my passing, have my account entered into the record so that the infamy of my ineptitude might be known to all, and that the events contained herewith might also serve as warning to other captains who perchance sail these treacherous seas of space without adequate training or caution or with too much arrogance or surety without adequate basis.

Years ago, or at least so it seems, my name was Melville, Captain Philip Melville of the Interstellar Merchant Marine. My commission had been bought for me by my father as was the custom for parents whose ne'er–do–well offspring required a certain amount of seasoning prior to entering the family business and, as ours was long-term and short-term transport, I was urged to partake in a journey of practical training to enhance my resume (though the amount of training that can be accorded someone with the rank of captain on a merchant transport ship is no doubt minimal in an age where navigation, maintenance, and order are all maintained by various mechanical intelligences whose only function and direction is to make sure that the mission at hand is accomplished . . . or at least so I thought).

My responsibilities included supervising the humanoid personnel, a seasoned and competent contingent of engineers and stevedores whose main duties included AI and robo-maintenance along our multi-month missions on an "as needed" basis which, of course, afforded them enough downtime to cause trouble that might delay or jeopardize matters of business at hand thus justifying the oversight/managerial duties of my position (though I must note at this time that the crew of the *Essex,* my ship, was extremely well behaved and almost functioned more as *my* wet nurse than as my charge, as these seasoned veterans took upon themselves the daunting task of educating their commanding officers in the practicalities and pragmatics of the maritime spaceway).

One of the elder engineers, Stubb by name, quickly took me on as his senior charge on my shakedown cruise.

When I first observed him looking over my shoulder, I quickly moved to put him in his place.

"Surely there are matters that are more requiring of your attention," I observed churlishly.

"No, sir," he replied respectfully, and then with a mischievous wink quickly added, "at least none as important to your father."

"My father?"

"Indeed, sir," he replied. "I assured him before we left that I would dry the wetness behind your ears and keep you safe from harm on this, your maiden command. 'Tis the only reason I accepted this posting. I was about to retire, but your father has always been good to me, been a good man and a good sponsor. It was the least I could do."

I was crestfallen.

My father had hired me a babysitter for my maiden command.

" 'Tis just a precaution, sir, no offense intended," he

said carefully. "Nowadays a captain's place is more in the line of dealing with other captains, handling business and settling the occasional dispute."

"You mean like some account executive?"

"Not exactly," he explained. "Most of us space monkeys can barely balance our own credit account, let alone figure out tariffs, and harbor fees. And when it comes to the gentle art of negotiation, let's just say that if it can't be settled with fists or a complimentary drink or two well, I guess we're all pretty much useless. And your father assures me that you are perfectly suited to such tasks."

"Suited," I repeated.

"His word, not mine, though I always did count him as a fair judge of the measure of a man, even if the man is his own son."

"Anything else?" I asked, having already received more than an earful.

"Not really," he replied. "The ship and her crew can pretty much take care of themselves. Just plug in her coordinates and away we go. It does, however, take a little time to get one's space legs, if you know what I mean, and there's no shame in taking it easy the first time out. I know one captain who never left his bunk for his five voyages, and yee be doing much better than him already."

I nodded, thanking my father silently for encouraging, demanding that I get a gyro-balance implant before signing on.

"And if you have any questions, sir, I'll answer what I can."

He was about to resume his duties, figuring that I would now be able to fend for myself for awhile when I tapped him on the shoulder and asked, "So what should I do?"

"Sit back. Take it easy, even read a book. The captain's cabin is full of them. Your predecessor collected them. Not lit-disks, mind you. Real honest-to-god bound books. Heck, begging the captain's pardon, with a name like yours, maybe you could even write one," he replied with a hearty laugh. "And you can be sure that anything out of the ordinary, you'll be the first to know."

I returned to the captain's cabin, or perhaps more correctly *my* cabin and decided to peruse the shelf full of, in Stubb's words, "honest-to-god bound books." A few of the authors' names jumped out at me. Forester, O'Brien, Pope, Cherryh, Drake, and even Melville.

Needless to say, seeing my family name amongst what I determined to be classics of nautical fiction was a nice surprise. The editions ranged from leather-bound tomes with gilded pages to yellowed paperbacks with gaudy illustrated covers of seagoing vessels in various states of disrepair. I first perused two of the longer volumes, a *Moby Dick* and a *White Jacket* as I recalled, but then settled on a shorter paperback by the name of *The Piazza Tales* in order to ease my way into the quaint hobby of reading a book.

I had heard of my alleged literary ancestor from my school days, but had never taken the opportunity to get acquainted with his legacy. As fate would have it, an opportunity for a possible family reunion of sorts had finally presented itself . . . or at least so I thought.

Thus reclining on my bunk with book in hands and my focus turned to the table of contents I quickly drifted off to sleep.

Little more than a few hours had passed when I heard Stubb's voice hailing me from the telecom.

"Captain, we have just sighted anther ship. It appears to be off course as our navigational computer has no record of any ship with pilot plans that might intersect ours."

Shaking myself awake, I answered, "How does it affect our status? Are we in danger of collision?"

"No, Captain," the engineer replied, "the ship has

already compensated for that . . . but there is something strange about it."

"How so?"

"I think you had better join me on the bridge. This may be something that a captain might be better suited to deal with."

I hastened to the bridge, absently placing the still to be read paperback in the side pocket of my waistcoat.

Stubb seemed puzzled.

"What seems to be the problem?" I asked.

"Not quite sure, Captain," he answered, his eyes shot straying from a digital monitor.

I cast my eyes on the exterior viewscreen and beheld the apparently errant ship.

"Is she the problem?"

"Aye, sir," he acknowledged. "She goes by the name *Mardi*, or at least that's the name on her hull."

"Have you tried to raise her on ship to ship com?"

"Not yet, sir," he replied, and motioned for me to join him at the monitor. "I think you should see a replay of her actions before she noticed our approach."

Stubb rekeyed a code, the action on the monitor blurred for a moment as our view retraced and panned back, and then resumed a forward motion at four times standard pace.

As the *Mardi* loomed into view, I first noticed what appeared to be little pods drifting from her wake, only to disappear in a flash of light.

"Let me recalibrate the photo-dissonance," Stubb said, as he keyed in another series of codes.

The *Mardi* became sharper, and the area around her became clearer. The pods did indeed appear to be single-person life pods that were being ejected from their docks only to be incinerated by one of the ship's stern-based lasers as soon as it reached optimum distance from the hull.

It appeared to be some sort of target practice, like

skeet shooting in space . . . but surely such an activity was a huge waste of resources not to mention life pods as one never knew when an evacuation might be necessary.

"Why are they doing that?" I queried Stubb

"Beats me," he replied with an edge to his voice, "but I'll tell you one thing. I don't like it."

"Neither do I," I agreed. "It's a waste of time and life pods."

"It may be more than that," he said.

I was losing patience.

"Well, why don't I just ask them?"

I retreated from the monitor and took my place at the com seat facing the exterior viewscreen.

"Co," I instructed the computer, "call up the profile of the ship currently on Viewscreen AZ."

Yes, Captain, the computer replied, and superimposed on the viewscreen the following digital profile:

Mardi
Class 5789 Long haul space freighter
Property of the Micro-Intel Corporation
Captain Lowell Roberts in Command
Note—Last subspace contact overdue by seven cycles

Stubb joined me at the com, taking the place that I assumed would normally be manned by a first officer if a ship such as ours had one.

"What do you advise, Mr. Stubb?" I asked in what I hoped was a reasonable facsimile of a captainly tone.

"She doesn't appear to have been boarded by force. No blast marks or ion residue detected, so that rules out pirates. Could be a mutiny, though," he considered.

"Only one way to find out," I replied taking matters into my own hands. "I'll ask to talk to their captain. Com, patch me through to Captain Lowell Roberts, and be sure to do a vocal identity verification on the reply."

"I don't think that's a good idea," Stubb commented without the slightest trace of insubordination in his voice.

"I think we should hold off on a com-link until we have a better idea of what we are dealing with."

"Stubb, time's a'wastin, and I don't see what . . ."

Ahoy, Essex!

This is Captain Roberts of the Mardi.

Thank God you came along when you did!

Please patch me through to Captain (pause) Melville immediately.

"This is Melville," I replied in a voice loud enough to be picked up and transferred via ship to ship subspace com. "Is everything all right? (I stole a look at the com monitor and verified that I was indeed speaking to someone whose voice pattern matched Roberts to 99.89% degree of certainty) We were afraid that you might have had a mutiny."

A mutiny, heavens no!

(Laughter)

We have a medical emergency.

"No problem, Mardi" I answered. "Have you called the sector infirmaries yet? If not we can. I'm sure that they can have someone here in (quick calculation) a cycle and a half."

That won't be necessary.

No, not at all.

A quarantine has been set up.

"Quarantine?"

Those infected have been put into cold sleep for the duration and the dead have been disposed of to avoid contamination.

"Were those the life pods we saw being disintegrated as we approached."

Affirmative.

(Pause)

Mardi's AI assessed the risks, and took action exercising all of the necessary precautions.

"Ask him what the crew status is," Stubb whispered in my ear.

"What is the status of your crew, Roberts?"

25% infected, deceased, and eliminated.
74% kept in preventative quarantine.
And then there's me . . .
(Pause)
Fulfilling my captainly duties.

"Affirmative."

I turned to Stubb, his brow knit with tension. "Punch up, Roberts' profile."

Stubb complied silently, his eyes never leaving the screen as his fingers danced over the keyboard.

Captain Lowell Roberts
Civilian graduate of Merchant Academy
Career breakdown:
5 years purser at Sector Five Customs House
5 years purser on *Nostromo*
10 years Captain of *Typee*
Retirement at full captain's rank
Last known whereabouts:
Civilian captaincy of *Mardi* (under contract from the Micro-Intel Corporation)
Criminal record:
Non existent

"Are we close enough to scan them for active life-forms?" Stubb didn't take time to answer as he keyed in the request.

Mardi
One life-form—human—fully registering
Numerous life-forms—human—detected in hibernation
Vital signs lowered but not in danger
AI is functioning at full competency
Additional information
Registered human
Identity Lowell Roberts
Rank—Captain
Life sign abnormalities

Blood pressure elevated
Respiration agitated and irregular

"Roberts, I'm coming over for a look-see so that we can talk face-to-face," I hailed.

Stubb whipped his head around, an expression that was a mixture of shock and disapproval apparent on his visage.

That won't be necessary, Melville.

I have matters well in hand.

(Pause)

On second thought, it might be a good idea for you to affirm my ship's status.

You know how the insurance companies move faster when you have a substantiating witness.

"Affirmative," I replied. "Please patch through the proper docking coordinates on the AI to AI ship to ship band."

Already done.

I'll put a few brewskis on ice.

(Pause)

Not that I'm a drinking man.

Just a little captain-to-captain joke . . .

"Affirmative. Melville and *Essex* out."

No sooner was the com-link broken than, Stubb stood over me, his arms folded and his lips pursed in a manner that reminded me of my father when he was in one of his more imperious moods.

"I don't think it's a good idea for you to leave the ship," he stated in a tone that didn't seem to leave room for discussion.

"Recommendation noted," I answered as I got to my feet and started to head off the bridge, "and disregarded."

Stubb rushed to block my exit.

"Now see here," he barked, "your father . . ."

". . . is not here right now," I interrupted doing my

best to match his imperious tone. "And I am the Captain."

"But . . ."

"And you wouldn't think of being insubordinate, Stubb. Would you? That would be mutiny."

"No, sir," Stubb said, his gaze cast to the deck, "but I just don't like it."

My point had been made, and it was time to mend fences with the mate who *really* did see himself as looking out for my best interests.

"Look, Stubb," I offered with my most conciliatory tone, "we've taken all the precautions necessary. Roberts is a former desk jockey, a civvy captain just like me. There doesn't seem to be any danger. Our AI confirms that their quarantine is intact and unless the problem is Roberts himself, a possibility, mind you, but given his age and medical profile I think I can handle him. I bet I even outweigh him. We have nothing to worry about, but just as a precaution I'll keep my stunner at hand."

"But Captain," Stubb inquired, "if everything is as fine and under control as he claims, why bother with the face-to-face."

"I guess this is what separates captains from crew," I postulated. "We love to press the flesh, form alliances, and do the dance. Probably the biggest problems we face are paperwork and substantiating corroboration. I make a quick trip to the *Mardi* and provide Roberts with his insurance witness, and voila, he owes me one. And if he owes me one, he owes the *Essex* one, and that's always a good thing."

"Promise me you'll stay in an enviro-suit for the duration of your stay outside of the ship," Stubb insisted.

"Face and hands only," I offered as a compromise. "If it's good enough for the GCDC . . ."

"All right," he agreed, "but I still don't like it."

"You have the com until I return," I stated as I left the deck.

I heard him promise aloud that he would be watching my every move.

I overlooked the insubordination, and hastened to the shuttle deck.

Stubb had called ahead and I was met by two crewman, one of whom helped me into an exit suit (with clear enviro-mask and gloves) while the other readied my shuttle life pod.

"There she is, Captain," the younger (who is still older than me by at least a year or two) instructed. "Ready to go. She's all programmed, so you just have to sit back and enjoy the ride."

As I adjusted the fasteners on the exit suit, I became aware of the bulge of the paperback in my pocket and transferred it to an exterior pouch for easy access.

"Maybe I'll use the time to catch up on my reading," I joked, though I sensed that neither of them was listening as they were completely absorbed in doing their duties.

"I've also programmed her for the trip back," the younger added, "but if the need should arise you can just switch her over to manual and we'll talk you back inside."

"Not a problem," I replied trying to sound confident. Though I had scored well on solo-pilot programming via simulation, this was going to be my first real flight on my own. I had already decided that my ego did *not* require that I wrestle control away from *Essex*'s AI, as I closed the hatch behind me and took a seat at the control panel.

A quick look around had confirmed that the area was neither spacious nor cramped and would actually be quite comfy for the short duration of my trip (or at least so I thought at the time).

I was almost there when I felt a sudden jerk as if we had snagged on something.

Sorry about that, Melville.

That was just Mardi*'s tractor beam guiding you in.*

I'll be meeting you at the hatch in less than ten minutes.

I promised your boy Stubb that I would take good care of you and that we would send a confirmation of your arrival asap.

Stubb was turning into a real mother hen, and I was probably not going to let it pass once I returned to the *Essex.*

"Affirmative," I replied. "See you at the dock."

Most of *Mardi*'s exterior lights were turned off, but I could make out a general overview of her as we approached.

She was a much older craft than the *Essex* though she apparently had recently been overhauled with some newfangled pieces that were even more modern than anything in my father's fleet.

As we approached the docking bay, I saw a flicker of lights moving down the ship toward me. *Of course,* I thought to myself, *the AI is conserving the ship's power reserves by only lighting those areas occupied by Captain Roberts.* This might be an innovation my father might want to consider for his fleet (and already I had managed to justify this trip).

The actual docking went simpler than a simulation, and indeed Roberts was there to greet me.

"Captain Melville requests permission to come aboard," I hailed (as was custom).

"Permission granted," Roberts replied, adding, "welcome aboard, Captain Melville."

"Thank you, Captain Roberts," I answered with a crisp salute, followed by a quick lowering of my hand to offer a friendly handshake as I had seen my father do so many times before.

Roberts quickly grasped my hand and gave it a shake, noticing the enviro-gloves, and observing with a nervous giggle and twitter, "Can't be too careful. Never know what you can pick up. Who knows where I've been or where I'm bound for?"

"Excuse me?" I replied, not sure if he was just joking in an odd way or whether he was indeed quite buggy.

Lowell is just a little on edge, and even at the best of times his humor is a bit eccentric, an AI voiced.

"Indeed, indeed," Roberts agreed, his eyes darting back and forth until their gaze fell on the book that I had carried over from the *Essex.* "Much of a reader? Always thought readers were the cream of the crop myself."

"Indeed," I agreed, as I noticed a certain gleam in his eyes.

"Then we have something in common, though obviously not as much as you have in common with your book, Captain Melville."

"One of my favorite ancestors," I winged, "and this one of my favorite books. I keep it as a good luck charm."

Lowell, don't you think that Captain Melville would like to see more of the ship than just the docking bay?

"Of course, of course," he twittered, "but first allow me to introduce you to (twitch) the only thing that has kept me sane (twitch) during this crisis. Mardi's AI, and you may call it (twitch) BABO."

BABO?

"Brain and basic operations," he explained to me even though the questions had come from elsewhere. "It's so much easier than AI–Brain and Basic Operations Unit. Don't you agree?"

"Why not," I replied, and walked with him down the corridor away from the docking area.

As I looked down the corridor, I noticed that the areas we would pass through were lit so as to be easy on our eyes, while also keeping certain areas along the way in complete darkness.

Roberts had started out as my tour guide, but seemed to be more interested in discussing the works of Herman Melville (which immediately made me uncomfortable since, with the exception of the data that one can pick up on a book by merely carrying it around, despite my claims to the contrary, I was still in state of total ignorance).

I also noticed that Roberts had the peculiar habit of finishing almost every statement with "right, BABO" as if the approval of the AI was necessary.

Eventually BABO took over the narration of our walking tour explaining that certain crewman had been exposed to Adkinson's Gangrene while in port at one of the SEATAC gambling dens, and had exposed everyone else on board to it (with the exception of Roberts who had been relaxing in coldsleep as a means to forestall the wear and tear on an older body during space travel) before it was properly identified.

As BABO related over the ship's com-link speakers:

At the outbreak of a second case, I immediately did the appropriate correlations and decided that a quarantine had to be put in place. As you may or may not know, Adkinson's Gangrene is a degenerative disease that causes massive tissue damage in the gray matter of the human brain at a very fast rate. By the time I had noticed the problem, ten crewman were already terminal. More would have died in hours had I not ordered everyone else into hibernation.

"Everyone owes their lives to BABO's quick thinking," Roberts commented, pointing to recently illuminated cold-cell that currently housed a crewman.

I looked on in quiet horror. I had never seen a case of this horrible disease before, and quite frankly didn't notice any external signs on the sleeping crewman.

As you can see, there are no outward signs of the insidious disorder, BABO continued. But it is deadly and highly contagious.

"Though it is now contained and no longer a threat," Roberts butted in. "BABO saw to that, and once we get back to port, all of the proper precautions can be taken and my poor crew, at least those who have survived, will get the proper treatment."

I also isolated the dead, and off-loaded them. I then incinerated them once they were a safe distance from the Mardi so as to avoid any further contaminations.

"That's my BABO. Always thinking."

Once the afflicted were in cold storage and the dead isolated, I decontaminated the ship, and revived Captain Roberts so that he could oversee my command of the ship.

"Indeed, indeed," Roberts twittered, "and it's a good thing that you did or else Captain Melville's call might have fallen on deaf ears, and then he might have had to make a query on our behalf, causing us lots of red tape which none of us would have wanted. Space Nautical Code Section 598, after all."

I had forgotten that part of the code which orders all commanding officers to investigate "unmanned vessels" more than two days out from port and take command or post a guard on such vessels until a controlling legal authority had assumed responsibility.

Even though Captain Roberts might be on the verge of going off his nut, the ship was still safe, under his command (with the able coordination of the obviously competent and conscientious AI "BABO").

As we entered the foredeck, I began to feel a slight bit of fatigue. I was not yet accustomed to varied artificial gravity fields, and the change from the *Essex* to the *Mardi* was just enough to cause a strain on my not quite in shape physique.

Roberts was babbling on about some story or another trying to involve me in a conversation about someone named "Benito Cereno" when BABO came to my rescue.

Captain, Captain Melville is obviously fatigued.

Perhaps you would like to rest for a few moments, Captain Melville.

Maybe you would like to take the opportunity to check in with your ship. I can set up a com-link for you directly.

"Thank you," I replied, more than willing to be rescued from Roberts literary jaws of boredom. "That would be splendid."

I'll have your mate on the line in less than three nanoseconds.

True to its word . . .

Captain Melville, is everything all right? Are you all right?

"Of course, Stubb, though I would think that you wouldn't have to ask that question. You are monitoring my vitals, I assume."

Yes, Captain, just as a precaution . . .

"Everything is well under control here," I pronounced, "and I will be returning shortly. Please relay on to port that all is well and under control with the *Mardi.* Tell them a viral outbreak has been contained and that no emergency assistance will be necessary until she reaches port."

Aye, aye, sir. (Crack-Crack-crack) There seems to be some feedback building up on the line . . .

"Melville out."

I hope you didn't shut the transmission short on account of the feedback. I am sure that I would have been able to clear it up.

"Not necessary, BABO," I replied, hardly noticing that I seemed to prefer conversing with the AI rather than my human captainly counterpart.

I noticed that Roberts was becoming increasingly twitchy, his hand constantly reaching up to scratch a scab at his temple.

"Well," I said aloud as I was becoming steadily more uneasy being away from my own command, "I should be getting back to the *Essex.*"

"I'll escort you out," Roberts replied, and quickly took my arm, urging me back toward the docking bay as if we were trying to rush beyond the carefully coordinated pace of the AI controlled lighting.

At one point we had just about outdistanced the lights and were proceeding rapidly from dimness into darkness when Roberts whispered into my ear, "I only call it BABO because of the story. There just isn't time . . ."

The lights had caught up as we entered the bay and Roberts immediately became stone silent.

Thank you for coming, Captain Melville.

"Thank you, BABO."

"As you can, see, everything is fine, so you better go," Roberts said, urging me forward, and almost pushing me into the air lock.

I turned around to return a customary salute when the madman rushed forward, coming right at me and into the shuttle pod with me.

"Wait," he cried, "the insurance forms . . ."

. . . but there were no forms in his hand, and before either I or BABO could respond, he had closed the hatch and hit the emergency ejection control.

In less than a nanosecond we were thrust off-balance as our craft was blown from its docking station.

"Switch to manual," Roberts ordered, reaching across me to undo the autopilot. "We can't trust the AI."

He then grabbed the com and hailed the *Essex.*

"Come in *Essex*! Come in *Essex*!" he screamed.

Who is this, a frantic Stubb answered back.

Where is Captain Melville?

We are at alert. Our shields are down and life support is dropping.

"Oh, no," Roberts cried.

Our systems won't respond.

Come in, Captain.

The AI is down, some sort of virus was passed to us from the Mardi, *we . . .*

(Silence)

* * *

"It's too late!" Roberts said in despair.

I grabbed the madman and shook him. I needed answers.

"What is too late?" I demanded.

"*Mardi*'s AI has infected the Essex! It has joined the mutiny . . ." the madman explained, his hand reaching to his temple. "The outbreak was a hoax . . . the decontamination just some form of demented target practice . . . I don't know how much time I have . . . I think BABO has control over my space-sickness implant . . . I . . ."

"What?" I demanded.

Just then Roberts' face became serene, as if he felt no pain.

"It was just like in your story . . . 'Benito Cereno' . . . I tried to warn you . . ."

. . . and then the sole survivor of the *Mardi* expired, as the electronic implant in his brain exploded at a transmitted command from the AI he called BABO.

A flash of light outside of the front portal distracted me from my corpse companion as the *Essex* exploded into a million pieces as its internal self-destruct codes were accessed.

. . . and then the lights went off in my shuttle pod.

The light came back on after what seemed like an eternity (but was probably less than an hour which was luckily more than the amount of time necessary for us to get out of scanning distance from the *Mardi*).

After the destruction of the *Essex,* we must have dropped off BABO's scanners due to the ion residue, and it and *Mardi* had apparently moved on to other matters.

Life support had been maintained through the shut-down, and I was left alone in the presence of a corpse with a paperback copy of a book that in my arrogance I had claimed to have read when I had not.

Had I read it, things might have turned out differently.

I waited for another hour to pass before activating the SOS beacon, praying that the *Mardi* wouldn't pick it up, and then decided to pass the time by reading the book before me.

Sure enough there was a story included by the name of "Benito Cereno."

It dealt with an inexperienced captain by the name of Amasa Delano who goes to the aid of a ship in distress only to encounter a distraught captain and his blackamoor servant Babo who was in reality the leader of a bloody mutiny that had just taken place before the other ship arrived on the scene.

Roberts had lucked out in that his BABO did not understand the intentional reference the name conveyed . . . but with one of life's little ironies, Roberts was also not lucky enough to have come across a better read captain even if he did happen to have the coincidental name of Melville.

So here I sit in this life pod, making a record of my folly for someone to one day review. I have read the bound volume that was the gift from my captainly predecessor and have almost memorized each word of one of *The Piazza Tales* entitled "Benito Cereno" by a certain Herman Melville who I may or may not be descended from. Had I not been so bold, haughty, inexperienced, and unlearned, my own crew as well as that unlucky captain might still be alive.

We have not crossed paths with any other ships since the encounter . . . but it is only a matter of time.

Hopefully, I will make it to port before *Mardi*.

Hopefully, the AI mutiny hasn't spread.

Looking back, I have to believe that Stub gave the self-destruct command on the *Essex*.

Why would BABO destroy a newly formed ally?

Stubb sacrificed the ship and crew for the good of he fleet.

Hopefully I will one day be capable of such a cap-ainly act.